They whirled as one, in time to see Elminster's body topple in a fountain of dark blood as a black blade scythed through his neck. The blade was held by—no, it seemed to actually *be* one arm of a tall black figure. The Old Mage's eyes stared accusingly at them as his head dangled, long white hair firmly in the dark man's grip.

"Futile fools!" the figure sneered, and backed away from them into a whirling green light that was growing behind it.

Heartsick, Shar took three running steps and hurled her blade. But as the weapon flashed end over end, the laughing figure faded away through the gate and made the portal wink out, so her steel bounced on dark turf in the night.

She felt the tears beginning as she turned her head and saw Belkram and Itharr looking down at the headless body. Belkram licked dry and trembling lips twice before he managed to ask, "What do we do *now*?"

FANTASY ADVENTURE

THE SHADOW OF THE AVATAR TRILOGY
Ed Greenwood

Shadows of Doom

Cloak of Shadows

All Shadows Fled
(Available Fall 1995)

Other Books by Ed Greenwood

Elminster, the Making of a Mage

Crown of Fire

Spellfire

FANTASY ADVENTURE

Cloak of Shadows

Book Two

The Shadow of the Avatar Trilogy

Ed Greenwood

To John, for Belkram's kindness.

To Ian, for Itharr's keen wits.

To Erica, for loving the Realms as much as I do.

Ignis aurum probat, miseria fortes viros

CLOAK OF SHADOWS

First Printing: June 1995
Printed in the United States of America.
Library of Congress Catalog Card Number: 94-61682

9 8 7 6 5 4 3 2 1

ISBN: 0-7869-0301-5

TSR, Inc.
201 Sheridan Springs Rd.
Lake Geneva, WI 53147
U.S.A.

TSR Ltd.
120 Church End, Cherry Hinton
Cambridge CB1 3LB
United Kingdom

***As the Time of Troubles came down upon the
Realms, dark things watched and waited their
chance . . .***

The Fall of the Gods had come to pass. The gods came to
Toril amid flame and destruction, and the world was riven
and changed forever. Amid all the flames and strife, the
Chosen of Mystra were hurt more than most guardians of
Faerûn, for the servants of the goddess of magic discovered
that spells were raging wild all over the world. Magic
would obey them no more than it did anyone else.

Just when they needed it most.

Against them stood outlaws, orc hordes, and fearsome
monsters that had long lurked on the fringes of the bright
realms and grown hungry indeed. Even the gods themselves were wandering Faerûn, slaying and plundering
and despoiling all that fell within their reach, and battling with reckless savagery whoever—or whatever—
stood against them.

It was a time for heroes to stand forth and fight to defend whatever could be saved of the splendor and strength
of the civilized Realms. Folk looked to the Chosen, who
stood helpless, with magic a treacherous thing in their
hands.

All save one . . . one who dared not act at all. Elminster
of Shadowdale, the Old Mage feared and revered across
Faerûn for nigh a thousand years, held so much of the
divine power of the dying goddess Mystra within him that
he dared not cast so much as the simplest spell, for fear of
shattering the Realms around him and being torn apart
in the world-destroying conflagration that might follow.

His foes, however, were on the move. Elminster's inability

to hurl spells against them must be concealed from everyone. One of his fellow Chosen sent two of her Harper pupils to guard him, and a brave lady Knight of Myth Drannor took the same task upon herself. Together the three young people aided Elminster as he plunged into the depths of Zhentarim plots in the High Dale that lay in the Thunder Peaks between Cormyr and Sembia.

Yet even as Elminster and his companions defeated Zhentarim evil once more, older and more sinister foes had their own dark designs on the Realms. The Malaugrym, masters of shadow, watched the chaos and ruin in Faerûn from their dark castle and grew hungry to conquer as much of Faerûn as might fall within their grasp. Shapeshifters and sorcerers of ancient power, they had long feared to challenge Elminster, who hunted and slew them whenever they ventured into the lands he held dear.

If Elminster was powerless, and the Chosen were busy trying to hold the Realms, the Malaugryms' chance had come at last. If they took the shapes of rightful rulers, the Chosen would actually defend their new-won realms for them! All that was needed, to make victory a sure thing, was shadow magic that would hide the Malaugryms' true essence, inside their stolen shapes, from any Chosen who survived the Time of Troubles.

All that was needed to conquer Faerûn was a Cloak of Shadows . . .

1
A Long Day Indeed

Faerûn, Raurin, Mirtul 29, The Year of Shadows

A dark shadow that had eyes drifted down unseen over a mist-shrouded battlefield where weary, snarling creatures hacked at each other with blood-drenched blades at the end of a day that had been long indeed. The Dark One looked around at hill after hill of destruction, and sighed. Waste, all this blood and dying. Waste on this plane and that, puny beings struggling to seize fleeting power, when might enough to shatter all their realms at once throbbed and strove all around them.

Magic. The power eternal, the energy behind all. He must have it. For centuries—eons, now—he had come back, again and again, to that gnawing need . . . and that stone wall blocking his hunger. Up against the shield that left him helpless once more. The Dark One snarled. Down the long years he had learned to be old, but not to be patient. Patience was for the powerless.

Restlessly, Bane turned toward the sun, corpses shifting under his black boots, and spun himself homeward through the shifting voids, back to the body that grimly paced the Cold Castle. Ethereal mists whirled briefly around him, and then he was striding again along the windblown battlements, looking far out over bleak Acheron. Magic, aye. Always it came back to that, and to *her*.

Mystra, the Lady who was magic. He must possess her, rule her—or destroy her—to gain true mastery of magic. But how? Many webs he'd spun to take her—some still hung waiting, even now—but the very power he sought warned her and shielded her, time after time.

In the ashen failures of his last few attempts, she'd even laughed at him. Bane whirled with a roar of sudden fury, there on the battlements, and drove his fist through a stout merlon, smashing it to stony rubble that rattled and sprayed down over his startled and fearful minions in the courtyard below. If only it had been her laughing face! The Overgod take her! She—

Bane froze in sudden thought, and a slow, dark smile spread softly across his angry face. Aye, let the Overgod take her.

Memories that were dim even for him flickered briefly, and he felt the stirrings of excitement. It might well work.

Yes. It was high time for the overproud, overreaching gods to be cast down again.

* * * * *

The Plane of Acheron, and a forgotten ruin in the Savage Frontier backlands, Mirtul 29

Cold laughter rang out through the castle, and scurrying servants of Bane paused in their scuttlings long enough to shudder before they hastened on again. Such sounds boded ill for all.

Still smiling like a wolf rising in bloody satisfaction from a fresh kill, Bane spun himself away from cold Acheron once more, heading for Toril. Of course.

Even gods need a playground. Because Faerûn was Mystra's, he had made it his—as had, increasingly, the others. The Dark One cloaked himself in shadows and sought the throne he liked to sit in, deep in the riven ruins of the once-proud city of Netheril.

In a moment he was there, surrounded by the drifting, sparkling shreds of forgotten spells. He peered around, feeling with his mind for living, watching things, but none were near. He looked around at the dim depths of the hall. Strange, how the shattered splendor of this place held his interest, awakening old memories and long-quiet lusts . . .

* * * * *

The Castle of Shadows, Mirtul 29

In a place of shifting shadows, someone else grinned like a blood-dripping wolf as he ended a spell and slid away from the dark thoughts of the god Bane, unnoticed and now traceless. It was done. At last.

Milhvar of the Malaugrym watched the gray and purple sparks chase each other endlessly over the spell-weave and nodded in satisfaction. He'd taken what he needed from the unwitting mind of Bane while it was blinded by arrogance and driven by dark passion. He allowed himself to relax, letting out his breath in a long sigh. The most dangerous part was done; all that was left was the fun.

He did not have to look to take down the razor-sharp waiting runeblade from the wall beside him. The naked priest of Mystra bound to the stone altar before him whimpered once, then stiffened in silent resolve—until the blade swept down.

Blood and screams rose together, and the gray and purple sparks leapt from the weave and raced down Milhvar's trembling arms, their power surging into the fading life he held, sweeping it away, absorbing it.

Slowly the power of the crowning enchantment gathered and swirled within him. Milhvar smiled coldly as the last of the staring clergyman's life-force flowed into the web, then turned to look at his creation.

As if in answer, the cloak hanging in the spell web stirred for the first time. Success.

Milhvar gestured, and watched the cloak rise like a silent specter to his bidding. He thought of his dead brother, and of a certain old wizard in a fair, forested vale—Shadowdale, that was it—and nodded slowly. Soon it would be time to go hunting. Soon.

* * * * *

Somewhere in Faerûn, Mirtul 29

Overhead, the dragon unfurled its wings with ponderous grace, and began to dance. The tall, silver-haired lady laughed in delight, and the music she'd conjured swelled around them all. Pegasi neighed their pleasure aloud as they swooped past her, and the spell-dance quickened.

The dragon managed a curving cartwheel across the sky, the wind whistling through its scales, and Mystra leapt to meet it, trailing bright silver stars in her wake. The wordless song rose with her, soaring, exultant—and was suddenly shattered.

In the air, the goddess of magic faltered, and her silvery light flickered. With little cries of unease, the cavorting creatures broke off their dancing to watch. Mystra drifted on until she touched the dragon and clung to it, but her face wore a frown, and her eyes gazed on something far off.

Suddenly she shivered. "Evil Art," she whispered sadly, waving her arms as if she could brush the moment away. Returning from wherever her sight had taken her, she shook herself and looked around the waiting sphere of gravely watching creatures.

"A great and dark Art has been worked," she told them calmly. "Not in Toril, but by someone who watches this world and thinks of it even now."

"We must be vigilant," the dragon said then, the deep, melodious rumble of its voice startling them all.

"Aye, that we must," Mystra agreed gravely, and swept her hands up. From between her long, graceful fingers streamed a bright shower of silver stars that made the watching creatures gasp and murmur in awe.

The music sang forth again. "I will not have the spell-dance ended," the goddess said with sudden fire, "by every evil deed of Art . . . or we should never dance together at all!"

Warily the pegasi, faerie dragons, sprites, swanmays, and the great form of the gigantic copper dragon circled her and began to move in time to the music again. Stars dove and spun around them as the music swelled, but there was a darkness among them now, a shadow of Mystra's mood that even the most spirited of her leaps did not dispel. "Bad times ahead," said one faerie dragon to another, and there was reluctant agreement. A note of proud defiance crept into Mystra's music as the dance went on. More than one troubled creature fell away from it and made for home, and safe lairs, and places where seeking-magic was stored. Bad times are better faced on the crumbling pages of tomes that relate histories of long, long ago—not as deadly events that tomorrow may bring.

* * * * *

The Castle of Shadows, Kythorn 6

Milhvar grew a long, tentacled arm that flattened into a leathery wing, and flapped it once. The power of his wing beat plucked him from his feet and took him a good way across the chamber. He noted approvingly that the cloak's gray and hard-to-see substance shifted shape along with him. His cloak of spells was truly a cloak of shadows, as suited to shifting as any of the blood of Malaug. Now tc test it against the Chosen of Mystra, to see if the enchantments he'd devised truly held. The cloak must foil all magic wielded or cast by any sworn minion of Mystra, from her mortal Chosen to Azuth himself! If it proved able, the Chosen wouldn't be able to sense the approach of the Malaugrym . . . and perhaps his kin would have their revenge upon the hated Elminster at last!

Milhvar made a certain gesture. The cloak shrank away from him, rolled itself into a ball, and dwindled into a thing of wisps and tatters. Smiling faintly, he took it in his hand and headed for his favorite hiding place. His cloak of shadows was best kept secret until it had served him in winning far greater power in the ranks of the clan than he commanded now.

Power he deserved. What, after all, had the Malaugrym done under the command of Dhalgrave? Elminster yet lived, and none who walked in the shadows dared set foot on Faerûn without great preparation—and greater stealth. All we do these days, Milhvar thought sourly, is watch from afar and brood. And the time for that is fast running out. Something was building among the gods, something that could be turned to advantage by those who knew how to bend both magic and shadows to their will.

"And then," Milhvar told the darkness politely, "things will change—rather violently, as they deserve to." He thought he heard an answering whimper, and stiffened for an instant before he recalled that the cloak in his hand *was* a priest of Mystra. Of course. He chuckled. "You serve me now," he told it with a savage grin. "Try to remember that."

As he cast it into a vortex of concealing shadows, the cloak did not answer. He chuckled again and turned away.

* * * * *

Shadowdale, Kythorn 14

The young lass in leathers screamed as a black-fletched arrow leapt from nowhere to take her in the shoulder. It hissed into her flesh before she had time to do more than gape at it, with its one red feather among the sable. The force of its flight plucked her from her feet, spun her about, and slammed her to her knees in the snow. Her face creased in startled pain as the vision wavered, like still water stirred with a hand, and then faded away, leaving only empty air over the table.

Itharr stared at the spot where the conjured image had been and shook his head. "Not a gentle way to die," the burly Harper said softly, one strong hand tightening absently on his tankard.

Sharantyr nodded and set down her ale, stern sadness in her gray-green eyes as she met his gaze. Itharr blinked. The lady knight's fine-boned beauty had made many a man stop and stare, and the firelight dancing on her face made her seem a creature from a dream. Itharr stared into her eyes for a long moment before the other man in the room spoke, and she turned to look at him.

"Whence came you by this magic?" Belkram of the

Harpers asked quietly over his own tankard. Sorrow to match Sharantyr's own glimmered in his eyes. He shifted in his chair, firelight flashing on his smooth-worn leathers, every inch the fearless fighting man. A well-used long sword shifted with him, riding his hip, always ready.

An onlooker would have judged Belkram more handsome than his fellow Harper, but like Itharr and the lithe Knight of Myth Drannor across the table, he wore the nondescript harness of a working ranger. They looked, Belkram was sure, like three weary hireswords at ease, not champions of good just back from saving the world from disaster and magical chaos.

The lady ranger lifted her slim shoulders and let them fall in a shrug, noticing a lock of gray hair at Belkram's temple—gray that had not been there a few days ago. "That vision was brought to me by a linking spell known to some elves and elf-friends. Flambarra linked to me when she cast it, so she could show me things of import, should it be necessary. It shows the caster in her last nine breaths before the spell is ended."

"In this case, by her death and not her choice," Itharr murmured, taking up his tankard again. "When do we ride to avenge her?"

Sharantyr shook her head. "That was a brigand's arrow, and a quiverful to match it were found on a man who chose to defy the wrong patrol, three days ago." She took up her wine and stared through it. "We live in dark times, friends."

Silence fell in that dim back room of the Old Skull Inn, and the fire in the grate sent fingers of light and shadow dancing across their faces. A roar of laughter came faintly to their ears from the distant taproom. Belkram stirred, grinned at Sharantyr, and said, "But not all is gloom, or should be. We're the great heroes who rescued Elminster, remember?"

"That sounds perilously like a cue for an impressive entrance," an all-too-familiar voice said from beside the Harper. They all started, whirling to look at the still-closed door of the room. A mist was coiling lazily in front of it. As they watched, the tendrils of mist grew suddenly darker, then seemed to drop and change in a whirl of colors and flashing movement. Elminster of Shadowdale stood regarding them, a twinkle in his eye.

The three companions at the table sighed—in Itharr's case, it was almost a groan—as the Old Mage shuffled unconcernedly forward. His pipe appeared out of thin air behind him with a *pop* and floated along in his wake as he came to the table, lowering himself with a grunt onto the bench beside Belkram.

The taller and more ruggedly handsome of the two young Harpers looked into the mage's old, bearded face with something approaching fond amusement. "How long have you been here listening?"

Belkram's tankard rose stealthily from the table and darted toward Elminster's waiting hand as the wizard of Shadowdale said mildly, "Long enough to tell this lass here—"

He gestured with a glance, and Belkram's eyes, following the wizard's gaze across the table to where Sharantyr sat with a dangerous look growing on her face, saw his tankard flying past. He made a grab for it, missed as it impudently shot straight upward, and overbalanced heavily onto the table.

Sharantyr's wine danced, and Itharr chuckled as she made her own—successful—grab for drinkables. As the lady Knight swept her goblet away from disaster, Elminster continued unconcernedly, "—that Flambarra was found by Elion of Talltrees, and by the grace of Tymora lives again."

Sharantyr stared at him for a moment in astonished silence. Then tears of joy rained from her, and she erupted across the table, crushing the stolen tankard against Elminster's cheek as she embraced the Old Mage. Around her tearful thanks he said gruffly, "Agh! Urgghh! I—The deed was not mine, lass, but if ye're bent on thanking me, well, my mouth is over *here*, and—"

Obedient lips found his enthusiastically, and his words trailed away in a confusion of frantic murmurs. One of the Old Mage's hands waved vainly above the lady ranger's smooth shoulders, gesturing frantically but not too frantically.

Itharr took in the sight with one bright eye. Turning deliberately to his Harper colleague, he remarked casually, "All in Faerûn is not dark these days, indeed. Why, I could not help but notice, as we came here to partake of this excellent beer tonight, that the price of potatoes has fallen a full two coppers the wagonload, heralding a goodly harvest without doubt."

Belkram nodded his head and replied heartily, "This is true, good Itharr, and yet surpassed by even more heartening news! Our internal ablutions cannot help but be aided by a similar drop in the price of ale, a drop that by the all-surpassing favor of the gods bids fair to coincide with a rise in the quality of the brew. Richer, nuttier, and more warming in the chest, by my halidom, and—"

"You can belt up now," Sharantyr told them both in dry tones. "I had to release him, to draw breath."

"And yet," Elminster put in merrily, in perfect mimicry of Itharr's conversational tone, "I find the surpassing memory of her kiss is a fiery balm upon the hitherto-cooling flames of my old heart! I could not help but notice, moreover, that her tears taste like the finest salt wine of Tashluta, and her eyes are like two dark and welcoming stars in th—"

Sharantyr plucked the gently smoking pipe deftly from where it floated in the air by the Old Mage's shoulder and thrust it into his mouth. "Glup," he added intelligently, ere smoke began to leak from his ears and nose.

The two young Harpers shouted their laughter at Elminster's slightly disbelieving expression . . . and then at the dangerous calm with which he spat the pipe out, watched it scud away trailing smoke across the room, and turned to regard Sharantyr.

The Lady of Shadowdale shrank back a little and brushed her long hair out of her face with one impatient hand as if preparing for battle, but met Elminster's gaze with a bold, silent calmness of her own.

Elminster's eyes blazed at her for a long, tense moment. Then the Old Mage turned his head and said lightly, as if nothing had occurred, "I observed the new-born pricing of potatoes too, and wondered in passing if it meant other goodly harvests, and a general time of plenty across the Dragonreach!"

"Well," Belkram said in a voice as dry as the bottom of the empty tankard he had retrieved, "if magic everywhere continues to fail and go wild, farmers'll certainly have less interference in taking their crops in, and we'll see fewer armies on the march to devour it all."

Itharr sighed. "You *would* have to drag things back to that."

Belkram spread his hands. "And is this chaos of magic not the true driving force of the times? And do we not share a victory, born of this very matter? A victory that bears celebration?"

"I'll ring for more beer," Itharr replied, pulling on the stout cord that hung by the wall near his corner seat.

"The simple solution to ill tidings," Elminster informed the ceiling. "Have more to drink."

Belkram shrugged. "With thirsty wizards at the table, I'm in little danger of getting *more* to drink, wouldn't you agree?"

Elminster's reply was a snort that seemed as eloquent as several speeches. They were still chuckling when there was a rap on the door. "Ale," came the voice of a server from outside.

"Ride in!" Itharr called in reply as Sharantyr took another sip of her wine and Belkram made an innocent grab for the floating pipe.

The door swung wide, and they had a momentary glimpse of a young boy's face, set in concentration over a tray laden with tankards, before he hurled tray and all at them.

Blue-white fire roared out of the heart of the tumbling pitchers and steins, thrusting into the face of the Old Mage like a bright, unstoppable lance.

Blue radiance flashed around the calm wizard, and the roaring shaft of devouring fire rebounded from him, snarling back at its source while the surprised and shouting Harpers and lady ranger were still hurling themselves back from the table and snatching at their sword hilts.

One tardy tankard melted away in the path of the fiery bolt and was hurled aside in the form of hissing droplets of molten metal. Beyond them there was a thin scream as the white light found its source and winked out.

Sharantyr and the Harpers were leaping forward by then, blades drawn, as the staggering, hunched thing that had been a serving boy a moment before sprouted long, snakelike tentacles in all directions. Coiling like a forest of serpents, the tentacles lengthened with terrifying speed, growing sharp edges and points like blades. Without pause they slashed and stabbed at the charging Harpers, slithering and looping around them.

Amid this sudden chaos, Elminster calmly pulled the bell rope for beer again, even as a single tentacle leapt past the shoulders of his three embattled companions, growing to an impossible stretch over the entire length of the table as it raced toward him. Its skin seemed to split and shrivel away as it came, revealing a needlelike, flashing sword. Elminster calmly murmured an incantation as the slim steel stabbed at him.

As he completed the spell, the Old Mage heard the tentacled creature grunt in pain as someone's blade struck home. Sharantyr gasped as a tentacle tightened around her, and then the sword that sought Elminster's life passed through his arm as if it were made of smoke and plunged deep into him!

He felt nothing as the blade plunged, probed, slashed, and was driven home again, cleaving the air freely as if he weren't standing there. El looked at his three friends, hacking at growing forests of tentacles around them, saw Belkram look back apprehensively, and snapped, "Drive your blades deep, all of you!"

An instant later his spell took effect. Blue lightning crackled from Itharr's blade to Sharantyr's, then from hers to Belkram's steel as the three swords quivered amid rubbery, shapeshifting flesh and hot, rushing blood. The creature they fought shuddered as smoke rose from it. Then it collapsed suddenly away from around their blades like the contents of a fresh-broken egg, flowing to the floor in an untidy heap.

"You're protected by an ironguard spell?" Belkram asked Elminster, watching the released sword pass down through the wizard's body to clang and bounce on the floor.

"Always," Elminster said, his eyes fixed on a disturbance in the air that had just sent his floating pipe tumbling aside.

As his hands came up to hurl blasting magic, the disturbance whirled and spun—and became a thin, wild-eyed woman in tattered black robes, her silver hair swirling around her as if it were made of lightnings.

It was the Simbul, Witch-Queen of Aglarond, who glared anxiously around the room, the red fires of an awakened slaying spell running up and down her arms, seeking the danger that had menaced her beloved.

Itharr tried not to shiver at the sight of her. Her gaze froze him on its way to where the Old Mage stood staring down at one smoking, shriveling tentacle as it shrank away from him in death.

"The Malaugrym?" she said in an awful whisper of fury and promised doom.

Elminster stroked his beard thoughtfully and nodded. "Again," he said as the door behind her swung wide. There was a startled gasp, and another platter of tankards crashed to the floor.

The sorceress whirled around, red fire blazing around one raised hand, in time to see a serving wench, face white in terror, moan and faint dead away, crumpling to the floor atop her spilled burden.

Behind the Simbul, the Old Mage's head came up, face brightening into a smile of welcome. "Will you take ale, love? It's richer, nuttier, and more warming in the chest, by my halidom, as a man I trust said not long ago!"

At the look on the Witch-Queen's face, Sharantyr burst into helpless laughter, followed by Belkram. It was a perilously long moment before the Simbul's dark gaze flickered. Then she too began to laugh, a low, raw, throaty chuckle that made both Belkram and Itharr think of leaping flames and hungry caresses and wilder things.

"Why is it," Elminster asked his pipe as it hung obediently nearby, fragrant wisps of smoke still rising from it, "that folk always seem to feel the need to laugh at my converse?" Fresh gales of mirth rocked the ruined room around him at his words. The Old Mage looked around at his friends sourly and then readdressed himself to his pipe. "Is it my looks, d'ye think? My sensually musical voice, perhaps?"

Wisely, the pipe chose not to answer.

2
This Wizard
Must Be Destroyed

The Castle of Shadows, Kythorn 14

The oval of light flickered and faded. As the dark and ever-hungry shadows crept and slithered back to reclaim the heart of the Great Hall of the Throne, those who'd watched death and laughter in the back room of an inn turned away from the darkening scrying portal. Some were hissing in anger as they went, and some were grim and silent, as their natures governed them.

"Poor entertainment," rumbled one lord, gliding through the shifting shadows in the shape of a cone of many eyes. He grew several long, spiderlike legs, two of which reached out to select a glowing bottle from a forest of glass containers in the vast black marble chamber.

Other Malaugrym muttered agreement, but a single clear, cold voice said, "We did not gather for 'entertainment,' Uncle."

Eyes swam swiftly around the cone to look back at the one who'd spoken so, but the cone did not turn or cease its gliding passage. "I know better than some young and loose-lipped kin, Halastra, why we're here," came the chill reply. "Guard your tongue, if you'd live to an age approaching mine."

"Another lecture? Are such words all you know how to speak?" a third voice put in. It seemed to issue from a coiling, serpentine form gliding half-seen through the mists, bound for the same destination as the cone. A low rumble of anger followed in the cone's wake as it went, expelling an empty bottle, but the lord did not accompany the rumble or the bottle with any words of reply.

Smoothly the cone began to rise through the mists, drawn up by the magic of the lift-spiral. Several half-human forms followed the cone in the ascent—bipedal figures that changed height and girth in a continuous, uneasy shifting but always seemed to have tails, clawed limbs, and spines or barbs here and there. The serpentine creature—sporting a succession of small pairs of leathery wings along its entire length but having no head—joined them, rising to where the mists hung darker and shadows seemed to drift menacingly like cruising sharks.

"Who was it who dared—and died?" a voice asked in hushed tones. The ascent seemed to be bringing a certain caution, or fear, upon all.

"Does it matter? Those who die fools are best forgotten," the conical lord said sternly, but another voice said clearly, "Thalart, get of Galartyn and Chasra."

"Another of us slain by the wizard Elminster," a new voice snarled. "His doom grows heavier by one more death."

"What can be heavier than an eternity in torment?" someone else asked.

"Such a small imagination," an older voice observed. "Learn to think on such things first, and speak after."

"We're very open with judgments today, it seems," the serpentine Malaugrym observed.

"I'd remind you," still another voice said, "that light or heavy, an eternity in torment is a price this mortal wizard hasn't yet paid."

From ahead of them in the mists came a deep, rolling boom, as if a great bell had tolled. Its echoes brought an end to converse for a time as the shapeshifters ascended. Bubbles occurred here and there in the shadows around them, brightening as they rose swiftly past. Dark shapes drifted beneath them. One shape strayed too near the spiral, and a Malaugrym made an exasperated sound and lashed out with a hissed spell.

There was a bright flash of falling sparks, a brief squalling, and the half-seen bulk convulsed away into the roiling shadows. A large, hooked black claw whose cruel curves stretched as long as the cone-lord stood tall tumbled into the spiral in its wake, severed cleanly by the searing magic. Trailing a last burst of sparks, it fell past a pair of Malaugrym in tall, gaunt human form before the power of the spiral took up the claw and it began to drift slowly around and upward. Another Malaugrym kicked the appendage aside, growing a clawed foot to do so. Driven out of the spiral, the severed claw fell from view, dwindling into the concealing mists, and was gone.

The bell tolled again, shaking the shadows, and the cloaking mists fell away in tatters. "Come," a deep voice rolled out, seeming to chase away shadows before it. "My time is not so endless that I can waste it on watching the vain parades of laggards." The last wisps parted, revealing the assembly high above the Great Hall to those drifting up the final arc of the spiral.

Sixty shapes, perhaps more, stood around the Shadow Throne, a vast, soaring spindle that pulsed its customary amethyst of magic and amber of bloodfire, and held the ruler of them all—Dhalgrave, head of Clan Malaugrym. Pale blue fire encircled one of his wrists as he leaned forward to watch the newcomers join the crowd around the floating throne.

In the shape he now wore, he seemed human—a naked, sexless human whose feet ended in a lion's pads; whose ivory body ended in a long, delicate tail; and whose flesh swam with many small fanged mouths that opened, snapped, drooled, and chattered soundlessly. His eyes were two dark, glistening pits that seemed to see the innermost thoughts of those he watched. And his kin, the greater and the lesser, looked upon him and were afraid.

Yes, Dhalgrave was dying, as all knew. Yes, the fires of fury that had seen him victorious through vicious kin strife down the ages were fading, leaving him placidly calm, almost cowardly it seemed. Yet he wore this weak human form—albeit handsome, even as the elves of Faerûn were comely, slender and fine boned—because doing so enabled him to control the greatest treasures of the clan. The very things that Malaug had crafted when he took the title Shadowmaster and strode from the strife of the dawn human kingdoms of Faerûn to conquer the demiplane of Shadow and build this vast and ever-changing Castle of Shadows. Or at least, the two items that had given Malaug and his ruling descendants mastery over the kin: the Shadowcrown and the Doomstars.

The first pulsed and winked on Dhalgrave's brow, darkness glimmering and sparkling in an endless, deadly chaos as it let him read the thoughts of any of the blood of Malaug he locked gazes with. More than that, it was the center of a web of spells and counterspells that waited to defend Dhalgrave against attack, or were set to howl through the castle at his death; and it gave him other powers whose secrets were much rumored but little known.

It was not reverence of Dhalgrave or respect for the Shadowcrown that had gathered most of the kin here today in answer to his summons. It was fear of the Doomstars.

They circled his left wrist endlessly, as they always did: four spherical stones of winking pale blue radiance, trailing motes of light as they orbited the bracer whose mighty spells—secrets lost with Malaug's death—tied them together, focusing their power into a weapon no shapeshifter could withstand.

The slightest touch of the rays—a dozen or more at a time—that Dhalgrave could call forth from the Doomstars could hold a Malaugrym unmoving, a powerless captive. With an extra caress of fear, some of the assembled clan recalled memories of an earlier disastrous treason-battle that had been settled in this manner. Properly wielded, the Doomstar rays could force a shapeshifter into any form Dhalgrave chose, from worm to mushroom, and bind the victim in that form forever by stripping away the power to shapeshift.

"Hear me, blood of Malaug," their ruler said formally, his old and wise voice rolling out deep and confident.

"Speak, O Shadowmaster High," the ritual response came raggedly, from most throats in his audience.

"You know the time left to me grows short," Dhalgrave said flatly. "Some of you have schemed to make that time even shorter. Thalart was one such schemer, though he saw the error of his designs and volunteered to serve the

Shadow Throne by destroying the mortal wizard Elminster . . . a task in which, regrettably, he failed."

The throne turned slightly at Dhalgrave's bidding, as he looked about at them all. "I say 'regrettably' because his failure leaves that task undone, for one of you to accomplish. Hear this. My successor as Shadowmaster Supreme, head of House Malaugrym, shall be the one who accomplishes the utter and final destruction of the mortal of Faerûn known as Elminster of Shadowdale, once Elminster Aumar of Athalantar, and the wearer of many other names in the years between. He is the greatest foe of this house, and I shall not go into the final shadow until I have seen him o'erthrown."

He looked around again, as if waiting for someone to fill the silence he'd left them . . . but no one did.

"There is a practical reason for this slaying, beyond the pride and passion of avenging the fallen of this house— too many, by far—he's destroyed down the years. An archlich of Faerûn, one Saharel, ceased to exist in a battle not long past. Her ending leaves Elminster, as far as we know, the only being besides myself who knows how to wield, empower, or destroy the Crown and Stars of Malaug I wear. He is, therefore, the only foe who can break our power over shadow and end the life all of us have known.

"For the younger and more arrogant among us, hear me and believe. Not only our dreams of greater power in Faerûn and in the Etherimm would be swept away—but all the lesser foes the Malaugrym have made down the ages would rise, here in the shadows and elsewhere, and rend us. You'd not then be striving with each other to decide who'd replace me, but fleeing as far and as fast as you could just to cling to life—existence, locked in some shape of lesser power that would begin as a disguise and might soon become a prison."

Dhalgrave rose to stand on air in front of the Shadow Throne. He grew taller, his ivory skin darkening as the batlike beginnings of wings stirred at his shoulders. He raised his left hand to show them all the fast-flashing, bright Doomstars dancing excitedly about it, and snarled, "Elminster must *die!* This wizard must be destroyed!"

Several of the senior family members echoed in thunderous unison, *"This wizard must be destroyed!"* and the very pillars of the castle flashed with sudden light as the Doomstars tolled once more. The ripple of chaos that burst from the circling gems and rolled outward in all directions through the shadows threw many of the assembled Malaugrym to their knees and terrified many of the younger kin—who'd never felt such power before—by clawing them, rudely and with casual ease, out of their carefully chosen shapes.

"If you would rule the house and realm of Malaug," Dhalgrave's voice boomed out over them all, augmented by the Shadowcrown until the echoes were painful in their ears, "go and slay Elminster, and speedily. For if I pass and he yet lives, the hand that wields this Crown and these Stars may be his, and doom will come to us all! Go, and work his death!"

"Death!" they cried in chorus and rushed off into the shadows, thrust away by the power of the Crown's compulsion, growing wings and tails and claws as they went.

Dhalgrave sat, his chin on his hand, and through his Crown watched them from afar. Where the compulsion faded, the younger ones sped on, hunger and fury in their faces. But many of the older kin slowed, and shifted shapes thoughtfully, and shook their heads.

Dhalgrave smiled a cold smile but did not use the Crown to further compel or rebuke them. Deep within, he felt as they did.

Many times that he could recall, Elminster's final and utter death had been a breath away, no more; but always he'd slipped away, cloaked in trickery and distractions and luck. Mystra's Luck. The favor of the goddess who watched over him, doted on him as he grew older and more bent to her will, a crabbed shadow of a man who served her with helpless loyalty. Always she shielded him and sent aid to snatch him back from his final doom.

Yet now her own power was failing, and her own foes were on the move. Bane for one. If only a small part of that one's schemes were accomplished, there'd be a time when the mortal wizard would be left to stand alone—and at last, at long last, Elminster's Doom could be accomplished.

It was time for the Malaugrym to earn their long-awaited victory, and past time for them to win and enjoy it. Then he could rest, his essence stealing into the Shadowcrown to join the other elders there, awakening only when he desired to, with the thoughts of the Shadowmaster his to whisper in and all the accumulated memories his to sort and seize upon, until the wearer of the crown saw things his way, and did as he bid . . . as even now he did the bidding of the whispering elders who'd worn the crown before him.

From time to time, Dhalgrave wondered, as they did, just what had befallen Malaug, the father and founder of them all. Dead, it was said, and by Elminster's hand, others held. Yet none of the elders had any memories of that death, only of a disappearance and many rumors cloaking it, like the fabled Cloak of Shadows, Malaug's lost secret, whose wearer would lead the house to true greatness.

He was looking forward to seeing that.

* * * * *

Shadowdale, Kythorn 14

"And you just left it there, all blood and tentacles, for Jhaele and her boys to clean up, and Shar and my two young blades to explain away?"

Storm Silverhand shook her head in disbelief, one shapely eyebrow raised, as she came around the table with a platter of fresh cheese-laced cornbread hot in her hands.

Elminster nodded as he reached for a slice. "Well, aye," he said, "but—" As he'd expected, she steered the platter deftly out of his reach to offer it first to the Simbul.

The Queen of Aglarond, hair and robes as wild as always, was frowning fiercely and muttering under her breath as she added a fourth layer of shielding spells to those she'd already woven around Storm's farm. She waved her sister away without even looking at the platter.

The lady bard sighed, rolled her eyes, and thrust the platter at Elminster. He smiled serenely, bowed with courtly politeness and, with delicate fingers, took a single slice. Storm set the platter down on the table and slid into the nearest chair to get out of the way. As she'd expected, she had sat down just in time to get clear of the flight of a pewter butter-crock and a knife, gliding in from the pantry to see to the slice he'd selected . . . as well as another dozen or so slices that rose one by one from the platter as the knife approached.

Storm was surprised when the Old Mage took the next chair and sent the first buttered slice drifting over to her, and the second to hang waiting by his beloved's still-murmuring mouth.

The Simbul finished her cloaking spells, smiled her thanks to them both, and attacked the bread with her usual voracious hunger. Storm watched her with a fond smile. Nethreen spent too much of her time rushing about the Realms as a raven or worse, eating nothing or things best forgotten. When she did dine, she had to approach many meals with cautious suspicion, thanks to the deadly designs of Thay.

Another slice rose from Elminster's plate to near the Simbul's mouth just as she finished the first, and Storm knew from the wizard's surprised expression that Syluné was at work, unseen but sharing the kitchen with them all. Dead she might be, but the Silent Sister had gone right on helping and caring for others.

"Well?" Storm prompted Elminster gently, leaning forward with her chin on her cupped hands.

"I look upon it as a Harper training exercise," the Old Mage told her airily, waving a dripping slice of buttered bread. He didn't notice when Syluné's ghostly hands tore it away to take to the Simbul, leaving him with just a crust.

"Explaining away dead bodies?" Storm asked, amused.

"Yes, I suppose—" She broke off with a snort of mirth as Elminster brought his slice down to take a bite, found he had possession of only a crust, and regarded it with deep suspicion.

"The problem with Faerûn these days," he said heavily, "is that ye can't trust anything to be as it should be, or once was. Anything at all." He glared at the offending crust darkly. Storm bit down on a knuckle to keep from laughing aloud at his baffled expression.

And then he winked and dropped the pretense and the clowning together, leaning forward to fix her with a disconcertingly level gaze. "I suspect that the Malaugrym spy on us all, often, watching for any chance to seize influence in Faerûn with little risk, and rushing in whenever events fall right for them."

The Simbul nodded. "I *know* they do," she said between bites, butter running down her chin. "Last summer, thinking to thin the ranks of the ambitious apprentice magelings of Thay, I set two slaying snake spells to seek out anyone who spied on a—well, on an attractive-looking trap I set up, that concealed nothing. Both of the spells struck within a day. When I followed them up, I found two headless bodies sprawled half in one shape and half out of another. Malaugrym, without a doubt."

There were grim nods, confirming similar experiences. Elminster pushed his plate aside and continued, "The point is, they're no doubt aware of the increasing chaos of Art in Faerûn, of Mystra's waning powers, of Saharel's final death, and of my own weakness. They must see this as a shining opportunity—perhaps the best they'll ever see—to rid themselves forever of their most annoying foe. Me."

The Simbul wiped her chin and said firmly, "It's just as gleaming a chance for me—for us—to destroy Malaugrym. If they're coming to Faerûn to destroy you—so long, mind, as you have the wits to stay here and not go running off to their shadow realm after every lure they set you—then they must come within my reach." She strode across the room to seize the back of a chair, and added softly, "And I'll destroy them."

Her slim hands whitened around the chair, trembled slightly, and abruptly the wood shattered, leaving her holding splinters. She stared down at the ruined chair. "Sorry," she muttered, stepping back.

Storm waved the apology and the damage away with the same gesture. "Are you sure it's the wisest course, battling Malaugrym across lands beset with growing chaos and lawlessness, what with magic fading and failing you?" she asked gravely, turning to eye both archmages.

"I'm tired of their attacks," the Simbul replied, forestalling Elminster's speech with a swiftly raised hand. "One of them just might succeed, robbing me of my beloved and Shadowdale—nay, all the Realms—of the best protector available. Moreover, Sister, I can't effectively fight Red Wizards if I must flee the fray often and abruptly to rush back across half Faerûn to battle Malaugrym. Who'll defend Aglarond when I'm not there? And how can I finish any foe if I rend his best defenses but must turn away, perforce giving him time to flee or replace his ravished Art?"

She looked at the twisted and shattered chair, and said with sudden cold force, "Destroy them, I say. Once and for all."

"If magic fails much more," Storm answered, "destroying them may suddenly be beyond our powers. Surviving might be a goal we find hard to grasp."

Elminster shrugged. "All magecraft—if one views it clearly and admits what truly befalls—is that sort of risky career. Not to dare is not to wield sorcery."

He got up and paced thoughtfully across the smooth flagstones of the kitchen floor, only to turn when he reached a wall, sigh, and add, "And yet—as always, it seems—I'm too busy to spend enough time on them right now to finish them. I know; this very thing has saved them many times—too many times—in the past. Yet in truth they're not worth it."

El spread his hands. "The Time of Troubles has ravaged Faerûn and is still doing so. I must repair this and that and the other—or what we know and love of Toril may be swept away and lost, and the war lost because I indulged myself in riding down a few pet foes."

"Look upon slaying Malaugrym as a repair," the Simbul offered calmly, setting forth the viewpoint in debate, her own emotions in check. "Weigh what they may do in Faerûn, left untrammeled, with the certainty of what they cannot do if you've stilled them forever."

Elminster frowned. "I'm too busy to get entangled in battle after battle, as they set their snares for me. And I'm far too busy to set snares of my own, using myself as a decoy to lure Malaugrym to their dooms . . . however richly deserved."

"Then you must be free to set things right in Faerûn, as before. Hidden by magic," Storm said to him, and then looked at the Simbul. "While the Malaugrym are drawn into attacking a false Elminster and open themselves to your attacks, Sister."

Elminster and his beloved both frowned back at her. "That will work but once," they said in unison. They exchanged glances, and Nethreen went on alone.

"Once they see they're facing a clone, or a simulacrum, or an illusion, they'll be far more careful in revealing themselves again. We might slay one, or three if they strike together to do the deed, but no more. I can't see how such a scheme will work in any continuing way, without demanding so much of our time that we might as well both be Malaugrym-hunting night and day through, and letting Faerûn fend for itself."

"I can see how it might be made to work," came a whisper from the empty air by her elbow. The Queen of Aglarond drew back a pace, raising a hand to unleash slaying magic, then blinked and said, "Sorry, Sister. How?"

The shadowy form of Syluné faded into view, smiling at her. "I can animate any body you create, and cast spells through it. As long as I don't have to smoke that awful pipe, I can be your Elminster."

"What's so awful about my pipe?" Elminster demanded, and was answered by three withering, silent looks. He looked around at them all, grinned weakly, and held up his hands in a gesture of surrender.

"Right, then," he agreed, "we have the makings of our false me. We still lack someone to watch over 'me,' someone capable enough to slay the shapeshifters Syluné's spells can't account for."

"We're all still too busy," the Simbul observed wryly, looking to Storm for inspiration.

The Bard of Shadowdale frowned doubtfully. "I've no Harpers close by who are powerful enough to hold their own against such foes, or who can be spared from whatever they're holding together in Faerûn right now . . ."

"Yes, ye do," Elminster said, the twinkle back in his eyes. "Two Harpers and a Knight of Myth Drannor, to be precise. In Shadowdale right now, fresh from ably demonstrating that they can slay Malaugrym with speed and cool regard for the spillage of good ale!"

Storm covered her eyes. "Ah, no," she said weakly. "They'll be slain for sure . . ."

"Aye, they will indeed, after this night," Elminster agreed briskly, "with all the Malaugrym who must have been watching that fight, if ye just let those three go about their business unprotected. Their best defense is to be a part of this ruse, hip deep in the serious Malaugrym-slaying business."

The Simbul grinned broadly. "It seems our only shining strategy, Sister," she said. Storm looked to Syluné for support, but the ghostly image floating beside her spread half-seen hands and said, "So it looks to these eyes, too."

Storm shook her head. "If they die . . ." she muttered, and then let out her breath in a deep sigh and waved her hand in dismissal. "Do it," she said heavily.

The Simbul inclined her head in understanding and brought her hands up, fingers spread. Tiny lightnings leapt between them, accompanied by a high, shrill singing sound, and she murmured, "El . . . ?"

Elminster spoke a few soft words of his own and pointed at three flagstones well back from the table.

Abruptly, three people were standing on the flagstones: two men and a woman clad in leather armor, long swords at their hips, half-full tankards in their hands, and startled looks on their faces.

Behind them the singing sounds ceased as the Simbul raised her shields again. After a few darting glances about, the three relaxed, relieved smiles on their faces, as Storm leaned forward across the table on her elbows, and began, "We have a little task for you . . ."

Sharantyr groaned. "I know these little tasks," she told the ceiling.

"So do we," Belkram and Itharr said in chorus, catching sight of Syluné's shadowy form and beginning to bow.

Sharantyr drained her tankard at one gulp and went on, cheeks reddening. "Unless I miss my guess, we'll be guarding a certain irritable old wizard against some sinister and ages-old unseen menace, with the fate of all Faerûn hanging about our shoulders."

Storm hid a smile by turning her head to address her own favorite spot on the ceiling (where she'd mounted a small round painting of a unicorn she'd done when she was very young, and was irrationally proud of) and replied, "Well, now that you mention it . . ."

3
To Battle We Go,
To Let the Blood Flow

Daggerdale, Kythorn 15

The horses snorted, as they always did, at the chill of the mists eddying around their ankles, the mists that cloak the Dragonreach lands of Faerûn before dawn. Shoulders and neck tight in the cold, Sharantyr knew just how they felt. "I'll set coins that no gods get up this early," she muttered.

Itharr, riding next to her, chuckled and said, "I'll not bet against you on that, Shar."

"Nor me," Belkram agreed from behind, the white vapor of his breath eddying around him.

Storm turned in her saddle to look at them. "What sort of Knights and Harpers is Faerûn breeding these days? Why, when I was your age . . ."

"I know, I know," Sharantyr interrupted her smoothly. "You went to bed at dawn after spending all night on your knees, cleaning the stables with your tongue, and enjoyed a deep and restful sleep for the time it took the stable master, roused by cock's crow, to walk the length of the stalls and empty his chamber pot over you. Then you had to run two miles to the river to bathe and draw enough water for all the horses to drink, run back with it, and get the axe to go out and chop firewood for the kitchen fires, before y—"

"When I was your age," Elminster said severely, "axes hadn't been invented yet. Nor horses. We *walked* everywhere to gather our firewood."

"Was it carrying armloads of all those whole, uprooted trees that got you all hunched over, graybeard?" Belkram asked merrily, steering his mount so that Storm was riding between him and the Old Mage.

Elminster swiveled a cold eye in his direction and

replied gruffly, "Nay, I got my hunch from fathering dynasties and fortifying kingdoms, a baby and a boulder at a time. Trees were no trouble to carry in those days, lad. The gods hadn't thought of them much before, y'see, and none of 'em'd grown much more than halfway to yer knee."

His reply was a chorus of sighs and groans. There was even one from Storm, as they rode onward in the last dark, misty moments before dawn. Then the lady bard tossed silvery hair out of her eyes with a lazy shake of her head, a motion so beautiful that watching it still made Itharr's mouth go dry, even the fortieth time around. She turned again to regard them all and said, "I can't ride with you much longer. Other duties call. Guard the Old Mage well, now."

Snorts and sardonic chuckles answered her. Storm stilled them with a lifted hand and reined her mount in as spear points loomed suddenly out of the mists before her. A gruff voice behind one of them said, "Hold, in Lord Mourngrym's name! Who are you, riding out before dawn?"

"Storm Silverhand," the lady bard told him calmly, "with two Harpers, the Lady Sharantyr, and—"

"Nay, lass, don't tell 'em my name," Elminster said gruffly, spurring forward. "Let 'em guess."

A helmeted face peered at him out of the mists, and visibly swallowed. "Lord Elminster," he said, "you may pass, of course . . ."

The row of spear points was suddenly gone, even before Elminster could snarl out any sarcastic reply, and they heard the clink and rattle of men in chain mail moving hastily aside to salute.

"My thanks, men of the guard," Storm said kindly into the mists. "Brion, isn't it?"

"Aye, lady . . ."

"I'll be back very shortly, alone," she said, and rode on, waving for them all to follow. Elminster inclined his head to her in sarcastic acquiescence and spurred past her into the mists.

"Ye bloody gods!" Storm muttered, rolling her eyes and

galloping after him, hand going to her sword out of long habit. Seeing that, the three who rode hurriedly after her reached for their blades, too. They rode on, hands on hilts but not drawing their steel, and soon heard ahead the thud of slowing hooves and Storm's soft "Hooo!" to her horse.

They came to an untidy halt in the mists, old wizard and all, milling around thigh to thigh in an open place where trails met. Storm pressed ahead a little way down one grassy ride until they followed her, and then reined in again. "Here I leave you. Follow this trail onward, and may you find fair fortune, all of you." She turned her mount, squeezed Sharantyr's arm for a moment as she rode past, and then was gone back into the mists.

As the thud of hooves faded away down the way they'd come, the first real gray light of dawn came stealing slowly in around them. "Whither now?" Sharantyr asked, peering at trees she could just begin to see on all sides.

"Forward, of course," Elminster said gruffly, and dug a toe into his mount's flank. It snorted its annoyance and moved off briskly down the new trail. The other three riders met each other's gazes, rolled expressive eyes, and followed.

"We appear to be heading into Daggerdale," Itharr observed carefully, as the first brightness of the coming day broke forth around them, and birds began to call and flutter.

"Perceptive, aren't ye?" the Old Mage replied without turning. His three companions, riding in his wake, sighed in unison.

"By all the lazily ruling lords," Belkram said under his breath, "it *is* Elminster."

* * * * *

The Castle of Shadows, Kythorn 15

Shadows shifted uneasily around them, seeming to sense the tension in the Great Hall of the Throne. A Malaugrym who bristled thorny spines from every inch of his lizardlike skin stood erect on the black marble beside the flickering scrying portal.

The portal was dim at the moment, showing only swirling gray mists somewhere in Faerûn. As always, the portal hung silent, floating immobile some way above the floor, but the Malaugrym drew away from it after a few moments. While near the endless flickering, he could not escape a prickly feeling of being watched.

He glared at the portal and then turned his back on it, feeling ridiculous.

A moment later, a tentacle brushed his shoulder and he jumped, spinning around with a wild snarl only to freeze amid the titters of his kin, standing around the hall, half-seen in the shadows.

"Don't drop your guard for a moment, not even here," said the tentacled giant mushroom who'd tapped him. Facing it, he recognized the voice. "Or rather, especially not here." Now he was sure.

"Bheloris," he said flatly, and the mushroom cap nodded. "Neleyd," it named him in reply and began to collapse, flowing swiftly into something else.

The words had been helpful, even friendly. Nevertheless, Neleyd drew away warily and grew a stabbing bonespike at the end of his tail, holding it up over his head, ready to stab if need be.

Bheloris ignored the threatening spike as he settled into the shape of a lion-headed man and stepped forward with his head cocked and a gleam in his eye. "Standing around waiting for a glimpse of the Great Elminster, are you?"

Neleyd shrugged, a small forest of spines shifting. "It seemed prudent," he said in a casual tone. Bheloris chuckled, and his tail briefly came into view, scratching the back of his neck.

"I'm glad to hear at least one of the younger blood of Malaug mention prudence," he said. "It would not be a grand day for our kin if all of you rushed into battle, falling over each other in proud haste, only to be slain by a foe anticipating just that artful tactic."

A strikingly beautiful woman glided forward through

the shadows, a goblet in her hand. As she came, barbed bone hooks grew along her forearms, and her head lengthened into a sharklike fin. "I've yet to hear anything but arrogance from the elders of the family," she observed coldly, "all of you sitting in judgment on the coming failure of us 'younglings' and doing nothing yourselves."

"And I have yet to discern anything but aggressive presumption in those younger kin like you, Huerbara, who speak against their elders and find fault with things done long ago, conveniently before such young, bright-browed heroes were on the scene to do things properly."

"Have a care, old one," Huerbara hissed, and Neleyd noticed the beginnings of a stinging tail to match his own, behind her back. He looked quickly at the leonine head beside him but saw only contempt in its eyes. Bheloris made no shifts in shape, made no move save for the very end of his tail, which switched lazily back and forth, seeming to await something interesting ahead.

"The warning is more appropriately received than given," he said flatly, and turned away from her to face Neleyd fully once more. "In this matter of the wizard, have you any plans that you feel moved to share, or simply discuss?" the older Malaugrym asked mildly, ignoring the furious Huerbara.

Neleyd kept a wary eye on her as he said, "Thoughts, yes, but anything approaching a plan or decision, no. I would look kindly on a chance to discuss such affairs freely with someone"—he bowed—"of more experience than myself."

Huerbara, eyes blazing with mounting fury, was shifting out of human form. Her beautiful head did not change, but the shoulders beneath it were sinking down into an insectoid body with many jointed legs. She was taking the form of a giant scorpion, stinger waving menacingly as she sidled forward.

Bheloris inclined his head and said, "I am pleased to see such wisdom and would derive still greater pleasure in being able to aid—even if only in a small way, through frank converse—the aims of so refreshingly intelligent a relative. When would you like to assay such a debate?"

Neleyd eyed the scorpion tail, licked his lips once involuntarily, and replied, "Ah . . . without delay, elder kin, though I feel it even more pressing to offer you a warning, an immediate warning of—"

Huerbara shot Neleyd a look of pure hatred, hissing loudly, but Bheloris waved a lazily dismissive paw. "I thank you for your regard for my welfare. Would that all younglings valued the resources of their kin so highly. Yet there is no need. The peril you seek to warn me of has the passion but lacks the daring. Observe her. She knows I am older, wiser in the ways of violence, and am expecting her attack. Thinking to awe me, she delayed action for a time . . . time in which she has inevitably begun to consider the consequences, and probable outcome, of any aggressive action. So it is that she has found she dare not attack, for swallowing an insult is a far less painful thing to do than dying—slowly, and in slavery to the pain and humiliations I can easily visit upon her. However reluctantly, she knows it and thereby takes another slow, unwilling step toward the self-discipline that marks the mature Malaugrym. Perhaps someday she'll have added enough steps along that path for her to finally acknowledge that self-control is necessary for those of our blood, and further, that she lacks it."

The elder shapeshifter spoke mildly, his words almost lost in the ever-louder hissing of the scorpion. Bheloris did not once look at Huerbara, however, but stood at ease, talking to Neleyd.

"Now, as to the matter of Elminster, any schemes you might foster are best hatched in private, lest the less prudent among us leap to the same ends and attempt unauthorized assistance—aid which inevitably will lead to the ruin of your plans and defeat for all kin involved. I speak now from rueful experience."

As the old shapeshifter continued, Neleyd saw Huerbara's fury abate. She backed up hesitantly, tail still wavering, then hissed again deafeningly.

Bheloris continued to ignore her, and she retreated again, dwindling suddenly into a woman's torso on a serpentine body. Neleyd tried not to look at her as she shot him once last venomous glance and glided away into the mists.

Several deep chuckles accompanied her withdrawal, and Neleyd saw her tail switch angrily before it disappeared from view.

"Shall we repair to another part of the castle?" Bheloris asked mildly. "The Great Hall lacks . . . privacy."

As if his words had been a cue, the scrying portal flashed once and brightened. Malaugrym all over the vast chamber glided or strode closer to afford themselves a better look.

Within the upright oval, it was bright morning, somewhere on a narrow, seldom-used trail through a forest. Four humans were riding horses along the path. In the forefront was an old, white-bearded man whose likeness had been shown to them all.

"*Elminster!*" came the snarl from a dozen throats. Several younger Malaugrym, who'd never seen the hated human mage properly before, moved right up to the portal to get a good look.

One of them gazed, smiled grimly, and moved one long-taloned hand in two intricate gestures. Then he strode past the portal, heading for a certain archway. "What are all of you waiting for?" he asked the chamber at large as he went. "Destroy him and be done with it!"

A Malaugrym who stood watching, in the shape of a darkly handsome man whose right forearm was a sword blade, turned to face the younger shapeshifter and frowned. "This we have seen before," he observed thoughtfully. "Have you given no thought to the possibility that this may be a ruse to lure us into attack? Is that truly Elminster or another, perhaps an empty husk, set up to lure us to our destruction?"

"*Another* craven elder?" From the shadows came a high, scornful voice that might have been Huerbara's. "Are you all cowards? How did you muster the courage to approach a human maid close enough to sire any of us?"

There was a stir around the hall, as if some listeners were stifling laughter or exclamations of approval, and others gasps or growls of outrage.

The Malaugrym with the sword arm only smiled coldly. "I've heard such words from several generations of kin before yours, rash one. Some of those who spoke thus still live . . . but no longer speak so foolishly." He turned and addressed his next words to the young Malaugrym by the archway. "Are you of the same mind as she?"

The young Malaugrym stared at him defiantly for a moment and then said boldly, "I am!"

"Come, then. You attack the human mage, and I'll watch. If you need aid, I'll pluck you to safety, so you at least will live to learn this lesson and not join our fallen too swiftly to think on it all."

"Trust you, Kostil?" the young Malaugrym sneered.

Kostil raised an eyebrow. "Trust, among us? Just how naive *are* you younglings?"

There was another stir, and at least one clear and deep chuckle from Bheloris. The young Malaugrym mage by the archway stiffened, eyes blazing, but said nothing.

Silence stretched for a breath, and then another, before Kostil added lazily, "Of course, if you're too afraid to strike at a mortal mage, I'll just have to find another of your contemporaries more willing to do so."

Almost spitting the words in his rage, the Malaugrym at the archway snarled, "Taernil son of Oracla fears *nothing!* Watch me, then, and render whatever aid you see fit—if you can find any way to aid me. I've not seen many elders wield spells that impress me."

Kostil smiled slightly and indicated the archway with a grand, leisurely gesture. Taernil gave him a wordless snarl of defiance, spun around, and charged through the archway.

Neleyd glanced quickly about the Great Hall and saw many older Malaugrym wearing smiles like the one on Kostil's face and shaking their heads. He turned away among the shifting shadowsmokes thoughtfully, seeking his own chambers and a scrying spell of his own. He must see this Elminster fight, if he or any of the blood of Malaug were ever to prevail against the wizard. As he left the open hall through an old tunnel that seldom changed its winding way, he passed two of the elders, standing in the shapes of griffon-headed giants, quietly wagering on the outcome of Taernil's foray. The bets were on how much magic he'd manage to loose at Elminster before being destroyed. Neither granted any chance that he'd survive.

* * * * *

Milhvar nodded. "The payment is accepted." He waved a hand behind him and the mists parted, swirling open in a softly widening whirlpool until Issaran could see the spell-stones that were going to cost him so much, winking and sparkling with their stored power. As he'd expected, they hung in a field of guardian magic. It would have been the sheerest folly to try any treachery upon the older Malaugrym who had hired him.

"I am ready," Issaran said, striving for calm, level tones. "Let it be now."

Milhvar nodded and waved his hand again. Another hole opened in the mists, revealing an empty, flickering upright oval of light. In size and radiance it seemed very like the scrying portal in the Great Hall.

Issaran strode toward the hole without hesitation.

"You recall the word for return?" Milhvar asked from behind him.

"Arthithrae," Issaran replied, not turning or slowing.

"Good. May you have Malaug's own luck," Milhvar said as the younger Malaugrym stepped through the magical gate—and vanished.

White sparks chased briefly up and down the portal's radiance. They were joined by others dancing in the emptiness within the oval, lights that grew swiftly into a glowing window on a scene of four familiar humans riding along a forest trail. The lights flickered once and then settled into silent immobility, identical to the scrying portal that many of the kin were now watching in the Great Hall.

Milhvar watched the scene within the portal shift as Issaran—no doubt walking on air for stealth—moved through the trees, following the four riders. Even if the bold youngling's Art—which Milhvar granted was stronger than most older kin expected or would readily believe—discovered Milhvar's conjured eye, Issaran could not destroy it without shattering the gate and stranding himself in Faerûn. Stranding him away from his spells, his kin, the protection of the castle—and the Shadow Throne he so obviously sought. One side of Milhvar's mouth crooked into a mirthless, twisted smile.

He would have been less confident had he been able to see Issaran's face. At that moment, in the woods of Daggerdale on a chilly morning, it wore the same ruthlessly assured expression.

* * * * *

Daggerdale, Kythorn 15

The sun was descending in the west when Elminster turned in his saddle. His pipe floated obediently out of his mouth. "We'll spend the night up ahead, in what's left of Irythkeep."

His companions nodded in silent acceptance and they rode on, as they had all day, through the ravaged wilderlands that had once been a proud and prosperous dale.

Rent by war for ten summers and more, Daggerdale was fast vanishing as the woodlands spread swiftly across untilled fields and deserted steads alike, reclaiming the land from the rule and hand of men who no longer lived to hold it at bay. In swampy places the trail they followed, once an important trade road, was almost gone.

Elminster, however, rode with the easy manner of a bored tour guide, never slowing to choose his way or change direction but proceeding as if strolling around his own garden, pointing out once-prominent landmarks as they went. Earlier, a gargoyle had risen heavily from the crumbling rampart of a small keep as they passed, but it had only circled once, high above them, and then descended again to the ruin, thinking better of attacking so purposeful a band.

The shadows were beginning to grow long when Elminster pointed at a pair of fingerlike stone pillars ahead. "Unless a dragon, lich, or something similarly energetic has decided to dwell there, that's our camp for the night."

"That's Irythkeep?" Itharr asked, peering through the trees. "There's not much left of it, is there?"

"A Harper needs no roof nor servants," Elminster told the sky overhead innocently, "but is happy to sleep under the stars, where the air is fresh, the living earth is closer, and the body has no chance to become pampered and weak."

Belkram and Itharr chuckled together. "Trust you to know *that* passage from the Code of the Harpers," said the taller of the two rangers, his eyes on the ruins ahead.

"Know it? Who d'ye think *wrote* it?" Elminster replied in aggrieved tones. Behind him, Sharantyr sighed theatrically, but when the Old Mage shot her a coldly meaningful glance, he found her staring skyward with a look of innocence surpassed only by his own recent performance. Elminster snorted and spurred his mount on, ignoring the cautious, weapons-out advances of the Harpers.

In the dust raised by the old wizard's hurrying horse, Belkram, Itharr, and Sharantyr exchanged glances, shrugged, and urged their own mounts on toward the ruins.

Irythkeep may once have been grand, but the winds and winters of passing time had not been kind to it since a besieging orc band had battered its walls from without, and the Zhentarim mage with them had summoned and let loose a fire-spitting hydra within.

All that was left now, amid fast-growing duskwood, pine, and shadowtop saplings, was a ragged stone ring outlining the outer walls, a few overgrown outbuildings and stables still clinging here and there to their roofs, and those fingerlike remnants of towers. Birds roosted on the stony pillars, and the crows that took wing as the four riders approached cried their anger at the intrusion loudly enough to alert ears anywhere near. Belkram cursed and then shrugged. What point stealth now? Several small furry brown shapes darted away from rocks where they'd been catching the last of the sun, and hurried off into the woods. Elminster watched them go, then rounded on Itharr.

"Well? Ye got that grand blade out and waved it about, lad. Aren't ye going to chase yonder scuttlers and do some carving to show thy manhood and deadly prowess?"

"No," Itharr replied brightly, and urged his mount ahead into the ruins. He tossed his grand blade into the air as he went, let it flash end over end up into the sunset, and then deftly caught it and sheathed it without slowing in his saddle or looking back.

Elminster's sniff was both loud and eloquent. Sharantyr hid a smile behind her own raised blade as Belkram and Itharr dismounted, tossed their reins over branches to serve as tethers for a few breaths, and jogged ahead into the shadows amid the stones.

The Old Mage watched them scramble and peer alertly about for a breath or two, then he turned in his saddle to fix Sharantyr with one clear blue eye. "Well, lass?"

Sharantyr raised an eyebrow. "As pouting maidens are wont to say," she replied, "'Well, what?'"

The wizard's stare became more forbidding. "What foolishness are *ye* going to favor us all with?"

Sharantyr smiled broadly. "Ah. Yes. Guarding you, actually." She waggled her drawn sword so the sun glimmered on one edge and then the other.

Elminster snorted. "Unnecessary folly, indeed. Why not put that steel away before ye hurt thyself with it?"

Sharantyr shrugged, more laughter in her eyes than in her face. "When Belk and Ith say the keep's safe, perhaps. We can talk about it again then . . . after I've told you how to cast a few spells."

"All right, all right, lass," Elminster said gruffly. "Point taken. Lash me with that pretty tongue o' thine later, eh? And put the sword away for now. Just do it."

Sharantyr gave him a puzzled frown as he vaulted from his saddle with sudden speed, sending his old dapple gray into a startled, snorting little dance. As she leaned forward to catch at its reins, the Old Mage dodged quickly past its head, snatched at her boot, and expertly pitched her backward off her horse.

Astonished, Sharantyr joined him on the ground, hooves flashing in front of her nose as both mounts decided that the shadows and stones ahead offered quieter grazing than the company of falling humans. She clutched at her sword to keep hold of it and opened her mouth to protest, but Elminster had taken two long strides to one side, away from her.

"*Well*, mageling?" he bellowed, staring back along their trail with blue fire in his eyes. He raised his hands in a deliberately flippant, showy gesture, and spoke a grand word.

Rolling up and staring hard, Sharantyr had a brief glimpse of a black-robed wizard standing on air amid the trees, excitement and fear on his face as his hands flicked and flashed in intricate spellcasting. She couldn't escape the impression that his fast-speaking mouth was sliding down into shapelessness. Suddenly, eight balls of bright flame erupted out of empty air and roared toward her and Elminster, drawing apart slightly as they came.

Sharantyr stared at the flaming death she knew she could not escape, heard the two young Harpers shout in alarm from the ruined castle behind her, and swallowed.

Is this how swiftly and easily death reaches out to take us all?

4
A Slaying Moon

Daggerdale, Kythorn 15

Sharantyr watched helplessly as flaming death roared
down upon the Old Mage. Long ago the spell had been
dubbed a 'meteor swarm,' castle-rending magic only the
mightiest mages could wield. And the wizard who'd
hurled it looked so young.

A Zhentarim? But all time for thinking was gone. She
was going to die. Sharantyr looked at Elminster as the
roar of the rolling flames grew louder around them.

The Old Mage was standing calmly, watching the racing fireballs. As Sharantyr looked at him, his eyes narrowed for a moment and he made the briefest of gestures
with two fingers. Little wheels of lightning were suddenly spinning in midair, in the path of the howling
swarm of fast-growing fireballs.

The lightnings blazed into sudden blinding brightness
as the flames flashed through them, but sliced apart the
blazing balls, drawing out their fury. The rush of stolen
spell energy made the spinning lightnings moan and
turn all the faster. Beyond them, eight failing, flickering
tongues of flame reached for the unmoving, watching Old
Mage . . . and fell away into nothingness, spent.

Elminster raised another finger imperiously, and the
whirling lightnings raced away from him, heading for the
mage in the trees.

The young mage cast another spell with desperate
speed, hissing and stammering words in clumsy haste. A
brief rain of green lances appeared in the air, slicing
down at Elminster's crackling pinwheels of captive fire
and lightning, but were shattered and absorbed without
pause. The lightnings flashed on.

The wizard shouted something desperately but hadn't
time to do more before the lightnings struck him.

Elminster leaned forward to watch with mild, academic interest.

Sharantyr had time to shiver at that as she turned to watch what befell their foe.

Trees cracked in the heat, hissed out all their stored moisture, and fell, smoking, as the writhing mage spun in their midst, small snarling bolts of lightning leaping around his body and scattering bright sparks where they touched.

He howled in agony, arching his torso, limbs splayed. Sharantyr stared, fascinated, as his arms grew, darkening and broadening into batlike wings.

Elminster uttered a satisfied hum and followed it with four quick, sliding words. The struggling figure of their foe spun end over end as the lightnings faded and fell away from it. The young mage seemed frozen, half-in and half-out of bat shape, bright eyes staring at them and brighter fangs gaping, as Elminster's magic whirled the attacker's body around and around. "Aye, I like thee better in half-shape," Elminster told the creature serenely, making a plucking motion with one hand.

The bat-thing abruptly broke out of its tumbling and seemed to leap across the air between them, directly at the Old Mage.

Sharantyr swallowed and rose up into its path, face set and blade extended. The bat-thing rushed forward as she held out her bright sword firmly in both hands. With a helpless, howling whimper, it impaled itself on her steel.

Shar staggered at the impact, icy blood drenching her hands, and stared in sudden alarm as the darkness and weight faded away from around her blade, taken to some other place by magic that flickered and tore at her, leaving her with a confused impression of shadows, watching malevolence, and a cold, dark somewhere filled with strange monstrous beings.

Someone said coldly, "Now do you see, Taernil?" but the reply, if there was one, was whirled away in a rising whistling, the noise of mournful, misty shadows streaming around and past her.

Sharantyr felt the magic that had taken the bat-thing

trembling through her. She stared at her bare blade and unmarked hands for a dazed moment before a firm hand encircled her arm above the elbow and an all-too-familiar voice rasped, "Did ye or did ye not hear me to tell thee to put thy blade away, lass?"

Sharantyr shook her head to clear the whirling shadows from it and gasped, "Who . . . *what* was that?"

" 'What' is right, Shar. A Malaugrym mage, young and careless with his power." Then the voice sharpened. "A fine useful pair the two of ye are! Puffing up here just a breath or six too late, as usual."

Belkram and Itharr plunged to a halt, breathing hard, and exchanged an exasperated look. "That's . . . our job," Itharr gasped. "Rushing in . . . we're Harpers, remember?"

Elminster snorted once more. "So am *I*, young and brainless one," he reminded them all none too gently. "And d'ye see me running about the landscape like a scared hare, trampling the crops and looking generally ridiculous?"

"No," Belkram replied bravely, "but I'm sure if we were a thousand years or so older than we are, we'd have seen you doing just that . . . probably with a maid or two fleeing in front of you and an angry father or two in hot pursuit at your heels."

The snorts of suppressed laughter that answered this sally didn't come from Elminster, who looked dangerously around at them all but spoke not a word.

None of them saw a figure watching from atop one of the ruined towers, a crooked smile on its face. "Laugh while you can," Issaran told the four standing far below him, and faded away.

A moment later, an oak leaf spun lazily down from that height, which was odd, for there were no oak trees near.

* * * * *

The Castle of Shadows, Kythorn 15

"Issaran goes to ground, would you say?" A goat-headed Shadowmaster chuckled, looking into the scrying portal.

"At least he's wiser than this flamebrain," rumbled a giant whose head resembled a warrior's helm, rising from his shoulders without pause for a neck. He was looking down at the smoking form of Taernil, shifting in slow pain from a puddle of black leather to something that had lizardlike legs. "By the Doomstars!" they heard him gasp. "It *hurts!*"

"I can send you back there, if you'd prefer," Kostil said calmly, watching the young Malaugrym shuddering at his feet.

"If any of you truly cared, you'd do something about this pain! Gods on their thrones!" Taernil spat, shifting slowly into something that had teeth to clench and eyes to glare around.

"Care, youngling?" The goat-headed Malaugrym sounded amused. "We do take care, which is why we watch and think before we rush in, trusting to a few spells that our foe learned to cast an age ago!"

"Clever, Yabrant . . . you're so clever, all of you," Taernil gasped, swaying upright and seeing Huerbara watching him mutely from the shadows not far away. He redoubled his efforts to quell the trembling in his limbs and look grim, calm, and strong.

The goat-headed Shadowmaster bowed his head sardonically. "At least you have progressed far enough to recognize cleverness, youngling. Keep at it, and perhaps in a century or so you'll have progressed far enough to be able to converse civilly with me for a moment. Add another century or so on top of that, and spending that moment with you might start to be worth my time."

"Well said, Yabrant," Kostil commented politely, taking a glass from the grasp of a paralyzed slave creature as it drifted past. He sipped delicately at the bubbling mint-green contents, his eyes shifting to match the hue of the drink, and turned to stroll away.

"You think so?" Taernil hissed, face white with fury, almost spitting the words in his rising rage. "You *agree* with him?"

"Why not? He's right," Kostil said serenely, walking unhurriedly off across the marble floor.

The helm-headed giant guffawed, and the recovering Malaugrym mage stiffened, turned, and snarled, "You too, Eldargh?"

The giant sighed and rose up to the full height of his snakelike lower body. He looked down at the young mage expressionlessly for a moment before he muttered, "Mature a little, Taernil. You're overdue for it," and slithered away into the shadows.

"All is not lost, lad," Bheloris said suddenly, stepping from behind a nearby leaning pillar shrouded in spiraling shadows. "You've learned something of value to us all."

"Oh?" Taernil asked bitterly, wary of more sarcastic criticism, his eyes on the grave admiring face of Huerbara as she approached.

"The spells he used against you told us all that you faced Elminster." He inclined his head toward the scrying portal. "Yonder is no false image or impostor, but a servant of Mystra."

Taernil's eyes narrowed.

Bheloris smiled ruefully. "Don't believe me?" He swept a hand at the shadows around. "*They* believe. See them go to work on their spells and schemes, now they know truly who they face?" Taernil turned to look at the misty gloom where the far reaches of the Great Hall of the Throne faded away to limits unseen, and saw his kin walking away, some drawn together in excited groups, others striding briskly.

The young Malaugrym drew himself up with something like pride in his eyes. "They are, aren't they?" His eyes flashed. "I traded spells with Elminster—and lived," he said quietly.

"Well, I wouldn't preen overmuch about that," Bheloris said mildly. "I've done that myself, as have most of us who style ourselves Shadowmaster. It's one of the ways we measured ourselves, when the kin were more rash . . . and more numerous." He turned to look at the scrying portal. "Why, I reca—"

The scrying portal flashed blindingly and burst into bubbling motes of light. There came a rumbling that shook every Malaugrym there, and the floor of the Great Hall—the very castle itself—heaved, shook, and tilted slowly and ponderously to one side for a moment. Abruptly, a score or more scrying portals burst into bright being here and there around the hall as an ancient web of spells responded wildly. The awed Taernil and Huerbara clutched each other instinctively, staring around, and were shocked to see naked fear on the faces of elder Shadowmasters as the legion of serenely floating portals showed them all the bright flash of something huge and fiery slashing through the sky of distant Faerûn. The shadows all around them rocked again, to the sound of many thunders, and someone screamed, *"Elminster!* The Doom is upon us!"

Someone else shouted, "Flee! Flee, or the House of Malaug is lost!"

"Not So!" roared a voice that echoed and re-echoed from every stone, goblet, and pillar of that vast chamber. Dhalgrave's voice shook with fury, and Malaugrym all over the hall cowered at the sound.

"This is no work of our foe, but something greater! Look, all of you, and behold: The gods of Faerûn are come, descending upon their worshipers in wrath. The land is torn! Look well, for this may be our best chance to seize as much of Toril as we can!"

Even as that great voice rolled out over them, one of the scrying portals burst into sudden blue-white fire, causing the nearest Shadowmaster to leap away from it and frantically shapeshift into something winged, flapping untidily in its haste. The portal spun around, blazing, and consumed itself, even as another portal exploded into a cloud of purple . . . flowers?

The Malaugrym barely had time to gape and peer at it before another meteoric descent rocked the Castle of Shadows, and its flash burst forth from every portal. Somewhere a pillar cracked, toppled, and fell with a thunderous, rolling crash. Shrieks of fear arose, and the tattered shadows were suddenly full of flying shapeshifters, adopting any form they could think of that flew and was fast.

Alone amid roiling mists, Huerbara and Taernil suddenly realized they were clinging to each other and hastily drew apart. Then they smiled at each other, tentatively, and joined hands again in a frantic dive for safety as another portal burst forth a gout of many-hued flame.

"Another god falling?" Bheloris murmured, strolling calmly through the ruins of rent portals and fallen drinkables. "Are we going to be able to trust *any* magic, in times ahead?"

"Ah . . . not all the wits of the kin have drained away or shriveled up," Milhvar murmured from the heart of a pillar nearby. "One, at least, has seen or felt the heart of the matter this swiftly."

Had a Malaugrym passed by the pillar in all the roaring chaos, it might have seen two dark, hooded eyes staring out of the stone. No more of the watching Shadowmaster could be seen, but somehow the entire stout stone pillar seemed to be smiling. Not that it was a particularly reassuring smile.

* * * * *

Daggerdale, Kythorn 15

As Toril rocked around them, Elminster stood watching the rain of stars with a smile on his face. Not that it was a particularly reassuring smile.

Belkram glanced at him once, as the flash of a star coming to earth somewhere south and east of them—in the Vast, perhaps—lit that craggy old face, and through the snow-white beard and moustaches saw that smile.

The Harper ranger shuddered, drew a deep breath, and announced to the Realms around, "Adventure . . . I know I asked for it. Thanks. Handsomely done. No more—got it?"

Sharantyr heard him and laughed rather wildly as the sky split apart above them and bright things fell in legions from a roiling rainbow sky that a moment before had been the soft purple of dusk stealing in.

"By all the gods, what'll the fanfare be?" Itharr shouted excitedly, staring up. Elminster shot him a look that had sent stronger men to their knees, but the young Harper was lost in trying to look at all the world at once.

The very air around them was alive, tingling and stirring. It felt as if all the world were awakening, rushing toward something exciting and splendid. The four friends felt exultant, on fire, and stirred as if by wild lovemaking all at once. They turned inward, looking at each other with shining eyes.

"What *is* all this?" Sharantyr asked the Old Mage, catching at his arm.

He swayed, almost falling, and for one terrified moment the lady ranger thought she saw him flicker and almost wink out. Then he was rounding grimly on her, as solid and as grumpy as ever.

"The Fall of the Gods," he almost whispered. "Come upon us at last. All of the gods will walk Faerûn before this night is out . . . and not willingly. We must be on our guards from this moment forth. Nothing is safe, and the land may well be laid waste or changed forever with each passing hour." He bared his teeth in a smile that had no mirth in it and added, "Just so ye know what to do with thy idle moments, from this breath onward."

Shar looked at him in sudden, quickening fear, her eyes wide. "Did the . . . the Shadowmasters have anything to do with this?" The two Harper rangers drew in close to hear his reply, swords out and ready but with no foes to fight.

"No," Elminster said shortly, holding up a hand to forestall further questions. Shar followed his gaze and saw that he was watching the rangers' drawn swords.

Small balefires flared and ran down the edges of those blades, and the four companions felt their hair rising to stand on end as the world lifted under them, hung for a moment, and then fell sickeningly through emptiness. As abruptly, the world returned to its normal state, seeming as it always had until moments before.

Cool breezes were stirring around them as night came down on Daggerdale, a night like any other.

They stared at each other and into the gathering gloom around them, hardly believing what had befallen and ended so suddenly. After a time, Itharr murmured, "What now, Old Mage?"

"Make camp, as we intended," Elminster said calmly, scratching the hair above one of his ears with the stem of his pipe. It was unlit and empty; Shar thought she'd seen him bring it out of a pocket only moments earlier. "Always keep an eye for the night around and blades at the ready. All the beasts of the wilderlands are liable to be up and about, stirred and upset by what just befell. First, see to the horses. They took fright, of course, and I can't hold them from bolting much longer." The Old Mage's voice changed. "Aye, that's another thing. Magic is no longer something ye can depend on. So don't set store by it. As of now, casting a spell is like starting a wildfire in dry wood; all things may be burned, not just what was intended."

"Without magic as our shield," Belkram asked very quietly, his eyes on the night around, "what's to stop these Shadowmasters from attacking in force and rolling over us?"

"Fear of me," Elminster said sweetly, clapping him on one biceps. "Now get ye to work. My old bones are looking forward to the softest cot ye can rig, this night."

Sharantyr raised a warning finger and eyebrow to forestall any jest in bad taste Belkram or Itharr might have been thinking of making, and after a silent moment they gave her identical grins and went away warily into the night, the first tongues of moonlight touching the edges of their swords.

"What will you be doing now?" Shar asked. "Should I be helping with wards or suchlike?"

"I must raise a shield and go within it, apart from ye for a time," Elminster replied. "Ye could do the heroic thing, of course, and stand guard with a drawn sword like those two heroes"—he snorted, jerking his head at where the two Harpers had gone—"or just sit down at watch for intruding beasts. I won't be long; just shout if ye need me."

Sharantyr inclined her head in a slow nod and stepped back, her sword hissing out. Never taking her eyes from the Old Mage, she sank down to sit cross-legged with her back against a sloping stone block that had once been part of the keep's wall. The lady Knight laid her sword across her thighs and settled herself into calm immobility.

"No snoring now," Elminster told her, waggling a finger in admonishment and farewell. An instant later, a ring winked and the world around vanished.

Then the shield rippled, wavered, and El frowned at it, pursing his lips and letting the tiniest part of his life-force slip out of him into the shield, steadying it.

That essence was gone forever now, and Elminster was the lesser for it. Which would have been a fatal miscalculation for the Archmage of Shadowdale—but for Syluné, the sister whom Faerûn thought dead, the loss was but a fleeting sorrow, lost amid so many more she carried already.

She shut the body's eyes for a moment, sighed, and then opened them again with a wry smile and went about what she had to do without haste or regret, for she was Syluné. First, the various depleted or partially spent rings, wristlets, and pendants that stored spells came off into a neat pile on the turf. Then she drew off one of the boots the body wore, did something to its heel, and spilled forth a fresh supply of enchanted baubles. She selected two rings immediately and slipped them on. Then she turned her attention to the other boot.

Its heel was empty and received the contents of her first pile. She put that boot back on and knelt for a moment in thought, selecting what would best serve from the small heap of fresh items.

There was so little magic here, and the lives of her companions—her friends—depended on it. So, to a lesser but not dismissable extent, did the freedom of much of Faerûn. Even so, conflicts of Art prevented her from wearing and wielding all of this at once. She made a few careful selections and put the rest away again.

Booted once more, she donned the various items, settled herself, and sat in stillness for a time, awakening things that had to be activated. Lines of force blazed through the lifeless body at her direction, linking this with that, building a web of interwoven magic as swiftly as she could. Now she could call up power after power without speech or gesture. This body didn't even need to breathe. The fire that animated it looped through the lifeless flesh, weaving tightly around enchanted items and muscles that moved limbs and gave expression to the now-slack face, and returned along a thousand channels to the stone nestled low between two ribs on the right flank. A stone from her hut, the anchor around which her spectral form could coalesce, the only thing that allowed her to animate this false Elminster. She felt for the stone with the body's fingers. When she could not feel it from the outside, she nodded in satisfaction and got up. The longer she stayed shielded, the more danger her companions were in.

Worse, the moment this imposture was discovered, they were walking dead. Syluné sighed experimentally, nodded again in satisfaction, and set her shoulders.

"Elminster once more," she murmured, raising a hand. The shield fell away, and she was gazing across moonlit space to the anxious eyes of Sharantyr, hand on the well-worn grip of her sword.

Being Elminster, Syluné did not smile reassuringly, but merely raised a gently mocking eyebrow and said, "Enthralled by the spectacle of my manly beauty, lass?"

Shar's face melted into a grin. "All the time, Old Mage," she replied happily. "All the time."

"Hmmph. Great advantage ye take of it, I must say." Elminster strode past her to peer hawklike into the night, locating the two Harpers. Belkram was curled up asleep in his cloak, drawn sword laid ready on its spare folds by his hand. Itharr was standing watch, looking around alertly. He raised a hand in salute to Elminster, who returned it and seated himself on the most comfortable-looking rock.

"All's well?" Shar asked, shifting her legs into a more comfortable position. Moonlight flashed on her blade as she moved. El watched it glimmer down the steel as an owl hooted somewhere not far off in the trees behind them.

"Aye. Should it not be?" Syluné made the words a testy challenge.

Shar gave her a quick smile of admiration for capturing the Old Mage's manner and said mildly, "Well, given that we've just seen the skies open and Toril wracked by forces that beggar even *your* mighty magic . . ."

Elminster snorted. "Be not so sure. Gods seem to feel the need to impress."

Sharantyr wrinkled her lips in wry disbelief. "Indubitably," she replied in cultured, courtly tones, "and yet the earth *did* shake, and magic is either failing us or going wild. Forgive me if, as a mere mortal, I find myself somewhat anxious as to what the future holds. Say, tonight and the morrow."

Elminster sighed. "The world has been falling apart for a long, long time. I know—I've been watching it. What particular part of this ongoing devolution concerns thee most, just now?"

Belkram rolled over and eyed them both. "Sleep fails me, amid all this chatter. Is this another version of his 'I'm older than the earth beneath ye, and have seen a thing or three' speech?"

"It is," Sharantyr said gravely. Belkram yawned.

"Ah, 'twas well I woke, then . . . wouldn't have wanted to miss *this* . . ."

"A little less biting sarcasm, ranger, if ye please," Elminster responded, looking around them at the night.

Tattered wisps of cloud were racing across the sky now, as if hurrying to a meeting they'd missed with all those divine falling meteors. When the clouds touched the moon, Daggerdale was bathed in a bright light of a violet hue that none of them had ever seen before. A little way distant, Itharr stared up at it in wonder, shook his head, and returned to peering into the dark trees around.

"What a sky," Shar murmured. Belkram gave her a look.

"It's all those Shadowmasters circling up there, interfering with the moonlight. Stop staring at it and get some sleep; I'll take over watch. If we start falling asleep where we stand, we won't even give the shapeshifters a moment's entertainment in battle."

"Cheerful, isn't he?" Elminster said to Shar, and added indignantly. "And what am I, suet pudding? Why must he take over watching from ye? Are my eyes so old and wandering?"

"Wandering, yes," Sharantyr mock-growled, and added sweetly, "besides, you're the one we're watching over, because you're the bad-tempered, witless wizard in this band."

And with that, she rolled herself in Belkram's cloak and sought slumber. The ranger and the wizard watched her in silence until they heard the faint rattle that served Sharantyr as a snore. Then Belkram leaned forward and whispered, "Old Mage, what's to stop these shapeshifters scrying us from afar and simply attacking when we fall asleep?"

"The Fall of the Gods. Magic will fail the Malaugrym as it fails us, in this e'er-growing chaos of Art."

"Aye, but without any magic of our own, how can we hope to stay alive against foes who can take any shape to elude our notice, escape us, or defeat us?"

"There is a way to make magic more reliable, if the need is strong enough," Elminster growled, and sat back as if dismissing the subject.

"How?" the ranger asked softly.

The Old Mage glared at him, but Belkram waited in unblinking patience.

Elminster made no move, but the singing of a quick cloaking spell was suddenly around them. "Spells ye cast can be steadied by feeding thine own life-energy into them, giving of thyself to make the magic as steady as it should be."

"Has a spectral one enough to spare, to so give?" Belkram asked, eyes steady.

"I shall do this when necessary, but only then," Elminster replied firmly, and let the cloaking magic fall away. The owl hooted again, and somewhere far off over the moonlit hills to the northeast a wolf howled.

They listened to the mournful sound until the wolf was done, and then Elminster stirred and spoke again. "Be more worried about attacks when relieving thyself is of paramount importance, or when you're hungry and downing weapons and wariness to eat."

"The monster who disturbs my meal," Belkram said darkly, "is liable to become my dessert."

"I shall devote myself," Elminster offered serenely, "to recalling the most superb sauces to accompany a platter of whole roast shapeshifter with apple in mouth."

"You could use the same sauce Lhaeo drenched those frogs with, a few nights back," Sharantyr murmured.

They both stared at her, but she was fast asleep, even through the sputters and chuckles of their suppressed mirth that followed.

Overhead, one last flaming star burst out of the night and flashed across the sky, heading west. It passed the waning "slaying moon" without pause or herald, and they did not see it fall.

5
Fallen the Flames

Daggerdale, Kythorn 15

When first it came, the violet moonlight made Arashta Tharbrow look up from her bitter reverie in alarmed wonder. What *now*, after a night in which she'd already seen stars falling from the sky and felt Toril shake around her? A night in which the small radiance she'd conjured to see what she was doing in the dark depths of these endless woods had twisted into a ball of worms and fallen to the earth beside her. A night in which the spell she'd hurled in disbelief to scorch those worms had produced a sprayed handful of ice pebbles instead.

"The gods are against me," she whispered despairingly, sitting down on what was left of a stone wall. She'd been a fool to come here alone, to wild, ruined Daggerdale. And if she couldn't rely on her spells, she'd very soon be a dead fool.

Who knew what beasts or brigands might be lurking near, watching her now?

She pushed down cold rising fear with firm anger and stood up, her robes swishing back to cover her high-booted legs. She was a sorceress of the Zhentarim, and folk feared her. Even veteran warriors deferred to her in the streets of Zhentil Keep—and sometimes in her bed. She took what she desired and did as she wanted, within the orders given by her superiors.

Those serpents! The mocking laughter of Thundyl echoed around her head one more time, and she saw again his amused face—and those of Rhaglar and Morgil, Master of Magelings, standing at his shoulder on the night of her humiliation, wearing smiles that vied with each other in open cruelty.

Arashta ground her teeth and banished those hated visions with a furious wave of her hand. Her long, unbound hair swirled around her head in the moonlight, and she caught at it with one hand, wondering what she must look like, wandering alone in these ruins.

She'd come hoping to slay Randal Morn and the handful of warriors loyal to him. They'd somehow eluded the best efforts of the Zhentarim to hunt them down. They slew encamped hireswords and Zhentilar troops in Daggerdale, striking here one night and there the next, slipping about like ghosts in the trees. They must have spell-cloaks to hide them from scrying, and they'd prevailed against some of the best blades the Zhentilar could whelm, leaving a trail of dead impressive even to an ambitious Zhentarim mage.

And here she was, alone, seeking to bring them down. Arashta smiled thinly. She had a wand, true. Its comforting weight, sheathed in her left boot, rubbed against her leg as she took a few steps out of the full moonlight, to make herself less easily seen by eyes in the trees nearby. The wand had little magic left in it, though, perhaps only a single strike. She also had herself, and men long without a woman might let a hard, wild beauty get closer to them than they'd suffer a peddler or pilgrim to venture.

She had to find them first, though, before a brigand arrow or a hungry beast found her. Even if she prevailed against such foes, it would not do to let a watching Randal Morn know she commanded magic that could slay so effortlessly.

The wings of her fury had brought her here so easily: a spell that, without her spellbooks, she could not regain here to take her home again. She had another magic that could change her appearance, but it was a sham seeming only, not a true change in shape. If she used it to hide herself while she slept, she'd be without it when it might be needed in battle.

Sleep. She yawned. Again. Soon she'd be too weary to stay awake. How to sleep in safety, in these wild woods?

Arashta sighed in exasperation. It had seemed so simple a mission when Thundyl—gods blast his arrogant smirk!—had charged her with it. All she'd have to do would be to avoid swaggering into Daggerdale with forty warriors or so, as her unsuccessful predecessors had done, and avoid being careless.

It struck her that she wasn't eluding carelessness all that well. Arashta shook her head, smiled ruefully, and took a few steps east, deeper into the dale, to where she could just see the glimmer of a small stream snaking across overgrown fields. Perhaps— She froze and then suddenly whirled around, robes flapping, to stare at the dark wall of trees. Someone, or something, was watching her. She could feel it. She raised a hand slowly, debating whether to cast her lone spell of revealing now or to save it for a more pressing moment.

In the trees, the man whose body looked like the dark trunk of a duskwood had grown tall enough to overtop most of the branches in his way. Steadying himself by grasping a nearby bough, he threw the stone in his hand high and hard, and dwindled again, sinking down as the stone was still in the air.

When it crashed down in the brush behind Arashta, making her whirl around again with a little gasp of alarm to face nothing in the night, the shapechanger had become a nine-foot-tall man with jet black skin and burning red eyes. As he stepped forward, his crooked smile changed and his features sharpened into those of a handsome man wearing spiked black armor and a superior smile.

"It would be best, Arashta Tharbrow, if you knelt to me." The soft, pleasantly menacing voice made the Zhentarim sorceress stiffen and brought her whirling around once more, hands raised to hurl deadly magic.

The figure facing her stood unmoving except for his hands, which stroked and toyed endlessly with something smooth and white . . . a jawless human skull. Arashta's gaze came slowly, almost unwillingly up from the skull to meet the stranger's blazing ruby eyes, and though she feared she knew the answer, she had to gasp the question.

"Wh-who are you?" As the words came out, she was already dropping to her knees in the grass and stones.

He smiled in cold approval. "Most mortals know me as

Bane." He left a little silence for her gasp of involuntary awe, and it came. The name seemed to echo and roll away from him when he uttered it. Something flickered across his face for a moment, but he stepped forward with a widening smile. "I've been watching you, lady sorceress, and have come to value you rather more highly than many of my mightier servants in the ranks of the Zhentarim. I have need of an agent who can serve me with true loyalty, and I believe you could be the one I'm seeking."

Arashta's face was the white of sunspun clouds, and her eyes glittered. "M-me, Lord?" she gasped.

"I can see you, in days soon to come," that soft voice continued, as the red eyes seemed to bore into her own, "as my highest servant in all Toril, a sorceress to overmatch the Witch-Queen of Aglarond, who rules more than one realm in my name and who need fear no man nor monster in this world."

A jet black eyebrow lifted. "Will you serve me with utmost loyalty, to the death?"

The sorceress stared at him for a moment, eyes huge and glistening in the moonlight, and whispered, "Lord Bane, I will."

"Speak my name seldom," came the reply, a hint of iron in the melodious voice now. "And hearken. If you'd become my most powerful and trusted servant, prove your worth now. Set aside pursuit of this Randal Morn—his fate is of no consequence, whatever certain Zhentarim believe—and slay for me instead the mage Elminster of Shadowdale and his three companions: the Lady Sharantyr of Shadowdale and two Harpers called Belkram and Itharr." The jet black giant took a step away from her and thrust the skull into his chest, where it vanished without a sound. His hand was empty when he drew it out of himself again and asked, "Will you essay this for me?"

Breathing as if she'd run a long way, Arashta licked her lips and replied, "Lord, I will."

He did not quite smile, but the sorceress, heart racing and excitement rising in her throat like leaping fire, knew that he was pleased. "The four you must kill are not far from here, in a ruined keep beyond yonder hills."

She looked southeast along the line of his pointing arm, marked a stony face on one slope she'd not forget or lose sight of, and quickly looked back to the god.

"You've heard of the magic of Elminster," he said dryly. "These days, my Zhentarim seem to talk of little else." She nodded, too eager to be hesitant, and he added, "Though he is always dangerous, the Art left to Elminster is greatly weakened. Right now even Morgil, Master of Magelings"—he allowed a smile to touch his lips—"could match him in battle, spell for spell." Bane waved a hand, and four life-sized figures were suddenly standing around her. Arashta almost hurled a spell at them before she was sure they were images and not the folk themselves, snatched here by the god's magic. "Look well," he said, "from all sides, if you wish. Rise and be free, Arashta. Know these foes and slay them for me, and more power than you can dream of shall be yours."

He hesitated, and then added softly, "It is not often I take a consort."

She was still reeling from that thought when he added, "I shall be watching you do this for me. Know this: It is the end that I value, not the means. Use hirelings, tricks, whatever. Glory is a foolishness others value, not me."

Sweat drenched Arashta in her excitement, and her body trembled unceasingly as she circled the four silent images as if in a dream, staring until she knew she'd never forget their looks.

Then she turned to Bane and went to her knees again. "Lord," she whispered, "I am ready."

"Good," said the dark figure looming above her. With slow ease, one sable hand drew forth a dagger whose blade did not shine but was a deep black with stars swimming in it. Bane held one flat side of it out in front of her face.

Trembling, Arashta put her lips to the dagger and found it cold. After a moment Bane took it gently away, and one cold black hand—he had long, pointed black fingernails like talons, she noticed—took hold of her left wrist.

He drew the dagger down her forearm gently, slicing a short line so deftly that only a few drops welled out. A finger wiped them away, and finger and dagger both vanished into that black mouth, to emerge clean again.

He handed her the dagger. It tingled in her fingers, cold and deadly, and the sorceress felt the chill force racing through her. "Always worship me thus," he commanded. "If I am not present to take the blood from you, consign it to a flame."

Arashta swallowed. "Y-yes, Lord," she managed to say. "Always." One of his hands suddenly flowed, widened, and became a mirror that showed her the face of Arashta Tharbrow strangely changed. In her reflection, at least, her eyes glowed with black-and-purple fire. She gasped, and looked up at him in wonder.

Bane gave her a wintry smile. "The mark of my power," he said. "It will soon fade." He raised a staying hand, turned away, and strode toward the trees. "Seek not to follow me," his voice came back to her, as soft and as clear as if his lips were by her ear, "but do as I have charged, without delay. The dagger you may keep."

Arashta bowed her head. As she'd expected, when she straightened up again, he was gone.

She stared down at the wickedly curved dagger in her hands. It was one piece of polished obsidian, like no other she'd seen before, its edges razor sharp. Wonderingly, she brought it to her lips again, and then held it up to the moon, panting in excitement. "Elminster shall die!" she told it fiercely, her vow echoing back from the ruins around her.

And then she was up from her knees and running southeast, across the grassy hills, the dagger clutched in her hands.

Moonlight shone back from it, and a tall tree saw the flash, smiled a crooked smile, and shrank back down to man shape. The longer he walked Faerûn, the more comfortable this form seemed. This must be why most elder Shadowmasters preferred it, after all.

Issaran of the Malaugrym smiled, shrugged, and twisted into the form of a giant barb-tailed bat. He took wing north into the night, and for greater speed shaped a second set of wings to beat in alternation with the first pair, cleaving the air with a soft moan. A little shifting, a few minor glamers . . . and a servant was his, to hurl her life away trying to work his ends.

Ruling Faerûn—save for dealing with his own kin—would be all too easy. His teeth flashed in a smile as he went. A moment later, a real bat shied away from him, squeaking in terror, and his smile grew broader.

* * * * *

The Castle of Shadows, Kythorn 15

"Issaran certainly makes it look easy," a pillar murmured, but no one was close enough to hear it. By the time the bell tolled again and other kin drew near, the scrying portal was once more showing Elminster's camp.

"Things seemed to have settled down, I see," Kostil remarked to Neleyd, as they came out of the Shaft of Many Stairs together and entered the vast Great Hall once more. "We're back to just one scrying portal."

"Why do away with the others, I wonder?" Neleyd asked, as the deep booming of the bell rolled over them again. Kostil gave him an amused look.

"After a surge of wild magic like that, youngling, every second portal could be the eyes and ears of some foe—or a maw waiting to spit out whatever death they choose to send us. Or to suck in whoever passes. Then again, the places they show may not be what you'd like to look at, or think you're seeing. There were a lot of such things in this castle, before Dhalgrave came to power. In those days, folk of our blood were concerned with ruling other planes. We saw Toril simply as a place to snatch up human and elven maids for breeding . . ."

"I saw old Rahorgha die that way," Bheloris confirmed, coming up beside them. "A manyjaws took off his head—down to the arms—when he looked too closely at a scene in a portal it was using as a lure . . . a friendly quartet of nude mermaids, as I recall."

"Who?" Neleyd asked, frowning. He thought he'd heard that name once before, but . . .

"Rahorgha the Brawler, we called him," Kostil said briefly, as they mounted the lift-spiral. "He was slain well before Dhalgrave came to the throne."

Neleyd swallowed. "You remember those times?"

Kostil gave him a despairing look. "Younglings," he muttered, a comment almost lost in the sound of Yabrant, Eldargh, and Bheloris chuckling in unison.

And then the orange and purple radiances flashed on their faces, and the gigantic spindle of the Shadow Throne was floating before them, a many-headed hydra the hue of shore mists seated in it. Several heads of dark, glistening eyes met Neleyd's wondering gaze, and he shivered despite himself. He didn't need to see the Shadowcrown or the Doomstars to know he was facing Dhalgrave.

Other kin were ascending swiftly to join them, more than Neleyd had ever seen gathered together before. He recognized Taernil and realized that the many-tentacled thing slithering along beside him must be Huerbara. When it glared at him, he was sure.

A tall, crimson-skinned biped covered with warts and questing tentacles of loose flesh oozed past, leaving acrid fumes in its wake. As it went, it rumbled to a lazily drifting fish with a snakelike tail that floated beside it, "There've been more assemblies these past few days than in the last few years. What's gotten up Dhalgrave's orifice now, I wonder?"

Bheloris grew a smile on his back, where Dhalgrave couldn't see it, but in front of Neleyd's face. Neleyd found his view blocked not only by Bheloris but by several increasingly bulky arrivals, and grew eyestalks to look over them. He wasn't the only kin to do so, he discovered, locking gazes with several other peering stalks bobbing above the crowd.

Then movement and noise ceased together as the Shadow Throne pulsed with a vivid amethyst radiance, and out of its heart Dhalgrave thundered, "Hear me, blood of Malaug!"

"Speak, O Shadowmaster High," came the ritual chorus, the gathered kin sounding a little resentful at the interruption of their various affairs.

Dhalgrave leaned forward, almost bellowing in his excitement. "At last—at *long* last!—magic seems to be weakening in Faerûn, and when most spells are cast, the magic goes wild. All is in chaos. Beyond the wildness of Art, avatars of all the gods walk Faerûn, sent there unwillingly and much hampered in their powers. Their magic overmatches us but is no longer absolute."

The Shadowmaster High leaned forward. "To some of us, sorcery is a strong weapon, but to most folk of Faerûn, it's their *only* weapon. Without it, they cannot stand against us in open strife. If we move more deftly, slaying certain rulers and taking their shapes, entire kingdoms of Toril can be ours without a battle!"

Excited murmurings were swelling. Dhalgrave quelled them with sudden thunder. "I know some of you hunger to *play* in Faerûn. Let me remind you that it is a resource for the use of all, under the protection of the Shadow Throne. Wanton destruction will not be tolerated, except against the person and allies of the foe Elminster. Treat Faerûn as our private garden, to be nurtured for later use."

The Shadowmaster High's many heads—Neleyd counted a dozen, but some of them seemed to be slumping down and shifting shape, as others rose elsewhere—looked around at the gathered blood of Malaug, and Dhalgrave added, "I have urged you to seize this bright chance to strike down Elminster, and further suggested that this could be our best opportunity to seize as much of Faerûn as we can, but as always, Shadowmasters are free to act as they see fit."

The Shadowmaster High rose from his throne and stood on empty air to look around at the assembled shapeshifters as he said forcefully, "Against our traditional freedom, I lay this sole commandment upon all: No one is to bring beings of Faerûn to the Castle of Shadows, or leave an easy route by which Faerûnians can find our home by following any of the blood of Malaug, without my prior permission. And be advised that such permission shall be forthcoming only in the case of approved breeding stock or captives who've been demonstrably rendered helpless, but who possess valuable knowledge—such as magic—you deem worth acquiring. I want this clearly understood. The supreme penalty shall apply for transgressions if I deem it appropriate—and I *will* deem it appropriate."

The Shadowmaster High raised his hands, and the assembled Malaugrym suddenly found themselves sinking, as the unseen floor beneath their feet dropped smoothly down into the swirling shadows toward the black marble floor of the Great Hall far below. The Shadow Throne and the floating figure of Dhalgrave were soon lost to view in the mists above them, and all the shapeshifters began speaking at once.

"He must be furious," Bheloris told no one in particular, "to dismiss us so. Word must have reached him of Olorn's plan to bring in all the Zhentarim, to pluck their spells from them."

"Hah," Kostil said, turning. "The last thing I want is several score of ambitious, ruthless little human mages scurrying about the place trying to slay us all. If such a risk is to be taken, let it be for one mage of real power, so we can learn magic of some worth."

"Such as?" Yabrant asked, snaking out a tentacle that sported a mouth and a trumpetlike ear to better converse.

"A Red Wizard of Thay, I intended."

"If the risk is to be taken anyway," Neleyd blurted, "why not bring in this Elminster?"

He was astonished and embarrassed by the respect he saw in the looks that all the nearby kin gave him—except one.

A gray, withered elder Shadowmaster in hobgoblin form thrust a belligerent face forward until his protruding lower lip almost touched Neleyd's own and snarled, "Have you seen Malator, Dhalgrave's bodyguard?" Neleyd nodded; who had not seen the battered giant Malaugrym who served as the Shadow Throne's champion? He was reckoned the mightiest Shadowmaster in combat, and often wrestled the worst of the marauding night-worms of the shadows.

"I am his older brother, Dlagim. I was always the larger and stronger of us two," the old Malaugrym continued, and smiled bitterly at Neleyd's obvious disbelief. "Aye, you can scarce believe it. Well, this is all that Elminster left of me, the last time he visited the Castle of Shadows. He just strolled in and started telling us what we must not do, and what we'd best stop on the instant—and all of us within earshot must have attacked him. He slew over forty of us before he left; only three survived. Let's hear no more talk of bringing Elminster to the Castle of Shadows."

"It was but a suggestion," Kostil said smoothly.

"A foolish one!" Dlagim said heatedly, but Kostil spread his hands and half-smiled.

"Ah, but that's all the younglings among us know how to make. And if all who make plots or suggestions that seem foolish were sent away from the castle, the place would soon be empty. Only you, I, and Dhalgrave himself would still be here . . . sitting staring at each other in the echoing emptiness."

"Look upon it as entertainment," Yabrant offered.

The old Shadowmaster's eyes blazed in sudden anger, but he took one look at the large and capable antler-adorned Shadowmaster and recalled that he had urgent business elsewhere that required immediate attention—after a last snarl of, "Bah! Fools and irresponsible rascals, all of you!"

"What'll befall now?" Neleyd asked Bheloris curiously. The elder waved at the groups of talking, gesticulating Malaugrym around them and smiled. "The cautious and the bold will make war on each other with their tongues, each seeking to prevail. In the end, most of us will go our own ways, unconvinced by whatever we've heard. 'Tis always thus. Dhalgrave will be sitting up there listening, mark you, and noting just who says what."

"The cautious being those who want to stay out of Faerûn until we know what's going to happen with the gods and magic and all?"

"No, youngling," Kostil corrected him, "we *are* Malaug's offspring, after all. The cautious are those who favor manipulation of Faerûnians, and goading or driving beasts and others to serve as our agents, so that our hand remains unseen. The bold are those who want to rush down there at once and attack everything they see, except that they all want someone else to attack Elminster."

"And the Red Wizards, and Khelben Blackstaff, and the Simbul of Aglarond, and a few others," Yabrant added with a grin.

"Precisely." The word had scarce left Kostil's mouth when angry voices shouted icily from the sneering, snarling mouths of two young and handsome Malaugrym who stood in human form, pointing and gesturing rudely at each other.

Neleyd stared from one to the other. "I've seen that one before, but never heard such words from him . . ."

"That's Olorn," Eldargh rumbled. "He fancies himself the next occupant of the Shadow Throne and is fool enough to think he can manipulate all of us into giving it freely to him."

"And his rival is Amdramnar—the wiser, I think, and smooth as oiled wine. A loner, where Olorn surrounds himself with the weakest witted among us, forming little whispering societies to make the nothings of the kin feel important."

"Olorn favors bringing human captives in, then?" Neleyd asked hesitantly, looking from one shouting shapeshifter to the other.

"Aye, but he might change his views several times before this day is done."

Neleyd looked at him in astonishment. "Why all the fury, then?"

"Those two?" Bheloris chuckled. "They'd disagree over what their own names are, just to be on opposite sides of something. They'll slay each other one day, for sure, if someone else doesn't get one of them first."

Kostil shrugged. "If they hold to their purposes behind Olorn there—see them storming off, all showy gestures?

—that someone bids fair to be Elminster, and soon."

Neleyd suppressed a shudder. "Have you seen many of us—of the kin—die?"

"Down the years?" Bheloris looked thoughtful. "Yes. A good threescore."

Kostil nodded. "More than that, before these eyes."

Neleyd looked from one of them to the other. "So what do you think we should do with human mages?"

"Destroy them," Kostil said calmly. "Once and for all."

6
Fire in the Night

Daggerdale, Kythorn 15

The rabbit stew that Storm had packed for them was all gone, and the fire out. Sharantyr and Itharr were licking their fingers for the last of the butter that had dripped from their hardbread, as Belkram scrubbed the pot clean with handfuls of sand. Elminster lay on his back, unlit pipe in mouth, and stared up at the circling stars overhead.

"Nnmm," Itharr said, licking his lips and wiping his hands on the turf beside him. "So how long are the gods likely to walk in the Realms and chaos reign?"

Elminster shrugged. "Too long." He lowered one elbow to peer past it at the young ranger. "If ye want a count of days, I know not."

"And we have to wander the wilderlands until then, playing nursem—ah, escorts—to a certain old wizard whom the shapeshifters regard as their Great Foe? Is this . . . prudent? Is this likely to end in anything else save disaster? Is—"

Shar put a playful hand on Itharr's chest and shoved him flat on the ground. "Stop sniveling, you thing you!" she said affectionately.

Itharr's reply was forestalled by Elminster's sharp warning: "No foolplay, ye two. We must be ready for them, always. Now is when they're most likely to attack!"

His words came too late. The Harper had tugged, twisted, and hauled all at once, and the helplessly overbalanced Sharantyr went over him, to her own landing. In the same movement he was atop her, tickling, as children tumble at play in muddy yards.

"*Itharr!*" Elminster roared over Sharantyr's breathless giggles and sobs of protest. The ranger turned a face of injured innocence to him.

"They'd have the good taste not to attack, surely," he asked, "when we are seriously engaged in wallowing in the heights of depravity?"

"They'll probably do *exactly* that," Elminster replied grimly, sitting up to give the Harper the full benefit of his forbidding glare.

"Wallowing in depravity?" Belkram asked in hurt tones, returning from the stream with the rinsed pot gleaming in his hands. "Without me?"

Elminster's snort awoke echoes from the stones around. "Truly the gods retain their curious ideas of humor," he observed, "giving me three jesters to ride around the Realms with."

Without hesitation, Belkram removed the lid and swept the upended pot deftly down over the Old Mage's head. Then he sprang back—just in time.

The pot shot up into the air, flashing end over end in the moonlight. It overtopped the stony needles of the ruined towers and fell again to earth, well clear of the flickering nimbus of light surrounding a furious old man who stood on air about four feet off the ground. "*Enough!*" the Old Mage roared. "Belkram, I'm astonished! *Ye*, of all here!"

Belkram spread unapologetic hands. "You can trust me to be loyal," he murmured, "but not predictable. Never predictable."

He'd said much the same thing to the Master of Twilight Hall almost ten years earlier, after Belkram had let a Zhent caravan crew swindle a few greedy and crooked local merchants in Elturel before attacking them. A furious Belhuar had demanded to know why. They had talked long into the night, and as dawn had come through the windows of that chamber, the stern old warrior who saw to the defense of Twilight Hall had clasped Belkram by the shoulder and said simply, "You'll do. You'll more than do."

Then a rare smile had split his face, and he'd added, "Mind you, madcap Harpers always seem to work better under Storm and Elminster, so I'll be sending you east for training under them, with your friend Itharr. I think all four of you'll deserve each other."

The gods had given Belkram Hardeth a merry spirit that was apt to rise up and seize hold of his tongue and his wits in times of danger, when other men grew grim and careful. This spirit had taken him across the Realms to the seas off the Sword Coast, where sailors valued such gusto. There he had made his living with his blade but stayed nowhere long, because he spoke plainly when masters gave foolish orders that cost lesser men their lives.

Foolish orders. He remembered stumbling along a wet night street in Athkatla, too much zzar riding heavily and uneasily in his stomach, when a haughty local merchant had sneered at him for being a good-for-nothing hiresword, loyal to no lord or company.

"Whereas you," Belkram had replied, "serve only your own purse—far higher and more noble a cause."

Grins had told him that the noble's bodyguard appreciated his sarcasm, but the white-faced merchant had curtly ordered his men to slay the outlander mercenary. A few anxious moments of slashing steel and swift shuffling in the street followed, and then six bodyguards lay senseless, dead, or dying as Belkram faced the now-terrified merchant alone.

The man took to his heels like a scared rabbit. Belkram had sprinted after him, catching up to say into his ear at full run, "You see? We hold the same values at heart. Each of us'd rather be a live coward than a dead hero!"

The merchant had fainted dead away, so a thoughtful Belkram had tossed him in a water butt to revive, and left the city that night.

He still believed that view made a swordsman more useful to the peace of Faerûn than any other stance. The mistake too many folk made—even the senior Harpers at Twilight Hall—was thinking him a craven, unprincipled man. Belkram of Everlund would keep after his foes and his goals, trying one way and then another, patient and inexorable as the years passed, tirelessly probing here and then there for a chink in the armor of those who stood against him, ever seeking a way through.

Of course, for such an approach to succeed, one must survive as the years pass. That was the task he was having trouble with. Twice now he'd been dragged back from the great darkness by the spells of priests hired by friends. On the other hand, his merry loyalty had won him those friends.

"What's the matter?" he asked the raging mage in innocent tones, holding the lid of the pot in his hands. "Don't you like helms? Warriors at least have sense enough to wear them when *they* go into battle."

"No, I don't like helms," Elminster said sourly. "And wearing pots over my head pleases my fashion sense even less."

That was too much for Sharantyr and Itharr. Their full-throated laughter as they rolled apart brought them the Old Mage's undivided attention. "And just what, pray to all the gods, do *ye* both find so amusing?"

"The sight of a . . . potty old mage," Itharr choked out, through fresh howls of mirth.

Elminster's mouth crooked. "The lot of ye have been on the road for far too long. The gods have been touching wits around here."

"Is that a bad thing?" Belkram asked. "New plans and items must come from somewhere."

"Aye, and most of 'em could go back there with much profit," Elminster grunted. "Back to the bottoms of the tankards that spawned 'em."

"Do you really believe that, Sy—Old Mage?" Sharantyr asked, her laughter subsiding.

Elminster gave her a warning look for the slip and said, "Nay, lass. But all of ye—the Realms entire, it seems—expect me to play the role of a gruff old wizard who yearns for shining younger times. It's a cloak that suits me, I'll admit. Wearing it oft gets me my own way in things, y'see."

"Don't you get tired of always playing the pettish, sour old wit?" Itharr asked, serious in his turn.

"To look behind such masks," Belkram said quietly, "is—too often—to destroy the wearer."

" *'Destroy,'* now that's a nice word!" a new voice rang out from above.

Four heads jerked up. A glowing figure was standing on air above the stone needle of one of the ruined towers, hands raised and moving. It was a man none of them had seen before . . . and a second man stood in emptiness beside him. As they watched, a third and fourth appeared, without herald's trumpet or flashing disturbance—just the starry sky one moment and a man standing in it the next.

Elminster's lips were moving. As the first bright and deadly bolt of magic flashed down into the ruins, it was met by a crawling net of light that rent it, sending angry lightnings sizzling and smoking in all directions . . . except down onto the scrambling companions below.

"Find cover!" the Old Mage roared, and took out his pipe. An instant later, the pipe flashed and he vanished.

The four lightning bolts that sought his life arrived too late, slashing through the darkening spell net in a shower of sparks to meet in a crash that sent riven stones spinning in all directions and toppled a section of wall. The structure leaned southward with slow grace, then fell apart in the air, spilling loose blocks of stone over a wide area of brambles and saplings.

Sharantyr ducked behind what was left of the tower, a frantic glance telling her there were now nine or more glowing mages aloft. A moment later she saw a purple oval of moaning light diving down into the ruin. As she watched, fumbling for the magic ring on its chain under her gorget, the spell-thing swooped through a gap in the walls and came around the corner, seeking her.

Shar cursed and sprinted back around the tower, catching one hand on the stones of the wall to wheel tightly and run close along the inside of the standing stonework. Then she put her head down and ran faster than she'd ever run before.

As the purple radiance howled after her, pulsing and gaining swiftly, the lady ranger caught at another stony edge and flung herself sideways through what had once been a window. Shar landed rolling as another lightning bolt crashed down nearby, its flash showing her Itharr's burly form in similar frantic flight. She sprang up to dodge behind a pile of rubble.

The radiance, whatever it was, tried to dart through the window, but didn't fit. The blast that followed took down most of that wall, showering the top of her rubble pile with stony fragments. Clutching her healing ring, Shar ran for the dark trees nearby as mocking laughter rang out overhead.

Balls of fire tore down into the forest to her right. Trees crashed to the ground, ablaze from top to bottom, and she heard a roar of pain. Belkram! She veered toward the blaze as fresh fire blossomed in the ruins behind her.

Then she heard screams from above, and something wet fell on her cheek. She wiped it away without slowing. Stickiness . . . blood! Reaching the trees, she saw another purple thing dodging among them, seeking Belkram. She flung herself flat on her back just in time.

This time, the spell blast showered her with jagged scraps of wood and hurled blazing cinders aloft. Watching them, she saw the glowing figures jerking and convulsing in a sky full of whirling blades that flashed and spun in the moonlight.

Some sort of blade barrier spell. It must be the work of Elminster!

Shar finally got her ring onto her finger and found her feet again. She was flung to her knees almost immediately as two explosions rocked some distant trees and a corner of the ruins quite close by. Itharr appeared, diving headlong through a window with his leathers ablaze, to roll and curse on the ground nearby. Staggering to her feet, Shar ran toward him as the ground rocked again, someone snarled, "*Die!*" high overhead, and a sudden amber light announced the fruition of another spell. Still at a dead run, Shar glanced up.

From out of that brilliant light swooped two gargoyles. Glistening, orange, and translucent, they seemed made of glass rather than stone—and were coming for her and Itharr fast, sharp talons extended.

Shar cursed, ran into Itharr—sending him sprawling—and then ran after him and rolled him hurriedly into the trees to give him some cover. Then she ducked aside with a shriek as one ice-cold talon laid open her leathers and shoulder together. As she sprinted away along the edge of the forest, Sharantyr heard the wind-whistle of the gargoyle wheeling in the air and then beating its wings, closing in on her.

At what she judged to be the last possible moment, she swerved into the trees and dropped.

A splintering crash told her the gargoyle had tried to follow her, and found a tree instead. She got up hurriedly and ran back the way she'd come, as a lightning bolt cracked across the ruins and lit up the night.

The brilliant light showed her the fallen, twisted form of one glowing . . . man? It seemed to have too many legs and something that might have been a wing. A Malaugrym? Strolling past it, out into the open heart of the ruins, was an unconcerned-looking Elminster, unlit pipe in his mouth and his hands empty.

A cone of shining white radiance leapt down out of the night at him, and an angry snarl came from the trees clear across the ruins, followed by a trio of glowing lances rushing right at the Old Mage with crackling lightnings dancing back and forth from one lance tip to the other.

A many-tentacled thing scuttled on spiderlike legs out of the trees behind Elminster, and a ring of scarlet balls of fire spun down out of the sky. Shar stared at them all, mouth suddenly dry.

No man—not even a thousand-year-old archmage—could stand against all this. And after Old Elminster was gone, she and the Harpers would surely die too. She drew a sword she knew was useless and thanked the gods she'd be dying with friends, and in battle, and that they'd shared a laugh or two this evening before death came for them all. "Lord of Battles," she breathed, watching death come for Elminster from all sides, "and Lady of the Forest, let us all die well—and not before we must!"

And then the Old Mage's pipe flashed again. An instant later everything crashed together, blinding her. The last thing she saw as the dazzlement overwhelmed her and the force of the blast flung her head over heels into the trees, was one of the ruined towers falling slowly, almost majestically, into the conflagration below.

* * * * *

"There's been no attempt to hide their trail, Lord," Brammur said, his old gray eyes grave.

"Yet only four, you say?" Like his men, the Lord of Daggerdale wore the leather armor of a forester and bore a sword covered with gum and soot to keep it from reflecting the light. And like his men, he spent his days sleeping in one of the caves they knew, and his nights out hunting Zhents, brigands, and other predators in his ravaged realm. Randal Morn sighed. "That means they're either confident as all the gods or trying to lure someone into attacking them . . ."

"Or just such fools that they don't know better." Thaern finished the sentence for him. His head archer looked as grim as Randal Morn felt.

"I don't like mysteries," the Lord of Daggerdale said shortly. "Fighting Zhents and orcs and such is bad enough. But we must know who they are and what they're about."

"Unless they're still riding through the night, Lord, it looks like they've holed up in Irythkeep," Brammur said through his gray-white moustache. "Shall we make haste, or walk wide to surround it?"

"The lure could be for us," Randal Morn mused. "We must go wide, quietly and with care. Bram—"

His next words were lost forever in a sudden flash that split the night. Then there were several flashes together, and the ground rocked under them. The last of Randal Morn's men exchanged glances, lifted eyebrows, and took tighter grips on their weapons.

"On the other hand," Randal Morn said lightly, "no one's likely to hear us if we go in bellowing drinking songs, through *that*." Another distant crash answered him, and a dead limb broke off a tree somewhere near and made its crashing way to the ground.

Irythkeep was outlined by amber radiance for a moment, and they heard shouting and saw glowing lights moving in the sky above its ruined towers. They watched the explosions, curling tongues of flame, and flashes of light for several awestruck breaths. Then the Lord of Daggerdale licked lips that had gone dry and said, his heart leaping with excitement within him, "That magic could slay us as swiftly and easily as the ones it's intended for. We must still use caution."

"I always do, lord," Thaern said, stone faced. Randal Morn punched him playfully on the shoulder and chuckled. "Right, blades!" he said to the others around him. "Onward! Follow the ever-cautious Thaern."

* * * * *

Daggerdale, Kythorn 16

Belkram came dazedly, painfully back to Faerûn, sprawled on his back over several broken branches of a scorched tree. Smoke curled up the cracked and smoldering trees around him, and something winged and taloned and made of glass was slashing clumsily at him from where it hung wedged in a tangle of leaning, half-fallen trees.

Belkram gave it a sour look and rolled away until he fell off his bed of branches and found his feet amid trampled ferns. His leathern gloves were inside his breeches as always, the cuffs protruding above his belt right behind him; they were out and on in three tugs. The ranger took up a scorched sapling and hefted it once. He swung it up for greater force, and then down as hard as he could.

Glass shattered and tinkled off branches. He snarled and struck again, until not only the talons but most of the arm had been struck off. Then he strode away, seeking his friends.

They weren't hard to find. Elminster was scampering around the clearing, hurling slaying spells up into the night and dodging the same sent back his way. Shar lay draped limply over a branch ahead, arms dangling, blood on her face.

He lifted her off the tree limb as gently as he could, flinching as a swarm of fireballs drifted through the now-blackened stones of the keep and exploded together, sending fresh tongues of flame roaring into the trees. He turned her over.

She was breathing. In his arms she coughed weakly, spat blood—she'd bitten through her lip, Belkram saw—and murmured, not opening her eyes, "Tempus . . . have you come to take me?"

Touched, Belkram knelt amid the tangled and smashed trees and laid her on the ground. Finding her sword, he put it into her hand, kissed her forehead, and said, "It's me, Shar—Belkram the Bold! I'll be back for you, Lady Knight. Lie still here . . . I'll be back!"

"Belk . . . ram?" she breathed, head lolling back. The Harper glanced back at her once, sudden moisture in his eyes, as he ran out into the clearing. Something that looked like a griffon or a giant eagle—but had three long tentacles curling out from each shoulder instead of wings—was writhing around on the ground, obviously hurt. Beyond it, something like an owlbear with a snake's body was hugging Itharr and trying its best to bite his face off at the same time. Farther off still, amid the stones of the keep, several men were blinking in and out of existence, hurling spells from time to time at foes who didn't seem to be there. One of these men looked like Elminster.

Darting magic missiles and flickering, slow-drifting motes of light from some other spell were streaming around the clearing, around them all, like a swirling school of fish. Belkram shook his head as he sprinted toward Itharr.

A bolt flashed down to the ground in front of him, splitting a stone block twice his size with a crack that left his ears ringing. Belkram fell sideways, rolled, and found himself coming up face-to-face with a robed man who had long fangs, rich-looking robes, and flickering globes of radiance around both hands. The man's startled face twisted into a sneer, and he raised one hand threaten-ingly—so Belkram thrust his blade through that mouth. A moment later he was hanging on through a squalling, bruising battering of blood and frantically shifting flesh. It melted away from his blade, ichor gushing out in all di-rections, and flowed around his legs, looking like the putty Belkram had once mixed to set glass in an Athkat-lan window. Cold fear rose inside the Harper, and he stabbed down frantically with his blade, carving at the thick, unyielding, slowly tightening stuff.

The mutating flesh shuddered and spasmed suddenly, then undulated away from him in snakelike coils. Bel-kram snarled, snatched out his belt dagger, and went after it, slashing wildly with both his weapons.

He was still slashing and hewing ribbons of the stuff away in all directions when a bright swarm of magical bolts swam down into the clearing and raced at him.

Once, Belkram had taken a dagger through the palm of his hand. The attacking bolts felt like seven such dag-gers in swift succession. The pain smashed the breath out of him as the force of the striking magic missiles drove him back into an untidy heap on the ground. It was like being struck in the short ribs over and over again, Belkram thought, struggling to get his breath. Through swimming eyes he saw some of those glowing mages still standing on the air above the keep. Itharr . . . he'd been going to help Itharr . . .

* * * * *

Rage burned in Itharr Jathram all the time. Slow and buried deep, but there all the time, like coals glowing under turf for the night. Once in a while—not often, but eventually—that building rage rose and warmed and boiled up . . . and the burly, quiet Harper slew things.

He'd said as much to Storm, that first day at her farm, sitting on two stumps in the forest behind her house. "Lady," Itharr had told her softly, "you must know this. I'd not be the best citizen in a land at peace. From time to time, I find . . . I must kill."

Storm had merely nodded, sober eyed, and said as gently, "I can see it in you. Yet know this, Itharr. You are welcome in my house, now and to the end of your days."

And for that, Itharr would love her forever. Her face then, and her words, came back to him now as he stood struggling in a grip much stronger than his own and felt the white heat of his rage blinding him. Those jaws snapped just shy of his cheek once more, as he twisted his neck desperately aside and snarled his defiance. His arms—and the weapons he thought he still held, though numbness was creeping over him, and he could no longer be sure—were pinned to his sides in an ever-tighter rope of flowing flesh. These shapeshifters could kill merely by wrapping part of themselves around you and crushing!

He tried to throw himself sideways, but the Malaugrym held him, swaying like a tree in a high wind, and he knew he struggled in vain. "Tymora, aid me now," he hissed, ribs aching under the increasing pressure, and the shapeshifter laughed out loud. Eyes dark with fury, Itharr tried again to overbalance the thing and bring them both to the ground, but the Malaugrym held him upright with easy strength and tightened its grip still more.

He was fighting for breath now, a far-off and faint roaring rising in his ears. Soon it would overwhelm him, Itharr Jathram knew, and he'd go down, raging still, into the darkness that waited for everyone.

* * * * *

The pipe winked more slowly this time. Syluné wondered if it would work once more if need be. Well, she'd best make sure she didn't need it.

The Malaugrym were learning. Instead of hurling more than enough magic at their foe and having it all go to waste when the pipe teleported Old Elminster away, they'd split up—a few blade barriers had taught them the wisdom of that—and were sniping at him from here and there around the ruins now, hoping to force him to transport himself away from one attack and right into another.

It had almost worked twice now. Syluné took quick stock of the spells left in the various devices that festooned the body she'd taken to calling "Old Elminster"—not a hard task, as so little was left—and decided to use invisibility.

She ducked through an arch, making sure one of the shapeshifters saw her, became invisible—the nice thing about these rings was their speed and silence—and darted right back through the archway again. She saw the shapeshifter confidently weaving a spell that would hurl a swarm of fireballs through the archway, to burst on the other side of the wall, and grinned. Two other Malaugrym were creeping through the ruins and should arrive at the other side of the wall at just about the right time.

Now to find Shar's blade. Belkram had laid it in her hand; he'd need her healing ring, too.

It might have to serve both Belkram and Itharr, if she could get this body where it had to go in time. Syluné was sprinting across the clearing, slipping on the dew driven out of everything around by all the fire spells, when a beam of flame swept across her path, too close to miss.

Someone could see Old Elminster. That was it, then, she thought, as the body plunged into roaring flames with hands clasped over its eyes to try to keep some sight. Old Elminster staggered and almost went down; Syluné kept the shuddering limbs going, trailing smoke, toward the trees.

Doom would be on them all soon now. She heard fresh laughter and the delighted exclamations of newcomers overhead but did not bother to look up. Of course the more craven Malaugrym would wait until the kill was certain and then come to watch.

The body's eyes were still swimming with tears. She could not see whatever it was that burst nearby on her left, flinging Old Elminster to the right like a rag doll. The body struck something—flesh—and she realized that it must be Itharr and the shapeshifter, still straining together. She snatched at the belt the body wore, found the burning-hot dagger as the burnt leather crumbled away and fell into ashes, and slashed at the ropy flesh she could not see, again and again, cutting at one spot, trying to make it release its hold on the trapped Harper.

Then the ground came up and struck the body's forehead. Bouncing helplessly on the turf, Syluné saw a fading flash and knew that a ruthless Malaugrym mage had decided his kinsman was expendable, and struck them all with a corrosive bolt. Would this body's limbs hold together? At least she felt no pain and could drive the body to do things when injured that no living man could have managed—but was getting up and reaching that sword and ring one of them?

7
Mushrooms and Revelations

"This is the great Elminster?" The Shadowmasters were laughing openly now, and quite a group was gathering in the air above the last tower. Forty or more looked down into the smoldering clearing where the blackened shell of Irythkeep more or less still stood, and watched the spindly ashen figure that had once sported robes and a beard stumbling toward the trees. Far too many of the blood of Malaug lay sprawled and lifeless or barely alive about the clearing, but no matter. The Great Foe was going to die!

And when the gods tired of playing in Faerûn, there'd be no one left to stand against the might of the Malaugrym . . . and at last Toril would be *theirs.* Gates winked in the air, and more kin arrived, swarming out across the air to stand above the clearing and look down.

"If we blast his body away from the knees up, will the feet keep walking?" one amused youngling asked, but another said, "No, no. Move what he seeks away just as he's about to grasp it, and keep moving it so it's always just ahead of him and he never gets it!"

"Don't toy with him!" an elder's voice roared out of empty air. Someone without magic, using the scrying portal's powers to speak through it. "Slay him *now,* or he'll win free somehow, and we'll have won nothing!"

The youngling who'd suggested blasting all but the Old Mage's feet turned to laugh at the voice, a sneer on his face. But then his form changed, his features holding a moment of shocked disbelief before they melted away into rubbery dun-purple nothingness and he fell away, tumbling helplessly toward the stones far below.

He was followed by another, and another. By now, the

Malaugrym were looking puzzled and alarmed. "What—?" one barked intelligently.

"Mushrooms," another said, watching them smash into the ruins and shatter into pulpy looseness. "Giant mushrooms!"

"But who—?"

Bewildered, angry Shadowmaster mages stared all around, seeking a foe. More of them fell away, helpless to cast spells or fly in fungoid form, to die below, while others snarled, "Some sort of spell to enforce a single shape? Blasphemous! Who would devise such a thing?" and still others warned, "Get back! Away from this place! It must be some spell of the Foe. It can't have a large range!"

More mushrooms fell, and suddenly a Shadowmaster snarled, "*You!* You're doing it!" and launched a rain of spell-lances at another Malaugrym standing on air not far away. A frantically conjured spell-cloak didn't form in time, and the accused one tumbled backward, transfixed by at least three lances, to spin slowly through the air, lifeless.

Mushrooms continued to fall, and one of the other Malaugrym raised his hands and pointed at the lance hurler. "No, it's *you!*"

The attack was struck aside by a shielding spell, but on all sides terrified and furious shapeshifters lashed out at each other. Spells flashed and burst all across the sky in sudden boiling fury until a great voice roared out of thin air, echoing all around them. "*Cease!* Hear me, blood of Malaug!"

Sudden silence fell. All Malaugrym knew the voice of the Shadowmaster High. "Attend me!" the deep voice boomed on, as a few more Malaugrym melted into mushrooms and fell away.

A mighty magic boiled in the air, and the blood of Malaug were swept through the sky as leaves tumble in a gale, flung aside until they found themselves in two ragged groups of a dozen or more on either side of an open space where a lone figure floated, a young Malaugrym sorceress known to some as Dralarca.

"*There* is the traitor!" Dhalgrave thundered. "*Destroy ᵃer! She's—*"

Dralarca smiled and waved cheerily—and Dhalgrave's booming voice was gone in midword, cut off as if by a knife.

The Malaugrym stared at her, and one more of them dwindled into a mushroom and fell.

After a moment more of shocked silence, all of the mages standing on air spat out incantations at once, waving their arms like a forest of crawling spiders. The air seemed to shatter under the force of so many cleaving, blazing, bubbling, and roaring magics.

Blue-black and vivid purple flashes leapt from where they met, and an instant later all of the spells came lashing back at their casters in a gale of tortured air that flung Shadowmasters across the sky for miles.

When the stars could be seen again, and the last ruined tower of Irythkeep had stopped rocking, the false daylight Dhalgrave had conjured above the clearing remained. In it, the awed Shadowmasters could see the small figure of Dralarca standing calmly, waiting for them. She waved a casual hand, and the nearest Shadowmaster became a mushroom.

As the fungus fell to earth, Eldargh turned to Huerbara, whose teeth were chattering in fear as she clutched Taernil, and rumbled calmly, "Is your magic good enough to hurl antimagic that far?"

She nodded once, white-faced and mute. The old giant turned to the Shadowmaster standing on his other side. "Yabrant?"

"Yes. Count us in together. And Taernil, if you have any sort of attacking spell, hurl it her way first, to mask us. Useless, mind. I'm sure it'll be coming back at us soon."

Eldargh counted them in. Three antimagic fields rolled out in the wake of a stinging cloud of red fire-mites, as another two mushrooms fell away from on high.

Other Shadowmasters had launched attacks, too. A scarlet flash, fading to pink, cut the sky before their own spells hit home, and for a moment there was a confusion

of whirling bones in the air around Dralarca as someone's spell went wild. Yabrant paled at the sight. "Magic's
starting to twist, here. This may be our only chance."

Then an explosion rocked them as old Halar was blown
apart by his own returning spell, not far away. One of his
hands tumbled past, trailing flames, and Huerbara
buried her face in Taernil's chest with a little scream,
shuddering uncontrollably.

A multitude of small flashes lit the air near Dralarca,
and Taernil's cloud came drifting back at them, fading
away before it reached the spot where they stood. At that
moment a gasp of fear and hatred from many throats
heralded their work. The false seeming of Dralarca was
gone, and in its place stood a wild-eyed woman whose silver hair danced around her like silver flames. She wore
black robes that were more tatters than garments, and
she laughed, hand on hip, and bowed to Eldargh. "Well
spun, sir!"

"The Simbul! It's the Queen of Aglarond!" someone
shouted, and the woman smiled and nodded.

Then she threw her arms up, her eyes flashed, and two
rings of crimson light burst from her palms to run slowly
down her arms and fade away around her torso. Something was growing there, a web of pulsing red beams of
light encircling her—no, encaging her!

"What's that?" Yabrant whispered slowly. "Has someone caged her?"

"No," said Eldargh in a deep, despairing voice. "Oh,
no."

From that web of light they saw a beam stab out, and
then another. One leapt across the sky and struck Eldargh before Yabrant or Taernil could move or speak, and
a cage of red beams sprang into being around the old
Shadowmaster.

Yabrant frowned and quickly wove a shearing force-
blade, but when he swept it across the humming, thick-
ening cage, there was a flash and he was hurled back,
minus his sword arm.

After a moment, looking both shaken and thoughtful,
he grew himself a new arm. By then the cage had begun

o shrink and darken.

"Farewell, old friend," he heard Eldargh rumble, and he giant's head turned toward him.

"You will be remembered," Yabrant hissed quickly, training to see and meet Eldargh's eyes as the giant larkened and shrank within the dimming cage. There vere other cages now, he knew, but this web of spells held ne of the few kin he cared about, and he could do nothng to save Eldargh.

The cage was shrinking swiftly now, as Huerbara vhimpered, draining Eldargh's life essence as it dwinlled. It shrank to a thumb-sized globe of light and then vinked out, leaving of Eldargh only a little drifting dust.

Yabrant turned to Taernil. "We must leave this place. Help me spin a gate!"

As they worked magic in feverish haste, they heard the Simbul's merry laugh followed by the call, "A little fire, Malaugrym?"

They tried to ignore the roar and crackle of flame—adorned with screams—that followed, though Taernil stammered an incantation that almost ruined their whole effort.

And then a green flame seemed to grow in the air before them, rising swiftly into a spindle. Taernil almost leapt for it before it was fully formed. Yabrant held him back with a hastily grown and ungentle tentacle, and snarled, "Take Huerbara through before you!"

Taernil snarled back at him in wordless fear, eyes wide and staring, but did as he had been ordered. Yabrant looked back once as he followed, and saw a handful of other gates opening in the sky. One of them suddenly blossomed into an explosion that sent Shadowmaster bodies tumbling through the air as the Simbul laughed wildly.

Yabrant shivered and let the gate take him. It was not a time to tarry, or he'd be just one more of the kin who would die this day—and just how many was that by now?—before that human witch was finished.

* * * * *

"Ye gods!" Thaern gasped to his left, face paling, but Randal Morn looked quickly to his right, alerted by an unfamiliar sound. After a moment, he realized it was Brammur, on his knees and praying to all the gods he could name.

He started to chuckle and then decided that prayer might not be such a bad idea. Before he could go to his knees, however, the world exploded in thundering voices and rolling balls of fire, and he froze with the dozen men around him and stared up into the sky, at the many dancing, spell-hurling figures that stood high above the ground in a drift of daylight that should not be there.

It was a long while later when Brammur got to his feet, slapped his dazed lord's arm, and asked matter-of-factly, "Use caution, did you say, m'lord?"

* * * * *

The Castle of Shadows, Kythorn 16

"Soulcages," Bheloris said slowly. "I haven't seen one of those— "

"Since Albarat died," the rolling voice of Dhalgrave put in from above, startling them all. Shadows shuddered and curled away into the corners of the Great Hall as they all stared at the scrying portal.

"I dare not reopen the portal," the Shadowmaster High went on, his voice raising echoes. "The witch-queen has spun an antimagic spell that someone foolishly cast at her across it. To strike at her or open a gate now would be to unleash that damaging magic here." His voice gained strength, so his next words would carry down distant passages of the Castle of Shadows. "We have a new foe, blood of Malaug!"

"I told you 'twould be a disaster," one old Shadowmaster said to another, who shook his head and replied, "And I believed you. I expected deaths, aye, but not *this!*"

"This is worse than Shimmerglade," still another muttered.

Neleyd leaned close to Bheloris. "Shimmerglade?"

"A place in northern Faerûn—in Impiltur or Damara or somewhere around there—where six of our strongest elders trapped Elminster, and were all slain in spell-battle." He sighed. "Once again, it seems that a trap intended to be the death of the Foe became a trap for us. Mushrooms! No mouth or limbs to work magic, no way to fly . . . and death before anything can be done. Worse than that, she has some spell that overmatches our shapechanging, to trap us in a form of *her* choosing."

"Perhaps now some of these flamebrains'll think twice about sneering at human mages and strolling out to attack Elminster on any idle afternoon," said a tired voice from the back of the hall.

As his words ended, a green flame flickered in the shadows, pulsed once, and widened into a gate. Several Shadowmasters took a step toward it, prepared for the worst, but out of the pulsing portal stumbled a Malaugrym who trailed smoke, and several others panting on his heels. Another gate was opening now, and another. An alert elder banished the first one with a hissed spell that sent shadows swirling around it in a swift spiral. Disheveled survivors poured into the hall, stalking grimly past an elder who smirked as he drawled, "Hail, conquering heroes of Malaug!"

Gates glimmered out of existence here and there, and the cursing Malaugrym who had come through them sought the comforts of their own chambers. As they hurried past, Kostil stared at the scrying portal and shook his head. "What did I say?" he offered. "Always we ignore the strengths and trickery of the folk of Faerûn."

"No more," Bheloris promised softly, staring into the distance. "No longer."

Neleyd shivered at the elder's tone, but infinitely worse was the look in Yabrant's eyes as one of the last gates disgorged a weeping Huerbara, a silent Taernil, and Yabrant, who stopped by Bheloris and Kostil and said shortly, "Eldargh didn't make it."

Then he strode away into the shadows, leaving them with Huerbara's tears.

* * * * *

Daggerdale, Kythorn 16

The light in the sky above faded to a soft purple glow, and the Queen of Aglarond rode it down to step lightly onto the smoldering turf in the heart of Irythkeep. She wrapped arms around the blackened form of Elminster with an exultant laugh. "Well met," she said happily, bestowing an impulsive kiss on lips that were no longer fringed by hair.

My thanks, Sister. Syluné's mindtouch lasted for only a moment before the Simbul stepped back, surveyed the Old Mage critically, and frowned as she raised a hand and gestured deftly.

White hair appeared on the scorched wizard's chin and upper lip, and raced across the skin, growing with almost comical speed, until the Queen of Aglarond judged its length and appearance right. Then she did the same for the old wizard's head. "There! Yourself again!" she said with a wink.

"The others need your spells rather more than I do," Elminster said dryly, waving a hand around the clearing. "And that Malaugrym"—he pointed—"may still live."

The Simbul nodded, mirth suddenly gone, and hastened to where Itharr lay sprawled amid ichor and many ribbons of slashed flesh. Belkram lay not far from him. The queen went to her knees amid the blood first. As the glow of her synostodweomer flared around the motionless Harper, she turned her head to watch Sharantyr rise stiffly among the trees, and said in amusement, "I notice you healed the pretty lady first."

Elminster's head shook in denial. "Nay. I never reached her. Her ring did the work."

"No matter. This one will be fine. He has a handsome face, I'll grant." She pinched Itharr's cheek, watched his eyes flutter open, and rose with a merry laugh to go to Belkram.

It took longer this time, and her laughter was gone when she came back to Elminster. "Much in the way of repairs was needed yonder," she said, "but he'll live—this time. He's been raised many times, that one." She tapped her lips thoughtfully. "Perhaps he's lost all fear of death."

"He's not the only one," Syluné said dryly, through the Old Mage's lips. The Simbul turned to stare at her and then gave her a sudden smile. "My apologies. I sometimes forget. You are very good at this, you know."

Elminster gave her a sardonic little bow. She dimpled and replied with a certain unqueenly gesture, and the Old Mage waved his resignation from the lists and sat down on a stone.

"The Malaugrym now have a new Great Foe, I daresay," he observed gruffly. "Ye'd best watch thy backside."

She smirked. "As attentively as you do?"

Elminster rolled his eyes and sighed. Her merry laughter was drowned out by a sudden thunder of hooves. He had half-risen in alarm before four lathered and familiar horses came into view around a blackened wall.

"Your mounts. Some people are so careless with their horses," the Simbul said with a flourish. El frowned at her.

"It's not as if we weren't rather busy . . ."

She waved his unspoken thanks away, looked around at the dazed lady Knight and the two Harpers coming slowly across the trampled turf toward the Old Mage, and said, "That was fun. Yet the Realms around await me, and there's much to be done, what with avatars and lesser idiots running around stirring up trouble. I must go." She turned eastward, took a step, and then turned back and pointed up at the fast-fading purple glow. "You need not fear attack from above for a time. Magic's all too apt to go wild up there, now."

Then she was gone, without sound or drifting spellsmoke to show she'd been there. Elminster stared absently at where she'd been for a moment, scratched one of his bony arms, and thought on what paltry magic he had left. The wisest thing to do would be to return to Shadowdale, to stock up, if that wouldn't be going into a worse trap than Irythkeep had turned out to be.

"What a battle," Shar said in a voice that was not entirely steady.

Elminster gave her a wry smile. "Ye missed the best part, lass," he said gruffly. "It was raining mushrooms."

"Mushrooms?" The chorus was bewildered, as Belkram and Itharr joined them, still peering critically at their weapons and looking around in apparent disbelief.

"Malaugrym who'd unwillingly taken the shapes of mushrooms," Elminster explained. "They burst quite thoroughly when they land on a rock. Or a tree."

Belkram frowned. "Did we . . . die?"

"Nay, nearly, but the Queen of Aglarond thought ye had a pretty face . . . or no, 'twas *him* she considered handsome"—Itharr managed to raise an eyebrow and sketch a courtly bow at the same time—"and healed ye. Sorry to disappoint thy sense of glorious tragedy."

"So what do we do now?" Sharantyr asked softly, looking around at the smoking ruins and at their still-restless horses. "You can't have much magic left."

"I was wondering if it would be best to return to the dale, or go looking for a Harper cache. There's one not too far from here."

"What?" Belkram asked innocently. "When we're having so much *fun?*"

His companions answered this observation with various rude sounds.

"We can't count on any more unexpected rescues, from the Simbul or anyone else," Elminster warned. "Certain Harpers have been told to watch out for us and aid us if need be, but most of 'em hereabouts are fast swords and little more."

"We need a little more," Sharantyr agreed softly, and shivered suddenly. "I did not think any of us would live to see these stars again," she added as they looked at her.

"*You need not!*" a voice spat, and from around the nearest tumbled wall came a woman in dark robes, running hard, her face contorted in hatred. A fey purple glow, tinged with black, blazed out of her furious eyes, and she held high a black dagger.

"For the glory of Bane—*die*, Cursed One!"

She flung the dagger as she came, and Shar couldn't draw her sword in time to strike it aside. It wobbled—a bad throw—but struck Elminster's cheek hilt first before spinning away into the night.

* * * * *

Behind another nearby wall, a tall black stone that stood by itself bent forward a little to peer at the fray with eyes that grew very bright. Then the stone hissed a soft word, and smiled a crooked smile.

* * * * *

As the dagger left it, Elminster's cheek fell slack, looking suddenly lifeless. The glow around the pipe in his breast pocket faded, and the three rangers in their burnt leathers, blades drawn to face the running woman, looked back in sudden alarm.

"A disjunction!" Belkram snarled, who had seen such things before.

"Gods *spit* on all!" Itharr added angrily, and strode forward to meet their attacker. Elminster backed away from them, looking horrified.

Behind the wall, the stone smiled wolfishly and grew an arm that gestured almost lazily behind him. *"Perast aum izeebuldree,"* he said conversationally, and Brammur, Randal Morn, Thaern, and all the men with them froze together, blades raised, in poses of cautious stealth.

"Thank you," the stone told them courteously as it melted into the shape of a man whose left arm ended in a sword blade instead of a hand. He peered at the motionless men for a moment to be sure he'd got them all, nodded in satisfaction, and dug his right hand into a pouch at his belt.

From the other side of the wall came the ring of steel and a scream of rage. "Some sort of magic shields this place!" a man's voice shouted.

"Aye," the man who had been a stone agreed pleasantly. "So it does." Bringing forth a handful of pebbles, he cast them in a wide fan onto the ground and muttered something else.

With terrifying speed, the stones began to grow. The dark forms rising from them had burly arms, tusked mouths, and were . . . hobgoblins!

"Come," he said simply, and jogged around the corner of the wall. Howling, the hobgoblins poured after him, jerking out brutal weapons and jostling each other to be first at the kill.

* * * * *

Spheres of vividly glowing air—of all colors, from a rather glorious ruby red to a putrid green—were drifting around them now, expanding from Elminster's person and various minor enchantments worn or carried by his three companions. The disjunction was working all too well.

The woman who'd hurled the dagger struck a pose just beyond the Harpers' blades and laughed in triumph. "When Elminster lies slain," she cried, eyes shining, "remember that it was I, Arashta Tharbrow, who struck his magic from him—for the greater glory of Bane, whose foremost servant I am!"

"Oh?" Itharr asked curtly, as his blade cut a line of shrieking sparks from the invisible shield protecting the sorceress. "He's reduced to hiring madwomen now, is he?"

She howled at him like a dog in fury. *"Blasphemy!"* she spat when she found control enough to form words. Shaking in anger, she threw up her hands to smite the hard-faced ranger with magic—and then her face changed, one of her hands flew to her mouth, and she went pale.

Her face contorted in frantic fear, and her hands flashed in the gestures Belkram knew would unleash a lightning bolt. Snarling against the pain he expected to come, he kept hacking at the unseen barrier that protected her, and suddenly realized it was giving way. Instead of ringing off something rock hard and unyielding, his blade was going a little way into something that rushed past it like floodwater, resisting but allowing the steel's passage.

And then he realized no lightning had come to snatch breath and life away from him.

"Look!" Itharr said. "Her eyes!"

All three of them peered past their hacking blades. The weird purple glow had faded away, and the green eyes behind it looked very young and very frightened as Sharantyr's blade broke through the fading shield at last and slid into the woman's breast with silken ease and speed.

The sorceress went down, blood bubbling from her mouth in a last, soundless scream, her mouth moving to shape words that would never be heard. The disjunction swept away the last of her shield as it had robbed her of spells, and with shield and spells went a cloaking wall of shadows, revealing to the rangers a snarling, hooting group of hobgoblins racing toward them across a few paces of open grass.

" *'Ware!*" Belkram shouted unnecessarily, and then battle was joined, the skirling clangor of steel on steel drowning out all coherent speech. The hobgoblins were reckless, snarling hackers of the sort skilled warriors disparagingly called "meat-choppers," but they were big and coming in fast, and there were a lot of them. If one Harper caught his blade against a hostile weapon, the slashing steel of the next foe could well be into his ribs before he could recover. Wherefore the three ducked, dodged, and dove as they never had before, swords and daggers together weaving a deadly wall of darting death that took down their hulking attackers with a stab in the eye here and a thrust through the ear or throat there, never slowing to parry and hack at chests or flanks.

Shar got a single glimpse of a tall black figure running easily at the fore when the charge began. Then the being thinned suddenly, like a wisp of smoke, and the hobgoblins thundered past and crashed into the three rangers without their dark companion.

That seemed like an eternity ago now, as she twisted and strained and set her teeth against the numbing force of the hacking blows raining down on her deflecting blade. Shar's lungs were burning with the effort of meeting those strikes, and sweat was running down her wrists and dripping from the end of her nose as she danced, leapt frantically out of reach of a roundhouse slash—which sank deep into the side of another hobgoblin, she noted with glee—and found herself spinning through the heart of the gathered hobgoblins.

A startled face loomed up at her, and she slashed just beneath it, opening a throat with her whistling steel as she launched herself in the other direction, hoping to stay ahead of any direct pursuit. Rounding to the left, she found herself behind an unwitting foe and hamstrung him with a ruthless slash along the backs of his knees. With a grunt of surprise, the next hobgoblin turned his head from trying to gut Belkram, and Shar drove her dagger hilt deep into one staring eye.

It lodged against the bone as she overbalanced, and she brought her sword up to protect her back as she jerked her arm back and forth wildly to haul her fang free.

It came away at last, but by then hobgoblins were swinging at her from three sides. Shar flung herself down flat on her back, and as their blades crashed into each other overhead, kicked out hard against a massive hobgoblin foot and got the momentum she needed to roll away.

She rolled right into Belkram, who leapt high to allow her passage under him. Sharantyr came to her feet in time to see a snarling Itharr take a slash along his ribs as he leaned to drive his sword into the tusked mouth of his assailant. The sword continued upward, pushing the hobgoblin's helm off on the top of its head. Itharr let go of the blade at once and tore the hobgoblin's own black-bladed scimitar from its failing fingers, bringing it back immediately in a swing that took two fingers off the sword hand of the next hobgoblin.

As that one screamed, it reeled back into another, who slipped and got Belkram's blade in its throat. Shar fenced with another, gritting her teeth, until Belkram reached out and put his dagger into its armpit.

Then it was over, and they still stood, three panting, sweating, bleeding humans among a confusion of groaning, writhing, or silently sprawled goblinkin. They sought each other, wiping sweat from their eyes, and then stiffened at a cruel laugh from beyond the battle.

They whirled as one, in time to see Elminster's body topple in a fountain of dark blood as a black blade scythed through his neck. The blade was held by—no, it seemed to actually *be* one arm of a tall black figure. The Old Mage's eyes stared accusingly at them as his head dangled, long white hair firmly in the dark man's grip.

"Futile fools!" the figure sneered, and backed away from them into a whirling green light that was growing behind it.

Heartsick, Shar took three running steps and hurled her blade. But as the weapon flashed end over end, the laughing figure faded away through the gate and made the portal wink out, so her steel bounced on dark turf in the night.

She felt the tears beginning as she turned her head and saw Belkram and Itharr looking down at the headless body. Then they looked up at each other. Belkram licked dry and trembling lips twice before he managed to ask, "What do we do *now*?"

8
To Get a Head in This World

The shadows swirled uneasily in the vast, gloomy Great Hall of the Throne as a shimmering occurred in their midst, a disturbance that—in light of recent events—was swiftly surrounded by a dozen grim-faced elder Shadowmasters, hands raised to deal magical death.

The roiling shadows they eyed so narrowly parted into a green flame. The flame deepened swiftly into a man-high spindle and then widened into a tunnel. A breath later, Issaran of the blood of Malaug stepped proudly out of the spiraling emerald depths with a severed human head gripped in one fist, a staring man's head with long white hair and a longer white beard.

He waved his other hand, calling bloodfire down from the Shadow Throne to illuminate himself—an act of insolence for any lesser kin when a Shadowmaster High ruled in the castle. Murmurs in the shadows reminded him of that, but he cared not a whit. This was his moment of glory, and everyone must see it lest the Shadowmaster forget the reward he'd promised. The amber glow drove back the darker shadows, making the center of the hall a grand and glorious place.

At the heart of the radiance, young Issaran stood tall, holding up his trophy for all to see. "Elminster of Shadowdale," he proclaimed loudly, "slain by my hand!"

"Oh?" Dhalgrave asked coldly, melting suddenly out of invisibility to hang in the air just above the proud young scion of Malaug. "So how do you explain *that?*" One of his powerful hands lifted to indicate the pale glow of the scrying portal, behind the dwindling disturbance that a moment ago had been Issaran's gate.

Something in that acid tone made Issaran pale as he spun, to stare openmouthed at the scene in the portal. Dhalgrave obligingly made the view expand to fill a wide arc of the hall's upper air, and made the young Malaugrym's humiliation complete.

The night sky over what must be ruined Dragonspear Castle, in the Sword Coast lands, was lit as bright as day by spell-glows. There, shuffling around in the air, wearing what could only be described as a satisfied expression, was a lone, lean figure. Elminster of Shadowdale, pipe trailing along behind him as he went, was treading empty night air as if he were walking the floor of his own kitchen.

The Old Mage was peering down into the darkness below, ignoring black arrows and hurled stones alike—as Issaran watched, some of these missiles came close to the human wizard and promptly perished in gouts of flame—and from time to time hurling spells down into the night.

Dhalgrave obligingly made the portal's view drift down to where Elminster's spells were going, just in time to show the watchers in the hall a spinning wheel of lightning plunge into the depths of a great host, an army of orcs clad in spired and fluted armor of ancient style—Netherese? Nimbralese, from the Dawn Days of that realm? No matter. That ornate armor did nothing to stop the wheel from bursting in an explosion that sent bolts of lightning sizzling off in all directions, hurling orc bodies for hundreds of feet and searing great swathes of ash-choked air, where all solid things had been burned away in an instant, through the massed army.

More than one of the watching Shadowmasters gasped or swore, and someone in the depths of the dark hall whimpered. There were more startled oaths a moment later, when Elminster's next spell scooped a thousand or more orcs skyward, whisked them some distance away to hang for a breath above another orc horde, and then dropped them all as helpless, wriggling missiles from the sky.

The portal moved again to show the small human band Elminster was protecting: an unarmed caravan fearfully struggling to pass the castle as fast as possible. Something that looked like a hemispherical shell of flying swords whirled endlessly around this small train of merchants, carving up any orcs bold—or crazed—enough to try to reach them. A scarlet mist of gore marked the edges of that deadly barrier, and the massed ranks of the orcs were starting to give way before its advance. The mutterings in the Great Hall grew louder and held a distinct note of awe, and of fear.

"Could . . . that be someone else?" Issaran asked, almost whining in his desperation.

"It could be," Dhalgrave said gravely, his eyes like two hard points, "but it's not. I've checked on the whereabouts of all the powerful sorcerers of Faerûn . . . unlike certain overconfident younglings."

There were chuckles and smirks from around the chamber as a crestfallen Issaran looked at the head he held and said unwillingly, "So this . . . isn't Elminster at all?"

The head's eyes swiveled up to meet his and winked, its mouth pursed into a kiss.

The watching Shadowmasters drew back in a wary hush, fearful that Elminster might have worked a slaying spell on the head. But the disembodied visage merely blew Issaran three kisses and then began to melt away like wax in a hot flame, dripping down into nothingness.

Fearfully Issaran flung the thing away from him. The head faded away before it could reach the floor, with one last mocking wink and a chuckle of its own that made certain elder Shadowmasters stiffen—notably the serpent-man who was Yabrant, and the wyvern who was Kostil.

"Try again," Dhalgrave said, almost wearily, and waved a hand. The portal sprang back to its original size and location and the bloodfire winked out, leaving Issaran in darkness.

Slowly he walked away across the black marble floor, never seeing the Shadowmaster who stood alone on a high balcony, cloaked in deep shadows. Milhvar watched the young Malaugrym go, and there was a tight smile on his face as he shook his head.

* * * * *

Deep in an inner room of the Castle of Shadows hung a gem, a sapphire as large as a man's head. Its rich blue depths glowed with captured fire as it floated above a pool whose thick black waters had yielded many potions. A spell library of ancient Netherese make, the gem held spells of great power ready to be used by anyone who dared to touch it. All Malaugrym knew the Shadowmaster High could instruct the gem to visit death on the deliverer of any touch but his own.

There was one small way, however, in which any learned Shadowmaster could call on the power of the gem. One did so now, causing the massive stone to chime softly in its private chamber.

A questing shadow shifted through a doorway and rose up to regard the gem, which chimed again and began to spin slowly, a pulsing light awakening in its lower depths. The watching shadow thickened swiftly as others joined it, and then sharpened suddenly into the large but human face of Dhalgrave. Staring calmly at the gem that no one should have awakened, he asked, "Who is it?"

And from out of the heart of the winking gem, a voice he knew said, "Milhvar of the blood of Malaug, Shadowmaster High. There is a plan I must lay before you."

"Say on," Dhalgrave replied, his face and tone unreadable.

"There are other gems like this one in Faerûn, hidden away in vaults that have survived since the fall of Netheril. Many more spells sit in grimoires and items all over Toril, and we have seldom dared to seek them out. The deaths that the Simbul caused underscore the prudence of this caution, but our younger blood grows ever more restive, and you rightly chose this opportunity of the godstrife to send them after the Great Foe. Yet I fear not just he, but all of Mystra's Chosen are our foes—as the Simbul is. We stand little chance of survival unless we can find some means of warding off their seeking magic, and the spells they send to slay us. The time is right for us to devote all of our skills—together, not as warring individuals—into crafting a cloak of concealing spells."

The voice paused, and then went on more strongly, "If such a thing can be woven, we could make forays into Faerûn and seize the magic long denied to us. If the Chosen confronted us there, we could fight them as equals—and better—and no harm would come to this castle around us. I have heard many kin speculating aloud as to how they'd lure Elminster here, and overwhelm him with our massed might and the power of shadows we can call on. I'd rather not see such a battle, with all its unavoidable damage, occur in our very home." Milhvar's voice fell silent.

"You have my permission and support for all you've said thus far," Dhalgrave said without hesitation, "but I sense you've more to propose. Say on."

"There is a grave danger in this proposal, a danger to one being. You."

"I know this," Dhalgrave replied patiently. "Go on."

"Our trust in each other must soon be absolute," Milhvar said, as casually if he were discussing the weather in Faerûn, "and I am prepared to submit to all of the scrying magic you care to use. When the concealing cloak of spells is shown to work against the wrath of one of the Chosen, it must also be demonstrated to all that the Shadowmaster High has the means to remove the cloak without warning, leaving the being who was using it vulnerable. I fear this demonstration will cost us one of our more ambitious—not to say rebellious—younglings. By this action you will reaffirm your power and quell the inevitable moves by the younger blood to go their own ways in the planes, armed with cloaks of our devising."

"Your words please me," Dhalgrave responded. "Will you submit to my probing immediately?"

"Of course," the voice replied. "Bring me through."

The Shadowmaster's head didn't appear to do anything, but the floating gem flashed brightly, and the slim man-form of Milhvar stood beside the pool in the chamber. He opened his mouth to speak, but sudden lightnings raged around him, stiffening him into immobility, and a singing, droning sound awakened in the gem, rising in pitch and volume until it abruptly ceased.

Dhalgrave nodded. "You spoke truth to me. I confess I am surprised and pleased. Your loyalty is rare indeed. Know that I have established scrying links to you that govern your very life. Go now and do as you have proposed. If you need my authority to call your team of spellcrafters together, use it."

"My thanks, Shadowmaster High. You shall not regret this."

Dhalgrave nodded curtly, the gem flashed again, and his visitor was gone. Silence returned to that hidden chamber as the floating head frowned at the space where Milhvar had stood. There had been just a shade too much triumph in that parting smile.

* * * * *

Daggerdale, Kythorn 16

The milky mists of approaching dawn had come again to Daggerdale, and Sharantyr shivered once as she stripped away the last of her clothing and stared down at the headless body, contemplating the grisly task ahead. Belkram deftly took the well-worn cotton halter and clout she handed him, as he'd taken her leathers before.

"Don't look," she commanded both Harpers with mock severity.

"Of course not," they replied with identical grins, keeping their eyes carefully on hers. Then they turned around together, walking well away around one soot-blackened wall.

Sharantyr watched them go, took a deep breath, and reluctantly let her eyes fall to the cold form at her feet. She swallowed and then knelt beside it, taking up her newly sharpened knife. This was not going to be easy.

"Be easy, sister-in-arms," nothing spoke, close by her ear. Shar nodded and smiled wanly as the voice of Syluné went on. "Place your longest finger on the ribs, on the right side. Feel them? Move up one . . . and another.

There. Take the knife and make a mark large enough to see clearly."

Shar swallowed. Then, deliberately, she did as she had been told, feeling her gorge rise alarmingly within her, a sudden hotness in her throat.

"If you spew on the body," Syluné said in dry but somehow sympathetic tones, "you'll make the job a lot more distasteful."

Shar nodded irritably, wiping sudden sweat from her brow with one swipe of her forearm. Cutting a foe in the heat and swiftness of battle was one thing, but . . .

How did chirurgeons—and butchers, for that matter—do it?

"The stone is deep," Syluné said calmly, steadying her. Shar thanked her with another smile, ran the knife point down Old Elminster's side almost to the ground, and then drove it in.

Blood flowed, more and faster than she'd have thought, bathing her fingers in warm stickiness. Sharantyr's stomach lurched.

Involuntarily her eyes traveled to where Elminster's head should be and was not, and a moment later she flung herself to one side and emptied her gut onto the turf, her own ribs aching as she shuddered and heaved uncontrollably.

"It'll be harder if you wait," Syluné said soothingly, but Sharantyr sung back to the bleeding body with an angry snarl, face white, and dug her blade in as if striking a blow in battle.

Her arms and breast were soon dripping, and she nearly squirted herself in the eye twice. One glimpse of her matted, dangling hair made her wish she'd tied it back before starting this, but she couldn't think of everything, by all the gods, and . . .

There. It slipped out easily into her fingers: a gray, unremarkable stone from Syluné's hut, the focus that allowed the undead Sister to speak, to *be*, this far from the place of her death. The means by which she'd been able to make this spell-crafted body move and speak and perceive—and ape Elminster so well.

The impersonation had been masterful, Shar reminded herself as she took another deep breath, her stomach a loose and floating thing, and got up grimly from her knees, the stone tightly clutched in her fist. Blood ran down her arms and dripped off her elbows as she headed for where the two Harpers stood talking. Modesty was just going to have to be abandoned for the nonce; she *had* to get clean!

"Goodsirs," she said tightly, "I must . . .

"Close your eyes and trust in us," Itharr said gently. "We won't lose the stone; just hold it out."

Sharantyr did as she was bid and felt the stone taken from her fingers, followed by a warm stinging on them and on her eyelids, face, and body as someone washed her carefully with . . . zzar!

She wrinkled her nose at the unmistakable almond scent, and someone chuckled. Before she could draw breath to speak, Belkram said, "Sorry, Shar. 'Tis all we could think of in haste." After a moment, he offered slyly, "We could lick you clean, after."

"You could run to Zhentil Keep and back before nightfall, first," she replied briskly, and all three of them chuckled. A moment later, she relaxed gratefully into the warmth of an energetic toweling.

"You won't be the only one smelling like a tavern, though," Itharr said. Shar opened her eyes to look a question at him and saw that both men had stripped to the waist—hairy beasts, the pair of them—and were drying her with their undershirts. She wrinkled her nose again at the thought of smelling like an unwashed, sweaty man, then smiled at their hurt expressions and said hastily, "You *are* sweet, both of you."

"I was wondering when you were going to say that," Syluné's voice said in her ear, in a faint, private whisper. Belkram proudly held out Shar's leathers for her to see the hasty but neat stitching where they'd sewn her rent shoulder panel more or less back together.

She took their work in her fingers and shook her head in delighted wonder. "How did you do this in such a short time?" She clutched the leathers to her breast and looked from one beaming Harper to the other. "You'll make wonderful mates, you two!"

"Oh, no," Itharr said firmly, backing away.

"No, indeed," Belkram agreed, eyes wary. "We're kind folk, not crazy men."

Sharantyr stared at them and then around at the gory body behind her, the soot-blackened rocks, the mushroom pulp strewn everywhere . . . and started to laugh. Not crazy. Indeed.

The snorting sound from the empty air at her elbow told her Syluné shared her amusement.

Shar shook her head again, her broad smile refusing to fade, and then a gentle breeze touched her with cool fingers, reminding her that she was— She looked down, then up at the carefully raised eyes of the two men, and said crisply, "You have my thanks, and my clothes. I'd like them back now, *if* you don't mind."

They bent and gathered her garments promptly. "There's a worn spot here on your halter," Belkram said helpfully, pointing, "where it's starting to pull apa—"

"I'll live with it, thanks," Shar told him firmly, taking everything in an armload and retreating hastily. "A worn part of my body customarily lives beneath it."

"*Don't*," Itharr said quickly, holding up a warning hand. "The body . . ."

Syluné added quietly, "To the right three paces, and there'll be no chance of slipping on gore or tripping over the . . . remains."

Shar sighed, breathed deeply for a few moments, and then turned her back on her two companions and marched around the body in a wide circle, heading for the other side of the ruins.

Belkram and Itharr exchanged glances, smiles, and shrugs. "Worth seeing, and that's all I'd best say," Itharr said quietly, reaching for the zzar bottle and its cork.

"I agree," Syluné's voice said sharply from the stone Belkram's fingers had just closed on. "Let's leave the comments at that fair observation, shall we?"

"Of course, great lady," the Harpers replied in swift unison, and were treated to the sight of a stone chuckling.

Belkram nearly flung it down a moment later when a startled scream rent the air from the far side of the ruin. The two men snatched out blades and sprinted to the rescue, running too fast to spare breath to growl, "What *now?*"—so Syluné voiced it for them.

They came around a rubble-strewn corner at a dead run, to see no nude ranger. "Shar?" Belkram called urgently.

"Here," their companion replied curtly, and they turned toward her voice. To find her, they had to pass through an arch and around the tumbled remnants of a wall, into a little sheltered corner. "Did you bring my blade?" demanded the woman huddled in the corner, shielding herself with her hands.

"N-no," Itharr said. "What befalls?"

"Turn around while I dress," Shar ordered, "but keep your blades ready. You may need them."

A few breaths later she joined them, breathing heavily in her haste. "What made you scream?" Itharr asked, feeling her hand on his shoulder. "You never scream."

"Well, thank you," Shar replied evenly, "but I do. And so would you, if you were a woman wearing nothing but a smile and walked almost right into *them!*"

"Who're 'them'?" Belkram asked her, puzzled.

Shar pointed in exasperation. "There! In the trees!"

The Harpers looked, and frowned—and then stiffened. Just inside the edge of the concealing trees, a dozen warriors stood frozen, weapons raised, faces tense, and eyes alight with frustration and appreciation. Belkram peered narrowly at the silent, absolutely motionless band. Only their eyes moved as he swung his sword idly in the air and stepped forward.

"Randal Morn, Lord of Daggerdale, if I'm not mistaken . . . and his court," he said, and bowed to one of the statuelike figures. "A moment, sir," he said, and then looked down to the stone in his hand. "Lady?"

"The second ring Sharantyr took from the body—from the left little toe—should hold the means to free them," Syluné's voice said, a little wearily. As Belkram turned to walk back to where Shar had been working, Syluné added, "They can help build a pyre. The body must be burned before someone gets a good look at it. Waste no time about this, mind."

"Of course not, great lady," Belkram said, sarcasm only the faintest of ripples in his tone.

The deep tinkling sound made in reply by the stone in his palm was quite the loveliest chuckle he'd ever heard.

* * * * *

The Castle of Shadows, Kythorn 16

Blue-tinged mists swirled hastily out of the way as Kostil of the Malaugrym stalked angrily through the Castle of Shadows. "Summoning us all to a council is a wise—if time-devouring—action at such a time, but how long must we wait for the Shadowmaster High to appear? I have plans—I daresay we all do—and now, with magic raging wild in Faerûn and godlings bounding all over the place, is not the time to tarry in bureaucratic power games!"

"I am of like mind," Yabrant said quietly. "What could he be about, to be so important tha—"

Under their feet, the shadows shook with the sudden boom of the great bell. They stopped, turned as one, and grew wings to speed back to the Great Hall as the rolling echoes died away.

Then the bell rang again, a single strike in measured time with the previous ring. Their eyes met. The bell tolling? This could mean only one thing—and Dhalgrave had been forceful, strong, and in full command of his powers not long ago at all.

Unlike Dhalgrave, neither of them—senior Shadow-masters both—had the strength of magic to levitate around a chamber, move the seeking eye of the portal around Faerûn, speak to an errant Malaugrym, bring one's own shape out of invisibility, and alter the portal's size and location in the Great Hall, overriding its spell defenses constantly and smoothly to do so . . . all at once.

Moreover, all the things that laid humans low—heart attacks, diseases, poisons, the failure of veins and lesser organs—were minor annoyances to Malaugrym able to change their bodies. Those of the blood of Malaug declined slowly, losing their shapeshifting abilities fitfully, usually along with their memories. Unless they were slain.

Kostil and Yabrant exchanged another grim glance and redoubled their efforts to get back to the throne chamber. The great bell tolled once more as the speed of their passage made the shadows they tore through rise in a continuous moan.

* * * * *

Daggerdale, Kythorn 16

"It has been a pleasure to aid you," Randal Morn said quietly, shaking their hands. Brammur smiled broadly and nodded his head in emphatic agreement, moustaches bobbing, but Thaern stood watchfully a little way to the side, an arrow fitted and ready in his bow. In these dark days, Daggerdale was hard pressed to keep its rightful lord alive.

The three rangers in worn leathers bowed in response. Straightening up, Sharantyr kept her features straight in the face of Brammur's longing gaze. The old warrior was obviously smitten with her. The eyes of the other loyal men of Daggerdale said plainly that they'd not forgotten their glimpses of her, either. She gave them all a cheery smile and said, "When the smoke begins to rise, I take it these ruins will become a very dangerous place to tarry?"

The Lord of Daggerdale nodded. "We are always watched," he said quietly, "by the cruel creatures of Zhentil Keep and by predators hungry for man-meals. Not that there's much difference between them as far as the few surviving good folk of Daggerdale are concerned."

"Then we are forcing you into flight once more," Belkram said, in tones so sensitive that no warrior of Daggerdale thought to take offense at his words.

" 'Tis what we're best at, these days," Brammur rumbled, and there were rueful chuckles from his fellows.

"Then let us part as trusted friends," Itharr said gravely. Then his voice changed. "Anyone have flints handy?"

More chuckles gave him reply, and several hands crowded forward to strike sparks onto the handful of kindling that all wayfaring Harpers carried in their bedding, and coax it into a flame for the torch-rag.

As the kindling flared, Randal Morn said, "We'd best be on our way and leave you to bid farewell to your fallen comrade in privacy. Know that Those Who Harp are always welcome in Daggerdale."

"If you need refuge, doors are always open to you in Shadowdale," Sharantyr replied.

"And more," Belkram said. "That Harper pin you have will allow you safely into a cache of healing potions and the like, in a cave big enough to shelter six, under a tree. Dig under leaves between the two largest exposed roots of the third shadowtop tree south of Dagger Rock, on the east side of the road. Don't stop if you uncover orc bones."

The men of Daggerdale exchanged glances and nodded to each other as they fixed the Harper's words in mind.

"That is princely payment," Randal said quietly, "for cutting a few tree boughs."

"You deserve all that the Harpers can give you, and more," Itharr replied as flame flared under his hands. "Most folk would have fled or thrown their lives away in stiff-necked glory-seeking long ago. Your struggle protects all in the Dalelands."

"It is good," Brammur said gruffly, "to hear someone say that, now and then. Thank you." He turned away quickly, eyes very bright, but spun about again to raise his hand in salute.

Randal Morn and the rest of his men joined in the gesture and then began to back away together, the watchful archer covering their withdrawal.

In two breaths they'd all melted away into the trees, and the three rangers in the ruins could see no sign of them.

"Shar?" Itharr asked, holding out the torch.

"You do it," Sharantyr said shortly, heart suddenly full and catching at her throat. She stepped back, fighting down the urge to burst into tears.

The Dales should not be lands where men's lives were torn away from them daily by fey shapeshifters and prowling beasts. Where brigands reigned and rightful lords lived like outlaws while arrogant Zhentarim plotted the overthrow of the next dale . . . and the next.

Belkram touched her arm. "Mount up," he said quietly, "and then you can cry at will."

Shar stiffened, turning blazing eyes on him, but he merely smiled and clapped her on the shoulder—the shoulder covered by leathers he'd mended. She gulped, threw her arms around him, and said tremulously, jaw hard on his shoulder, "I'm . . . not . . . going . . . to . . . weep now. It was only a false seeming of a mage, anyway, not our old friend."

The pyre crackled and then caught, damp wood hissing loudly as smoke rose from many places in the woodpile. Itharr tossed the torch onto it and sought his mount.

Flames began to show themselves, dancing here and there in the pyre.

The horses danced under their riders, the flames making them restive, so the three rangers pulled back a little way to watch.

"We should be leaving," Belkram said, "before eyes we won't welcome turn hither."

"Let us have a real pyre," Syluné's voice said, from the pouch in the Harper's breast pocket where he carried her stone.

An instant later, the growing crackle of flames leapt into a bright white roar, and a pillar of fire clawed at the sky.

The horses snorted and stamped. After a moment of awed watching, the three riders turned their mounts away and settled into a gallop, heading northwest. No one felt like talking.

9
Another Day Spent Saving the Realms

The Castle of Shadows, Kythorn 17

Shadows danced and shivered around the edges of the scene in the portal. Six sweating elder Shadowmasters, under the gasped directions of Bheloris who stood among them, trembling with effort, fought to hold its view so large and clear.

Most of the kin—sixty or more—were in the Great Hall of the Throne now, but the bell tolled on. Everyone but the struggling elders was talking excitedly, eyes glued to the portal, which showed Dhalgrave sprawled on the gleaming tiles of his private audience chamber. His eyes were two smoldering, empty holes. A long forked tongue trailed from his mouth, and his brow and wrists were bare. The Shadowcrown and the Doomstars were gone.

There was more. A word had been written on the tiles beside the head of the Shadowmaster High . . . written in his own blood. That word was "UNWORTHY."

The talk was growing excited, as hope to seize the Shadow Throne grew in the hearts of two dozen Malaugrym, tempered only by fear of what might befall anyone who tried to hold that throne without the Shadowcrown and the threat of the Doomstars. Even if the ambushes and treacheries of open rivals were quelled, whoever had the missing items could appear without warning and slay any new Shadowmaster High, to take the throne in turn.

"*Who* could have done this?" Taernil asked for the sixth time, his voice as awed and outraged as it had been at first. Beside him, Huerbara sighed.

"Someone has," she said simply. "Accept that and go on. What now, for the two of us?"

"*Accept* that someone—" The rising rage in Taernil's voice broke off abruptly, and he fell silent and looked at her. "You're right. We must decide what to do, and not rage or dither." Then his sharp features changed, and he added softly, almost wonderingly, "The two of us, you said . . ."

Huerbara blushed, eyes glittering into his, and then abruptly turned her head away.

"Young idiots," Kostil said under his breath, flapping his wings down to reabsorb them into his body, eyes on the quivering scene of Dhalgrave dead in his chambers.

Yabrant shrugged beside him. "We all were, once." He seemed about to say more, but at that moment Bheloris shuddered, cried out, and pitched forward on his face— and the scene of death flew apart into shards and streamers of radiance, fading swiftly into the mists.

"He managed to force the portal's eye through Dhalgrave's defenses?" Kostil muttered. "I'm surprised he held it together so long."

"Dhalgrave wasn't resisting him or directing the shield spells," Yabrant said thoughtfully. "The feat is not that impressive. Doing it with such swiftness *is*."

"The young she-kin's question remains a good one," Kostil said. "What to we do now, the two of us?"

"Rescue Bheloris, before one of his old rivals decides to take advantage of his condition. We'll need him," Yabrant said, shouldering his way forward. "I believe the killing's about to start."

As he spoke, shouts arose across the Great Hall, and there was frenzied movement. The flaring radiance of a spell followed, accompanied by a scream, as the unleashed magics returned to their caster.

"Didn't that idiot pay *any* attention to Dhalgrave's words about the defenses he'd added to this hall? He made enough noise about 'a truly safe meeting-ground for all of the blood of Malaug' and such!" Kostil's voice was disgusted. "Do we really share kinship with total idiots?"

"It's a common fate in the multiverse, I'm told," Yabrant replied wryly as they forced their way to Bheloris. They found Neleyd there before them, his body shifted nto a shield of many curling tentacles. "Well done, boy."

Neleyd flushed at the words, then sighed and asked,
Am I to be 'boy' forever?"

"No," Kostil told him kindly. "You get to alternate be-
ween that, 'young fool,' and 'brainless youngling' for a
ew hundred years yet."

"I'll enjoy that," Neleyd told him dryly, as the chamber
ocked under the impact of two warring explosions, and
in all around them grew weapons out of their limbs and
egan shouting and hacking. "Let's be gone!"

"Wisely said, young fool," Yabrant told him with a
nany-fanged smile.

His expression was matched by a figure none of them
aw, who stood watching the tumult from a high, shadow-
loaked balcony. Milhvar smiled only that once, then
urned silently away. There was much to do.

* * * * *

omewhere in Faerûn, Kythorn 17

Elminster paused for a moment on a hilltop, his eyes
ull of swirling stars. The sight that showed him the
lows of Art—that is, where magic could be expected to
wist wild—was an exhausting thing to use for long, but
e had to be sure of his next move. He had a long, hard
ay ahead, what with avatars stalking around Faerûn,
gos first, trying to destroy anything and everything that
o much as looked askance at them.

A thought brought his pipe whizzing around his head
o his lips, and he puffed on it thoughtfully. Over *there*
vas the next battle to be fought, aye, but first . . .

He leaned forward, banished the mage-sight, and
alled on farseeing for a moment. A gnarled tree, bark
rumbling off a dead limb that curved just so . . . and the
round beneath . . . a-hum. Enough. Do it!

Abruptly the hilltop was empty except for a silently
ircling pipe. An instant later, the pipe vanished too.

* * * * *

Faerûn: a camp on the High Road south of Tunland, then Hawkgauntlet, Kythorn 18

"I *told* ye to strike at the goblins, an' leave the orc to *me!* Tempus take thee for a softskull, lad! Now we'll have to . . . leave him lie."

"To die." It was not a question.

"Get out of my sight!" the old warrior roared, rounding on the younger with his eyes blazing almost-visible flames. The younger man fell back, fumbling for his blade in fearful habit. "If ye knew how to rotting take orders as well as ye know how to rotting well ignore 'em, we'd not have to be leaving anyone! Go now, afore I *really* lose my temper!"

The young warrior gulped, spun about, and ran.

The older armsman spat after him and then turned back to the injured priest of the Wargod, who lay clutching at a lapful of his own steaming innards where an orc scimitar had bitten deep. "Roarald?" he asked roughly. "Are ye with us yet, man?"

"I . . . I suppose," the reply came dully, the priest's eyes not seeing him. "Beware, Symon. I may be the luckier of us two. The days ahead will be dark. I have seen gods walking Faerûn, and whole cities laid waste, and the land much changed. Titans clash with their heads among clouds and their feet trampling us poor folk beneath, and rivers run black with poison . . . and more death than any war has brought to this world. No good. No good I've seen . . . no end that Tempus would show me." He caught his breath for a moment, and then gasped, "Symon! I am much afraid. Speak gently to the boy, for my sake. He was only . . . a helpful fool, and we've all been that a time or two."

The old warrior took him by the shoulders. "Don't leave us, Roarald! Call on Tempus, man! Surely he owes ye *something*, after all these years! Surely he'll—"

"Speak not of the god that way!" Roarald was protesting feebly under his hands. "The way of Temp—"

"Surely he does," a powerful, melodious voice thundered around them.

The two men gaped, dumbfounded, at the man-high, glowing battlesword—of one piece of deadly blue-black metal, standing vertically with its point not quite touching the ground—that stood beside them. A sword that had certainly not been there before. That thunderous voice issued from it again.

"Stand clear, good Symon. Thy loyalty to a comrade pleases me."

White to the lips, the old warrior hastily scrambled back, going to his knees in the mud. "M-my pardon, Great Lord! I meant no presumpt—"

"I know this. Be still now." The sword began to move, and the old warrior gulped once and was silent.

The black blade drifted silently through the air to hang with its point above Roarald's hands, where they clutched at his bloody vitals.

"I need ye, faithful servant. I need thy obedience and strong arms to keep order in this Time of Troubles. I need thy continued service, Roarald of Tempus. Will ye obey me still?"

"L-lord," the priest gasped, "I will . . . if I can."

"Then go to Luskan, and put down a rising of dark wizards who seek to plunge all the North into bloody slaughter not sanctioned by me. They seek to whelm all the Uthgardt tribes, rule their minds with potions and spells, and hurl them upon the cities of the North, Neverwinter first. Ye will gather my faithful against them, and Symon here will aid ye. The strife will be hard, and there may well be death in it for ye both. Knowing that, will ye do this?"

"I will!" Roarald gasped, a pink froth rising to his lips. "But, Lord, I—"

"Be still! Symon, will ye do this?"

"Lord of Battles," the old warrior said, face to the ground and teeth chattering, "I *will!*"

"It is good. Roarald, draw thy hands away from thy belly."

Hastily the priest did so, and the sword plunged down.

A blaze of white fire shrouded the priest's agonized scream.

When he could see again, Symon struggled to his feet. "Roarald? Roarald, do ye live, man?"

The priest was rising whole and strong, the stains of blood and dirt gone from his body. "I do," he said, wonder in his voice. "I *live!*"

"Praise be to Tempus!"

"Praise *be!*" the priest agreed, and clapped his comrade on the shoulder. "Speedily, now—find the boy and our horses. We ride on Luskan without delay!"

As Symon hurried off, the priest went to one knee and whispered, "Thank you, Tempus. I shall not forget."

"See that ye don't," a quiet voice came from the empty air, startling the man. He gulped, got up hastily, and ran after Symon.

And behind him a black sword melted out of the air, wavered, and became a thoughtful-looking old man, worn and much-patched robes draped about his thin frame. The morning sun gleamed on the man's long white beard and whiskers as a pipe floated into view from somewhere in the trees nearby and drifted gently up to the old man's mouth.

"That's done," Elminster muttered. "Too good a man to lose, Roarald, even if he is as stubborn as an old post. Hmmph! A certain Queen of Aglarond has used those same words to describe *me* a time or two, hasn't she?"

He strolled away, calling to mind the next place he'd viewed from the hilltop—and abruptly he was there, worn boots stepping onto the soft ground behind a tent.

"Another one dead? Have all the gods cursed this caravan?" The voice was proud and angry. "Who is it this time?"

"Mider, sir. He's—eaten away, sir, like the others. Only his feet left, and his scalp. In his tent, still in his blankets."

"Was he the only one of us alone in a tent?"

"Yes, sir. Albrar was his tent mate, until . . ."

"I know. Maybe it's something they were carrying, the two of them. Burn that tent and everything in it, just as it stands. Now!"

"Yes, sir." There was the sound of hastily receding

ooted feet, followed by a rustling of canvas and tent silks.

"Do they suspect?" a new voice asked in a whisper that did not carry beyond the ear it was said into.

"Mider did, but it's just a little too late for him, now," was the amused reply. The shared mirth that followed was silenced by the meeting of lips, a mouth-coupling that soon became a frantic, muffled screaming as the doppleganger couple found themselves locked in their embrace, immobilized by something that had twisted them into their true, monstrous shapes, and frozen them there. Something that drifted up from the tent like a ghostly mist and whirled back into the shape of Elminster.

"It shouldn't take long for someone to find them," he said, turning away in satisfaction. "Live by trickery, die by trickery. That'll be my ending too, no doubt, when at last it comes."

He stepped through the trees to where his pipe hung. "Now I'd best hurry," he murmured. "Galdus hasn't much time left." And then he was gone, an instant before a guard, drawn sword in hand, came warily down the path in search of the privy bench.

The Hawkgauntlet Arms was distant indeed from that privy bench at the back of the caravan camp, but it was the pride of Hawkgauntlet, a hamlet north and west of Tipur too small to grace any map. And too poor to loot, unless one was a brigand too hungry to care.

Elminster shoved open the groaning front door and stepped into the gloomy taproom beyond. The old man behind the bar blinked at him in the sudden shaft of daylight. "We're not open yet," he said gruffly. "Come back at sundown."

"I'm not thirsty, Galdus," the Old Mage replied, coming to the bar. "I've come to give ye something."

The old man's eyes narrowed, and he peered at Elminster in the dimness. "I know you, don't I?" he asked thoughtfully. "That voice . . ."

"The magefair when Almanthus tried to make the mountain fly," Elminster reminded him gently. The man's head snapped back.

"Elminster?"

"The same," El said, sliding a coin across the bar with one finger.

The old man stared at it, and then up at him. "What'll you have?"

Elminster shook his head. "I need ye to do something for me. Four things, actually."

The old man blinked again, and grinned. "*That* sounds like the Elminster I knew, to be sure."

"Ye have only a few minutes left to live, if ye do these four things wrong," the Old Mage said softly. "So heed."

Galdus glared at him, then swallowed and nodded. It had been years since he'd worked magic, and he knew he'd been no match for Elminster even at the height of his striving. "Say on," he said shortly.

"Armed men are coming this way—hungry and ruthless wild-swords," El said, "and they'll be here very soon. I need ye to stand still whilst I cast two spells on thee."

Galdus sighed. "Do it," he said simply. El nodded, and made two quick sets of gestures, touching the old bartender at the end of each.

"What—what did you do?"

"Made ye immune—for a little while—to all harm from weapons of iron and to all thrown or hurled things, like arrows. The same cannot be said for anyone else ye may employ or dwell with here. So the second thing I need ye to do is to keep all such folk from harm. Warn them now, but be quick!"

Galdus stared at him for a moment, then ducked his head through the door behind him and spoke quickly and sharply. Then he closed the door, and Elminster heard a bar being settled across it from within. "Done," the old man said simply.

"I need ye to give this coin to the men when they demand money of ye. Best give them a handful to go with it, so they don't suspect a trick."

Galdus reached down behind the bar, opened a cupboard door, and dumped the contents of an old, cracked earthen jar onto the bar. A gleaming fan of silver and copper coins slid out. "I'll be counting coins when they come in, then."

El nodded. "I couldn't help but notice, on my way in, that thy outhouse is a bit of a ruin," he said, nodding his head in its direction.

"That one?" Galdus grinned. "We don't dare use it. When it falls in, I'll have the lads take away what they want, for manure. If you have to feed the gods, the real one's out back."

It was Elminster's turn to smile. "Feed the gods? I hadn't heard that expression!" He chuckled, then stopped at the look on the old man's face. "Ye call it that because of what befell ye at the temples?"

Galdus nodded, face set. It had been forty summers ago that his health had been broken and his magic torn from him by two warring priests in Sembia. Their temples had grown in size and splendor, and doubtless they'd grown fat and powerful with them, but Galdus had been left with only one spell he could use. There's not much future for a mage who can create magical radiance at will, and do nothing else.

Elminster leaned forward across the bar. "If it makes ye feel better, old friend, know that all the gods have been cast down into Faerûn. That's what's behind all these troubles—the wild magic and roaming monsters, outlaws and armies everywhere. The gods are wandering Faerûn with little more up their sleeves than ye or I have. A lot of folk will get hurt, aye, but at least the gods'll be feeling just what ye went through."

Galdus stared at him, slack jawed. Then a deep red color slowly rose in his face, and he leaned forward with the first enthusiasm El had seen in him. "Is this true?" he asked excitedly, and then paled. "I-I didn't mean . . ."

El smiled. "Be easy, Galdus. Yes, it's true."

And then the old, balding bartender threw back his head and bellowed with laughter. "Yes!" he cried. "*Yes!*" He whooped, jumped around behind the bar, and with sudden resolve snatched up a cracked tallglass and hurled it exultantly across the taproom. Watching it shatter into a thousand shards in the empty fireplace, he looked up with fierce exultation in his face and said,

"Where are these brigands? I'll face 'em, and fifty more besides! Bring 'em on!"

Elminster grinned. "There's the fourth thing," he added.

"What?" Galdus grinned back.

"Ye may have to lose that old outhouse," El told him. "And I hope ye have a fire in the kitchen ye can get to swiftly, with some logs on it that're well and truly alight, but have unburnt ends ye can carry 'em by."

Galdus stared at him for a moment, and then laughed again. "I have, and can. What's this all about?"

"Well," El began, "just be sure ye say 'With Elminster's regards' to whoever touches that coin, an—"

The door banged open suddenly, and the Old Mage was gone, as if he'd never been there. Galdus blinked at where he'd been and then at the drawn swords coming across the room at him, followed by the stench of old sweat and desperate men.

"Counting the coins, were ye? Well, I think that right kindly of ye, to save us the trouble of finding 'em. Go and get yer *real* savings, old man, with Baerlus here beside ye to save tricks, while we have a pull or two at a keg o' yer best!"

"Who—? What're y—" Galdus began, struggling to keep a smile from his face. Then he saw the man's hands raking the coins across the bar, and knew the enspelled one might bounce and roll on the floor in a moment, so he stammered, "With Elminster's regards!"

"You fools," he added a breath later, watching the coin erupt into wildly coiling black tentacles. The five brigands shouted in alarm, and the one who must be Baerlus snarled and drove his blade into Galdus, under the old man's ribs, jerking his steel savagely up and sideways.

Galdus stared down in wonder as the weapon slid through him as though he were a ghost. He didn't feel a thing! The outlaw stared up at him, face paling, and then hacked wildly at him, the blade whipping back and forth like a flail on the threshing floor.

The blade seemed not able to touch him, though he felt the man's knuckles graze his shoulder on one wild swing.

Baerlus stared at him, dumbfounded. Galdus snatched a wooden salad bowl from its wall peg and brought it down smartly on the man's sword hand.

Baerlus howled and stepped back, dropping his blade with a clatter, so Galdus leaned in and walloped him across the side of the head with the edge of the bowl. The outlaw staggered and stepped back, right into his four fellows.

They were thrashing and grunting in fear, staggering around his taproom helplessly in a confused tangle of arms and legs. The coin had become a black ball with many long tentacles that stuck to flesh as a sucking eel sticks to fish. The tentacles were wriggling and probing constantly but didn't stick to clothing, weapons, or wood. The four outlaws—no, five now, with Baerlus—were firmly bound together, unable to straighten up or even turn to face each other as the tentacles pulled them in closer together . . . and closer still . . .

Galdus watched the brigands struggle, slipping and sliding on the coins and swords that lay dropped and forgotten all over his recently cleaned floor. They crashed aside chairs and even a table, yelling in muffled fury and mounting fear, and rolled about, their struggles taking them vaguely away from the bar.

The front door groaned open again, and Galdus looked up warily, wondering if he could reach any of the swords on the floor. The man who stepped inside, however, was Elminster.

"My apologies, Galdus," he said. "I'd something else to attend to and no time to do it in. But 'tis done now."

"Can I—may I ask what it was?"

"I had to talk a few frightened archpriests in Baldur's Gate out of starting a religious war—on each other."

"Why bother?" Galdus asked, frowning. Then his frown deepened. "Did it work?"

"No, of course not, so I had to scare them into a truce by showing them what I'd do if they didn't make peace."

"You flattened both temples," Galdus said hopefully.

Elminster grinned. "I see ye know the basics. I did indeed. Rebuilding and trying to keep folk from looting will keep both sides busy for a time." He stepped carefully around the tangled knot of rolling, kicking brigands and continued. "And to answer thy other question, I bothered because I didn't want to see a lot of homes burned and innocent folk slain in the Gate over some disagreement that had nothing to do with them." He sighed. "This is going on all over Toril, right now. First thing this morn, I had to do the same thing to head off rival factions of illithids, in a city in the heart of Raurin."

Galdus stared at him. "Mind flayers? You stopped *mind flayers* from killing each other? *Why?*"

"They're intelligent folk too, just as ye, I, and these dolts here are. And besides, they're sitting on enough battle spells there to destroy half the eastern Realms! I didn't want any tentacle-heads to remember that and start tearing open vaults and using 'em. A few hundred years more, and most of the scrolls will have crumbled away to nothing . . . and it'll take them half that time to dig out all the stonework I piled up on top of those vaults!"

Galdus grinned. "Make sure you check back with me in a few hundred years, then, to let me know Faerûn is safe to live in at last. In the meantime"—he gestured down at the tightening mass of bodies on the floor—"what do we do with these?"

"Roll them into thy outhouse and burn it," Elminster said calmly.

10
Talking to Gods

Daggerdale, Kythorn 18

The Mountains of Tethyamar rose like a distant wall
ahead on their left as the three rangers in worn and
patched leathers rode warily into another soft-shadowed
evening. They were headed into the heart of lawless
Daggerdale, Randal Morn had warned them; reaches
where steads lay abandoned to the forest, orcs and hobgoblins roamed the land in raiding bands and clashed
whenever they met, and monsters lurked in the ruins
and woody tangles for the unwary. For all those dire
warnings, they'd ridden all day and seen nothing more
deadly than birds. Of course, Itharr reflected, they had
no idea just what might have seen *them*.

"Oh, but the land is beautiful," he sang softly as they
forded their third tinkling stream.

"And the living carefree," Belkram sang the next line,
heavy irony in his tone.

Sharantyr chuckled and took up the song. "So come, ye
fairest of dark-eyed maidens . . ."

"And come dwell in the greenwood with me!" Itharr
and Belkram sang together. Ahead of them, a gore-crow
took wing heavily from a dead branch and flapped away
with a derisive caw.

"What are you, a bard?" Itharr called after it. The bird
circled, winked at him once with a very steady black eye,
and flew away.

"The Simbul?" Belkram breathed the question as they
all stared after it.

"Without a doubt," Syluné's voice came to them from
the stone in his breast pocket. "She probably appreciates
your singing about as much as I do."

"A little less sarcasm there," Belkram told her. The
stone thrummed against his chest in reply. The hand-

some ranger stood up in his stirrups to look all around and sighed. "I suppose we'd better start looking for somewhere we can defend—and protect the horses, too—and camp for the night."

"Agreed," Sharantyr said, drawing up beside him on her patient steed. "But after we're out of the saddle, I'd like to talk about the wisdom of riding aimlessly around the most dangerous territory we can find, now that we lack a false Elminster to escort. Surely these deadly shapeshifters can find us wherever we are?"

Belkram sighed again. "To hear good sense spoken so directly and clearly is always disconcerting. It makes debate seem so . . . foolish."

"Spoken like a man!" Itharr agreed in robust tones.

"Exactly," Shar and the stone that was Syluné said in perfect unison. After a moment, everyone laughed.

Belkram rose again in his saddle still chuckling, and pointed northwest. "Is that a suitable place I see before me?"

"Pray, good knight, ride ye and see," Itharr quoted in response.

Belkram looked quickly at the lady ranger who rode with them, cleared his throat, and said loudly, "Ah, no, Itharr. Not *that* ballad. Really."

Shar gave him a smile, a twinkle in her gray-green eyes, and sang steadily, "For I crave a bank by a stream running softly, where ye'll lay me down and make love to me!"

"Oh, no!" Itharr said in shocked tones. "You were right, bold Belkram. Not a suitable ballad at all!"

"Belt up and stow it," Belkram told him dryly. "Well, what say you? Does anyone know what that place might be?"

"It's a little hard to see from inside this pocket," Syluné said sweetly. "Perhaps if we get closer and you dismount, I could tell something about it. We'd best poke about a bit first, to see if that's a prudent course of action."

Itharr and Sharantyr both spread eloquent empty hands in answer to Belkram's query. "We're out of the bits of Daggerdale I know," Shar added. "It looks more like a manor on a hill than a keep, but just as far past its proud days as Irythkeep. We'll be lucky to find any part of it still with a roof."

"Well, we've been very lucky in avoiding rain thus far," Itharr observed brightly.

"Hush!" both of the other riders said severely.

"Do you *want* to bring it on?" Sharantyr demanded, scowling. "I've heard of lump-headed idiots before, but—"

"You weren't prepared for what a couple of Harpers can do," Syluné said loudly enough for them all to hear, startling Belkram into nearly falling out of his saddle.

"Steady on, there," Itharr commented. "The bit of the horse that snorts and has ears is the front. Now, all you have to do is keep a leg either side of the beast and that front bit pointed—"

"You can belt up any time, friend," Belkram said easily. "Your tongue runs on almost as much as Elminster's!"

The stone in his pocket laughed heartily.

"Enough," Sharantyr said, her eye on the lowering sun. "Trap or no, let's look at this place before darkness leaves us no choices at all."

The ruin they were fast approaching stood on a grassy hill whose steep slopes fell away into thick, tangled woods to the east and south. Broken land, all hills and copses, lay beyond it to the north, and there seemed to be a patchwork of woodlots and meadows—the former manor farmlands, no doubt—to the west. An overgrown road of sorts crossed the rolling country before them, leading down into the woods and thence up that oddly bare hill to the ruin. Why had no saplings sprung up on the hillsides?

"I don't like the look of it," Itharr said.

"Nor do I," Belkram said, "but I must remind you that I've heard those same words from you about seventy times since we began faring together."

"And how often was my concern justified?"

"Umm . . . twenty times or so."

"Well?"

"But if we strike out the times we were looking at

known Zhentarim holds, brigand camps, and undead holds, Itharr . . . four times."

"Perhaps this'll be five," Itharr offered, almost hopefully.

"You don't really have too much doubt, do you?"

"No. The backs of my hands itch," the burly Harper said, as if that explained everything.

"The backs of his hands itch," Belkram told the sky. "Shar, you're closer. Scratch them for him, will you?"

"I go out riding with a pair of hairily handsome men," Shar told her horse conversationally, "and what do they want me to do? Scratch the backs of their hands. You certainly meet some crazed-wits in the ranks of the Harpers, don't you?"

"Enough levity," Itharr said in quite a different voice, and drew his sword. A moment later he was riding down a green tunnel beneath the interlaced branches of the trees, slowing his mount abruptly and looking warily at the trees ahead. "Lady of the Forest, be with us," he breathed, knowing an arrow could take him in the face or throat before he even saw it.

He glanced back once. Sharantyr was catching up to him swiftly, her beautiful brown hair flowing free around her shoulders and her blade naked in her hand. Far behind he could see Belkram, head turning from side to side and then twisting to look back the way they'd come, in a steady, watchful cycle.

Knowing just what reckless fools they were, Itharr sighed as he faced the woods and rode on. Ahead, the road dipped to ford a small stream. No—a sagging bridge, gray with age and neglect, sloped across the bright ribbon of water. Past the bridge, the road climbed out into daylight, up the hill.

He expected an attack where prudence forced him to dismount and lead the horse through the shallow waters just above the ruined bridge, but none came. He thought he saw a small dark figure turn and scuttle away through the trees well downstream, but brownies and halflings could almost always be found in country like this, and might well leave a few humans alone.

Or might not, as their inclinations took them. Itharr's shoulders felt very exposed as he rode up the hill and circled the ruin at a careful trot, seeing his companions come up the hill in turn.

Someone had burned the manor house a long time ago. Roofless walls were all that was left of two barns and the house itself, which had a semicircular flagstone terrace commanding a very pleasant view from the hilltop. Anything with eyes had seen them approach, but the ruins looked safe enough in themselves. Sharantyr was already dismounting to check the corners.

"Human bones here," she said almost immediately, "and orcs, too. Long dead, and scattered by something that came along later, something hungry that had big teeth."

"Ah, the expertise of the trained ranger," Belkram said jovially. "Have you decided on the best place for the horses?"

"Indeed," Shar told him pleasantly, "but I'm not sure if all three of them'll fit there; you'd probably struggle and squirm."

Itharr's barked laughter spilled out his relief that no attack had come, and it was Syluné's turn to sigh. "Crude, children . . . very crude. I'd best come out and look about. I can see undeath and things invisible where you can't."

"Please do," Belkram replied. "Teasing aside, I've just as odd a feeling about this too-pleasant place as Itharr."

The stone seemed to turn over in his pocket, and Belkram felt the softest of breezes against his cheek. "Try to behave while I'm gone," came a whisper in his ear, and he frowned in puzzlement at the word "gone" until he recalled her first act as Elminster, when coming to a camp: checking the trees all around for spies, brigands, game trails, and the like. He stretched, trying to relax shoulders tight with tension, and looked around the ruin.

The place must have been a cozy house when it was whole, not a grand residence. There were no halls, forechambers, or defensive ring walls, just a stout building of rooms opening into rooms. They chose one for the horses and another for themselves, and built a fire as soon as Syluné drifted back unseen to tell them the woods around were safe for as far as she'd cared to look.

Belkram had bent his ear her way in suspicion at something subdued in her tone, but Syluné saw him and said firmly, "Nothing is amiss that need concern you, Belkram. Relax, and have that debate you were so looking forward to. I'll stand watch the night through, if you'll all sleep clothed—or at least with your boots on—and with weapons to hand."

"That's hardly fair to you," Shar objected, and was rewarded with light laughter.

"Child, I don't need to sleep anymore . . . remember?"

"True enough," Sharantyr conceded. "Well, then, let's have our tongue-wag now, and stow it all when the food's ready."

"Aye, I've noticed that works with these two," Syluné agreed. "Speak."

"The question," Sharantyr said promptly, looking to her companions for confirmation, "is whether we're better off out here in the wilds or back home in Shadowdale, now that the Malaugrym have slain Old Elminster."

"It's safer for us back in the dale, surely," Itharr told the food he was preparing.

"Yes, but if we return there, we'll bring danger to Shadowdale at the hands of any Malaugrym who show up to attack us," Belkram put in from where he was seeing to the horses.

"Well, then, what about going to another defensible place?" Sharantyr replied. "One we don't care about, but which shelters us from brigands, hungry beasts, and other wandering perils—including marauding avatars, I suppose."

"Umm . . . got any such place in mind?" Itharr asked, looking up.

Shar shrugged. "My experience of these lands is limited," she reminded them. "I'm merely suggesting a strategy."

"What I'd like to know more about is our foes," Belkram grunted, checking the hooves of a horse who saw no reason for staying in a stony pen when there was a lovely grassy hill out there under the setting sun, and was firmly telling the nearest human its views. "Syluné?"

"The Malaugrym—a race of shapeshifters descended from the sorcerer Malaug, who have traditionally kidnapped women of Faerûn and taken them as mates—dwell in a vast, ever-changing Castle of Shadows on the demiplane of Shadow," the disembodied voice told them. "Some of them are powerful mages, but none dare to walk Faerûn openly because of Elminster, whom they call the Great Foe."

"Because he once foiled one of their kidnappings or slayings?" Itharr asked.

"Precisely. Centuries ago, they stole spells and enchanted items from all over Faerûn—competing with each other, I've been told—and quite often killed wizards so as to have a free hand in plundering their magic. When they tried to do the same to Elminster, he slew one of them and warned the others present to stay out of our world, but that just made them determined to eliminate him. It's been a running battle between the Malaugrym and the Chosen down the long years since especially a year back when spellfire appeared in the Realms, in the hands of Shandril Shessair. Elminster and the Simbul between them kept her alive and out of Malaugrym hands, more than anyone else."

Sharantyr nodded slowly. "I know, now, why the Knights decided to let Narm and Shandril go unescorted, but for Torm and Rathan riding after them."

"Yes," Syluné said. "Elminster didn't want any of you slain by the Malaugrym because you got in their way. The Shadowmasters, as they call their eldest and most powerful, think themselves superior to all folk of Faerûn. We're cattle, to be slaughtered or stolen from at whim."

"Charming," Shar commented, lifting her lips in a sneer. "Remind me, dahlings, to slaughter the cattle out of hand tonight . . ."

"Now, now," Belkram said, "don't give them any ideas. They may well be listening to us now."

"They probably are," Syluné confirmed calmly.

"What puzzles me," Itharr said, "is why they haven't taken to ruling the Realms long ago. How many of them are there, that a few diligent archmages can stop them? And what else do we know of their powers? What can slay them?"

"We don't know how many of them exist," Syluné replied. "As you can appreciate, it's difficult to do any sort of body count on secretive shapeshifters who're engaged in intrigues against each other as well as battles with folk of the Realms . . . except for, of course, a literal body count."

"Hoo-hah," Belkram agreed. "So what's Elminster's best guess?"

"He thought there were about seventy of any consequence," Syluné answered, chuckling at the calmly pressed question, "but that's before the Simbul had her little disagreement with them back at Irythkeep."

"Killing them," Itharr said. "Get back to killing them."

"Well, they're physically very strong—hardy is perhaps a better word; they'd have to be, to change shape so often—and so fare well in falls and the like, though it seems Malaugrym who've taken another shape *can* be slain by whatever would usually be fatal to the shape they're using. Cut off the head of a Malaugrym horse"— one of the horses lifted its head to give her a hard stare, and Syluné darted over to mindtouch and be sure it *was* a horse and not something more, before proceeding— "and you'll slay the Malaugrym, unless it's moved its vital functions somewhere else by starting to shift into another shape. Apparently they're suspicious enough of each other to shift body shape all the time, and go about their castle in forms that have several heads, tentacles all over the place, and so on."

"Definitely charming," Itharr said. "Go on."

"They like to take human shape but tend to put their vital functions in unusual body areas, so stabbing one in the eye might not blind it, and there may be no brain behind the eye to harm. Malaugrym who have magic can, of course, hurl spells if need be, in any body shape, and can cast protections on themselves before venturing out, just as human wizards do. They're also, as far as we've been able to learn, immune to all poisons fatal to men."

"So what is poisonous to a Malaugrym, I wonder?" Belkram asked softly. "There must be something."

"There is," Syluné confirmed. "The touch of silver in their blood—so on a blade, for instance—is corrosive to all of their tissues it reaches."

"It would have been useful," Itharr said quietly, "to have known this a little earlier."

"My apologies," Syluné said. "You are right, and right to be angry. We—Elminster, of course—didn't want you to alert the Malaugrym to a possible deception when we rode out, by demonstrating that you knew all about them. He's . . . he can be ruthless too, in his own way."

"We know that," Sharantyr said with feeling. "Believe me, we know that." The two Harpers laughed easily.

"Ah, Shar, 'twas a grand adventure that befell us in the High Dale!"

"*You* had each other," Sharantyr pointed out. "*I* was paired with Elminster."

"There're ladies across Faerûn who'd swoon for a chance to be where you were," Belkram reminded her.

"Right, you can call some of them in next time . . . but enough," Shar said briskly. "We'll trade salacious stories another time. Correct me, please, if I err in the following admittedly brief analysis. We have a handful of half-spent magic items and Syluné's wisdom and watchfulness to use against an unknown number of powerful shapeshifting wizards who come from another plane . . . and presumably can flee back there, out of our reach, whenever they desire."

"No, I think you've said it pretty well," Belkram agreed. "Despite our cause being heroic and our hearts pure, we've been very lucky to survive thus far. Sooner or later, if they bother with us, we'll be caught and overwhelmed . . . as we almost were before the Simbul showed up."

"As we *were*, I must remind everyone, by nothing more than hobgoblins," Itharr put in soberly. Then he laughed, a sudden light dancing in his eyes. "Why not take the battle to this mysterious castle hideaway of the Malaugrym? If we're dead anyway, what's to be lost? Why not take some of them with us?"

"Spoken like a true Harper," Belkram agreed.

"Spoken like a true idiot," Sharantyr retorted.

"There is often a great similarity, yes," Syluné said diplomatically, and they all chuckled. After a moment of silence, an owl hooted somewhere off in the woods, and Itharr asked, "Well?"

"Well, what?"

"Who's for attacking this castle on the morrow?"

"Are you *crazy?*"

"Why don't you sleep on it until morning, all of you?" Syluné suggested. "We can talk again then, when there isn't food spoiling."

"*Itharr!*"

"Sorry!" Itharr promptly burned his fingers at the fire, nearly dropped most of the food into the flames, and gave vent to almost as many colorful suggestions as were offered to him.

The scorched rabbit was, surprisingly, very good.

* * * * *

Hawkgauntlet, Kythorn 18

Across the gloomy taproom of the Hawkgauntlet Arms, the balding bartender stared at Elminster and slowly grew pale. "Burn them alive?" he gasped. "Right . . . here?"

"Would ye prefer I did the deed?"

Galdus gulped. "I'd prefer . . . it didn't happen at all."

Elminster nodded at him. "I hear ye," he said softly. "I'll take them far away instead. If I leave them nearby— believe me—ye'll have them back here soon, carving up thy folk, looting thy tavern, and then going on to the next place."

Galdus nodded. "No doubt. Yet if you burn them here, I'd have to move on myself. I couldn't walk past their ashes every morn . . . I just *couldn't.*"

The Old Mage nodded. "I understand," he said quietly. "So be it." He murmured something and waved a hand, and the struggling brigands were suddenly gone.

"Are they . . . dead?"

"Not yet. If they behave, not for many years yet. But I'm afraid I don't expect them to behave."

The bartender gulped. "I . . . ah . . . you have my thanks, friend."

"Fair fortune follow thee and thine," Elminster said in formal reply. Then he smiled, went to the bar, and extended his hand.

Galdus took it. "Thanks for saving our lives—myself and the wife and the three lasses the other side o' that door, my two daughters and one I hire in. Thanks for the magic, too."

"Oh, aye," Elminster said, and leaned forward to touch the old man's shoulder.

Galdus stiffened. "What did you do?"

"You have a year, now, of taking no harm from slung stones and fired arrows and cutting blades of iron and steel. A year, mind. Use it well to make the folk who're going to be fleeing here from Westgate in the months ahead respect ye."

Galdus tried to smile. "Those brigands . . . You have to slay like that often?"

"All the time," Elminster said simply. "Today's been quite a busy day for it, but yestereve was worse." He turned toward the door.

"Is all this slaying the price of becoming an archmage?" Galdus asked from behind him, almost whispering.

"Nay," Elminster said, fixing him with tired eyes. "This is the price of keeping the Realms alive. I've been paying it for more than a thousand years."

Galdus paled again but held up a hand to stop Elminster's departure. He drew two tankards of bitter from a keg and wordlessly slid one across the bar. Elminster took it, and from his empty hand a stack of gold coins slid onto the polished wood.

" 'Tis free, El!" Galdus said almost angrily, looking

down at the coins, then up at the Old Mage, and then down at the coins again, mouth dropping open.

"Ye have two daughters to raise, and maybe three, if the year ahead is cruel to the parents of the other," El said. "Put those away—bury 'em in a pot nearby—and ye'll have what ye need, later on." He grinned suddenly. "Perhaps even enough to rebuild that outhouse."

Galdus turned very red and then, a long moment later, grinned back.

"Right, then," he said, carefully taking up the coins. His hands trembled slightly as he put them in a sack and tied it at his belt. Then he took a pull at his tankard and looked at Elminster with almost pleading eyes.

"I'm a fool for asking this," he said quietly. "You could burn this place down, and me with it, probably by uttering a single word."

El inclined his head in a slow nod. "But ye're a man and were once a mage, so ye'll ask."

Galdus grinned slowly, shook his head, and said, "Yes. Well . . . Right, then. Why is all this killing necessary?"

Elminster shrugged. "Because I haven't yet succeeded in talking anyone to death."

"What?"

"I can't get folk to agree with others in peace. Always swords, spells, poison, or just fists come out . . . and are used." He sipped thoughtfully at his beer and said, "For several hundred years I tried to forge treaties here and handshakes there across Faerûn, and trust rulers to keep 'em. Some did so for as long as a year or two, seldom more."

He stared into his beer and added, "I grew tired of threatening and pleading, over and over again. Folk lied to me, smiled, and laughed at my back the moment I'd left. So I did what I had to: told folk clearly what the price'd be if they didn't keep peace in this or that way they'd agreed to. And I made them pay the price when I had to. Sudden respect, or sudden death, was the result. Some folk learned, and that won us peace enough for humankind to rise above scrabbling in the dirt to feed ourselves between goblinkin raids and monster attacks."

El drained his beer. "So men grew rich, and arrogant, and spread across Faerûn, making me wonder if I'd *really* done wrong, as the glorious old peoples, the elves and the dwarves, grew few and hunted. I started to worry about having to slaughter entire realms of men to keep us from laying waste to all Toril, burning down every tree for fuel, and eating all else, and finally each other—and then starving in the desert we'd left, dying off with a world wasted."

Galdus stared at him, swallowed beer without tasting it, and waved at him wordlessly to continue.

"I needn't have worried," Elminster went on, rubbing his sharp nose and looking off into the distance. "Humankind took advantage of its power and leisure to go to war with itself . . . and still does, year after year. I sometimes wonder if they've managed this any better, in other worlds where there are men, elsewhere in the multiverse."

The Old Mage fixed Galdus with calm eyes. "My job now—with the other Chosen, and the Harpers I helped found, and all the rulers I can dupe or threaten or bargain with—is to keep wars small and the real villains in check so that little folk, like thy family, can grow just a little better off year by year."

Galdus finished his own beer and held out his hand for El's tankard.

"From anyone else," he said heavily, refilling them both, "I'd call this deluded raving. A thousand years . . ." He shook his head. "Yet I believe you." He said it almost wonderingly and shook his head again as he set a full tankard down in front of the Old Mage. "Say on, please."

Elminster raised his beer in a silent toast. As the two tankards clinked, he asked the bartender, "Have ye never wondered why, year after year, the cruel mages in Thay, Zhentil Keep, Calimshan, and half a hundred other places don't destroy half the Realms in spell duels? Or just lead armies to roll over all of ye and meet to hack each other up in the smoking ruins that're left? Or why those orc hordes out of the northernmost mountains, that cover the land for mile upon mile of grunting goblinkin, don't just sweep over everyone?"

He drained his beer at single gulp. "Slaying," he answered himself, "that's why. Slaying when needful, and only when needful. Some realms have armies to do such dirty deeds. Shadowdale has Elminster."

Galdus swallowed. "When I was young and thought I could rule the world in just a few years, with just a few more spells, I used to talk about the way of the world and how I'd change it. I think all young wizards do, if they've someone to talk to. Later on, I never thought it'd all be for real, or that any halfway sane wizard spoke so, when he grew older." He shook his head and looked up at Elminster. "I thought they all just got twisted with power and greedy for more, and spent their days selling scrolls for gold or stealing spells from tombs or their enemies, or locked themselves away to go slowly mad making spells to open doors silently, or get wet laundry dry, or open stuck corks in old bottles . . . or blew themselves and their towers to the skies trying to perfect army-reaving magics."

"Most of them do just that," Elminster said softly. "Yet their very self-interest helps the rest of us. They're turned inward to small things, not trying to change the world, but they're *in the way* of conquerors and monsters. Intelligent folk rightly fear that they'll awaken and do battle if threatened, and beasts find that out the hard way."

Galdus grunted. "It makes one want to have more to drink, thinking about it."

Elminster grinned. "A lot of wizards do that, too."

He straightened in his seat and said, "My thanks for the bitter, Galdus, and the converse. 'Tis seldom I get to talk so freely to someone who'll understand, and more seldom yet that I find someone I dare say such things to. All too—"

And then the very air around him danced with blue sparks, and Elminster saw the bartender freeze in midstep, mouth hanging open to speak, eyes fixed on nothingness. The front door groaned.

Elminster found that he could still move in that surging web of magic—more than he'd ever felt unleashed before—so he turned toward the door to see who'd wrought it. He might as well see whatever god his words had angered, before they destroyed him.

A thin woman in a black gown was just closing the door behind her. She was alone, and her raven-dark hair, red-and-black eyes, and ivory skin made her look like a vampire. Her gait and movements, too, echoed the sultry, almost pouting manner of many she-vampires Elminster had met, but her eyes were somber as she walked toward the Old Mage.

"Your words have saved you," she said quietly, "and found me the teacher I need—and need to trust. Well met, Elminster."

"Well met, lady," Elminster said, bowing to her. "Who are you?"

"Midnight is the name I am known to most by, but you may call me . . . Mystra. We must talk."

11
Two Edges to Every Sword Blade

The Castle of Shadows, Kythorn 18

The three Malaugrym stood waiting like patient statues as Milhvar said, "The Shadowmaster High had great hopes for this project. Try not to let him down. But above all else, we want you back safely. If anything goes wrong—anything—use the power of your belt buckles to get back to us. Even if the foe is under your blade or in your hands, break off rather than be taken—or slain. There will be other forays, and other chances."

The three kin nodded, and one of them added a visibly nervous swallow. Milhvar did not smile or shrug. If they lived through this, perhaps they'd grow into Shadowmasters of some use. Huerbara almost was already, only her inability to bridle a too-oft-blazing temper holding her back. But Kuervyn and Andraut were nothings, all swagger and undisciplined thrill-seeking. They still found nightly fun in shapeshifting their ways through Faerûnian brothels, and took their greatest satisfaction in leaving without paying!

Dead growth, the pair of them. Milhvar let nothing of this judgment show as he told them all to willingly draw at least a drop of their own blood with a talon, claw, body spur, or other part of their own shape, and signaled the team of Shadowmaster mages to begin weaving the cloaks.

He'd deliberately woven the chain of interlocked spells to be more complex than it need be, take longer—and require more mages—than it needed to, and to be more than a little unstable. He'd no wish to unleash an army of unbeatable flamebrains like Kuervyn and Andraut on Faerûn or anywhere else.

When the long chanting and gesturing was done, and a

shimmering and dark singing in the air above the three told him the spell-cloaks were done, he stepped forward and added the "secret spell" that linked each magical construct to its wearer, through the drop of blood. This false enchantment added nothing useful to the process, but kept Milhvar essential to the crafting of every spell-cloak of the Malaugrym. A useful, if dangerous, status to hold.

But then, there were no safe positions to hold in the ranks of the blood of Malaug. Milhvar lifted his lip in a mirthless grin at the thought—and seeing this, Kuervyn toppled over, fainting dead away.

Milhvar laughed aloud as he strode toward the fallen Malaugrym, ignoring the smoking glare Huerbara gave him. There were still amusements to be found, if one waited patiently for them. It would be funnier still if these three went into Faerûn and found Elminster waiting for them. Perhaps he could arrange it sometime.

* * * * *

Daggerdale, then Myth Drannor, Kythorn 18

The face bending over her was a ghostly mask. "Shar," the familiar voice said kindly in her mind. "Shar, awaken. Quietly, lass. There is a deed you alone must do."

"Syluné?" she whispered.

"As always." The voice was warm and reassuring. Shar sat up and looked around at the blue, moonlit dimness. One of the horses shifted slightly, but the two Harpers lay still, breathing softly, a blanket thrown over each of them. Syluné stood beside her, a pale wisp of shifting nothingness in the night, like the memory of a white flame. Something called in the woods off to the north, something small and mournful that she didn't recognize. Shar laid aside her blanket, took up her blade—its grip cold and hard, bringing her fully awake—and got up as quietly as she could.

The ghostly figure beside her reached out, offering something to her. A ring. "Put this on."

Shar did so, her fingers tingling as they touched what was left of the Witch of Shadowdale. Syluné smiled at her reassuringly. "Come."

"I don't know *why* I do these things," Shar breathed as they walked west into the woods. "I get into more trouble . . ."

Syluné, her bare feet walking in utter silence an inch or so off the ground, turned and smiled at her reassuringly. Shar rolled her eyes in response but followed, blade at the ready.

Far, far away ahead of her, a wolf howled. It was answered, from somewhere much nearer, off to the left. Shar shivered and cast another look all around her at moonlit Daggerdale. She must be crazy, to follow a ghost into the woods, away from their camp. She looked back at it searchingly, half-expecting to see another ghostly form standing guard over it while some false shade led her to a horrible, lonely doom.

"Be not afraid," Syluné said softly, as if reading her mind. "Just go well out into that meadow, there, and touch the ring with your free hand."

Sharantyr looked ahead at the moonlit clearing and then back at the ghostly face beside her. "Will I see you— and Belk and Itharr—again?" she asked.

Syluné smiled. "Of course. We all need to get a lot more work out of you yet."

Shar made a face. "Of course," she replied, a grin playing about her lips. "Silly of me . . ."

" 'Twas, yes."

Shar shook her head at that, lifted her hand in salute—Syluné returned it—and walked away into the meadow. The moonlight was bright on the grass, and the night was very beautiful. Shar looked around at it, drew a deep breath, and smiled. Some folk never get to see this.

Syluné's voice came to her, as if borne on an unseen wind. "Plant your blade in the ground before you touch the ring. Don't take it with you."

She found a spot she liked and stopped, planting her booted feet firmly. Then she looked back over her shoulder.

Syluné was still standing there, a frozen flame floating in the nightdark under the trees.

Shar took another deep breath, thrust her sword upright into the turf, watched moonlight gleam down its length—and laid her fingers over the ring.

There was a wink, and the world changed. She was standing in a smaller, darker glade, dim blue moonlight filtering down to her through the tangles and mossy boughs of huge, gnarled trees much older than the woods she'd left in Daggerdale. It smelled . . . like the Elven Court woods, near Myth Drannor.

She looked around, not moving. Mosses glowed eerily here and there, and the trees stretched away into utter darkness all around. She was in the heart of a large forest.

Something winked, softly, between two trees. She stared at it, shifting slightly to get a better view, and obligingly it drifted nearer, sparkling as it came.

A will o' wisp, beautiful but deadly. Her hand went to her empty scabbard and then drew back. She hadn't a hope, even with her sword. Scrabbling after daggers and boot-knives just didn't seem worthwhile. She hoped Syluné hadn't made a mistake, and that her awakener *had* been Syluné. Could a Malaugrym take a ghost shape?

Why not?

Too late to wonder now. The will o' wisp, blue-white and awesomely beautiful, shone like a little star in front of her. "Take out thy dagger," it said, in soft, feminine tones.

Shar stared at it for a moment and then did so, never taking her eyes from the floating sphere of light.

"Follow," it said softly, and retreated across the clearing the way it had come. Shar did so, casting a quick glance around as she crossed the damp, fern-studded ground. There was no sign of other life.

The wisp was hovering above a tangle of brambles. "Cut away enough to pass," it told her, "and go down."

"Go down?" Shar asked, but there was no reply. She went to her knees and sawed at the thorny branches obediently, laying them aside in a neat pile as she cut herself a tunnel. Beyond, there seemed to be an emptiness in the gloom. Before Shar could will her enchanted dagger to glow and give her light to see by, the wisp drifted silently over her shoulder. Its radiance showed her a hole in the ground, half-covered with fern root creepers. She drew them aside and stared at worn stone steps and darkness beyond.

Shar wiped her dagger on her thigh and sheathed it—the wisp bobbed approvingly—and put her legs forward, onto the steps.

Then, cautiously, she shifted forward, holding on to the edges of the hole, and began to descend. The wisp drifted past to hang just in front of her, lighting her way down those old stone steps . . . down a dozen feet and more, then turning to the right—to avoid the roots of a huge duskwood she'd seen, Shar judged—and plunging down more steeply, another eight steps, before opening out into a damp, stone-floored chamber.

A tomb. A stone coffin stood on a bier before her, almost filling the room. Around it, the walls were of cracked and fallen tiles, unadorned squares that bore no inscriptions, scenes, or heraldry to tell her who was buried here. Their smooth run was broken by the roots that had dislodged some of them.

Bones littered the floor beyond her boots, scattered human bones. She could see at least three skulls, and there were probably more around the back of the coffin. Adventurers had come here to plunder, and met some sort of doom.

Shar drew back onto the lowest step. The will o' wisp winked sharply beside her. "Lift the lid and take the sword within."

Shar tilted her head to look obliquely up at the beautiful sphere. "It's not a good thing, to disturb the dead."

She shivered suddenly, her words taking her back to someone else speaking that same phrase—a cold, cruel voice offering a mocking warning not to try to flee through a crypt in the Underdark.

And suddenly, as the memories so often took her, she found herself back in that glow-cavern with the barbed lash curling fire about her bare thighs, trying not to scream as she heard the dreadful promises spoken so softly and lovingly by the priestesses who wielded such whips, the loving daughters of Lolth with their crazed plans.

The plans that had kept her alive. Long after they'd broken her, making her crawl to kiss their booted feet at a gesture or command, posing herself to accept the lash automatically when they appeared, they kept her alive. Kept her alive for their darkest plan after they'd slain men who could give them greater pleasure—slain them by flogging the skin right off them and then exchanging their whips for long flails with barbed iron bars, or whips with hissing, hungry living serpent heads, to work on the fleshless, moaning shapes that remained.

She was to be bred to a spider. A giant, hairy spider whose limbs bore barbs and saw-edges, whose bulk almost crushed her when they'd experimented, lashing its mandibles together with their whips to keep it from beheading or slashing open the pale-skinned victim chained beneath it, slick with sweat and fear, writhing helplessly.

A spider whose spell-twisted brood would have hatched in her paralyzed body and eaten her from within to nourish themselves into life as manspiders—"biddable driders," as one priestess had called them, her face alight with excitement at the thought. Manspiders who could serve as loyal, intelligent fighting steeds for drow warriors paired with them, in a war against rival drow cities deep in the lightless Underdark.

Sharantyr shivered again, recalling days of pain and humiliation, and nights of eerie terror, as the glowing, gelatinous fungi had crept slowly down the stone walls where she lay chained by the throat to a huge ring in the wall, bedded on hard, sharp human skulls, and *flowed* over her, their translucent pseudopods covering her with glistening slime as they lapped at her wounds and body openings, healing and cleansing her, absorbing her wastes and blood and energy alike, leaving her too weak to work toward any escape.

The touch of jelly or jam on her skin still left her drenched with sweat, and quivering with fear—and excitement.

"Trust me in this, and do as I bid." The voice was musical and assured, almost amused. Shar closed her eyes. "Trust me" had been one of the taunts used by the priestess with the strongest liking for her pale-skinned human prisoner. *Trust me*.

Shar opened her eyes deliberately, swallowed, and stared at the winking globe of light. "Who are you," she asked softly, "that I should trust you?"

"Mystra," came the soft reply, and it seemed that an echo arose from that softly spoken name and rolled across the chamber to recede into vast distances, as if they stood in an immense void and not a small tomb smelling of damp earth and the roots of the forest above.

Shar shuddered. Syluné, she complained in her mind, what have you gotten me into *now*?

The wisp drifted closer, and the echoes seemed to roll and thunder again in the distance. "Well?" it asked, its voice a sudden challenge. "This is no drow trick."

Shar shuddered; it must be reading her mind. Oh. A goddess. Of course it could. *She* could. Shar shook herself, smiled, and stepped forward. "Why didn't you say so?" she asked almost petulantly, as she laid her hands on the cold, crumbling lid and shifted it aside.

Stone grated, and Shar peered cautiously into the darkness within, but the wisp flashed across the chamber to hang where she needed light. The coffin held heaped dust and a wild-weave of cobwebs, but no body that she could see. A scabbarded blade lay in front of her, shrouded in dusty gray webs. Without hesitation she reached in and took it.

A cold tingling ran up her arm, and fear awoke to accompany it. What if the blade turned her into some sort of monster or visited a curse on her? What if— Enough, she told herself firmly, stowing the blade under her arm to free her hands for replacing the lid.

The wisp seemed to bob approvingly again, but as she turned toward the stairs, it flashed through the air to block her path. "Draw the blade," it told her.

Shar nodded and held the scabbard out horizontally before her, drawing the sword slowly. It was a magnificent, gleaming long sword, curved more than was the fashion in the Dragonreach lands. The hilt, grip, and blade seemed to be all of one piece, polished mirror bright and glossy smooth. As it came free of the scabbard, the sword awakened with its own blue radiance, a light that grew and grew until it blazed.

"This is yours to bear, Lady Knight," the wisp told her.

Shar turned it slowly, feeling its weight, and replied feelingly, "An honor."

"Indeed." The wisp sounded a little amused. "You may not always feel so. You hold a weapon against the Malaugrym. Return to your camp, and in the morning go down to the bridge that Itharr mistrusted so. There draw this blade, and it will show you a gate that will transport you to the plane of shadows where the Malaugrym dwell. When drawn, this sword will show you all gates nearby, and work them for you if you will it so. Take your companions and go and slay Malaugrym for me."

Shar took a pace away from the wisp to gain room, and swung the blade experimentally. It hummed as it cut the air, and a delighted smile came to her face. What a magnificent weapon! It matched her as if made for her, and its rippling weight made her feel like a dashing young hero, the excited girl she'd once been when she first sought adventure, long before she'd ever seen the endless Underdark . . . or drow.

Shar laughed, her unbound hair swirling about her as she leapt lightly around one corner of the tomb, fencing with an imaginary foe. The blade felt alive in her hands. *Yes!* With this, she could rule the world!

At swordplay, at least. She turned to look at the will o' wisp, and asked, "Will I see you again?"

"No," came the flat reply, and to Shar's ears it sounded sad. But when the voice came again, it was calm. "No mortal shall ever see this aspect of me again in Faerûn. It is a fading thing I inherited, a shell of ghosts and shadows. I cannot wear it well."

The wisp drifted toward the stairs. "Go now, Sharantyr. Make us all proud of thee."

As she went up into the glade and saw the white glimmering ring that must be the gate to take her home, Shar thought she heard a familiar old voice, a mere whisper behind her. "Well said. Very well said. Ye'll do fine."

Elminster? She was still frowning in excited puzzlement when she came out into the moonlight of Daggerdale and found Syluné waiting for her.

* * * * *

Silverymoon, Kythorn 18

Milhvar's spell tapped into existing gates—or so the sinister, smiling Shadowmaster had told them. Huerbara didn't trust him one whit, but she had no choice but to place herself in his hands, and watch him like a hungry hawk for any sign of treachery.

It would come. Oh, it would come.

Hopefully not on this foray . . . probably not. The cold truth was that the three of them weren't important enough to be rivals whom the Shadowmaster might want to eliminate. But enough speculation.

Milhvar's whirling magic had just taken them somewhere dark. As the spell-motes of the gate they'd linked into scattered around them, the three cloaked Malaugrym stared around, looking for any sign as to where they might be. Their mission was to find Alustriel, the High Lady of Silverymoon, and attack her. They were to slay her if possible, but the real test lay in finding out how much the cloaks concealed and protected them against her.

First to find her.

Ignoring the startled gasps and hissed warnings from behind her, Huerbara strode across the darkened chamber to the only door she could see. This had better be Alustriel's palace, or Milhvar would soon be hearing about his overblown cleverness.

The door was unlocked. Beyond stretched a short

passage whose left-hand wall soon became a row of tapestries, implying a larger room in that direction.
Huerbara walked forward without hesitation.

Behind her, the two male Malaugrym exchanged
glances, shrugged, and followed.

Voices were coming from beyond the tapestries. Male
voices, at ease.

"She never seems to know what she wants to buy, but
she always comes back with something. Or rather, a pile
of somethings." A glass clinked down on a table.

There was a chuckle. "You can sell more to a woman
who knows not what she wants to buy but is restless to
have new things in her hands."

There was a snort. "You make her sound like a brothel
cruiser, not the lady with the largest collection of once-
worn gowns in Silverymoon."

"And *you* want to wed her. Have you thought this
through?"

Kuervyn and Andraut smiled silkily at each other and
turned toward the tapestries, hands going to the slim
blades they wore at their belts.

Huerbara shot out two long, silent tentacles to wave
them to startled stillness. She glared at them and gestured down the passage, beckoning them on. There'd be
time for such amusements later, unless, of course, they
had the whole palace after them by then.

Bringing two such flamebrains along on this mission
could prove very dangerous to her, she reflected, following the passage through an archway and into the rear of
what seemed to be a gigantic wardrobe.

And then a slim hand reached out in front of her and
unhooked a dust-shroud-covered gown from its place on
the crowded bar. Huerbara smiled tightly and shot a slim
tentacle around that corner, high up. Eyes swam down
the tentacle to see her quarry, and guide that appendage
around its throat before it could utter a sound.

Huerbara stepped around the corner with a pleasant
smile on her face, another tentacle snaking out to take
the gown from suddenly desperate fingers. The maid
whose throat was wrapped in her tentacle—a pretty

wench with great dark eyes and a pert little lace-framed bosom—stared helplessly at her for a few moments in terrified bewilderment before Huerbara broke that pretty neck with a deft twist, and the light in the eyes faded away. Then she handed the body back out into the passage to amuse the two louts, felt them take it with low laughs of anticipation, and shifted to match the maid's form perfectly.

A moment later, Shantra the Underdresser stepped unconcernedly out of the wardrobe room, dust-bagged gown in hand, and looked up and down the corridor she found herself in. Two magnificently mustachioed guards in opulent uniforms were seated before a closed and barred door at one end of the passage, playing leap-knights at an ornate octagonal board. Light, soft voices spilled from two open doorways in the other direction.

The guards looked up, so she gave them a half-smile before she turned away. One guard looked back to his game immediately, but the other guard frowned. His eyes narrowed as he watched Shantra—his beloved, who'd never looked at him with such pleasant lack of recognition before—walk away and pass through one of the doors. She'd never walked like that, either, all sinuous glide and none of her happy bounce.

He got up, saying softly, "A moment, friend Silder. I'll be right back, but come with your sword if I bellow."

He left the other guard frowning up at him and went down the passage as quickly as stealth would allow, hand on the hilt of his blade.

In the room he was approaching, three ladies were looking up at the maid with surprise on their faces. "Why, Shantra, what's amiss?" one of them asked, gliding forward.

Huerbara looked at her as if bewildered. "L-lady?"

"The dust bag . . . why've you brought the gown still in its dust bag?"

"Ohh," Huerbara said, trying to look confused—easy enough, she thought wryly—and bent her knees, sagging forward and clutching at her head. "I feel . . . not right . . . I . . ."

"What befalls?" The quick, anxious male voice came from behind her. One of the guards?

"Shantra's been taken ill," said a voice very near, as gentle hands took her forearm and elbow and guided her to a stool.

"That's not Shantra," the male voice said firmly. "Her walk is wrong, and she didn't recognize us."

"And she spoke differently," said one of the women slowly. Then the third woman said quietly, "Speak, Shantra. Name us."

Oh, shadows take them! Not three rooms into the palace! She shook her head. "I . . ." she said, trying to sound broken.

Then she heard the soft swish of a sword being drawn. Huerbara turned toward the guard with a snarl, extending her breasts into tentacles to hold his eyes, while a third shot out to take his feet from under him.

"*Doppleganger!*" he bellowed, fear and anger in his eyes as his sword slashed down. Huerbara struck it away with her tentacles, shifting her innards hastily to avoid a lucky blow, and then stiffened with a real shriek of pain as something slim and hard went through her from behind, burning . . .

She looked dully down at the sword tip protruding from her breast and saw that it was silver. Huerbara wept in agony and did what she had to do, let half her body fall away and be lost to her. With the only arm she had left, she firmly grasped the belt buckle embedded in her flesh and said, "Brathaera."

As the guard battled her writhing tentacles, she simply melted away. He crashed forward helplessly into the wall as Silder came charging around the corner to find three ladies staring down at an amorphous mass on the floor that had one human arm protruding from it—and a slim silver sword cane through it.

"A doppleganger, here?"

The double-chinned, haughty lady who held the handle of the sword cane shook her head. "No. Much worse than that."

"Oh?" Silder asked, raising his eyebrows. "And how

would *you* know, Mistress Iraeyna? Fought many monsters in the nurseries of the palace, have we?"

Mistress Iraeyna, Chief Dresser of the Ladies' Wardrobe, fixed him with cool eyes as she calmly undid the front of her gown and pulled the fabric wide. The two ladies on either side of her gasped.

Both guardsmen gulped—not at the formidable bosom exposed to their gaze, but at the black silk waist-corset just beneath it. Its straining fabric held a too-large tummy firmly in check and sported a silver pin: a harp between the horns of a crescent moon, surrounded by four stars.

"You know this, Silder? Haerarn?" she asked crisply. Both guards nodded dumbly.

"Then follow my orders, as the High Lady's decree binds you to. Into that wardrobe! There may be others— and suspect *everything* of being a foe, from stool to garment. They're shapeshifters far more deadly than any dopplegangers! Strike to slay, and thrust a silver piece into any wound you make, if you can!"

She bent swiftly and retrieved her sword cane. As she strode forward, Mistress Iraeyna snapped back, "Dansila and Ormue, go straight out that door and lock it behind you. Take your keys and don't tarry for anything! Go to Lady Amathree. If any guards try to stop you, tell them it's Harper business and order them to escort you. If you can't find Lady Amathree, ask for Alustriel herself. Say that there are Malaugrym in the palace! Got that? Malaugrym!"

The wardrobe door banged open, and Silder and Haerarn burst into the room. Silder's eyes were wide with amazement, and Haerarn's were wild with the awful realization that he probably wouldn't find Shantra alive.

It was worse than that. Her body was dancing between two laughing Malaugrym, suspended on tentacles that ran through the maid's corpse from one body opening to another. As they commented on how odd or delectable this feature or that organ looked, the Malaugrym were devouring her. Swooping tentacles that ended in eel-like jaws were tearing at her bared flesh, and blood was raining down on the dusty floor.

Weeping, Haerarn charged savagely into one shape-shifting monster, and Silder gulped and cautiously approached the other. Mistress Iraeyna strode forward and simply slashed a tentacle with her sword cane. The tentacle writhed and flopped in convulsions, slapping the floor, and she stepped past it and drove her cane deep into one flowing form. It stiffened, convulsed, and abruptly let go of the choking Haerarn. As he crashed to the floor, his face a dangerous purple, Iraeyna turned toward the other shapeshifter.

It slapped Silder into one wall with fearsome force—amid the crash, Iraeyna heard the sharp crack of ribs giving way—and then was gone. There one moment and vanished the next.

The Chief Dresser of the Ladies' Wardrobe frowned. With pursed lips she whirled back to the first Malaugrym and thrust her silver cane into it repeatedly until all sign of movement had ceased. Then she sat down on its gray-brown bulk and began to lace up her bodice.

When she saw Haerarn's eyes focus on her again, she said briskly, "Well done, armsman. Now get up and unbar the door, will you? A lot of folk will be rushing in here shortly. Ring for service, too; Silder's hurt. Oh, and you'd better put away that leapknights board before your swordlord sees it, hadn't you?"

Haerarn hadn't managed to carry out more than one of these instructions before a dozen armed men boiled into the wardrobe, weapons drawn.

"Thank you, gentle sirs," Mistress Iraeyna said serenely, "but it's all over now. You'd best check along the back passage, though, in case there are more lurking about."

"The day that Swords of the Guard take orders from ladies' dressers," the oldest and burliest swordlord told her, his moustaches bristling, "is—"

"Belt up and stow it, sirrah," she told him sweetly, causing some of the men who were goggling at the dead tentacled thing under her to look up and grin. "I give you orders by the High Lady's decree."

"Oh, aye, and how did you manage *that*, with her at the other end o' the palace from here?"

With a sigh, Mistress Iraeyna began to unlace her bodice again.

12
Marshaling the Madfolk for Battle

Daggerdale, Kythorn 18

Sharantyr held up the blade admiringly. Its blue outshone the moonlight and turned the center of the meadow into a ring of eerie beauty. Syluné flew out of the tree-gloom toward her, and Shar smiled in welcome and said, "Look what the Lady Mystra gave me!"

Syluné danced around her in the air—the first time Sharantyr had ever seen her do so, rather than drifting or walking along upright—and then smiled and said, "I'm proud of you, Shar. Yet perhaps it'd better be sheathed instead of waved about, here in the wilds by night. What say you?"

Sharantyr sighed and shook her head. "Foolish Shar. Back down to the everyday with a crash."

Syluné chuckled. "Be not so downfallen, Shar. Have I called you 'child' yet?"

"No."

"Nor will I again," the Witch of Shadowdale told her, "now that you've faced a goddess and held your bladder."

Shar grinned and shook her head but slid her new blade obediently into the scabbard at her side. Though it seemed far too large to fit there, it went in. Syluné shook her head.

"No. Better back in its own sheath. Don't forget your own blade, either. It's served you well for years, and will again."

Shar looked back at the blade she'd driven into the turf, standing forgotten in the moonlight, and blushed. "How could I—?"

"Relax, lass," Syluné told her gently. "You've faced divinity and are apt to be mazed in the wits for a while yet. Recover your blade and draw the new one again. There's something I want you to see."

Shar did as she was bid, and as she held the blue blade up again, she became aware of a flickering white ring in the trees that she was sure hadn't been there before. She pointed at it with the blade, which immediately gave off a satisfied-sounding little hum. "Is that what you wanted me to see?"

"It is," Syluné said. "Use the blade to work it. Don't fear, for it will not take you far."

Wondering, Shar approached the ring. It flickered, and the blue radiance of her blade pulsed as if in reply. As she stepped into the ring, white motes of light circled her, making her skin tingle. The blade pulsed again, as if asking her if she wanted to call on it.

She willed the gate to take her wherever it went, and the sword flared a bright blue before her eyes.

When the light faded, Shar looked hastily around. It was warmer—much warmer—but she seemed to be standing under the same moon, at night in an open ruin. The manor!

She looked down and found herself standing in the midst of the campfire, which had been banked over with turf for the night. She sprang back hastily, boots scraping on the stone, and saw Syluné floating into view around a wall.

"Some folk," Shar said sternly, waving her blade, "have a very strange thing where *I* carry a sense of humor."

Syluné's light laughter tinkled on a night breeze, and a sleepy male voice said, "All day you have to gossip, and you must do it when honest men are trying to sleep?"

"Belkram," Shar told him smugly, "there are no honest men here, only you and—"

"What's *that*?" Belkram cried, pointing at her blade. "You didn't have *that* when I went to sleep!"

"Fast, isn't he?" Syluné observed lightly.

"Not half so fast as he's going to have to be, if I find he's awakened me for no good reason," a deeper, more sour voice said from another corner of the roofless room.

"Well met, Itharr!" Shar said gaily, waving her blade at him.

"Where'd she get *that?*" Itharr asked Belkram irritably. The Harpers, both propped up on their elbows in the moonlight, exchanged glances and shrugs.

"I haven't a scrap of an answer to that," Belkram said testily. "Tomb-robbing, probably. That's usually how such baubles turn up. But she's been waving it around like a young maid displaying a doll at her birthday feast since I woke up!"

"And still is," Itharr said, tossing his blanket aside. "Where'd you get it, Shar?"

"In a tomb," Shar said lightly, tossing it from hand to hand. "Like it?"

"Here," he replied, coming toward her, "let's have a look at it!"

She sprang back, fetching up against a stone wall suddenly enough to make one of the horses snort in its sleep, and told him, "Looking is generally performed with the eyes, Itharr. Only thieves need to 'look' at things with their hands!"

Belkram chuckled. "Right enough, Shar. Tell the man."

Itharr halted, raising his hands in a gesture of surrender. "Seriously, Shar . . . where've you been?"

"In the Elven Court," she told him quietly, meeting his incredulous gaze with level eyes, "in a tomb somewhere close to Myth Drannor."

"And how did you find this tomb?" Belkram asked softly, disbelief heavy in his tone. Sharantyr saw his gaze dart to her empty blanket, to be sure he wasn't facing some apparition—or shapeshifter.

"Mystra took me there," Sharantyr told him, wonder in her eyes, "and gave the sword to me. A weapon against the Malaugrym, she called it, and charged me to use it against them. Are you with me?"

"Shar," Itharr said gently, "we've been with you since we met in a ruined castle by the desert, and watched a crazy old mage kissing a rotten old archlich. We're still with you." He tilted his head to regard her coolly. "But are you sure your wits are steady?"

Sharantyr held up the blade. In response to her rising exultation, it blazed bright blue fire around her. "You think I'm imagining *this?*"

"Well," Belkram told the nearest wall brightly, "it's certainly nice to share the same delusions as one's closest friends . . ."

Syluné chuckled. "She's telling the truth, Harpers, and she's not crazed. Excited, yes, but meeting Mystra does that to one . . . as you should both remember."

"I believe," Belkram said, getting up and folding his blanket.

"*We* believe," Itharr corrected, going back to retrieve his own bedding. "So what now? You want us to follow that bright blade of yours through a gate into the castle of the Malaugrym and start dicing them up for morningfeast?"

"Yes," Shar said sweetly. Belkram rolled his eyes and groaned loudly, waking the horses.

"Look . . . we're a mite leery of swords that appear in the night—even with you holding them—and strange tales that go with them, so tell us plainly what you intend."

Itharr grunted. "And then we'll tell you plainly 'no.' Or at least, not until morning."

Sharantyr and Syluné laughed together, making the horses snort and stamp. "Well said," Belkram told Itharr.

"Thank you," the other Harper said, sketching a courtly bow.

Shar drew in a deep breath and then let it out slowly. "My apologies, friends," she said softly, "for rousing you. Mystra *did* tell me to wait until morning. There's a gate to the Castle of Shadows down by the bridge, where you felt so uneasy, Itharr. When it's drawn, this sword shows me any magical gates nearby, and works them if I reach them and will it to. Mystra told me, 'Take your companions and go and slay Malaugrym for me.' So here I am."

"Now *that* I can believe," Belkram said with a shake of his head and a smile, "because it sounds so unbelievable that it must be what Mystra did."

Itharr nodded, a rueful smile on his face, and said, "I'm forced to agree." He sighed. "They didn't tell me there'd be nights like this, back in Twilight Hall."

"They didn't tell *me* there'd be nights like this," Syluné told him, "back in Elminster's kitchen."

"Elminster's kitchen? Didn't the man have enough class even to show you his bedchamber?" Belkram demanded.

"Harper boy," Syluné told him severely, "I was referring to when I was a babe, and a different kitchen than the one you've seen. And spare me your jokes about Elminster and young babes, too."

"I'm beginning to realize," Sharantyr said carefully, "just why so few Harpers live long. They get angry swords right through their clever tongues."

Belkram and Itharr both looked hurt. "Critics," Itharr said, "everywhere we go in Faerûn, we find ourselves surrounded by critics . . ."

"Get some sleep," Syluné told him kindly. "We've a castle to conquer in the morning."

* * * * *

Another forgotten ruin in the Savage Frontier, with a side trip to the Flame Void, then the sky somewhere over Thay, Kythorn 18

"Nothing is worse than promises that are not meant and deeds that are not accomplished," Midnight said quietly. "I need folk who stand behind what they say and do. Such as Azuth—if he survives—and you."

They clasped hands then, the man and the goddess. Both were white, drenched with sweat, and shaking. Long they had lain side by side, hands clasped, while Elminster's memories—his long road with Mystra, and what of her secrets and power he held—poured into Midnight, and she grew old and wise in a day and most of a night.

They walked out of the tomb together, an old, long-plundered tomb of Netheril whose stone biers had served the living as couches. If anyone saw them emerge, they did not tarry to offer a challenge.

Midnight wiped her mouth as if she'd eaten something

foul. "I . . . I've swallowed overmuch," she murmured. "I must go apart and think."

"Seek Evereska, here," Elminster suggested, "or Evermeet, over the water. The elves will let ye alone. When ye've thought, return and tell me your will. Until then, I'll spend my days as I've always done, darting here and there about Faerûn, saying this and meddling with that, slaying here and building there . . . less grand than some godly servants, perhaps, but the tasks get done." He faced her, eye to eye, and said gently, "It may be, when ye return, that ye'll want me to lay down life and service together, and make room for your own style, and your own messengers."

"No," Midnight said softly, and then again, more firmly, "No. I shall need your counsel in the ways of Faerûn—and in plain common sense—to guide me for ages to come, or I shall be a worse wildheart than Talos, Lolth, Loviatar, and Malar have ever been, ruling by whim and wrecking all I touch, ending twisted and bitter, no doubt, or sinking down into madness and despair."

Elminster bent his head. "Then I shall be here, Lady, for as long as ye need and want me. I and all the Chosen, some of them gentler and grander and better than I."

Midnight smiled and laid a hand on his arm. Blue fire swirled briefly around them both. "Truly, I doubt that. You have walked the hard road, been the old gnarly rock, faced the worst moments. You did the work Mystra set you, and did it well. And in all Faerûn, there's none of us, god or mortal, can do grander deeds than our duty."

Elminster coughed. "Ye'll be turning my head, next, las—er, Mystra. Go, and do thy thinking, and I'll try to set thy temples in order so ye'll find a good gaggle of priests to chant ritual profanit—er, litanies yer way."

Midnight giggled at him and then growled in mock severity, "By me ever-thunderin' vitals! Away with you, mortal! How canst I maintain my godly dignity when you mock me so?"

Elminster grinned and scratched his head. "I've always wondered that, myself, lass, and—"

He stopped, looked thoughtful, and said, "I'd not

thought of this before, but ye could go to my Safehold. It's well away from the reach of any of these avatars and such, and has all the spells and potions and items ye're likely to want to play with. Two of its doors: the one into the wood with leaves tinged blue—that's Evermeet—and the one into the stone passage that leads into a cellar of my tower in Shadowdale, steps away from a flowshaft that'll take ye up to . . . ah, my bedchamber . . ."

Midnight giggled again. "None of that. I'm Mystra now, remember?"

Elminster rolled his eyes. "My reputation, I fear, has been somewhat enhanced by wagging tongues down the passing years."

"Not from what I saw in your memories, it hasn't," the goddess told him tartly. "Take me to this Safehold, then. It sounds ideal."

Elminster nodded, stroked his white beard for a moment, and then extended his hand. "I have but to cast this spell, and—"

Abruptly they were somewhere else, but not the cozy room Elminster had been seeking. They were tumbling together in a void, a darkness lit by drifting stars. Midnight was curled up as a small child sleeps, eyes closed and mouth gaping open, face blank and hair streaming like night shadows around her. Elminster laid a comforting hand on her, but she did not stir. Magic that he could not break held her in thrall. The same titanic Art, presumably, that had twisted or broken his evasion spell to bring them here. "To the Flame Void," the Old Mage mused, "but how—?"

"By *my* will, mortal mage," said a voice from close by. Elminster turned and saw a man whose hair and beard were whiter than his own, whose face was unremarkable, but whose eyes and robes were both a dark swirl of stars, so that he seemed to be the heart of the Flame Void.

Elminster sighed. "And who, sir, are ye?" he asked mildly.

"Some men call me the Overgod . . . others, the Hidden One."

"Ao," Elminster named him, leaning forward with

interest. "I've much to ask ye—"

The Overgod frowned. "I am not here to give ye answers, presumptuous mortal. Ye have tried to hasten the elevation to full powers of my choice for Mystra's replacement, and take her from Faerûn!"

"Magic goes wild across the lands," Elminster said sternly, "and I would restore as much peace and order as I can. 'Tis bad enough for the common folk, what ye've wrought, with hordes and brigands and avatars on the loose, earthquakes and eruptions and typhoons and all. For magic to be stable again, we must needs have a Goddess of Magic. Must I point such an obvious thing out to ye? I sought to take her to my Safehold, to sit and think . . . and learn. Rare for a god, I know, but long overdu—"

"Such temerity!" Ao thundered.

"Is the way of mankind," Elminster replied gently, spreading his hands. "Have ye not seen this?"

Ao sighed, and then chuckled. "Enough. So you meant well. So have many tyrants—and gods—before working their worst."

He raised a hand to point at Elminster and said in a voice of doom, "Midnight I am returning to Faerûn. She will forget what you gave to her, for a time. You I charge never to speak of this, or what she will become, until the Testing is done. And to keep you busy, oh most energetic of mages, I send you to deal with—*this!*"

And the world changed again. Ao, Midnight, and the Flame Void were gone, and Elminster found himself falling through the night sky of Faerûn, somewhere east of the Sea of Fallen Stars, where a wall of mountains rose around vast plateaus, and . . . Thay!

"Thay?" Elminster said in disgust. "The Land of Mad Mages? If Ao's sent me here, it must be to deal with some idiot mage who's trying to make himself a god, or set up some particularly nasty doom for all of us under cover of all these Troubles. Ah, blast all gods and their Overgods, too!"

And then something rose up through the clouds and stretched out shadowy arms to claim him.

Elminster saw how many miles its arms spanned, and

swallowed. As he felt for his least powerful means of flight, he said through his teeth, "Allfather Ao, if I live through this little affray, ye and I will be having words!"

And then the shadowy figure howled, and from its mouth leapt ravening magics to claim him. Ah. Of course. Two spells at once, to his one. Just another little job for Elminster.

The Old Mage snarled and selected the best spells he could think of, under the circumstances. And then the shadowy hands closed in around him.

* * * * *

The Castle of Shadows, Kythorn 18

Another three Malaugrym stood waiting impatiently, striking dramatic poses, hefting their forearms, and patting at where their weapons rode, as Milhvar delivered his little speech.

"The Shadowmaster High had great hopes for this project. Try not to let him down, but above all else we want you back safely. If anything goes awry—anything—touch your belt buckles and will yourselves back to us. Even if the foe is within your reach, or you're just a blow away from a victorious finish, break off rather than be taken or slain. There will be other forays, other chances."

The three kin nodded curtly and went on with their restless posturings. Milhvar smiled bleakly. If nothing else, testing this cloak of spells would temper some of the untried blades among the blood of Malaug, and break off others before they wasted much more of the time and attention of their betters.

Out of this lot? They were all so arrogant, they just might make it. Or considering the way they swaggered through things, they might all perish at the hand of some half-asleep mortal guard with a rusty halberd. Taernil was a lean, dangerous type, and knew it. If he lived, if he stayed Huerbara's partner, they could be trouble together . . . or the best pair of Shadowmasters to rise in a long time.

Balatar was simply a bad, wild one, who loved cruelty and killing too much and taking orders too little. He was the only one, so far, who'd openly sneered when Milhvar invoked the memory of Dhalgrave. Hmmph. To the waiting grave with him!

Jarthree was a cold, controlled one. She always looked through you as if she knew just what you were about, and had already planned your doom, but it was all manner and nothing behind it. Yet.

Keeping his face bland and his voice calm, Milhvar instructed them to willingly draw at least a drop of their own blood with some sharp part of the shape they wore, and signaled the Shadowmaster mages to weave the cloaks.

The lengthy chanting and gesturing began. Milhvar watched the three carefully, wondering who'd perish—or prevail—on this foray. They were off to Blackstaff Tower this time, a far stiffer challenge than the first three had faced. The cloak of spells hadn't helped a whit against simple guards and servants who happened to have luck—the luck of a little silver weapon—on their side. This time, it'd be more magic against magic.

The cloak of interwoven spells was more complex than it needed to be, and far from stable. But then, no Malaugrym had ever worn invulnerable armor into battle, and these three arrogant younglings had no right to be the first.

The shimmering and dark singing of the completed cloaks mounted into the air, and Milhvar was pleased to see that at least Taernil had the wits to look momentarily impressed.

Folding his arms, Milhvar of the Malaugrym stepped forward and cast the "secret spell" thrice, linking each cloak to its wearer through the shed blood.

"You are ready," he said calmly. "Stand together, so my next spell can take you all as one."

"Take us where, exactly?" Taernil snapped, trying to assert mastery of the situation.

"To a gate that links Blackstaff Tower with Evermeet, most likely," Milhvar replied gravely, "though there is some small chance that you'll be drawn to one of the other gates—we know of at least three—that open into Blackstaff Tower from other places in Faerûn and elsewhere. Try not to get lost."

"Don't patronize us, old one!" Jarthree snapped.

"Oh, you'd be in far worse straits, were I ever to do that," Milhvar said softly, and was rewarded by seeing Balatar blanch and Jarthree looking just a little unsure of what insult she should hurl back at him.

While she was still sorting through those she had ready, he brought his hands together with a smile, whispered the word that launched the gate-link spell, and said benevolently. "Go now. Bring glory to the Malaugrym."

* * * * *

Daggerdale, Kythorn 19

"I hope the horses'll fare all right," Itharr said anxiously, watching them trot purposefully away into the woods.

"They'll be fine," Syluné assured him. "One of my woodland friends is watching over them."

"Don't worry about *them*," Belkram said, shouldering the two largest saddlebags, the ones holding the food. "Spare some worry for us. We're the ones undertaking a madwoman's mission into the very fortress of our foes. It'd be crazy if these villains dwelt in Faerûn, and didn't have mighty magic and the power to change shapes at will. As it is, it's sheer carve-our-tombstones insanity time!"

Sharantyr sighed. "Was he always this cheerful?" she asked Itharr. "Before he fell on his head, I mean."

Itharr blinked. "The first time, or the second?"

"Bah!" Belkram said. "Dost thou respect my trenchant view of the whelming you've undertaken? Nay! Well, then. Ready? *Away!*"

"That's more what he was famous for, back at Twilight Hall," Itharr said. "The bold rush into oblivion, I think they called it, in tactics lectures."

Sharantyr looked at him, wrinkling her brow. "You had lectures at Twilight Hall?"

"Just to separate the feasts," Belkram called back to her. "And the org—"

"Ahem!" Itharr called loudly. "Hey, there! Brave companion—hoy! Come back here! The lady with the blade is *here*, remember?"

" 'Twould be best, I think," Syluné said quietly from the handsome ranger's breast pocket, "if you calmed down, Belk, and did just that."

Belkram looked down. "Thank you," he said quietly.

"For the advice?"

"No, for calling me 'Belk' instead of 'Harper boy' or the like. It's . . . good to hear."

"My apologies, Belkram," the stone said. "Chide me as I chide thee, if I seem too high and mighty. It was the way of things in speech, when I was young. Elders spoke down, and others looked up." Her voice became dry. "It seems the world has changed."

"As always, lady," he muttered as they rejoined Itharr and Sharantyr. The three stood looking at each other, bent under the weight of their saddlebags, and then down at the softly singing blade in the lady ranger's hand.

"Ready?" she asked softly.

"A moment, if you please," Syluné's voice came to them. "It would be best if you kept me a secret until I am most needed. So speak not to me, or of me, whenever possible."

"Aye, good thought. Agreed. Yes," the living three said, voices mingling, and then Sharantyr asked again, "Ready?"

"*Away!*" they shouted together, and the blue blade flashed. The tingling that had been rising around them took them all, and they were . . . gone.

The lopsided bridge looked as lonely and forgotten as ever, for a time. And then dark shapes came loping down through the trees in some haste, golden slanted eyes looking balefully this way and that, and padded across the bridge, sniffing suspiciously.

Abruptly one barked and headed along an unseen trail, shoulders hunched and moving fast. The others poured after it, picking up the scent themselves, only to circle to an uncertain halt and lift their heads in puzzlement. They cast around and then loped up the hill to the manor, only to come reluctantly back down the hill, following three scents, to the same spot.

One wolf rose on its hind legs and then seemed to glow, gray furred and tall, rising into . . . a naked man. He peered around at the bright morning in Daggerdale and shrugged. The wolf next to him rose into the shape of a long-tressed woman and looked around in turn.

"The horses ran free," she said in irritated tones. "I scryed them to be sure the humans weren't with them, cloaked in magic, but—nothing!"

"I know that," the man said, growing wings. "We'd best take to the skies and look again. Trails can't just end like that. They must have flown away on something!"

"What's that, over there?" one of the wolves asked, growing a human mouth and arm to speak and point with.

"Maybe they're riding it!" said another, and there was a general flurry of feathers into falcon shape. The Malaugrym leapt into the sky, heading north to where the distant, sinuous shape was flying.

It was unfortunate for some of the younger, weaker kin that the flying beast they'd seen was a wyvern, and a hungry one at that.

But these were dark days in Faerûn, and every shadow held danger.

13
Guests of the Blackstaff

It was a dull morning outside the windows of Blackstaff Tower. Storm clouds hung purple and heavy over Mount Waterdeep, and pearly gray sea mists rolled in under them from the harbor. The clop of hooves echoed up from the street below, but the usual cries, rumbles, and other incessant noises of the City of Splendors were muffled. It sounded as if the city were half-asleep.

It was always quiet inside Blackstaff Tower, the velvety, waiting quiet of shielding magic that robbed footfalls of their echoes and shouts of their resonance, and gave to everything a heavy, unbroken hush. Many an apprentice had fallen asleep while studying in the tower, and many an experiment had ended explosively without disturbing the occupants of neighboring chambers.

Laeral hoped this wouldn't be one of *those* experiments. With Khelben away in Elturel, sitting in spellcourt over a long and entangled dispute between two feuding archmages, Blackstaff Tower felt empty, like a throne without its king. Laeral was acutely aware that no one but she was on hand to repair things if her two senior apprentices really botched their work.

Tath was overly shy and almost as overly nervous, but his painstaking check-things-and-check-them-again safety precautions had probably prevented a dozen minor disasters thus far. Baerista, on the other hand, was the impulsive, even reckless, let's-try-it sort. Her occasional flashes of brilliance were the stuff of which real advances in Art were wrought. For the first time in decades, Laeral thought that apprentices might craft something of true worth in the tower, advancing what was known to all workers with magic, and not merely go over well-known ground one more laborious time.

Wherefore the Lady Mage of Waterdeep was quite willing to work late at their sides, the night through if need be—and she just had.

Laeral stifled a yawn as she saw the morning sun climb past the windows, and turned to peer again at the flickering, shadowy edges of the shields Baerista had devised and Tath was struggling to control.

A strange, leaping . . . well, growth of sparks and bubbling spinsmoke was clawing and rebounding around a small sphere of swirling green-gold radiance in the open end of the laboratory, the limits of the wild magic area Laeral had called into being. Normally, Khelben forbade such evocations anywhere in the city, let alone in the tower, but Art is not advanced without making exceptions. Laeral had swallowed once or twice and gone ahead with it.

Now her apprentices, who'd not long ago been safely in the realm of excitedly discussing the possible, probable, and theoretical, were elbow deep in a very real, very dangerous, and possibly runaway experiment. Having created the wild magic field, Laeral could do nothing to control it. Had she not been one of Mystra's Chosen, but merely a mortal archmage of mighty powers, she would have stood no chance of reliably and safely banishing it. She stood watching silently, awaiting the disaster that might all too easily come.

Soon, perhaps, for the wild magic was tirelessly trying to spread, and Baerista, teeth bared in a fierce grin of concentration, was trying to keep it enveloped in the shields she'd raised, without letting it get free or having the shields collapse. Tath was trying to keep Baerista's struggles to direct the lively shield-stuff here and there from tearing the shields asunder, and was just barely holding his own.

The shield was an amorphous area in which bolts of magical force endlessly and chaotically whirled about, something like the blade barrier used by certain priests, wherein blades of all sorts whirl and flash about. The unique feature of the shield was the tight turns and collisions of the bolts along its edges, which caused a humming, crackling energy discharge that seemed to repel the chaos of wild magic. Laeral wasn't sure just how this worked, and she knew as well as any of the gods that neither Baerista or Tath had more than hazy theories to explain it, either.

But that wasn't stopping the shield from working, after a fashion. "Steady! . . . Steady . . ." Baerista was snapping, sweat standing out on her forehead as she stared at the shield, stretching it by redirecting individual forcebolts. She'd almost completed the englobement now, shaping the shield into a sphere that lacked only a small area of coverage to be complete, but Laeral had more than a hunch that the wild magic would explosively resist being completely surrounded, or the shield itself would collapse through ever-increasing instability.

As if to confirm her fears, the hum of the shield began to climb in pitch, rising steadily into a scream. Tath blinked away sweat and hissed, "Slow down, Baera!" It was the first time he'd dared speak so, and betrayed just how nervous he was about the shield's survival. His arms were trembling as he conjured spell-hooks and murmured wardings, struggling to hold the flashing webwork of bolts together.

Not good. Laeral looked to the ceiling to be sure the vent hatch to the roof was unlatched, so any explosion could roar skyward and not burst out sideways to hurl fragments of Blackstaff Tower into nearby buildings. Satisfied, she glanced again at the windows and murmured the word that brought plates of stone and of metal sliding across them, walling out the world. It was crucial that nothing disturb them now.

* * * * *

A closet door swung noiselessly open somewhere in the cellars far beneath Blackstaff Tower, causing an alarm to flash. Ushard of Athkatla frowned at it in annoyance and passed a hand over the sphere, causing it to wink out. Elminster or one of the more restless wizards of the Alliance come visiting again, no doubt. He muttered a word and looked at the scrying stone in time to see Rylard of Neverwinter cross the chamber, waving merrily at Ushard, and vanish toward the stairs, followed by a pair of patrician, gray-bearded master mages of that city whom Ushard hadn't been introduced to. They nodded impassively in his direction and followed.

Well, if they'd come to talk to Khelben, they were going to be right out of luck. Too tiggarty bad, and all that. Ushard shrugged and turned back to the forty-third volume of Pelmurt's diaries. In the long and yawn-inducing account of the eighth magefair, Ushard was sure crafty old Pelmurt had hidden some clue as to just how he had opened The Door Obler Had Forgotten and got into The Lost Library of Funderdelve, where Eltaran Earthshaker and six other powerful mages of Netheril had stored their spells.

But where was the clue? Was it in the catalog of names given as winners of the illusion-crafting contest, in which six names appeared, but only four prizes had been awarded? Or was it in the description of the victory feast that followed, with its wealth of attention to smells, colors, and shapes of the food served?

Hmmm. "Blurturt," Ushard said rudely, uttering the ancient Sword Coast obscenity with crisp gusto, and drummed his fingers on the desk top. It was here on these few pages somewhere, he just knew it, but going from a certain inner feeling to finding and opening that fabled door was a journey that mages had failed to make long before Ushard had seen the route.

Blurturt indeed. Ushard bent forward to read the all-too-familiar passages again, hoping that somehow what he was seeking would leap up and grab him by the throat.

Of course, even lowly apprentices should be careful what they hope for.

Had Ushard watched the image in the scrying stone an instant longer—as he was supposed to, for it dimmed only when the closet door that had activated it closed again—he'd have seen the spectral doomguard emerge from the door frame and follow the two master mages.

And he'd have known that they weren't what they seemed to be.

Had Ushard been attending to the scroll-copying he'd been assigned to do, he would have noticed the glowing globe over his desk bob and dim for the briefest of moments, and known that the dumbwaiter had been called down from beside the desk (where it was holding his evening snack of mulled cider, smoked oysters, and a melted-cheese-sliced-pickles-and-mustard bun—now cold because he'd forgotten them) to the nether regions.

Had he cared about welcoming uninvited guests and summoning Laeral to receive them, as he was supposed to do, Ushard would have wondered why they hadn't come up the stairs, passing through any of the various detection fields and screening spells, and wondered about the eccentricities of six-foot-tall mages preferring to somehow fold themselves into a square box about two feet long on a side to ascend into the tower instead.

And had he possessed half the brain he thought he did, Ushard would have slapped every alarm he could lay hands on when the dumbwaiter's door opened by itself to reveal a very squashed bun and a complete lack of both oysters and cider tankard. As it was, he glanced up, frowned, and said "Damned ghosts. Why can't they go bother the girls? At least *they'll* scream."

He'd actually turned back to his book, whistling the melody of "She Was Only A Mermaid In Waterdeep Harbor" between his teeth—badly off-key—when it struck him that something odd might be going on.

A moment later, he concluded that something most definitely was, as his book erupted into a pair of steely talons that shot up and grasped him by the throat, propelling him firmly backward away from the alarms.

His back arched painfully, Ushard of Athkatla fought for breath, choking and flailing his arms futilely about, flapping hands that might one day hurl spells to humble all known Faerûn . . . or might not. The gods weren't telling.

An instant later, the chair and Ushard overbalanced and crashed to the floor together, but the talons merely closed, tearing out the apprentice's throat. His body bounced and flopped once as everything faded, and then his eyes brightened. All that rhapsodizing about frog salad! The name of the frog was really . . . But he had no throat to speak, and there was no one to hear, and he was sinking into darkness that rushed in from all sides, and—

"I believe that melody, properly sung, goes like this," an icy voice told the unhearing apprentice. But a second voice interrupted the speaker with an urgent, " 'Ware, Taernil! Behind you!"

Rylard of Neverwinter was rapidly ceasing to look like himself and more like Taernil of the Malaugrym, even before the intruder spun around to face the spectral guardian rising from the underside of the dumbwaiter. The box was rising up its shaft despite its open door.

"Stop that thing!" Taernil snarled, meaning the box, but Balatar's arm grew into a spike that rushed across the study with impressive speed to pin the guardian to the wall.

"Hah! Die, bone-bag!" Balatar laughed, enjoying himself immensely—and then his laughter twisted into something else.

If the guardian had been solid and tangible, it would have perished on the spot. Instead, it merely let the Malaugrym's arm pass through it and coalesced around that arm, eating away at the flesh with its chilling unlife as it extended its own ghostly arms into overlong scything blades and began to hack at Balatar.

He howled and shrank back but couldn't get out of the guardian's reach without sacrificing the large part of his body that he'd poured into making the spike. Though he was retracting that spike as fast as he dared, the undead thing was riding on it, refusing to let go, and eating away at it steadily.

Balatar son of Alcarga had never felt such agony before, nor had he felt the cold clutch of real fear. He collapsed, shaking, and Taernil looked at him in disgust. Then he met the gaze of the third cloaked Malaugrym and snarled, "Come on! If we tarry here to help him, the whole tower'll be roused and come down on us. Through this door!"

Jarthree stared at him, then down at Balatar, and then lifted her head and nodded, shedding the last of the dignified white beard and stately dignity of a master mage of Neverwinter. She frowned as they went through the door together, leaving a sobbing Balatar to his fate. He began to shriek and curse them as they went, and Jarthree jerked her head back at the noise and complained, "I thought doomguards couldn't do that."

"It's not a doomguard. More a watchghost, I think." Taernil frowned as the curses behind them died into incoherent moans, and then shrugged and grew two tentacled arms to probe ahead of him as he crossed a darkened parlor—where a trio of driftglobes helpfully brightened into soft life and then faded again as they hurried past—pulled open another door, and mounted a circular stone stair. "There're probably other strange things ahead of us," he added helpfully. "Besides Khelben, I mean."

At the sound of that name, something thrummed nearby, something just above them. They hurried around a bend, ascending, and saw what it was.

The stone pillar that formed the heart of the stair broke off cleanly beside a certain glowing stone step, and resumed again perhaps eight feet higher. In the cylindrical gap that should not have existed (without the staircase collapsing!) floated a vertical black staff. It was covered with runes and gnarly protuberances studded with small silver glyphs and inset metal studs. Tiny lights winked here and there down its sinister length. Its power hung heavy and silent around it. The very air tingled.

"The Blackstaff!" Jarthree's exclamation was a hoarse whisper of longing, and without thinking she reached forth an impossibly long, growing arm to seize the ebon-hued staff.

Taernil's tentacles struck her arm roughly aside. "Are you mad? It might burn you to nothing or call Khelben to itself if touched by anyone but him! Don't you know how suspicion-crazed human wizards are?"

"I know how suspicion-crazed Malaugrym mages are," Jarthree replied, with the first smile Taernil had ever seen on her lips.

He shook his head. "Then you know you shouldn't touch it. Don't . . . just don't." He advanced cautiously and added, "We'd better not touch this step, either. It might awaken anything."

Jarthree sighed. "We're here to slay Khelben if we can, remember? Stop shying away from mere traps and shadows." Her tone was cold and scornful. She sounded almost bored.

Taernil looked back at her sharply, his lips thinning. "These 'traps and shadows,' as you term them, could trammel us just long enough for Khelben to call on any number of friends and guardians. Milhvar's precious cloak didn't save Balatar from the first undead he met with. I don't trust it to make us immune to everything the Blackstaff can throw at us!"

Jarthree waved a dismissive hand. "I merely meant that we'll do best if we strike quickly and keep moving. These are only mortal mages. They can't possibly be as powerful as Milhvar, or—"

"Oh, no? Then how did just one of them kill so many kin that Dhalgrave kept us out of Faerûn for centuries?"

And with those grim words Taernil launched himself up the last few stairs and into the room beyond at a dead run, his arms widening into glide-fins to allow him to cleave the air in a clean turn as he swept in, hands raised to hurl destroying magic.

The end of the room he was so grandly menacing contained a simple but large bed, with maroon bedding and a dark, polished wooden headboard. A pointed hat hung from a hook on one side of it, and something slim and silky hung from the corresponding hook on the other side. A single forcebolt crisped whatever it was before it could stir to strike, as the rush of Taernil's charge brought his feet into contact with the headboard.

He kicked at it and rebounded in a backward somersault to land catlike, facing the bed. Jarthree sloped her body into something ropelike to get out of his way and said dryly, "I'm sure the lady mage's best black silk stockings were *very* threatening . . ."

Taernil whirled to face her, hot death in his eyes. "Do you mock me?" he demanded.

Jarthree shrugged. "I'd call it only a lighthearted observation," she said easily, "but if you're so desperate to dominate me that you must press a challenge here in the heart of a hostile wizard's tower, perhaps I should leave." Her long-taloned hands went to her belt.

"No!" Taernil said quickly, too quickly. Jarthree's slow, catlike smile told him that she'd taken her measure of him and knew the real interest behind his seemingly casual glances at her. He grimaced and turned his head away, then straightened with a snarl to fix her coolly mocking gaze with his own hot stare.

"While we're here, with Milhvar judging what we do," he said heavily, "the only course prudence allows us is full cooperation. Do I have your agreement on this?"

"You do," Jarthree said simply, and the catlike smile was gone.

"Then let us be about it," he hissed, and his skin bulged out into plates as rugged as armor. As he strode to the door facing the foot of the bed, his form broadened until an umber hulk—with the long-fingered, nimble hands of an elven conjurer and fingertips to match those of the apprentice he'd strangled downstairs—laid hands on the ring in the center of that door and pulled.

The door swung out and up, revealing a swirling blueness beyond. The two Malaugrym stared at it, startled to see something so nearly the image of the shadows that swirled about the battlements of the castle they called home.

Neither of them saw the black staff on the floor under the bed—a twin of the one they'd passed on the stair—wink to life and vibrate in silent urgency, turning over once as it rose a few inches off the dusty floor to hang there, quivering.

* * * * *

Two rooms away, Laeral felt the staff's awakening as it sent a warning thrumming through her body. She glanced quickly around the room, seeking anything that should not be there. Intruders! By all the gods, why now? Then her lips twisted in a rueful smile. Of course, now, because of the fall of all the gods, no doubt.

She closed her eyes and whispered something that made a man half a world away stiffen and heed her. *Khelben*, she called silently. *Oh, my love, where are you?*

* * * * *

The two Malaugrym stared into the room before them. This bedchamber was larger than the one they were standing in, and its walls were half-hidden in blue-white mists that swirled amid darker shadows, like the shadows of home. Whoever had conjured up the shadows almost had to have seen Shadowhome, the demiplane ruled by the blood of Malaug.

"It's some sort of trap," Taernil snapped, eyes dark.

In those swirling mists anything could be concealed, but Jarthree suspected nothing more immediately menacing than hanging cylindrical wardrobes were prominent among them. The glossy, unbroken black rectangle of a door could just be seen across the room. Between that door and the one they were looking through, filling much of the room, was a huge circular bed floating three feet or so off the fur-covered floor. On its silken sheets sprawled two smoky-gray furry things that raised heads to favor the intruders with unblinking, inscrutable stares. Cats.

Or worse, perhaps. A forcebolt lashed out from Taernil's hand, angled with careless ease to scorch both beasts out of existence at once. There was a flash, a feline voice raised in mild annoyance, and a sudden fury of force that tumbled Taernil back against the foot of the plainer bed, limbs tingling in seared pain. Scorched by his own forcebolt!

Jarthree stifled her mirth before it became audible, which was a prudent thing. A reflective spell-shield.

Well, why not? As the awakened cats rose lazily and stretched, her eyes drifted up to the ceiling and she gasped in half-mocking admiration. "Oh, look at *this*," she breathed, reaching back with a tentacle to beckon at Taernil.

"What?" he growled, rolling his massively muscled form upright once more.

"Wouldn't you like to have *that* above your bed?" Jarthree asked him, pointing.

Taernil looked up and scowled. "No," he said shortly, staring at the circle of star-studded darkness. He knew little of Faerûn's night sky and cared less, but he recognized the gleaming trail of Selûne's Tears drifting off to one side, and knew what he was looking at. It was breathtakingly beautiful.

"Hhmmph," he said, stomping boldly through the doorway. "I'd rather have one that showed me what I directed it to, like Dhalgrave's scrying portal."

"Dhalgrave is no longer," Jarthree reminded him softly as he glared at the cats, stomped past the bed, and reached for the handle of the room's other door, a door that looked to be made of a single piece of smoothly polished obsidian.

Jarthree faded quickly and silently to one side, shifting her form to look like the blue-white swirling shadows, and took up her place among them.

She was coiling in almost perfect unison with the other shadows when Taernil flung the door wide and launched his most powerful spell into the room beyond. Nine arrow-straight, needle-thin ravening beams of fire leapt from his breast, sizzling across the room into the heart of the strange whirling magic that hung there. Three faces stared at him, two gaping in astonishment and the third grimly expectant.

And then things happened very quickly. The room seemed full of whirling forcebolts, darting and ricocheting in all directions, with something flashing and writhing in their midst. As Taernil's beams tore into the heart of this confusion, the two startled people were snatched back against the far wall as if yanked by tentacles, and the grim-faced woman stood serenely facing him, her hands rising out to either side as if tracing an invisible wall. She did not seem to see him, but rather was staring down his beams, trying to perceive their source. Some of them were striking her—she should be falling as flaming ash! Other beams were striking the whirling confusion of lights and roiling mists, and seemed to be turning into . . . other things.

Tumbling bones and mauve bubbles . . . boulders and single shoes, many-eyed sea jellies and sparkling, rain-dewed flowers . . .

As the beams began to fail, Taernil frowned in bewilderment and hurled another spell, a fireball that should scour that chamber and all within it, leaving him free to face Khelben Blackstaff, who must be in the room beyond.

Behind him, he heard Jarthree gasp—a short indrawn breath of utter terror—even before his fireball twisted in the doorway, meeting that whirling chaos of shoes and bones and things, and spilled back toward him, expanding hungrily across the bedchamber.

The woman still stood facing him, her arms a barrier to the expanding wild magic—by the blood of Malaug, *that's* what it was! The magic was all around him now, blowing blue-white shadows away like wisps of smoke to tumble suddenly revealed cylindrical wardrobes to the floor, and grounding the bed with a thump. It whirled Jarthree and himself back into their true shapes, with the shimmering of Milhvar's cloak of spells suddenly gone from around them.

Taernil gulped, then shuddered uncontrollably as a firm hand stabbed through him, parting his flesh like melting butter, to grasp and crush his organs, one by one.

"So now they're sending young Malaugrym to Black-staff Tower, are they?" Khelben's voice was calm and level, and profoundly unimpressed. "I'm quite particular about whom I invite into my home. And you, Taernil son of Oracla, would not have been among my first eighty thousand or so choices. Out with you!"

And as a last, shattering pain exploded through him, those were the last words Taernil ever heard.

"I suppose you're going to plead for clemency for this one?" Khelben asked, eyes softening as he looked at his lady love.

Laeral looked down at Jarthree and then slowly shook her head. "No," she said. "Ushard was a lazy idiot, but he did not deserve to die as he did. This one is the brightest and most dangerous of the three Malaugrym who came here this night. I am learning, slowly, not to let kindness be taken for weakness, and through such kindness let the ranks of our enemies slowly but surely grow. The Malaugrym understand only the cruel use of power, and learn only lessons of death. Teach her."

Khelben shook his head grimly and brought his hand down. Jarthree did not have time to scream as her body convulsed once and then slowly rose from the floor, floating toward the conjured fire that would consume it.

As the awareness that was Jarthree faded, she tried to weep, for Khelben had taken his lady's words literally, and the last moments of the Malaugrym were a whirlwind of images of the love and beauty, the things wondrous and exciting, to be found in the Realms. Things she might have had, and now, never could.

Khelben watched the flames dwindle and fade away, going to the same place—a demiplane of shifting shadows, with an ancient castle at its heart—as he'd sent the dying whirlwind of wild magic. When the flames were gone, he straightened to watch Laeral restore the last of the floating wardrobes to its cloak of concealing mists. She stood quite still beside him, only the stirring of her hair about her shoulders betraying the complex magic she was wielding. Gods, but she was beautiful.

Khelben took one tress of hair in his fingers and curled it absently, stroking its softness. She turned toward him with that dark smile that still awakened excitement in him, after all these years, and asked, "How fared your spell-court, my lord?"

The Lord Mage of Waterdeep shook his head. "If I'd had the sense to take my ready-staves with me, I just might have been overcome by the desire to ram them both swiftly upward in places that might have painfully removed two mages from the Realms, and thereby done wider Faerûn a lot of good. However, my foresight remains weak."

"Oh, I think it does well enough," Laeral said softly, curling herself into his arms as her magic floated them both toward the bed.

"Ah, my lady," he said, blinking. "The—your apprentices! They—"

"Have to start learning the most important things sometime," she murmured, her mouth against his.

Khelben lifted his eyebrows. Then he recalled the spell he needed and brought his hands down, precipitously transporting startled apprentices and indignant cats alike to a room lower down in the tower.

It just wouldn't do, twice in one night, to plunge apprentices elbow deep into a very real, very dangerous, and possibly runaway experiment.

14
Visitors to the Castle

Thay, Kythorn 18

Elminster caught only glimpses of the stars over Thay
as shadowy death loomed around him, blotting them out.
The smoky clouds of dense gloom were alive and reaching for him. As he frowned and willed his magical undergarments to let him descend at a slightly less precipitous
rate, he wondered just what this giant was, who'd created
it . . . and why.

Just once, 'twould be nice to know.

* * * * *

Thay, Kythorn 19

It is hard to become a Zulkir of Thay. Someone always
holds such a title already and must be willing to give it
up voluntarily—or be made to die. A final death, that is,
admitting of no resurrections, clones, or death-cheating
contingencies. As most of the present Zulkirs enjoy the
powers their titles bring (if not always the responsibili-
ties) and have honed their magical powers—and accumulated allies and magical safeguards, traps, and useful
items—for centuries, bringing final doom to one is no
easy task.

It is quite possible to become a very powerful Red Wizard without ever seeking the mantle of Zulkir, and indeed many "Bloodcowls" (as certain mages of other lands
derisively call Red Wizards) have no interest in the expo-
sure—not to say danger—of the position.

It is not easily possible, however, to reshape the teach-
ings, habits, and direction of an entire school of magic
without either being its Zulkir or having his full support.

Consider, then, the plight of a man who feels he must

accomplish such an end, and is neither Zulkir nor has much chance of gaining the support of the incumbent—centuries-old Szass Tam, Zulkir of the School of Necromancy—or unseating that infamous and awesomely powerful lich, archmage, and master of undead. According to most observers, Szass Tam hasn't sunk into the decadent ennui of many lichnee. He still enjoys besting rival Zulkirs and Red Wizards, and remains driven by an elusive goal: the destruction of Rashemen. This makes both his resignation and destruction unlikely—his death is irrelevant—and leaves a Thayan necromancer who'd like to change the interests of the School of Necromancy in an untenable position, the more so when his tentative approaches to colleagues in the craft are received with cold rebuffs and open suspicion of being an outlander agent or spy.

So he withdraws into apparent bitterness (real) and aimless researches (for show), and behind this mask sets about accomplishing an almost impossible goal: gaining power enough to destroy Szass Tam and anyone else who stands in his way, and force Thay to follow the road he sees for it. He stages an apparent disaster in his spell laboratory, that reportedly weakens him and leaves him disfigured, and becomes The Masked One. Colleagues foolish enough to try to take advantage of his apparently failing powers fall victim to his one real accomplishment, the magical ability to dissolve the person—and subsume the powers of—anyone his most secret spell can envelop.

A few Red Wizards vanish, and The Masked One grows in power until he can craft a giant to ensnare wizards. Then he must wait, for he dare not use it openly and invite attack from all sides by terrified Bloodcowls. He must wait until a time of chaos, when wizards can be trapped alone . . . or avatars, falling from the sky!

When the Fall of the Gods becomes living truth, no longer empty prophecy, the Masked One exults in a hidden place and raises his giant to stalk the avatar he's detected roaming Thay, the mortal who holds the lessened powers of Hoar the Doombringer, Hurler of Thunders. The avatar is very near, and even the lessened power he wields shames the vaunted might of the greatest Red Wizards.

The giant rises and stretches forth his hand, attracting the attention of the One Who Is Hidden (and therefore unknown to The Masked One and his calculations). Ao deems the giant a creation of evil far more dangerous than the status quo in cruel Thay, and looks for something to foil such a dark scheme. Something that always seems to drop into the midst of troubles in Faerûn . . . something called Elminster.

* * * * *

The Old Mage waved a hand to direct his pipe smoke out of his eyes and grunted, "So here's a hearty thankee to thee, Ao, for dropping Elminster into the midst o' things again! Bah!"

As these kindly words left Elminster's lips, the giant seemed to see him, turning a head as large as a good-sized castle to regard the falling wizard, and emitting a thunderous rumble. A distinctly unfriendly sound, Elminster thought, his fingers already weaving a complex pattern in the air. At a certain point, he murmured an incantation that left his pipe behind. As he beckoned the still-smoking item to follow, silver spheres began to coalesce and grow in the air around, like a stream of gigantic bubbles falling to earth with him.

His suspicions were soon confirmed. From the outstretched hands of the dark, menacing mass streamed fire, two lines of eight spinning balls of flame per hand. They loomed up at him very quickly, howling and crackling as they came, and El sent two of his spheres drifting out to meet them. He'd best intercept the fireballs before they could burst. The days when he could serenely survive the fiery blasts of two meteor swarms at once were long gone.

He spun another spell thoughtfully but left it hanging, lacking but a final word to call it into being and send it on its way. Best to wait a bit and let this titanic construct exhaust a few spells more before battle began in earnest. Above and around him, balls of fire met silvery spheres and winked out of existence together in velvet silence.

The giant destroyed the last few fireballs itself, banishing them to spreading steam by the touch of gray-white rays of conjured cold. They hissed out from its hands like angry drifts of cloud, and Elminster's eyes narrowed. Lesser strikes, so soon?

Those must be one of the forms of a freezing sphere spell. Did the thing hurl only duplicates of the same spell? Perhaps it was some sort of projected image raised by an over-clever Red Wizard, and merely aped spells-in duplicate that the Thayan was casting, somewhere far below.

As silver spheres spun and darkened before him, drinking in drifting cold, Elminster let loose his hanging spell. The ruby ray stabbed down, right between the two whirlpools of darkness that served the giant for eyes. Wisps of cloud blocked his view of its striking, but an instant later, when El tumbled out of the pale, clinging cloudy drift, the giant stood unchanged.

It stepped forward, shaking the earth far below, as if goaded by his spell, or as if it now knew just where he was and intended to finish him. Elminster sighed, gathering silver spheres around him in a falling wedge, and pulled them all to one side with him, to see if the giant would hurl its spells at where he should have been.

It did not. From one hand flashed a spreading arc of lightning, leaping from cloud to cloud in a blinding needle to spear a sphere that Elminster hurriedly thrust its way. The sphere lit up blue-white for a moment, then slowly faded into darkness, flickering once, and was gone.

Elminster barely saw it. His eyes were on the giant's other hand, which had made a throwing motion but seemed empty. What could—? Then his eyes narrowed, and he shifted spheres into a line, out from himself toward the giant.

One sphere flared almost immediately, lit from within by tongues of fire, and was gone. A delayed blast fireball.

"So we think ourselves clever, do we?" Elminster asked the night almost absently, and launched his response.

The spell was one he'd always thought unfair, one called "disintegrate" that devoured matter as if it had never been, wiping out struggling creatures and things of beauty alike, visiting such prompt oblivion that El thought it something no mage should habitually use. Ah, high principles. The Old Mage shrugged, and used it now.

One vast arm was his target, to see if an overbalanced giant would fall, or if a one-armed giant could hurl only one spell at a time. He peered into the falling night, and obligingly, the arm that had hurled the stealthy fireball vanished.

* * * * *

Not far away, The Masked One lifted a sweating face and gasped out a heartfelt curse on Mystra and Tymora both—fickle women, to turn their faces away in the moment of his triumph. Now the old man falling from the sky had a chance, when his memories and mastery should already have been flowing into an impatient Thayan necromancer. The Masked One snarled and raised his hands to cast a spell he hadn't expected to have to use.

* * * * *

And in a place of shifting shadows, Milhvar of the Malaugrym stared into his scrying globe and smiled, stroking the shimmering stuff of the cloak of shadows in his fingers. Soon would come the time to use it. Soon.

* * * * *

Thay, Kythorn 19

To a warm and scented pool where several pairs of soft hands stroked a bored Zulkir with oil, there came a sudden commotion. The cause of this commotion rose up,

alarm on his face, spilling silent slaves away from him,
and said aloud, "My cloak and towels to the Turret of
Stars, at once!" Not waiting to hear their murmured
replies, he uttered the word that took him there. Someone was hurling around more magic than any man
should be able to harness, out there in the night, in the
very heart of Thay! Even if this was no attack or act of
treachery, thousands of bindings could be broken! Why
had no one informed him? Why was he always the last to
learn of such things?

* * * * *

As the stars over Thay glittered and swam, the giant
lurched and turned ponderously, raising its remaining
arm in silence to point at the Old Mage, who shrugged
and began the casting of a firestorm.

The weaving he was attempting was a slow and complex thing, denying it much use on battlefields or in sor-
cerous duels, but this strange drifting struggle was
unlike most duels. This might well be the fire spell's best
chosen time.

The giant struck first. A fiery comet streaked skyward,
well above the Old Mage, and burst, raining down fiery
death from above. El finished his casting with a flourish
and looked up to enjoy the show. He'd not seen a Rain of
Fire light up the darkness since three magefairs ago.

And then he saw the spreading rainbow that was his
foe's other sally, and muttered a curse of old Myth
Drannor.

* * * * *

Thay, Kythorn 19

In a tower whose spires stroked the stars, a tall robed
figure turned sharply away from the battle he'd been
watching—the wrestlings of a captured couatl and a
winged devourer he'd conjured into existence not long before—and said aloud, "Something's amiss!"

He turned to the west, in time to feel the surge again. Greater magic than he'd ever felt on the move before, even in the battles where massed Red Wizards had together hurled storms at the witches of Rashemen. Greater magic than any mortal should be able to control.

Perhaps it was out of all control, or perhaps a god had come to Thay. The robed archwizard shuddered and tapped a crystal sphere, awakening it to floating life. He *must* know what doom might be hurtling toward them all.

* * * * *

El willed his undergarments to take him to one side again and thrust himself backward, twisting his fall into an eddy in the air that gave him time enough to cast a spell he'd used before. Bringing the spell up one word short of its close, Elminster fell through the night—more quickly now, as he willed it—and watched the giant's disjunction suck in the spheres of his epuration spell, drinking them one by one.

He glanced up. The spheres had absorbed the entire rain of fire before being destroyed, and he should be out of range of the disjunction by now. He spoke that last word, and silver spheres bubbled out around him once more. Now he had no more epuration spells left.

He turned in the air, his clout and undervest tugging at him in response to his direction, and sent himself on a long glide toward the giant, trailing silver spheres. He had to get a better look at things.

It was the work of but a moment to send a flaring eye away from him, whistling away like a tiny tear of flame. He watched it dwindle speedily toward the giant as the titan's next attack came.

Roiling purple beams that would have wracked and forcibly transformed his body lanced past. Elminster rolled aside to be well clear of them and watched the flight of his probe.

It plunged into magical shadow and lit up the smoky form of the giant from within. In the spreading glow, Elminster saw the tendrils of conjured matter expanding, moving slowly to re-form the missing arm, and also saw the flashes of moving energy that sustained and animated the shadowy titan. Flashes emanating not from a man, but from . . . an item, a small bar or baton that hung in the giant's heart, winking and turning as it strove to move the giant to grasp at Elminster again.

Aha. So this giant was being directed from elsewhere. That—scepter, was it?—might be worth a look, if he could ever get to it.

Elminster summoned up his mage-sight as he plunged ever closer to his gigantic foe. "Far be it from me to cast aspersions on your origins, mighty Ao," he murmured, "or even to inquire too closely about such things, notions of blasphemy being what they are, but . . . Ao, *you bastard!*"

He screamed those last words as he saw silver spheres crumbling close around him under the assault of an attack meant to transform his body to stone, and a second attack, breaths behind the first, intended to shatter his petrified form.

This was enough, and more than enough. Folk were dying in the Realms while wild magic raged and avatars walked, as he wasted time playing with this ungainly wizard's nightmare. Well, at least there'd be no more spells of open rending sent his way—not *now*.

At that thought he plunged into the giant's smoky body, spheres close around him. Sudden lightnings raged, but the spheres bought his life with their own, one after another, and held breathable air between them, and he went on.

Down, down, spiraling in the lightning-lashed gloom toward the quickening, rushing lights that marked the consternation of whoever was making the giant move. Silver spheres were falling away like mist before an open flame now, but he was close, very close . . . and falling like a flung stone, hands outstretched.

Then a sphere flashed into being around his goal, a shimmering, rainbow-hued sphere of light right in front of him, banishing the shadowy heart of the giant like tattered smoke with its power, pulsing as it promised his death.

A prismatic sphere. Thanks again, Ao.

Elminster put his hands back and then swept them together sharply before him, and silver spheres flashed willingly past him to their doom, flaring into vivid flashes of red, orange, and yellow as they bored through the deadly multilayered barrier in his path.

The fourth sphere spun past him, expiring in a vivid green flare, and Elminster called on his underthings one last time, bidding them slow his fall. Fabric sawed at all his joints, protesting with raw pullings and tearings that were more felt than heard, and the fifth sphere died in front of him, the blue flash of its passing making his eyes flood with tears.

The deeper flashes that followed shook him soundlessly. Then, through swimming eyes, Elminster saw the crackling scepter turning in front of him.

He put forth a hand and grasped it firmly, saying calmly, "Thaele."

And the world seemed to stop. There was a frozen white instant of pain as he hung motionless in the air, feeling lightings surge through him; then he felt the giant begin to collapse. Abruptly the night sky was gone, and he was standing in a familiar, cozy room more than a world away.

* * * * *

Thay, Kythorn 19

The Masked One shook as the last lightnings roiled through him, and the shadows that had been his titan tumbled and rolled away. Gods curse the Mage of Shadowdale! The scepter was gone, and without it . . .

The door behind him split from top to bottom with a thunderous crack. The necromancer whirled, snatching at the serpent-headed rod that was his last and most secret defense.

"*What're you playing at, traitor?*" came the cold question from the light beyond. The glowing head that drifted into the room was as tall as a man, but its features were those of the Zulkir Lauzoril.

The Masked One opened his mouth to reply, but whatever he might have said was lost forever in the crash of raining acids and bursting forcebolts that came through his scrying stone and his secret gate respectively, and crashed together with him at their heart. The chamber rocked, and the necromancer's struggling figure vanished.

As smoke rose from what had been a room of splendor only moments before, the floating head said irritably, "Stay out of this, both of you. *I'll* deal with affairs that occur on my own lands!"

"We await your starting to do so," came a reply. "All of Thay awaits."

The head raised an eyebrow. "Does it? And how comes your perfect knowledge of this?"

"Lauzoril," another voice said carefully, "has it occurred to you that being Zulkir might occasionally involve other talents than the ability to make clever remarks?"

"We're waiting," the first voice agreed, almost smugly.

The conflagration that followed hurled stony fragments for miles, but Zulkir Lauzoril suspected that The Masked One was long gone. He wondered briefly just what Szass Tam was going to say about this, and decided he really didn't want to approach that dark tower in Delhumide and ask. Whatever the necromancer had tried was done, a failure that had cost him his abode and much of his power. A fitting punishment could wait for later—a decade or two, perhaps.

* * * * *

Elminster's Safehold, Kythorn 19

The softly glowing globe that usually hung above the table in the center of the octagonal room had drifted over to one side, to hang helpfully over the shoulder of the white-bearded man lounging in Elminster's best chair, his feet up on the edge of one of the many crammed bookshelves that lined the room. A small array of wine bottles and half-empty tallglasses hung in the air around him, his rarest and best wines.

Elminster hated uninvited guests, but his expression did not change as his eyes flickered over the scene. He stepped forward with a twinkle in the depths of his old blue-gray eyes.

"You wanted this dealt with, sir?" the Old Mage asked in the calm, cultured tones of a servant as he set the scepter in his hand gently on the table in front of the Overgod. His tone was innocent, but the words hung in the air as firmly as any challenge.

Ao raised calm eyes to meet his but said nothing. Challenge answered.

Elminster met those dark, star-filled eyes steadily and laid the torn remnants of his undervest and clout beside the scepter. "See? Clean," he announced calmly, and waved a hand.

A second chair melted out of the air in silent obedience, and El sat down, swinging his own feet up to the table.

Ao glanced at the scepter, and it disappeared. His eyes flickered for a moment as he considered the implications of the powers he'd just absorbed. Then he raised his eyebrows and his glass together. "Perhaps *you* should be the god of all magic in Faerûn."

El put his hands behind his head and frowned. "What? Would ye ruin my life and my usefulness both at once?"

Ao regarded him thoughtfully for a moment and then nodded. "You're right . . . all too often, Elminster Aumar. *Try* to stay out of the grievous sort of trouble that beset the gods of your world. I'd not want to have to return here to destroy you."

He held out a hand, and after a long moment Elminster took it—to find himself shaking only empty air.

The Old Mage collapsed into a chair, noticing his wines were all back on their shelf, stoppered and arranged as he'd last left them. "Foosh!" he said in shocked tones. "A 'be a good boy' lecture and half my wine gone! I don't think I can *afford* to entertain Overgods!"

* * * * *

The Castle of Shadows, Kythorn 19

Deep green and serpentine were the shadows coiling around them as three rangers in leather blinked at each other and at their surroundings. It was cool and damp and smelled . . . strange, as if the smells of an old and deep forest were mingled with sharp scents of burning. It was some sort of high-ceilinged chamber or hall, longer than it was wide and built of stone, the massive blocks smooth with age and unadorned.

They were alone, though small things seemed to be alive in the ever-swirling shadows. A sudden flurry of fogs made Sharantyr look down quickly at the blade she held, to find it cloaked in a quickening spiral of concealing shadows. An attack?

"Gentle sirs," she said warningly, "we may have a problem. I—"

Belkram leaned in close. "Syluné's doing it, to hide the blade. Ah, don't put it away."

Shar nodded and looked around again.

"Well," she said, wriggling her shoulder blades to loosen some of the tension, "it certainly feels . . . strange. Whither now?"

"My arm," Itharr said quietly. "It's . . . changing."

Shar heard the tightly chained fear in his voice. His left arm seemed to be growing a row of barbs and shifting from patched and seamed leathers to a bluish fur, rising over bones that should not be there.

"Is it happening to any other part of you?" Shar asked, glancing involuntarily down at herself. Nothing looked or felt strange, but . . .

"It's—I'm changing, too," Belkram said grimly, and they all saw that the booted foot he thrust forward had become a taloned, curling claw. He scratched his shoulder with an arm that had begun to sport scales here and there, and muttered, "Can your blade take us home again, if need be?"

"I don't think I want to see a guard's face at the bridge in Shadowdale when he looks at *this*"—Itharr thrust his arm forward, and Shar saw that the barbs had become a row of curling, questing tentacles—"especially not a guard I know."

Sharantyr grimaced. "Does it . . . hurt?" she asked, looking from one man to the other and wondering if she'd soon have to strike one or both of them down. As if reading her thoughts, the blade in her hands lifted a little.

Shar shivered and took a pace away, to get out from between the two Harpers. They gave her hurt looks. "Syluné's not doing this to you, is she?" she asked Belkram. "This isn't some sort of disguise."

"No," he said grimly, shuffling forward. "It's this place, working on our bodies. I guess this is how the Malaugrym became shapeshifters."

"Can you . . . manage?"

Belkram gave her a rueful smile. "Have to," he said briefly.

"I'm trying to tell my body what to shift into," Itharr said quietly, "but it doesn't seem to be working. Am I turning blue?"

Shar peered at him. "Not any part of you I can see," she observed carefully, "but—"

"Trying to get her to disrobe you again?" Belkram asked, rolling his eyes. "Haven't you given up on that *yet?*"

The laughter they shared then was a little wild, but the smiles that ended it were real ones that remained as Shar took a few tentative steps across the chamber. "We might as well start looking around," she said.

"Do we have to find this place again, to gate back home?" Itharr asked. Shar shrugged. "I . . . don't know. I guess so." She raised the blade, and they saw the air behind them wavering in confusion. After a moment she lowered it. "It will show me gates, I think . . . even here."

"So why isn't there a clear door, or oval, or whatever?" Belkram asked, waving at the spot where they'd appeared.

Shar frowned. "I don't think that gate is there anymore," she said reluctantly. The two men traded glances.

"Then we'd better go exploring," Itharr said, "or we'll never find a way out of here. If we just stand here, either someone'll find us—and no doubt offer violence—or we'll die of starvation!"

"You may not want to wait for that," Belkram told him. "Have you looked at yourself?"

Itharr regarded him sourly. "Now how could I do *that*?"

Belkram shrugged. "If your eyestalks grow a little longer, you should be able to swivel one around and get a good look at yourself."

"I'd refrain from such talk if I were you," Itharr responded. "You may have started out more handsome than me, but I doubt Shar's going to be overly thrilled with a man whose back is growing a row of breasts, a *moving* row of breasts . . ."

Belkram tried to twist around to look at his back, but couldn't. He shot a look at Shar. "Tell me he's bluffing," he demanded. The lady ranger could only shake her head sadly.

"Why hasn't it affected you?" Itharr asked, frowning. As he did so, his eyes flickered a deep mauve and began to slide slowly toward red in hue. "Could it be linked to sex?" Then he added quickly, "No jokes, Belk."

Belkram turned to him as the line along his back moved slowly up his neck and onto his scalp, lifting his hair in an odd-looking crest. "I wasn't planning any," he grunted, "but I think it's more likely the sword. Without the shadow weaving being done around it, it'd be standing in a little gap in the mists, a place these shadows don't care to go."

"They're alive, aren't they?" Itharr murmured.

"Yes," Shar agreed briskly, "and so are we." She strode away into the curling mists, raising the blade like a prow before her.

"Well, for now, yes," Belkram agreed mildly. He and Itharr looked at each other, shrugged, and moved tentatively after her. A slithering sound made them both freeze, until Itharr realized it was coming from the tail he'd begun to grow, whispering along the stone behind him. They traded grimmer glances and went on.

* * * * *

Elminster's Safehold, then the Castle of Shadows, Kythorn 19

"I really must give the Shadowmasters something to think about besides laying waste to Faerûn," the Old Mage mused. And then he smiled suddenly and snapped his fingers.

Obediently, in a place of ever-shifting shadows distant indeed from the room where Elminster sat, above the unbroken black marble floor of a vast chamber that was never empty, a severed head that looked very much like Elminster's own faded back into view from its stay in otherwhere, winked at a startled Malaugrym striding importantly across the Great Hall, and was gone.

A breath later, in a passage where candles flickered and wavered but never went out, fed by always-circling shadows, Old Elminster's head suddenly appeared. Floating between two pillars, it politely said, "Boo!" to a pair of startled Malaugrym conspirators, spat lightnings that left one shapeshifter rolling about in agony and the other a smoking heap, and was gone again.

In a chamber where several Malaugrym chanted and slithered, shifting shape in a ritual forbidden by Shadowmasters High for some centuries, a disembodied human head suddenly appeared, floating above the center of the sacred ring of flames, smiling down benevolently at the startled kin of Malaug.

"A sign!" one of them said excitedly, pointing with a flipper. "A sign!"

"What should we read in it?" another asked, almost suspiciously, as they all gaped at the smiling head.

It winked. " 'Abandon hope,' perhaps?" it suggested, as the blood dripping from its underside became a stream of silver lances that spun and erupted around the chamber, ricocheting energetically among Malaugrym blood and screams. By the time a Shadowmaster had lifted shaking hands to ward death away, the head was gone again.

" 'Twas Elminster," he mumbled grimly to the gape-mouthed corpse beside him. "He's back."

Wisely, the corpse chose not to answer.

15
Tumult and Affright

The Castle of Shadows, Kythorn 19

Blue-black and sinuous the shadows coiled, rising
thigh high around the three rangers as they moved warily down the hall. Soon the parting mists showed them
an end wall, and in its center a door flanked by two spitting serpents of stone.

Sharantyr eyed these gape-fanged sentinels warily as
she approached, and thrust her sword carefully between
them, probing back and forth, but there was no response.
They seemed to be no more than lifeless stone ornaments.

Which made a nice change.

"Where shall we head for?" Sharantyr asked her companions softly, turning before the closed door. "Upward,
or down? Head for large and grand rooms, or small and
dark?" Two shrugs answered her, so she added, "Is there
something we should be looking for?"

"Food," Itharr said brightly. Shar gave him a look, but
Belkram held up a hand to halt them while he bent for a
moment and listened to the stone he bore. Then he
looked up. "We will need water to drink, first, and food
eventually," he said, "but I've been told we're not to put
anything in our mouths that *she* hasn't touched—been
immersed in, whatever—first. Try to avoid even *touching*
Malaugrym; they know all about what's poisonous to us."

"So no biting," Itharr commented, and added slyly,
"Not like our last visit to Waterdeep."

Even before Sharantyr could give him a disgustedly
despairing look, he'd adopted graver tones, adding,
"Which brings to mind why we've come. Do we attack
everyone—every*thing*—we meet? Do we avoid battle if
we can, and try to scout about? Do we try to befriend
someone, to learn all we can or to earn a place here?"

"Perhaps next time," Belkram added in a small voice, addressing the unseen ceiling, "we could answer a few of these good questions *before* we leap into the heart of danger."

Into the rueful little silence that followed, Itharr said, "I like that. 'Leap into the heart of danger.' Quite impressive. There's a ballad in that . . ."

"*Don't*," both of his companions advised, in chorus. He spread teasingly apologetic hands in silence and then gestured at Shar, wordlessly bidding her speak.

Sharantyr eyed both men, seeing several horns growing out of one side of Belkram's head, and small eyes that should not have been there blinking at her from a cavity in Itharr's shoulder. She closed her eyes on these sights for a moment and took a deep breath. Letting it out slowly, she looked at them both and said, "If we begin by fighting, we're sure to be slain as soon as we meet anyone too powerful, or a group. I don't even think we should be talking like this; they might be able to hear. Just act as arrogant as they did, back at the keep, but be casual . . . and mysterious."

"When you don't know what you're doing," Belkram agreed solemnly, hefting his saddlebag, "that's not too hard."

Sharantyr gave him a half-smile and a shrug in reply, and reached for the door. As her hand approached it, the door gave way silently, pivoting back into dim shadows beyond.

Shar gave her companions a raised-eyebrows look of wary, impressed-despite-myself surprise and peered into the chamber beyond.

It seemed empty of life, though it held shadows that flickered and clawed at each other in a fitful semblance of life. Blade first, Sharantyr advanced, looking this way and that, and saw that this smaller chamber had two doors to their right and one ahead. A massive metal fish bolted to the far wall spilled out light from its mouth, like a tap that flowed radiant air rather than water. They peered at it suspiciously and then advanced across the room. Something echoed in the mists, far ahead beyond the single door . . . a tapping sound. It came to their ears once but was not repeated.

"They're here, all right," Itharr murmured, trying to ignore the eel-like thing his left arm had just become. "I don't know just where, but they're here."

The other Harper looked at him and sighed. "Act like we belong here," Belkram suggested firmly, "not as if we're creeping around an enemy stronghold."

Itharr looked innocent. "But what if we *are* creeping around an enemy stronghold?"

Shar chuckled despite herself. The mist swallowed the sound as if it were hungry, and she stopped short and looked around once more. "I feel like I did in the Underdark," she said softly, "creeping around, hoping I'd not be found . . ."

The two Harpers exchanged glances. Belkram laid a kindly flipper on her shoulder and said, "Shield high, Shar. We're—"

He broke off at the rather nauseated look she was giving her shoulder, or rather, at the part of him that was wiggling obscenely there, well on its way to changing into something else.

Her look was so comical that both men chuckled—long, deep chuckles that built into shaking mirth. Sharantyr gave them both a hurt look.

"Do you two giggling idiots *mind?*" she asked indignantly.

And the door in front of them swung open.

They hadn't even time to look apprehensive before an apelike, shambling thing with the head of a handsome young man and one hand that ended in a cluster of tentacles moved through the door and headed past them, over toward one of the doors on the right. He gave them a cold glance and then stiffened, turned, and looked Sharantyr up and down.

"Shapes of Faerûnians? Are you practicing for a foray after this Elminster mortal, or just having"—his gaze traveled back and forth between them, and his grin acquired a few needlelike teeth—"a little fun?"

Sharantyr gave him an easy shrug. "A little fun," she

drawled in soft, lazily menacing tones. The Malaugrym seemed to hesitate, and she added pointedly, brushing one arm along Itharr's now-pustuled flank, "*Private* fun."

The Malaugrym seemed about to say something more but merely nodded and went on. As the door opened, he looked back and was favored with a trio of faintly mocking, faintly challenging half-grins, just the look Belkram had seen on the lips of Elaith Craulnobur, the notorious elven adventurer, in a spell-scene shown to him by a Harper in Waterdeep. Itharr remembered that look from a lady brothel-keeper he'd arrested in Elturel, just before half her girls returned to their true doppleganger forms and she'd started to scream. And Sharantyr would always see the almost-smiles on the faces of drow bending over her, whips in their hands.

Seeming satisfied with what he saw, the Shadow-master vanished through the door.

"It almost seems as if we know what we're doing," Belkram commented, flexing his right arm, which was lengthening steadily into what looked like a gigantic crab claw.

Itharr nodded. "Just behave as if you know what you're about and have every right to be doing it, and most folk will accept you." He looked critically at his own arms, one of which was a deep red in hue. "A fairly simple deception at heart," he observed. "I suppose that's why so many kings have managed it down the years."

* * * * *

Elminster's Safehold, Kythorn 19

Elminster paced back and forth in the bookshelf-lined Safehold, frowning and stroking his beard. From time to time he lifted his head to stare at one of the room's four doors, noting absently that Ao had shuffled through the spell-stored animated scenes he displayed as hangings on those doors, and put on display the most alluring of each. He gave one of them—a lady who had been dust for almost eight hundred summers—a half-smile as he ban-shed her, shaking his head. "Distracting," he muttered, and returned to his pacing, striding up and down the room, face dark with thought.

"This is ridiculous," he muttered after a time, coming to a halt by the table. "I *must* know."

He waved a hand. The chamber darkened obediently except for a small point of whirling light above the table, which grew and grew until it became as large as his face . . . whereupon it spun a book out of itself and vanished with a satisfied sound.

Elminster took the floating book and stepped on the floor tile that would whisk him at will onto the seat of his private privy. 'Twas time for some serious reading, before some bespectacled twit at Candlekeep noticed this tome was missing, and called on magic to trace it. Oh, he had his own copies of Alaundo's predictions, but the *Commentaries of Iyrauthar*, the book in his hands, was the only text to gather related records, rumors, legends, and testimonials about the Mad Sage's thunderings. Moreover, Candlekeep's copy had been annotated by First Reader Paltro some six hundred years ago, collecting even more useful lore on the Endless Chant and its various fulfillments—much of it errant nonsense, but one can't have everything.

"Oho," he said softly, after a while. "Oh ho ho, indeed." He summoned his pipe with a crook of one finger and sent the book back to its rightful home with a wave of his other hand, rising up through the floor from jakes to study in slow, stately majesty. Tablets of Fate, my wrinkled old behind, he thought sourly. Did even the divine lack taste and inspiration these days?

* * * * *

The Castle of Shadows, Kythorn 19

The door through which the Malaugrym had come proved to open into a long gallery, with pillars and a railing on their right. The view over the railing looked down into a shadow-shrouded hall where various robed folk—

Malaugrym, presumably, in largely human form—strode
back and forth from door to door. A smell wafted up that
could only be described as something fishlike being fried.

They did not tarry to watch, for fear of attracting attention. At the end of the gallery, a door opened into a
room dominated by a deep, echoing well. They dared not
confer in that room, in case the well took their voices to
unseen ears far away. So they chose one of the other
three doors leading out of the room and found themselves
in a little closetlike space lined with benches. A hole in
the floor made them suspect this was a Malaugrym
garderobe, and useless to them for the same reason as
the well room. Retracing their steps, they chose a different door and entered a room with a stair descending in
front of them, curving off to the right as it did so.

"What did you make of that cooking smell?" Belkram
murmured from at the head of the stairs. "My stomach
just growled."

"Is that what I heard?" Itharr asked, eyebrows dancing.

"Belt up and stow it," Shar murmured with menacing
softness. "The question is a good one." As if in agreement,
her stomach turned over with an audible sound of
protest.

The look she gave them both just dared them to comment, but at that moment someone began to ascend the
stairs. Itharr propelled his two companions downward
with gentle pressures on their backs, muttering as he did
so, "Well, to *my* nose it seemed like someone frying a gigantic oyster or mussel in herbed butter, and I can hardly
wait to sink teeth into it. Seeing what it looks like, mind,
stands not so high on my list of dreamy desires."

The Malaugrym reached the large midstair landing a
pace before they did and halted to watch them, his eyes
glinting in suspicion.

"Who are you?" he asked coldly. "What shapes are
these?" And then his eyes fastened on the shadow-
shrouded blade in Sharantyr's grip and he hissed and
raised his hands in gestures that could mean only spellcasting.

* * * * *

Elminster's Safehold, Kythorn 19

Selune sailed serenely among the stars outside the window in the ceiling of the Safehold, and cast her cool light down on the table where, after many long hours, the Mage of Shadowdale still sat slumped in thought. Elminster stirred as the full glory of the moon cast ivory fire around him, and stroked one of the knots in the richly polished tabletop.

His moving finger awakened an old magic, and a small crystal coffer was suddenly floating in front of his nose. It held a locket, a few exquisitely beautiful earrings—kings' tears at the end of sapphire spindles, keepsakes he'd given Lansharra and found again after her death—and a lock of blue-green glossy hair. His fingers took it up. This was all that was left, now, of Essaerae, once so young and beautiful in Myth Drannor.

Mystra had forbidden him to use Art on this glossy remnant, he recalled, to try to bring her back. Sitting alone in the moonlight, Elminster turned the silken hair over and over in his hands, remembering dark and laughing eyes in that long-ago moongleam, and nights that stretched softly on forever . . . and he came to a sudden decision.

"Overgod or no Overgod," Elminster murmured, "I must do as I see right, for the good of all Toril."

He laid the hair gently—someone watching might have said reverently—back in the coffer and banished it again to its place of hiding. Then he reached out his foot to a certain floor tile and uttered a word that was all hissings and inbreaths. Under his boot a rune flashed into momentary brilliance, and the tile slid aside.

The tentacles that emerged from the void below were long and delicate, and in their curled tips they held a box of polished, rainbow-hued abalone. Elminster took a circular silk-wrapped bundle from inside the box and thanked the tentacles gravely. They closed the lid and withdrew as softly as they had come.

The silk was black and crumbling with age. From its folds Elminster drew forth a circlet of silver-blue metal that looked almost as decrepit. Setting the crumbling crown on his head, the Old Mage beckoned a crystal ball down from its role as a bookend on a dusty shelf, to float over the table in front of him.

Then he leaned forward and stared into the scrying crystal, and the crown on his brow began to wink with tiny moving lights. The same light danced in the old wizard's eyes as he whispered, "Midnight . . . Midnight . . . Ariel Manx . . . Mystra to be . . ."

And where she slept under the cold light of Selûne's watchful eye, Midnight whimpered in her sleep and twisted onto her side as a gruff voice softly whispered in her dreams and she began to see places, and folk, and things. A tablet swam into her view, and the voice told her, "A useless thing, this, but one of three such playing pieces in this game forced on all the gods."

There was more, but the young sorceress had been very tired, and much of it whirled around old memories of ardent young men and older mages she'd seduced to gain their magic. The rest was lost to the sound of the gruff voice saying, "Bah!" more than once.

In the end, she came sharply awake, sweating in terror, with the image of a yawning grave stark and bright in her mind. From it echoed that testy voice, saying, "Beware, lass. Gods who dare not pursue a tablet will not hesitate to use mortals who can, even such a one as . . . Midnight."

* * * * *

The Castle of Shadows, Kythorn 19

The Malaugrym was swift, and there was no telling what sort of spell he was weaving, so Belkram regretfully shot out his tail, wrapped it around the Shadowmaster's ankle, and pulled. An instant later, a flash of violet radiance washed over them all as the magic took hold, and the two Harpers found themselves swaying and dazed but in their true forms again, tails and horns and such gone.

Their state made Sharantyr's cold reply to the Shadow-master's question about the shapes they wore an unintended irony. "Our own," she said crisply, tossing her saddlebag aside without taking her eyes from him.

Suddenly released from Belkram's grip, the Malaugrym swayed but thrust out half a dozen sucker-covered tentacles to brace himself against the wall and steps. He snarled in anger, a snarl that became a lunge of snapping fangs as his neck lengthened with lightning speed. Sharantyr turned her face away from those gleaming fangs and struck at him frantically. The serpentine neck reared back, but once her blade had flashed past, the Malaugrym struck, plunging his teeth toward Sharantyr's breast.

Inches before the shapeshifter's fangs would have touched home, a Harper lunged to the rescue. Belkram's punch glanced off Sharantyr's forehead as it drove the Shadowmaster's head aside, and the lady Knight staggered back as the Harper and the Malaugrym struck the wall together.

The shapeshifter put a hand on Belkram's face to pin his head against the wall, and grew talons to put out his opponent's eyes, but Belkram sat down suddenly and vanished from under the shapeshifter's grasp just as Itharr's blade burst through the Malaugrym's body, sword tip spraying blood.

The Malaugrym merely sneered and stepped back, his flesh flowing away from around the blade to leave it bare. "Mortals in our castle?" he hissed incredulously, and seemed almost gleeful as he added, "There can be only one proper punishment for such effrontery!"

"Death, I suppose?" Belkram asked, launching himself from the landing in a kick that drove the feet out from under the Malaugrym.

The shapeshifter fell on the stone steps and rebounded, rising to keep Itharr's blade at bay with a flailing wall of saw-edged tentacles.

"Blinding, dismemberment—and other enjoyable

diversions," he replied pleasantly, pressing forward. His tentacles fenced with both Harpers, and behind the wall they wove, the Malaugrym raised his hands almost leisurely to cast another spell.

Sharantyr set her mouth in a grim line and sprang forward, her blade flashing. Where it touched a tentacle sent to intercept it, smoke rose and the shapeshifter grunted in astonished pain. The lady ranger dove through the hole she'd cut and found herself face to face with the furious Malaugrym as her blade whipped through his throat once, and then back across it again on her backswing.

Blood sprayed her, and the shocked Malaugrym staggered back, choking on his incantation, wisps of smoke curling up from his throat. "Usss—" he hissed. "Oorthhh . . . ," and he coughed weakly and shook his head, backing away.

"Do we dare let him go?" Belkram muttered, sword in hand.

Itharr shrugged. "I don't think it pr—watch out!" The Malaugrym sank down swiftly into an octopuslike sprawl on the stairs, shooting out a small forest of tentacles that snatched at the ankles of all three rangers. Belkram fell helplessly and heavily, hacking at whatever he could reach, and found tentacles slapping over his mouth, striving to suffocate him.

Itharr went to one knee but caught hold of a stair post for balance, sawing at the tentacles wrapped around Belkram.

Sharantyr plunged into the heart of their foe, hacking and slashing. Although tentacles rose up all around her in an effort to snatch or twist the blade from her hands and bear her down, she kept hold of her weapon with both hands and cut glowing blue lines of death through ever-thicker smoke.

Where Belkram and Itharr cut the Malaugrym, its cuts flowed together again and healed, but the wounds made by Sharantyr's humming blade gaped open and smoked.

Other Malaugrym had come upon the struggle. One

even descended the stairs past them all by the simple expedient of shifting its body up onto the rail for the few paces it needed to stay clear of the fray. Few of the observers seemed interested or tarried to watch, save one.

He took up a relaxed position against the stair rail lower down and watched calmly as the blazing Malaugrym began to shrink away from the two Harpers, concentrating all of its energies on slashing Sharantyr with barbs it had grown on the ends of its tentacles. As she chopped and slashed those rubbery appendages down to a few, the Malaugrym dwindled and suddenly rolled away from her, down a few steps, to lie asprawl, gape mouthed and very human.

"Impressive," said the new arrival, levering himself up from his elbow to stand facing them. He looked like a youngish, handsome man with wavy brown hair that threatened to fall right over one eye. The only sign that he was a shapeshifter was an extra arm, half-hidden in the folds of his loose, open-necked shirt. A third hand could be seen at his belt, fingers endlessly stroking the pommels of the ranked throwing knives there. Silver-bladed throwing knives.

This Shadowmaster spread his other hands in an "I mean no harm" gesture and came up a step.

"Keep your distance," Sharantyr told him, breathing heavily, her eyes afire. The sword in her hand pulsed once, warningly.

"Of course," the Shadowmaster said. "But please believe me, all of you. I mean you no harm. I see that you're mortals and may be unaware of our ways here in the Castle of Shadows. Be advised: This kin you slew— Phenanjar by name, if you're interested—was long a foe of mine. You have done me great good by his removal, and I regard you as friends." He advanced another step. "I would be pleased if you looked upon me as a friend, too."

Shar moved her blade menacingly, and the Malaugrym sighed. "Lady, please! Have I threatened you? Do you look upon every man you meet on a stair, here or in fair Waterdeep or in any inn of the Dalelands, as a foe to be cut down rather than spoken to? This place"—he waved at the mists around—"is, after all, my home. May I not walk its halls freely? I was, in fact, returning to my own chambers, and I'd be happy if you'd accompany me there as honored guests."

"Guests?" Itharr asked quietly, his voice neutral.

The young man smiled pleasantly. "Guests. Here in the castle, that means you are free to come and go as you please, but are under my protection and not to be mistreated by"—his gaze fell to the still-burning Phenanjar at his feet—"those of us with, ah, careless tempers."

"Are you adept in magic?" Belkram asked.

The Malaugrym smiled. "Hardly. That has been my undoing, thus far. Yes, I work at magic and can hold my own in most company, but not here in the castle. You three need not fear my spells. They are not suited for smiting enemies low or hurling stones about in battle. Come. Be my guests. Learn what one of the blood of Malaug is truly like."

He met Sharantyr's hard gaze and shrugged. "You are suspicious of me, of course. Well, then, accompany me for as long as you like, and we'll part when you choose. Of course, thereafter I cannot speak for your presence and purposes in the castle, and some of my kin *will* seek to slay you on sight."

"We shall accompany you, sir," Sharantyr said with a smile that touched her lips but not her eyes. "Walk ahead of me, if you will, but my blade will stay in my hand."

"I would not have it put anywhere else, good lady!" he joked, and stepped smoothly past her, inviting the wary Harpers to fall in beside him with a gesture. "I am Amdramnar, son of Chasra, by the way. And you are—?"

"Hungry," Itharr said with a beatific smile. "And he's"—he indicated Belkram, striding along on the Shadowmaster's other flank—"very hungry."

The Malaugrym chuckled. "I . . . see." He looked over his shoulder at Sharantyr, who was walking warily just behind him. "Are they always like this, good lady?"

"No," she replied calmly, a twinkle deep in her watchful eyes, "they're on their best behavior just now."

* * * * *

"Alja! Did you hear?"

"Something about Phenanjar being killed, aye? So who finally got tired of him?"

"Mortals did it, they're saying. Folk from Faerûn!"

"What? How did they get into the castle?"

"Talk is it's some plot of Amdramnar's. He's parading around the halls with them now, three of them, and the wench has a blade that burns when it cuts. That's what killed Phenanjar . . . he couldn't heal."

"Really? I'll bet there's more than a few kin Amdramnar would like to see her put that sword through. He gathers enemies the way you and I collect good gossip!"

"Aye, that's for—*whaaaa*?"

A startled, wordless exclamation followed, and then all that could be heard in that lonely hallway was the hissing of burnt flesh and a chuckle as Old Elminster's head passed over two blazing bodies and flew on, deeper into the shadows.

16
The Unbidden Guest
Knows Not Where to Sit

The Malaugrym led them a long and winding way
through the castle, through rooms that swam with shadows and rooms where the air was as clear—and as dank
—as any they'd seen in a Faerûnian keep. After a time,
their route led down and down again, into a many-
galleried chamber thick with shadows. As they walked
its muffled gloom, Belkram ventured to ask, "What room
is this?"

"Some call it the Well of Shadows," the Malaugrym
told him without hesitation, "but to most of us—I don't
know why—it's Deep-pool. There's no actual pool of water
here, just shadows, always as thick as you see. Some elders call this the heart of all Shadowhome."

The three rangers could well believe it. They moved in
close around Amdramnar to ensure they wouldn't get
separated. It would be a terrible thing to wander here,
lost and alone.

It was an eerie place. Night dark and tinged with
purple, the tattered shadows slid past, shaping eyeless
faces, prancing unicorns, and trees whose whispering
leaves were human hands, all grasping and grabbing.

Sharantyr shuddered, shifted the saddlebag on her
shoulder, and hefted the comforting weight of the blade
Mystra had given her. Its glow was dull here, and moisture clouded its steely length. More than once she turned
it sharply behind her to menace the unseen source of
some half-heard sound—a slithering or the thuds of monstrous footfalls—but there was never anything visible
through the endlessly boiling mists.

Shadows. Just what were they, anyway?

"Amdramnar," she said carefully, almost stumbling

over the unfamiliar name, "what are these shadows? You
speak of them almost with reverence."

"Not here," the Shadowmaster replied quickly. "We'l
talk of this in my chambers. It's no secret that some o
my kin believe that only two sorts of beings should know
the ways of shadow—those of the blood of Malaug . . . an
the dead."

An old and ornate stair post of black stone loomed up
out of the mists, and beyond it a flight of steps climbed ar
unseen wall. They ascended, Shar grimacing at the carv
ings on the post as she passed. It was ringed witl
chained human maidens, bodies bare and mouths oper
in endless silent wails of despair. The stair itself seeme
to moan as they trod its worn, mist-shrouded steps. From
time to time, a step would glow with awakened magica
light as they stepped on it. Uneasily the three compan
ions went on, wondering just when their guide's treach
ery would come, and what fatal form it would take.

"What's that?" Itharr snapped, at a sudden movement
on the stair ahead. Beads of light swam out of the shad
ows like a string of little lanterns, slid across their path
and plunged over the stair rail into the shadows of the
Well. They watched the glimmering radiances plunge
into the falling darkness where the dreamshadows
spun—and then burst, one by one.

"Just shadow at play," Amdramnar said with a shrug
"There are a lot of things around here that even our el
ders can't explain. The shadows are alive, you see."

* * * * *

Blackstaff Tower, Waterdeep, Kythorn 19

"Alustriel's back chambers first, my tower next. It cer
tainly seems as if the Malaugrym are visiting Chosen."

Elminster frowned at the Lord Mage of Waterdeep
and they stroked their beards in unison. Laeral stifled a
giggle at the sight.

"Aye, so much is obvious," the Old Mage agreed slowly
"but why have they sent such young dolts? Zhentarim

may test their younglings in order to kill them off, but not everyone is *that* stupid. Why plan for almost inescapable failure?"

"Perhaps they're not testing the Malaugrym, but something else," Laeral offered. "Something they mistrust, so they'll risk only the young—and enthusiastic—to try it. That would square with what befell me."

Khelben and Elminster turned their heads and lifted an eyebrow each, in perfect unison. Laeral managed not even to smile this time.

"Befell you?" Khelben prompted, which was unusual impatience for him. Beneath that calm gravity, he must be excited.

"I could not see who attacked us, until the wild magic broke over them," Laeral reminded him gently. "The spell attack, yes, but it seemed to be born from empty air, not a foe. What I could see of the bedchamber beyond the doorway seemed empty, and the body of the Malaugrym should have blocked all view of the bedchamber from me."

"A cloaking magic, then," Elminster said, nodding. "They're testing something that hides them from us."

"And only us," Laeral added. "The 'prentices could see the Malaugrym normally. Poor Ushard may just have been distracted."

"His attention was permanently elsewhere," Khelben said darkly.

"It certainly is now," Elminster agreed, his lips twisting into a mirthless smile. "Servants and guards readily saw the Malaugrym who got into the palace in Silverymoon, too. So this cloak is set against *us*—the Chosen. The 'how' we can wonder about later, and the answer to 'why now' is almost certainly to take advantage of chaos across the Realms, so guards won't be guarding and watchers not watching—"

"And great power walks the land for those who can devise some way of taking it," Laeral reminded them.

Khelben looked at her. "I doubt I'm archmage enough to tear divine powers from an avatar, master them, and hold on to them—and most of the Malaugrym aren't half the wizards we are."

"Ah, but we're not half the arrogant dancing idiots *they* are," Elminster told him, a bleak smile growing on his face. "That's what they'll be after, all right, the ambitious ones. The older, craftier ones will probably settle for sliding into Faerûn and taking over a kingdom here and a region there, by slaying kings and envoys and taking their shapes, using this cloak to hide themselves from our prying eyes."

"They might have picked a quieter time in the Realms," Khelben said grimly.

"But they did not, love, and 'twas ever thus," Laeral replied quietly, "and you know it."

"Yes," Khelben growled, getting to his feet. Floating in the air across the chamber, the nearest of his blackstaves moaned in sympathy. He glanced at its pattern of winking lights to be sure that nothing was amiss and then looked down at Elminster. "If that cloak works," he growled, "they'll be able to hide from us with impunity. They'll come after us to slay us, one by one and time after time, until Tymora smiles upon them. We've got to find out just who knows how to raise the cloak, and destroy them and all their work so that no clever Malaugrym or other foe coming along later can craft other cloaks."

"It's not the best season for touring the Castle of Shadows," Elminster murmured with the beginnings of a smile on his face, "but I may already have eyes and ears—if not much else—there."

Laeral gave him a look. "I'd not call those Harpers and the lady Knight of yours little more than eyes and ears," she said reprovingly.

"Nor would I," Elminster agreed. "I meant something else."

Khelben gave him a look of failing patience and asked, "*What*, O grand and mysterious one?"

"Well, 'tis often said ye must get a head in this world . . ." Elminster began innocently. Laeral, who knew what was coming, nudged his ribs with one shapely boot and groaned.

* * * * *

The Castle of Shadows, Kythorn 19

"Wine?" Amdramnar held out the slim, fluted bottle, but three heads were shaking firmly.

"No, thank you," Shar said calmly, her fingers laced about the hilt of her still-drawn sword as she sat with its point grounded on her boot. "We're not thirsty."

The Malaugrym half-smiled. "Inform me when that situation changes, please," he said smoothly, as a velvet-shrouded seat glided up out of the floor behind him. "I can assure you that whatever I offer will be safe to consume."

He poured himself a glass and sat, adding, "Hard as you may find it to believe, trust *is* something that can grow between us."

"Well, then," Belkram said, a trifle less smoothly, leaning forward in his seat, "perhaps we can begin by trading information."

"An excellent idea," the Malaugrym said, growing another hand. As they watched, fascinated—for it looked identical to his other limbs and to their own—it deftly took his wineglass, leaving his other hands free to gesture. "Pray state what it is you'd like to know, and what you offer in trade for it."

"Who and what the Malaugrym are," Itharr said calmly, "and what your folk intend to do in the—in Faerûn."

Amdramnar nodded. "An inquiry bound to touch on sensitive areas before it is done. And for such lore you will give me—?"

"Tongue-fencing is not a sport all of us here favor," Sharantyr told him bluntly. "What do you want to know?"

The Shadowmaster raised an eyebrow. "Oh? You show mastery of it, though. As to my desires, they approximate yours. I want to know who *you* are, and why you're here. What are your intentions in Shadowhome?"

"Clear and civil enough," Itharr said. "Who begins?"

"As host," Amdramnar said smoothly, "I feel under some obligation. A little, then, you shall have. My name you know. I am a male of the blood of Malaug, a family who can shapeshift, descended from the sorcerer of that name."

"Who was this Malaug?"

Amdramnar shrugged. "I'm not a historian, and we tend to speak the same few admiring phrases about the family founder, without really knowing overmuch. He's been dead a long time." He sipped wine. "All I really know is that Malaug was a human mage, the first in Toril to find his way here and master the use of shadow in magic."

"What *is* shadow, anyway?"

"It is the formless, ever-changing stuff of this demiplane. Sages—even among our kin—argue a lot about what shadow really is, but most of us consider the matter something like this. Shadow is the mobile, mutable essence of Shadowhome, a fog that is everywhere, as air is everywhere in Faerûn. It absorbs energies and traces of whatever it flows past, and uses these energies to move about. Shadow can easily be harnessed—as a power source and as a raw material—to make things, or used to change things or do things. Its unevenly stored energy gives it lighter and darker areas, although it usually looks sort of gray, like sea mist or moon shadows in Faerûn."

"You can make things out of it—solid, permanent things?"

"Well, nothing is permanent. The shadows are ever changing by nature. But yes, some of us can craft items, tools, furnishings, even weapons from it. Much of this castle is made of shadows, and it changes, most of it, only slowly. Learn to fear shadow here, for those who do not learn may die, killed by creatures out of shadow or by their own foolhardy actions."

"Some of you use magic, too," Shar said slowly.

"As with other humans," the shapeshifter said with a smile. "A few of us are mages; most are not."

"Forgive the manner of my asking," Itharr said quietly, "but you are . . . human?"

"Of course. We can take other shapes—as you yourselves have found, shadow tugs at everyone who enters Shadowhome—but we are humans underneath the shapes we take."

"I was wondering about that," Belkram said, looking at his own hands.

Amdramnar spread his hands. "Here in my chambers, as in most inhabited rooms of the castle, the wild effects of shadow are lessened by enchantments and habit and . . . the force of our wills. Out in the passages, shadows play, though Malaugrym learn to counter unwanted effects until it becomes a habit. Your shifting marked you as mortal. Only the young of my family care to indulge in uncontrolled shifting as they go about the castle."

"I see," Belkram said. "Can we learn to control our own bodies?"

The Shadowmaster's shoulders lifted in a shrug. "Perhaps," he said, "perhaps not. Some have come to join our ranks and mastered shadow readily. Others never do."

"Some have come to join you?" Sharantyr asked. "From Faerûn?"

"From many places," their host replied, raising his glass.

"Well then, why haven't we heard of you, across the Realms?" Itharr asked, frowning.

"Realms-wide recognition of us, and knowledge of our natures, is not something we welcome," Amdramnar said, his smile dimming a trifle. "So many folk in your world fear and hate others who have power they do not, or seek to seize such powers for their own purposes. The sorcerers of Thay and Zhentil Keep, in particular, have hunted us. Common folk from the Sea of Swords to the Celestial Sea think we're dopplegangers come to eat them, when our paths cross. We've grown rather tired of always finding swords thrust through our innards."

"But you do come to the Realms," Belkram said slowly, as if listening to some inner voice, "and take away women. Several sages have told us this."

Amdramnar raised his eyebrows. "Oh? It's not an amusement I'm personally aware of. Were they sure Malaugrym were taking maidens? This sounds like one of those 'dark dragon' tales old nurses scare young brats with."

"You need them for breeding," Belkram said inexorably, "because female Malaugrym are barren."

Their host shrugged. "Forgive me. I must reveal ignorance of this because, as you may have gathered, I am not a woman." He sipped at his wine and added, "I should warn you, however, that from what I do know—and know well—of the temperament of the ladies of my family, this is not a wise topic of conversation when you're in their hearing." He smiled faintly. "Ah, we do have a family tradition of duels—on the spot—to answer what are regarded as insults."

He set down his glass and added, "It seems you've made a good beginning at getting to know my kin, and I'd like to learn as much, if I may, about yourselves. It's not every day I meet visitors from Faerûn upon the stairs."

Amdramnar leaned forward. "This much I can tell. You are friends, companions-at-arms, and know each other. You are adventurers, or at least more comfortable on forays into the unknown than say, a potter or cowherd might be. There my useful information ends. Tell me more, if you would, such as your names and where you hail from and whatever led you from there to Shadowhome."

"Belkram is my name," Belkram said calmly, "and that's Itharr. We're both rangers, wandering the Realms getting to know its ways, a common thing for folk in our line of work to do. One travels the wilds of Faerûn, looking for the places one is loved and needed." Itharr nodded his agreement but said nothing.

"And I am Sharantyr," the lady Knight told him. "I dwell in Shadowdale, and yes, I am an adventurer. We grew restless and accompanied a friend of ours on a journey as his sword escort. The Realms have become dangerous this last year, and he was headed through Daggerdale, which has been a perilous land for some time, thanks to the Zhentarim."

"Ah, yes," the Shadowmaster said with a bleak smile, "we've had our own occasions to thank those ambitious wizards of Zhentil Keep." He bent his head to one side. "*Through* Daggerdale, you say?"

Sharantyr shrugged. "He didn't . . . live to tell us his destination."

Amdramnar's eyebrows lifted. "Oh? Some misfortune befell him?"

"He was killed," she said flatly, "by some rival mages. A day ago. This morning, wandering open country in Daggerdale, we stumbled through some sort of glowing door and found ourselves here, in your castle."

"Oh? Where in the castle?"

They gave him three shrugs. "Somewhere shadowy," Itharr told him, straight-faced. The Shadowmaster almost smiled.

"I . . . see," he replied. "And who was your friend? 'Rival mages,' you said. Was he a mage of some reputation?"

"Oh, yes," Belkram replied quickly. "Quite famous, in the Dalelands at least. His name was . . . Elminster of Shadowdale."

Eyebrows rose. "I *have* heard of him, yes," Amdramnar said mildly, reaching for his glass. "He must have been, oh, several hundreds of years old, at least."

Itharr nodded. "We believe so." The Shadowmaster fixed bland eyes on him and seemed to be waiting for him to say more, but the burly ranger spread his hands to indicate he had no more to say, and kept silence.

"Would you judge that the gate that brought you here was of his making?" Amdramnar asked. "Could he have been taking you to it, perhaps?"

Sharantyr and Belkram spoke together, "No." After exchanging quick glances, Shar went on. "We don't think so. The place where we camped was not in quite the direction we'd been faring, and he'd said nothing of such things to us." She let a note of sadness creep into her voice and added, "He . . . liked to talk. There were very few things about magic that he didn't warn us about, not just on this venture but always, in all the time I've known him."

The Shadowmaster frowned. "I'm sorry to hear of his passing," he murmured, "though not all of my kin would share that view, I'm afraid. Some of the elders here in the castle are—were—sworn foes of his. Just what disagreements they had with him were very much before my time, so I've never known just why this . . . coolness . . . existed between Elminster and my kin." He stirred. "Nevertheless, Shadowdale—Faerûn—has lost a great mage, and that's something all should be saddened by. 'Tis only the advances in magecraft that make life, in whatever small ways, better and better with the passing years. Are things seen this same way in Shadowdale?"

"They are." Sharantyr agreed. "Though the power of sorcery corrupts far too many men, and far too often, some good always finds its way down to the farmhands and the honest tradesfolk. His death diminishes us all."

Amdramnar frowned over his glass, then looked up. "What you say leaves me downcast, but also curious. If Elminster of Shadowdale knew nothing of the gate that brought you here, how came it into being, and when?" He smiled thinly. "It's no secret that we haven't seen any stream of visitors from Daggerdale before you."

It was Itharr's turn to shrug. "Truly, we went through the gate by accident. We've heard of such things before— fireside tales of wizards fighting wizards are full of them—but we'd never seen one. At first, well, I thought it was some sort of trap to lure us, or even something to do with mating, that a will o' wisp had spun."

The Shadowmaster chuckled. "Oh, that's something I've never thought of. How *do* they mate, I wonder?" He set aside his glass again. "Can you find this end of the gate again, to get back home?"

Sharantyr shook her head. "No," she said simply. "We don't even know for sure if they work in both directions."

"Well, some do, and some . . . ," their host replied, tilting his head from side to side in a gesture of resignation. Then he leaned forward again. "Some of my kin certainly know sorcery enough to get you back to Faerûn, though just where you'd emerge is another matter. I must warn you, however, that such powerful spells are regarded as valuable, and the caster will expect payment"—he eyed the sword Sharantyr held—"in the form of a service, if you have nothing more tangible that you're willing to part with." He smiled and leaned back again, waving a dismissive hand. "However, that can be a problem for another day."

The Shadowmaster spread his hands to indicate the room around them. "Now that you're here, however accidental your journey, what are your plans?"

"Uh, to get home again safely," Belkram said with a tentative smile. The shapeshifter nodded approvingly.

"A wise ambition," he said. "I must warn you that, were you to wander freely about the castle, you might well be attacked by those of my kin who fear you're spies for an army of mages from Thay or elsewhere. Or you just might talk too loosely of what you've seen when you get back home, and spur someone more greedy than prudent into trying to take magic from us."

He held up a gentle hand to indicate he suspected them of no such failings, and added, "Moreover, shadows are strange things, as you've seen. There are some among us whose wits have . . . shall we say, been changed by their experiences with shadow. They aren't safe to themselves or to the rest of us. For some of these unfortunates, the sight of mortals is a goad that enrages them into attacking in beast shape or hurling the most damaging spells they know, or . . . similar behavior. You'll readily see why wandering about the castle with no good plan is asking for trouble."

Amdramnar stood up. "Please don't misunderstand me," he continued, walking slowly to a sideboard, "if I say that it might be safest for you if you remained here in my chambers. In fact, I'd like you to stay here tonight, if you will. I've room enough to spare to afford you private rooms, all three, and your own bathing and cooking facilities. I must confess I find you entertaining, and welcome a chance to talk more with you about life in Faerûn and, I suppose, tell you more of things in Shadowhome."

He turned, a platter in his hands, and smiled. "On the other hand, I know you're curious about the castle—who wouldn't be?—and I'll quite understand if you'd like to explore it. It would be cruelly remiss of me, however, to let you walk out that door without providing you with my protection, or some small magical defense, or something to keep you from another distressing encounter such as the one during which I first met you. And I must stress that not all of my kin would be as easily defeated as Phenanjar."

"Well," Belkram began, "w—"

"We'd be happy to stay with you this night," Sharantyr said firmly, giving the Shadowmaster her first real smile in some time, "and talk further. Is there a place we could . . . ah, refresh ourselves? And is there anything we could do to help with a meal? We don't want to be a hindrance to you in your living, or in your affairs."

The Shadowmaster waved a dismissive hand. "As to the first, go through that door, though I fear you'll find the facilities somewhat . . . different. We usually leave wastes behind us through changing shape, you see, and let the shadows take away what we don't want." He smiled broadly and went on. "As to the second, be at ease. We can prepare food together if you'd like, or you can leave things to me, as you prefer. It's no hindrance, and I'm delighted to have you."

He set down the platter and turned to the door. "Here," he said, "let me show you. You might find that your sword—"

"Feels best if it stays with me," Sharantyr murmured softly, and he gave her a surprised look.

"Ah, yes, of course," Amdramnar replied, and opened the door by holding his palm up in front of it. He indicated a dim passage beyond. "You see," he said. "Now, if you'd feel more comfortable venturing down it together, by all means. Your travel arrangements are your own."

"That won't be necessary," Sharantyr said, whirling about to stare hard into Belkram's eager face. The ranger had already opened his mouth to offer. Staring at her eyeball to eyeball, he shut it again, blinked, gave her a weak smile, and sank back into his seat.

The Shadowmaster turned quickly back to the platter with what sounded suspiciously like a snort, and announced, "I'll just get the meat and bring it back here. I won't be much time at all."

And he strode away through the mists, another door

opening for him in what had seemed to be a dark and solid wall. Belkram promptly leaned over to Itharr and said in his ear, "If I hear much more of this smooth-as-silk politeness, I may spew! Have you ever heard the like? Not a word wrong. He's worse than a Waterdhavian courtier!"

"*Better* than a Waterdhavian courtier, Belk," Sharantyr told him severely, bending over them both. "Better, do you hear me? I'm rather enjoying it, for a change. Heed ye, gentle sirs!"

"Ye gods, he hasn't got you believing him, has he?"

"He's probably listening," Shar hissed, shaking her head to indicate "no." She straightened, strode quickly across the room, paused in the doorway their host had shown her, and looked uncertainly back at them. "Itharr!" she hissed, and beckoned. He came.

"Stand in this doorway," she said, "as if you have to . . . go, you know . . . and don't let the door close. I don't want to be trapped on the other side of a stone wall that won't open for me, fighting to the death, while you two sit in here with him swapping 'and then I changed shape and she swooned' stories!"

Itharr looked hurt. "I don't know any such stories to trade. You'll have to tell me some."

"*Itharr!*" she wailed under her breath.

"Go," he whispered, nodding as he took up his position in the doorway. "And . . . be quick!"

"I intend to," they heard her soft voice floating back to them. "I certainly intend to."

Sharantyr was as good as her word. She arrived back through the door, panting and with the sword pulsing sullenly in her hands, a scant instant before their host returned, his platter piled high with what looked like slabs of pork cooked in a variety of green herbs.

"Boar?" Belkram asked, sniffing the unfamiliar, faintly lemony scent.

"Ah, no," Amdramnar replied, looking a little uneasy. "Actually it's . . . roast shadowslug." He watched them draw back and added, "Er . . . from an earlier meal, too."

He took up a fork and speared a piece, saw them all

watching, and muttered, "Excuse me," as one of his hands grew into a needle-sharp knife of bone. Sawing off a long strip of meat, he fed it delicately into his mouth, put forth a shockingly long tongue to lap some of the herbed sauce from his chin, and murmured in appreciation.

"It's very good," he said, "and it's not harmful to you . . . really. Try a little." He offered it to Itharr, who held up a warding hand wordlessly. Then he offered it to Belkram, who leaned forward with a smile, astonishing his companions, and said, "Yes, I think I'd like to try. It looks wonderful!"

The Shadowmaster gave him a genuine smile, and Belkram realized something. Taking the proffered small piece, he sat back, turning his head slightly so Amdramnar couldn't see the wink of reassurance he gave Shar, and bit into the shadowslug with gusto.

The stone that was Syluné vibrated soundlessly, telling him that—so far as she could tell—the meat was safe. He chewed, aware that their host was watching his face almost anxiously. It *was* good.

"Did you cook this?" Belkram asked him eagerly. "It's great!"

Amdramnar beamed, and Belkram knew he'd guessed right. "As a matter of fact," the Malaugrym said proudly, "I did, and—"

And then the door they'd come in by slid open by itself, and his face changed. Belkram's head swung around, and he suddenly wished he hadn't eaten a piece of shadowslug—or anything else.

The passage outside was full of Shadowmasters in human form, standing tall and grim and silent, their faces hard. One shouldered into the room and glared around at them all.

Amdramnar saw Shar's hands tighten on her sword and put out his hand in a quick quelling gesture.

The newcomer's eyes slid coldly over all of them, lingering for a moment on Sharantyr's sword, and came to rest, as if nailed there, on Amdramnar's face.

"I had heard," their Malaugrym visitor said coldly,

"that you were entertaining humans in your chambers, but I hadn't thought even you to be quite so foolish. It appears that, sadly, I was wrong."

"And not for the first time," Amdramnar said coolly, "though this is the first time I've had an *uninvited* guest cross the threshold of my chambers."

"I don't like such dangers being harbored—even embraced—in our midst without all of us being informed," the newcomer said tightly, ignoring Amdramnar's words. "Such offal must be"—he raised a hand that slowly became a thick, powerful, sucker-studded tentacle—"destroyed!"

17
Hot and Cold Running Receptions

The midmorning sun laid dappled patches of golden light and shadow across the forest trail. Elminster appeared out of empty air behind his favorite boulder. He sniffed, frowned, and looked critically at the nearby evidence that some wolf had been using it as a boundary marker. Ah, well. Life in Faerûn was at least never dull.

He looked to one side, frowned again, and rubbed his nose. Small wonder the wolves had been about. Enough fresh-gnawed bones to make up at least a dozen folk lay strewn down the hillside in the lee of the rocks. Hmm. It had been his experience that feeding hungry wildlife wasn't usually the goal of so many kindhearted folk in one locale, during peacetime. He'd found the spot, right enough, so 'twas time to stow the 'prentice philosophy. To work!

Stepping out from behind the stone, the Old Mage strolled down to the path, hitching at his robes so that it might look to an observer as if he'd had urgent business in the bushes off the trail.

Reaching the cart ruts, he stepped up onto the worn grassy strip between them and trudged along. As he'd expected, one of the bushes beside the path ahead trembled slightly.

"Oh, a wizard may well find time for much fun (for much fun), but an old rogue's work is seldom ever done (ever done)!" Elminster warbled, taking up a tune he'd heard a world away from this one.

"Aghh! Do ye *mind!*" A deep voice growled from the bushes. "I was plannin' just to rob thee, but if ye don't'en belt up, I'll be happy to gut ye instead."

"*Gut* me?" Elminster looked properly terrified. As expected, he drew back and turned to run, only to find himself staring into the grinning, unshaven visage of a half-orc whose parentage was attested to by one broken-off tusk, flat, piglike features, and a cruel smile.

"Don't mind Glorym. He's not hungry today, so he probably won't nibble on ye, being as ye aren't a pretty maiden." The brigand leader stepped into view, guffawing loudly at his own jest and scratching himself with his free hand in an ongoing quest for fleas. The other hand held an axe that might have once served to chop down trees—young saplings, that is, and several hundred years ago.

Elminster looked from one outlaw to the other and suppressed a wild urge to hoot with laughter by quavering, "Wha-what will ye be doin' to me?"

"Well, minstrel boy," the brigand leader drawled, displaying teeth that might have made a boar envious—an old and very sick boar, mind—"the proud army of which I'm swordlord hasn't been paid in a goodly while, and—"

"Pike," the half-orc rumbled from behind Elminster, "what army? There's just ye 'n me, near's I can tell—"

"Hush!" the brigand leader said severely, and favored Elminster with another crookedly reassuring smile. "Pay no attention to my friend behind ye. I—hem hem blaugh ahum—chose him for this duty because of his, ah, kindly ways toward donors we meet on the road. Donors, I say, because 'tis our habit to, at this time, ask ye for some small tokens for passage on our road . . . a toll it pains us to request, mind ye, but—"

Elminster forestalled more of this by scaling a gold piece into the man's grubby outstretched palm.

Pike's eyes widened as he looked down at it, and then narrowed. He scratched his nose and stepped forward.

"Well," he said jovially, " 'tis a beginning, right enough, an' I'm right grateful to see ye've got the idea of the th—"

Elminster added a second gold coin to the first and turned to face Glorym. "Would ye like the same? I'm in a hurry . . ."

"Aye," Glorym rumbled, but Pike's eyes had narrowed again. "In a hurry? That's an awful shame . . ."

Elminster smiled pleasantly at him and said, "So it is, friend Pike, because I perceive ye and Glorym here share the same fondest wish. Ye both want to die rich."

He gestured, and both brigands wriggled in midair, their faces telling the world of their sudden terror at discovering they could no longer move. As the white-bearded, gaunt old man between them crooked a finger, one of the gold coins in Pike's palm drifted smoothly through the air to settle into Glorym's grasp.

Elminster smiled at them both and steered their frozen, floating bodies together, gently arranging their hands on each other's throats, tossing away their weapons, and closing the fingers of their free hands firmly around the coins. Then he snapped his fingers. Magic made none-too-clean fingers tighten, and the trapped, frightened eyes began to bulge almost immediately.

"And so ye shall," he added brightly, and went off down the road whistling.

* * * * *

The Castle of Shadows, Kythorn 19

"Oh? They must be destroyed?" Amdramnar's tone was lazily unconcerned as he set aside the platter of shadowslug and rose from his chair, his form swelling visibly. "I think not."

The Harpers made as if to rise, but Sharantyr laid a quick restraining hand on Belkram's arm, her eyes on the motionless Malaugrym out in the corridor, and Belkram froze. The three of them stared out at the watchers in the passage, who stared right back, faces impassive.

Between them, in the small open space encircled by the velvet-shrouded seats of Amdramnar's forechamber, tentacles and surging rubbery pseudopods and knots of muscled bulk were boiling and trembling in a tight mass. Sparks and brief sprays of radiance burst around them but seemed constrained by an invisible cylinder surrounding the entangled Malaugrym. A continuous din of snarls, barks, roars, and hisses came from a score of dripping maws that both combatants had grown— eyeless mouths on the ends of wormlike stalks that bit at each other in mindless savagery, rising and falling like surf around the heaving bodies.

Shar and the Harpers had never seen such savage energy sustained for so long and contested in so small a space. The foes began to grow within the cylinder as one found a strangling grip on the other. The trapped one—the three Faerûnians could no longer tell them apart—tried to reach air by throwing out breathing tubes, and the other sought to overtop and ensnare these. Entwined, they soared up inside the cylindrical shield, growing quickly toward the mist-shrouded ceiling of the chamber, and all the while, the stone-faced Malaugrym stood silent and unmoving in the corridor, just watching.

And then, suddenly, it was done. In a cascade of abruptly freed sparks, the cylinder collapsed and fell away from around the two gasping, heaving tentacled forms, to be followed, blurring instants later, by the dwindling of the two Malaugrym into human forms once more. The panting men glared at each other until the newcomer found breath enough to snarl a stream of curses that the listening humans could barely understand.

Then he whirled suddenly, lashing out with talons that shot to long-sword length in a trice, stabbing at Sharantyr's eyes.

She flung herself back in the seat and brought her blade up sharply, and the black, seeking talons melted away before the sword's quickening blue glow as suddenly as they had come. Shar stared over them into the Malaugrym's eyes and saw her death in the look of cold promise he gave her.

She replied with a wintry, silent smile that seemed to amuse him. He lifted his lip in a sneering answering grin as he backed toward the door.

"My thanks for the invigorating exchange of views,

Olorn," Amdramnar said in a voice that sounded like a sword blade softly sliding through a stomach, "but I'll expect a request to enter next time."

The other Malaugrym started to hiss a reply, but Amdramnar waved a hand and the door boomed closed with lightning speed, no doubt coming close to striking Olorn's face.

Their host held up his hand and muttered a quick incantation, then quickly touched the door that had just closed and the one Sharantyr had used earlier.

Then he turned, bowed to them, and sat down again. "My apologies, friends—if I may be so bold as to call you so, now that I've fought in your honor—but it appears that you're now enmeshed in our family disputes, like it or not. As you might have heard, that was Olorn, and he's an even more charming individual than Phenanjar. Was."

He gave them a little smile and added, "He's a tireless foe, I'm afraid. If you see him again, strike first—and to kill—or he'll slay you. It is also important that you know one thing more: Olorn's strong allies are two similarly young and ambitious Shadowmasters, Iyritar and Argast, though they try to keep their affiliation hidden from most of the kin. Both are good at sorcery—by your standards, very good—and you'd better consider yourselves at war with them both, as they'll no doubt behave as if you are, the moment Olorn tells them of what just occurred."

"What about you?" Itharr asked, eyeing the platter of shadowslug. "Are we a danger to you, now that others know we're here?"

Amdramnar shrugged. "Not really. I am thought odd by many of the kin, but so are many others, and tolerance must needs be the order of things in many family dealings. You saw how they watched but made no move? They were telling me of their neutrality in this, by that very action. It is how things are done in the castle."

* * * * *

Somewhere in Faerûn, then the Castle of Shadows, Kythorn 19

No one was around to see, so Elminster stepped behind a tree, became a bedraggled-looking crow, and leapt lightly to a leaf-shrouded branch. There he nestled up against the trunk and grew still.

And far away, in a corridor where shadows drifted idly in the ever-present gloom, a pale, grisly object that trailed white hair and a long white beard behind it like a tail faded slowly into solidity, flew purposefully forward through the shadows to a certain spot, and then rose up into the concealing gloom and waited.

A breath or so later, figures came into view down the passage. One was a man whose fingers were a nest of small eels wrapped securely about a scepter whose pale red glow parted the shadows like a slicing sword. The other was a loping, shambling thing of many snouts and protruding ears and eyestalks, a creature that whuffled and tapped the stones of the passage floor and walls with long, spidery fingers as it came.

"So have any of these idiots survived?" it asked sourly.

"I don't believe so," was the curt reply. "Well, perhaps one from the first foray, but no one's talking about it. Milhvar goes about grinning and saying arch things, almost as if he intended them to fail!"

"Why wouldn't he? If he kills off all the most rebellious or hopeless younglings, he won't be the only one who'll be going about grinning, either! Believe you me, there's parents in this castle who'd be relieved to see their own young gone . . ."

The two figures waved very different hands in front of a certain section of wall and it split in twain, drawing back to reveal an opening. The moment they'd passed through it, the humanlike Malaugrym turned around to survey the passage behind suspiciously but did not see the head floating above him, in the heart of a concealing drift of shadow.

The door whispered closed, and for some moments the

head stared down thoughtfully at where the Shadowmaster had been. Then it faded away.

* * * * *

The moment the Shadowmaster stepped back through the door that led to his larder, Belkram stretched and brought his hand down over the stone in his pocket. *Syluné*, he thought at it, concentrating hard.

Gently! The silent voice in his mind sounded reproachful.

Sorry, he told the Witch of Shadowdale, *but we've some urgency. Can we trust the food and drink here? Thanks for reassuring me about the shadowslug, but he's bringing a lot more. How will we know?*

I've told Shar to plead a delicate stomach, and Itharr to eat slowly, she replied, *so you're it, Harper bold. I'll vibrate or even sting you, like this, if something's dangerous.* Belkram nearly jumped out of his seat at the jolt he felt then, and favored her with a silent growl, which earned him a giggle in return. *And don't talk when he's out of the room. This lad leaves more spying spells lying around than a castle full of Zhentarim!* Her mind voice changed. *Whoops—'ware!*

Belkram just had time to bring his hand down and look casual before Amdramnar reappeared, several steaming platters balanced in his arms. "Feast is served, friends," he said, extending several arms out as if they were expandable poles to set platters down on side tables all over the room. Sharantyr grinned despite herself at the sight.

Itharr looked at the platter beside him and drew back. "Thanks, Amdramnar," he said steadily, "but . . . what is this? It looks . . . alive."

The platter held a bed of rice, and on it some sort of chopped and seared green vegetable rather like peppers. Among those deep green shells were brown, fried things that looked like worms in sauce . . . squirming worms.

Amdramnar leaned over. "Worms in sauce," he explained eagerly. "Tombworms, they're called. They live in the castle foundations. Taste like roast almonds, only better. You'll love them!"

The look Itharr gave him then almost made Shar choke forth all the wine she'd just sipped, but it was obvious that the Shadowmaster wasn't jesting with them. He genuinely loved good food and wanted to share his enthusiasms with someone. Three someones . . . even if they were rather wary guests.

If we live through this, Belkram thought silently, *I'm going to get you for this, Elminster, I really am!*

Syluné laughed lightly in his mind. *Do you know how many folk have said that, down the years?*

No, and I care not, Belkram told her sourly. *With what I'm planning to do to him, only one of us has to succeed.*

". . . And this," Amdramnar was saying enthusiastically, waving a platter, "is a special delicacy. Netherbird brains in shadowdark wine!"

Remember, Belkram reminded her darkly, *it takes only one.*

Sharantyr shuddered delicately, but when she looked to Belkram, he gave her a very slight reassuring nod. He'd better not be enjoying this, she thought to herself, and gingerly took a spoonful.

It *was* good, and Shar told herself, for perhaps the hundredth time that night, to relax. Her ribs and shoulders ached with tension, and yet the smiling young Malaugrym that she knew they could not trust was being a charming host, plying them with food and wine, and partaking just as heavily himself as he kept up a smooth and witty flow of conversation, deftly slipping in sly digs when talking to Belkram and Itharr until he had them insulting each other with the easy grace of yore. The seat was comfortable, the room warm, and . . . suddenly Shar stiffened and sat up once more, slapping a hand to the comforting hard length of Mystra's sword, where she'd propped it against the inside of her right thigh. Had that been a stealthy tug on the blade? She leaned forward to look, but found no tendril or tentacle. When she looked up sharply at Amdramnar, she found herself looking at the Shadowmaster's back, as he pointed out to Itharr a particular scene etched on the wall.

Not Amdramnar, then. What could have jolted her so? Did the Castle of Shadows have . . . shadow rats?

Shar sighed and set down her glass. Stop doing this to yourself, lass, she told herself sternly, hunching forward in her seat and laying a hand on the hilt of her blade.

And then she felt it again, a gentle probing near her ankle. She kicked back sharply and got up, whirling to see what could have touched her, and bumped Amdramnar solidly, thigh to thigh.

Their Malaugrym host looked at her, startled, and Sharantyr had to catch her breath. Gods, but he's beautiful, she thought. And then a tiny voice within her replied: Of course. He can make himself look like whatever you most want. It's how they catch their prey.

"What's wrong, Lady Sharantyr?" Amdramnar asked, real concern in his stormy gray eyes.

They hadn't been that hue before. They'd been blazing red when he fought Olorn. Enough of this! Sharantyr shook herself mentally, wondering if she was falling under some sort of spell, and said firmly, "I'm sorry. I was startled. The seat . . . it started . . . to touch my leg."

"Wise seat," Belkram told his plate, and Itharr chuckled.

The Malaugrym shook his head at them. "Are they always like this?" he asked, mild amusement in his eyes.

Sharantyr nodded serenely. "Yes," she said. "I pay them no mind. They're my swordbrothers."

The Shadowmaster seemed to freeze for a moment, then said, "You'll have to explain that to me sometime, after we deal with your seat." He leaned forward and pushed on the fabric. "All of this is shadowstuff," he explained to them, "and it responds to magic. Some shadows flee strong magic, and others try to merge with it. This seat is of the latter sort. Your blade is powerful magic indeed. May I ask where you got it?"

He straightened, holding her eyes with his own, his deep and somehow hungry gaze locked with hers. So this was it, at last, Sharantyr thought, heart suddenly racing. Belkram and Itharr watched her, their faces expressionless.

And then she thought: He has spoken truth to us since we met. Lied with truth perhaps, but cleaved to truth. Very well. I shall do the same.

"This blade was given to me by the goddess Mystra," she said. "I am here under her protection, and she watches what we do even now."

The Shadowmaster stood as if frozen, and she wanted —suddenly wanted desperately—to see him show just the smallest amount of shock. Or surprise. Anything but that smooth, almost mocking confidence.

His mouth did not fall open, but he did lick his lips and hesitate before choosing his next words, almost whispering, "And your true mission here, Lady Sharantyr?"

"Is not something I can reveal to you," Sharantyr told him gently, "if you would live." She saw his eyes flicker and added almost pleadingly, "It is not something that should bring doom upon you, if you behave well toward us."

Amdramnar bowed then, and they saw his mocking confidence return. "Then I shall strive to be the perfect host, Lady," he murmured, bending over her hand.

Smoothly she took her hand from his grasp, pretending not to see the little barbs that were showing just above the skin of his fingers, and smiled at him. "I have no complaints at all about your behavior," she told him softly.

"Uh-oh!" Belkram told the ceiling loudly. "We know what *those* words mean, don't we, Itharr?"

Itharr nodded. "We get to sleep in the passage tonight," he said forlornly. "I hope it's softer than the last hallway was."

Sharantyr gave them both murderous looks and tried to keep all hints of the laughter welling up within her off her face. These two Harpers! What a pair! Catching sight of the Shadowmaster's quizzical expression, she lurched a dangerous step closer to open laughter.

And then she saw the first glint of what might have

been fear in Amdramnar's eyes, and her heart surged in triumph. They'd just won the respect they might need to stay alive this night.

Of course, it was also the respect that might drive him to betray them on the morrow.

* * * * *

Somewhere in Faerûn, Kythorn 19

"Warriors of the Nose Bone obey no coward's orders!" The hobgoblin askarr almost spat the words. "We run only to hunt down those who flee from us! We do not run—ever—to flee from battle!"

"Then warriors of the Nose Bone are fools," growled the other hobgoblin, "and are better off dead, leaving the fields of Thar to those more worthy."

"More *worthy?*" The askarr followed that last snarled word by swinging his rusty-spiked morningstar with all his strength.

It whistled past its target's shoulder with a rattle of chain and crashed to the stones underfoot as its wielder fell forward, the blood-drenched point of a broadsword protruding from his back.

"Aye," its wielder said, snatching a replacement blade from the fallen askarr's scabbard. "More worthy, I said. Are yuh *deaf*, too?" He laughed harshly, made a rude gesture with his new sword—and with the long, dirty knife in his other hand—at the ranks of the Nose Bone, and trotted away.

And with a ragged roar, the hobgoblins of the Nose Bone turned from the cowering warriors of the Thentian caravan they'd attacked, and charged after the running hobgoblin who'd slain their leader.

The battlegar of the Splintered Sword, he was, and if they had their way, he'd soon be shattered bones on a cookfire, with all his band on side platters!

In moments, the crest of the hill was a shrieking, hacking mass of dying hobgoblins. One of them, who'd come up that hill running, just kept on going, flinging his captured Nose Bone blade away . . . and then his knife . . . and then his helm.

He seemed to dwindle as he ran, and by the time he reached the nearest tree, a trail of greaves and bracers and armor plate marked his route, and he stood almost naked, his unlovely hide dark with dirt. Then he grinned at the sky, scratched at his ribs, and became Elminster again for a moment before he shrank into a crow once more and leapt into the sky. He circled over the hilltop, cawing loudly to give any surviving hobgoblins an ill omen, and watched the Thentians hastily hitching up their beasts again and trying to move off in frantic, almost comical haste. Another caravan saved, another scrap of order salvaged from all this chaos.

Ao was going to owe him a lot, Elminster decided, before this Time of Troubles was through.

* * * * *

The Castle of Shadows, Kythorn 19

"The time has come, Milhvar, for some explanations," Ahorga said coldly, and the row of candles in the Great Hall of the Throne flickered as if in agreement.

Milhvar smiled that slow smile of his and spread his hands. "The cloak of spells was a project ordered by Dhalgrave before his unfortunate passing. Obedience to the will of the Shadowmaster High is the cornerstone of order among those of the blood of Malaug, something recognized by all of the diligent participants in this work, not merely myself. Many of us labored long and hard to weave a web of enchantments that would shield users fully against the perceptions—and the launched magic—of any of Mystra's Chosen. Only with such a shield can we hope to bring doom to Elminster."

"Yes, yes," Ahorga growled, rising against the candlelit shadows like an angry giant. "We've heard this self-serving 'I am loyal' speech before! I'm—"

"Going to hear it again," Milhvar said, his voice suddenly steely. "Come, Shadowmaster Ahorga. That is the least you can do to honor the memory of your daughter Huerbara, who sacrificed her life testing this cloak. She fell in battle nobly, striving against the might of the defenders of Silverymoon. Let her sacrifice not be in vain."

"Strutting mage," Ahorga snarled, advancing menacingly, "I've heard enough! For the loss of her life, yours is forfeit!" He flung four Malaugrym out of the way as if they were dolls and mounted the steps to where Milhvar stood. *She was worth ten of you!*" he roared in anguish, in a voice that shook that vast chamber. "She was the hope for the future of us all! I'll scream her name from every battlement of this castle as I break the bodies of those who wrought this wretched cloak, and every one of them shall *die!*"

Milhvar nodded to the cowled figure beside him. It stayed motionless for a long moment, as a trembling Ahorga hurled kin after kin out of the way, ascending the guarded steps of the stair, until Milhvar began to fear that a trick was being played on him, and that Ahorga was going to reach him after all while cool eyes watched slaughter through that cowl.

And then the robe fell away, and Huerbara stood revealed, nude in the candlelight so that her father could see the true, twisted form of her birthing and know her for his own. "Father!" she cried, delighted at his vow of revenge and his judgment of her worth. *"Father!"*

"Huerbara!" the giant Shadowmaster cried in a disbelieving shout of wonder that shook most of the castle. A gigantic tentacle swept her from her feet to his breast, under his searching gaze, and then he cried exultantly, *"Yes!* My daughter *lives!"*

Milhvar stood watching with a small smile on his face until a tentacle slithered out of the affectionate embrace of father and daughter, grew a small fanged mouth, and said to him in a soft, menacing rumble, "The cruelty of your tricks impresses even me, Milhvar. Watch your back hereafter, and spend no more Malaugrym lives on this fool's game of hunting down Elminster. Every one of us who dies is someone's son or daughter. You would trade all these lives for that of one old human wizard?

We should all be glad the House of Malaug is not a fruit stall, and you the vendor! How long would the stall survive?"

Milhvar stood very still as the tentacle withdrew, staring after it thoughtfully, and said nothing. When Huerbara looked back at where her mentor had stood with her atop the steps, exulting in the sure knowledge that her father loved her, Milhvar had faded away.

18
Shadows on the Castle Walls

Shadows swirled around them, blue-green and laced with white, and even Belkram had to admit the spherical room was beautiful.

"I worked on this for years," Amdramnar said proudly, "after I—" Abruptly he fell silent, and his three guests looked at him curiously. Under their gazes, he continued with some embarrassment, "after I saw a similar room in a satrap's pleasure palace in Calimport. Ah, through my scrying stone, of course."

Belkram hooted. "In use, was it?"

The Shadowmaster nodded, the ghost of a smile on his face. "I've not yet found sixteen willing and tattooed ladies to share it with me—with little gold rings and bells set into their skin all over—as the satrap enjoyed, but . . ."

"Someday," Itharr agreed.

"You're working on it," Belkram offered.

The Malaugrym shook his head slightly and smiled in spite of himself. "I see what you mean," he said to Shar, who smiled ruefully in response.

"They're handy for soaping your back, though," she offered. Amdramnar shrugged. "A man with tentacles has no need . . ." he said almost sadly, and then added, "I always like to have music when I bathe, and wine. Will you join me?"

"Join you? Ah, in the water?" Itharr asked.

"No, on the ceiling! . . . In the water, yes," the Shadowmaster said with mock severity. Looking straight into Itharr's eyes, he added quietly, "If you're fearing I'll grow tentacles like an octopus and pull all of you under to drown, fear no more. You are my guests and, I hope, my friends."

ED GREENWOOD

"Of course," the Harper answered hastily.

Why does this shapeshifter go on with all this? Belkram wondered. He'd forgotten that Syluné was with him, riding his thoughts, until she replied, *He plays a deeper game, with patience. Some men do, you know.*

His derisive reply had no words to it.

Sharantyr appeared to have come to a decision. "Is the water ready?" she asked. The Shadowmaster nodded, and waved a hand. "Warmer at this end, colder over there, and the floating pods hold soaps. Smell them until you find a favorite. I'll set out trays with some wines."

"Then let us begin," Sharantyr said, and held her sword up horizontally over her head. She whispered a word to it and let go—and it hummed a bright blue and hung motionless above her. Beneath its glittering edge the lady ranger bent over, put her hands to her leathers, and calmly began to disrobe.

The Shadowmaster looked at the hovering blade expressionlessly for a moment and then turned toward the door.

Itharr was out of his clothes and into the pool in a flash, coming up to rest his elbows on the edge and watch Sharantyr in frank and open admiration. She wrinkled her nose at him and flicked her fingers in a 'so?' expression she'd seen haughty Waterdhavian ladies use at feasts, but he went on staring, with a big grin on his face. She sighed, smiled, shook her head, and continued.

Belkram was also staring at her when a sudden thought struck him. *What am I going to do with you?* he asked Syluné.

Go to Sharantyr and bind me into her hair, came the reply, quick as a flash. *Haste!*

He made haste around the pool, and Sharantyr stiffened under his hands for only a moment before Syluné's mindtouch revealed all. A breath later, the deed was done.

Belkram stepped back smoothly and took her clothes as Amdramnar reappeared behind a small forest of floating bottles, but inside he felt suddenly alone—and afraid. Syluné's comforting voice was gone.

Stow it! she said in his mind then, as his fingers momentarily brushed Sharantyr's, came away with her chemise—and dropped it, distracted, as he saw what he was holding.

He made a snatch for it as it fell to the waiting waters, missed the grab, and saw a tentacle snake out over the pool to snatch it inches above immersion. The tentacle held up the garment delicately. Belkram said, "My thanks," and took the garment as if he thanked tentacles every day.

Then he realized what he'd done, and wore a curious expression as he set Sharantyr's clothes neatly aside and straightened up to work on his own.

Shar plunged into the pool with a gasp of pleasure, feeling cool liquid wash away the stickiness that always plagued her under body leathers. When she rolled over onto her back to float and listen to the softly welling music —where had a Malaugrym heard hill flutes and harps together?—she found a wineglass full of smoking blue vintage under her nose. She smiled in thanks and pure pleasure, and asked in her mind, *Must we kill them all?*

No, Sharantyr. You can keep one or two for . . . entertainment . . . but choose carefully, came Syluné's wry and surprising response. *Choose very carefully.*

* * * * *

Faerûn, The Misty Forest, Kythorn 19

Ramtharage, Keeper of the Fastness, almost whimpered in his seething rage and had to gasp out two long, shuddering breaths to calm himself enough to recall the words he'd need. These blasphemers must die!

It had been a day and a night since the Great Evil, and these men could not be allowed to live through this second day. For every moment that passed, the hurt to divine Eldath grew greater. Their sin must be purged before nightfall, that the cleansing of the Fastness could begin.

At about this time yestermorn, the Great Evil had occurred. The night sky had been wracked by the thunders and flashing evocations of mighty spells: showers of lightning lances, great cauldrons of skyfire, and near-blinding clashes of strange radiances. Surely gods had been contesting in the heavens, one with another. Such terrifying outpourings of magic had continued through the dawn. With full light, a smoking star had plunged from the heavens and crashed down like a hurled axe into the heart of the Fastness itself!

The clear, tranquil waters had been hurled skyward, the small sacred creatures who dwelt within them rudely slain, the carefully nurtured mosses and reverently placed stones of the banks flung about like handfuls of refuse and gravel. In one awful instant, the Fastness had been riven and despoiled.

The faithful of Eldath had not even finished tending to those of their number who'd been struck senseless or dashed and broken against the rocks and nearby trees when intruders had come through the woods—local rangers Ramtharage knew by sight, men who worshiped that *other* Lady of the Forest.

And these Mielikki worshipers hadn't even asked his permission for their intrusion, only arrived in grim haste with nets and long hooked poles and a shamelessly clad witch in their midst. And then these desecrators had dragged the pool! Profaned the ruined Fastness anew!

When their hooks and ropes and probings failed to bring up what they sought, the witch had summoned up a dark spell that lifted the tortured waters once more, only this time all of a piece, floating upward as if held in a vast, invisible bowl.

With the polluted sacred waters hanging dark and heavy over their heads, those rangers of Mielikki had torn the sky rock out of the muddy, naked depths of the Fastness and borne it away. The witch even had the temerity, the utter flaming gall, to complain about the weight of the waters, the sacred pool of the Goddess!

"A sign of the goddess," they'd called the man-high stone as they hauled it away, gouging a trail through the sacred earth that still cut away through the trees, raw and bright, like a wound made by a slashing sword

There was only one goddess whom rangers could speak of so: Mielikki. Our Lady of the Forest.

Ramtharage's lips twisted in fresh anger at that name. He strode to stand beside the stone's trail and look along it, deliberately letting the anger build in him again, for he was not a violent man, and fury all too soon made him feel sick. But he must be strong; this desecration of Eldath's holy place must be avenged.

He'd begun the work he must do. Three of the blasphemers hung helpless across the pool, entangled in a webwork that Ramtharage in his fury had spun no less than seven trees into, and more vines than he'd bothered to count. He stared at their fearful, sweating faces stonily as his people gathered behind him, for priests of Eldath did no violence, and yet these men must die.

When the crowd was large enough, Ramtharage began the long walk around the torn edge of the pool. Behind him, someone began the Chant of the Fastness, and it swelled as he walked on, his bare feet plunging into mud that should not be there. Uncaring, he strode over sharp stones and tangled, broken branches alike, to bring doom to the desecrators.

When he stood below them, he held out one hand for the knife and raised the other. Around him, the gathered faithful of Eldath froze into utter stillness, and it was so quiet that a thin breeze could be heard rustling the leaves in distant trees.

"You have all seen the desecration of our holy Fastness, sacred place of Eldath," Ramtharage said, lifting his voice only a little. "Sacrifices of atonement cannot begin to make up the slight to our Lady. So evil an act can only be seen as the first blow in a war between two faiths that can no longer walk Faerûn as friends. The Sundering has begun. Let it now proceed!"

He raised the smooth-polished knife so that it flashed back the sun, and tried not to notice how badly his hand trembled.

"Eldath calls upon her priests to refrain from slaying and the work of war," Ramtharage continued, "and so it may be that what I do now will cost me the favor of our blessed Lady . . . and my powers. Yet my duty is clear!"

He looked to the three rangers in their living bonds and folded his arms, calling on that deep well of calm within him to quell his raging anger. He had to reach far deeper to find it than had ever been the case before.

But find it he did, and control with it, enough to work the spell and begin to rise from the tortured earth, a foot from the ground . . . and then another . . . ascending slowly until he was within striking distance of those he must sacrifice.

"This is not something I undertake lightly," he told them.

"Nor us," one of the helpless men told him grimly. "Nor us!"

The priest glared at the man who'd spoken. "Do not presume to profane this moment!"

"Ramthar," the eldest of the three asked him quietly, "why are you doing this?"

"Aye," the third ranger spoke. "What does shedding blood have to do with stones falling into pools?"

"Enough!" the priest spat at them. "*Be still!*" His hands were shaking again as he lifted the knife on high. "Your blood must be your payment for what you did here!" He whirled in the air to look down on the crowd and thundered, "Is this not right? Is this not *just?*"

"*Aye,*" many voices thundered. But in the silence that followed that impressive shout, another voice spoke from the ranks of the faithful, a voice that was not raised, yet somehow carried easily to the ears of all present.

"Ramthar, I've never heard such idiotic raving in my life! What are ye, mad? Since when do priests of Eldath spill the blood of those who embrace other forest faiths? Does Eldath know what ye're about?"

"*Blasphemer!*" the priest thundered. "Who are you, to use Her name so lightly?"

The man who'd challenged him was rising now, rising into the air as Ramtharage had done, passing the shoulders of the staring worshipers. He was an old man with white hair and beard, who seemed familiar.

"Elminster of Shadowdale, I am," the old man told the assembly. "Perhaps ye've heard of me."

Ramtharage gulped and turned scarlet and gabbled, "Leave this place! This is not your affair! This is a just and fitting punishment for a wrong to holy—"

"Ahh, belt up and stow it," Elminster told him crisply. "It's murder, that's what it'll be, and I'll see that the swordcaptain hangs ye from yonder tree for it, if ye're foolish enough to go through with this nonsense!"

"Be still!" the Keeper of the Fastness thundered. "You have no right to speak here! Y—"

"Ye're *wrong*, Ramthar," Elminster said in a voice of cold iron. "All folk of Faerûn should have the right to speak as they please, anywhere. 'Tis not the duty Eldath laid upon thee to forbid speech, or anything else. Thy task is to nurture and aid, not to restrict or punish. Ye forget thy proper place."

"You *dare*—?" Ramtharage was purple now and struggling for words. "I—silence him!" Struck by this sudden thought, he leaned forward and told the faithful, "Silence him! Strike him down!"

Angry voices rose in agreement, and fists waved in the air, but no one near the archmage quite dared to leap up and lay a hand on his booted feet. They had all heard tales of the might of the Old Mage of Shadowdale.

"Bring him down with stones!" Ramtharage snarled, waving his fist in the air. "Strike him down with boughs! Strike for our sacred Lady's sal—"

"This has gone far enough," Elminster said quietly, but his next words rolled around the Fastness with the force and volume of a thunderclap. "Let this madness be at an *end!*"

He waved one bony hand, and stillness came again to the clearing, the utter stillness of the magically bound. Elminster looked around at the crowd, frozen in midmovement, only their eyes and lungs free to move . . . and they looked helplessly back at him. Then he turned slowly, treading air, to squint at the priest who held the knife raised and ready. Elminster shook his head in disgust.

"Ye wouldn't listen to them," El told Ramtharage, "and ye wouldn't listen to me. Who *would* ye believe, if they told ye flat out in words even ye, Ramtharage Druin, can understand, that ye were wrong? Who would ye heed?" He touched the priest's lips with a finger. "Speak."

"The Goddess herself speaks to me," Ramtharage told him proudly, "and I will hear the counsel of no other."

"Right," Elminster said briskly. "Thankee." He stepped back and turned to face the crowd. "Ye all heard the solemn words of the Keeper of the Fastness, I trust?"

They struggled to reply, and could not. In their enforced silence, they stood and listened to the old wizard chant something long and low and full of words that echoed strangely and yet seemed to clang and slither upon the ear. And then Elminster stretched his arms wide and brought the chant to an end.

Two women appeared, one by each of his outstretched hands. One was tall and shapely yet robust, clad in leathers like the three pinioned rangers. Her garb was of muted green and brown, and her russet hair curled long and free. Her eyes were large and of the deepest brown, and when she moved, she drew the eye of every man there.

The other woman was as tall and as shapely, but thin, and her hair seemed like spun glass or flowing ice—the tresses of a ghost, that one could see through. She stood still and at peace. Her eyes were of the deepest green, and she wore green silks that did not hide what lay beneath them, yet she brought awe and stillness upon those who looked at her.

She nodded gravely to Elminster and then to the other lady, who smiled back at her. Then the lady in leather walked on air to where Ramtharage stood frozen. When she moved, it was with the surge of the leaping buck and the casual grace of the prowling panther.

"Do you know me, Ramthar?" The voice was low, even purring. The priest trembled, sighed, and spoke. "N-no, Lady," he husked, and licked dry lips. She stretched forth a long finger and touched him.

Sweat broke out upon his brow in a flood and washed down his cheeks. "I am Mielikki, and I tell you truly, diligent priest, that you err in this. I call upon you to free the men you have thought to sacrifice."

"Uh . . . ah . . . I do not worship thee, Lady," the Keeper of the Fastness managed to say, almost gabbling in terror. Then he whimpered at the flash of her eyes, and flung up his hands as if to ward off a blow.

The Lady merely curled her lip and drew back from him, turning her head. "Datha?"

The other apparition nodded and stepped forward. "But you do worship *me*, Ramtharage Druin . . . do you not?"

"M-my Lady?"

"I am Eldath," she said gently, "and you have done me much honor down the years. Will you deny me now?"

"No! Ah, no, divine Lady . . ."

"Then do as I bid. Free those men and apologize to hem for what you intended. Then go forth in the world and tell all who care that Eldath and Mielikki are friends and sisters, now and forevermore." She looked deep into his eyes and touched him with a finger. "Will you do this?"

Ramtharage shuddered and closed his eyes for an instant, then seemed to see the knife in his hand for the first time. He flung it away in disgust and went to his knees in the air. "Oh, Lady, I *will!*"

Eldath smiled almost impishly. "Good. That's settled, then." She turned briskly and embraced Mielikki, and hey both turned and shook hands with Elminster before Ramtharage's dumbfounded eyes.

"This was well done, mage," Eldath said, and Mielikki reached out and tousled the wizard's long but thinning white hair.

"Thanks," Elminster said dryly, bowing his head to hide his grin. He was still doing that when the air swirled like stars around him, and the sudden hubbub of movement and sound told him that the goddesses had gone, and banished all bindings in the Fastness in their going.

The Old Mage and the Keeper thumped unceremoniously to the ground in unison and looked at each other. Around them shouts and sobs and excited talk rose and swelled.

"Well," Elminster asked wearily. "Do ye believe *now?*"

"I . . . I do," Ramthar told him, and there were tears i꜍
the priest's eyes. "I came so close . . . to such a grievou꜍
mis—"

"But ye see that, and didn't do the thing," Elminster tol꜍
him briskly. "Good. About time. Now stop pontificating
free these very patient men"—he grinned up at the thre꜍
pinioned rangers, who grinned happily back—"and go d꜍
something useful." The Old Mage whirled around to poin꜍
at the pool. "Ye can clean up Eldath's Water, for a start."

"The Fastness, you mean," Ramtharage corrected hi꜍
almost happily.

"Lad, 'twas Eldath's Water nigh a century ago, when
first bathed in it," Elminster told him gruffly. As th꜍
priest stiffened in dawning indignation, the Old Mag꜍
waved a cheery hand and vanished, leaving them a꜍
staring at the empty air where he'd been.

"Gods!" the youngest ranger gasped. "He summone꜍
Our Lady—*two* goddesses, no less—just for us!"

"That, lad," said the grimy, sweat-soaked ranger besid꜍
him, "is why all Faerûn needs Elminster of Shadowdal꜍
He aids us, great and small, one at a time. All the god꜍
keep him from harm, I say."

The third ranger chuckled. "By some of the things
hear he's pulled, down the years, I don't doubt they d꜍
More'n that—I'll bet you the task keeps them right bus꜍
some nights!"

* * * * *

The Castle of Shadows, Kythorn 19

The shadows seemed to drift more slowly at nigh꜍
sliding with stately grace around the three sleepin꜍
Harpers. They lay sprawled on the floating silks an꜍
cushions Amdramnar had provided, outflung hands an꜍
feet just touching each other for reassurance. By th꜍
frowns on their faces and their shifting movements an꜍
murmurs, it seemed that such reassurance was ver꜍
much needed.

Over them all hung the blue blade, humming its quie꜍

endless song, and the questing shadows parted around it as they came. Otherwise, all was quiet.

Until the wall not far from Itharr's feet melted away with the faintest of sighs to reveal a dark figure beyond.

It stood motionless, watching, for a long, patient time before it stepped into the chamber. Catlike, long tailed, tentacled, and with broad, soundless soft pads for feet, yet it was somehow recognizably Amdramnar.

It did not go far, and eyed the sword warily as it padded forward to stand by Itharr's head. There it halted, looking down.

And then, with infinite slowness, its shape began to shift. The tail and tentacles drew in, reabsorbed by the body, whose catlike bulk grew lighter in hue and less furry before straightening toward an upright stance. With each passing moment it grew more and more like Itharr's sprawled, hairy, comfortably naked form.

Soon all that could be deemed different in the standing, silently shifting figure were eyes that gleamed opaque in the gloom, and those broad pads of feet. And then the figure reached down.

That's just about enough, Syluné thought crisply, as she floated over Sharantyr on silent, unseen watch. Sharply, she brought down a hand that none but she could see, and her spell snapped out.

The Malaugrym recoiled as if he'd been stung, as a wall of black, seeking tentacles suddenly appeared under his fingers, spanning the entire chamber and sealing him off from Itharr and everything beyond.

He stared at the black barrier, shaking his head in disbelief as its eager tentacles probed for him, reaching out seeking tendrils until he batted one away in annoyance—and then, of course, discovered his hand was caught.

Another tentacle came cruising up like a hungry shark, and the Shadowmaster hissed a spell in sudden fear and tore free. Wild-eyed, he stumbled quickly back through the wall and restored it to solidity in panting haste.

Syluné laughed soundlessly as she floated above the three Harpers, and thought again about just how much *fun* it was to go adventuring.

* * * * *

Ancient, deep shadows shifted out of the way with un-caring slowness, drifting in this hidden place like proud old ghosts. They ignored the black-bladed, gleaming new weapons that hung watchfully among them—weapons waiting to flash to the attack and deal death to an in-truder who never came.

In an old and ancient chamber that few knew existed, inside that ring of vigilant death, stood the four beings who'd set the enchanted blades to their silent task. One was a black, glistening globule as large as a house, whose only distinctive features were a pair of green-and-black bat wings large enough to have lifted a dragon. It an-swered to a terse greeting of, "Bheloris." The second was a swift, many-legged lizard whose bulbous head was a thing of a thousand staring eyes, bulging in as many di-rections. This grotesque cluster was surrounded by a ring of starfish arms ending in snapping mouths, like the maws of snapping turtles, and was greeted as "Yabrant."

The last two Malaugrym, Milhvar and Kostil, stood in their human shapes and confronted each other with soft menace in politely cultured tones.

"Though the cloak seems technically flawless," Kostil commented, "the inexperience of the test subjects and the protection surrounding the Chosen at the locales se-lected for forays has not only proved fatal to most of the test subjects, it has brought jeopardy on both the secrets of the cloak and on the security of the Malaugrym them-selves."

"Oh?" Milhvar asked coolly. "How so?"

"What if one of these Chosen sets up a killing brew of linked-by-contingencies spells, or even memorizes a goodly array of ready combat spells, and uses those belt buckles to trace us? I don't want spell-bombs raging through the castle twice or thrice a day!"

"Yes," Yabrant rumbled. "This foolishness must end."

Milhvar spread his hands smoothly. "But we are so close to achieving our aim and striking down one of the Chosen, a victory we need right now, as a people, to hold up our heads in confidence as we prepare to choose a new Shadowmaster High!"

"Pretty speech," Bheloris said mildly, shifting smoothly toward human appearance and size. "Are you planning to seek the Shadow Throne?"

Milhvar shook his head. All of the Malaugrym in the room knew he wielded greater influence right now than any Shadowmaster High.

Or *had* wielded it—until now. The thousand-eyed lizard who was Yabrant pressed on. "No, Milhvar, the blood of Malaug aren't close to grasping any victory of consequence. I have watched much and said little these last few months, and I believe it's *you* who stand close to achieving some personal goal." His voice changed, thinning to the cold clarity of a stabbing knife. "And just what, your elders gathered here would like to know, would that goal be?"

Milhvar shook his head again. "You are mistaken. My aims lie in perfecting ever-more-powerful shadow magic, and my progress in this is a very slow thing, not something whose achievements are near or within my—or any being's—grasp."

"So you have pretended, these last ten years," Yabrant went on, his body slowly shifting in shape toward a human build and size, "as you've played the role of studious but dangerously capable mage, but I know you to be more than that. Much more than that. What, for instance, befell that priest of Mystra you captured? You slew him, didn't you? To work one of the forbidden magics, no doubt. What is it, Milhvar? Human shape or dragon shape at will? Breeding with baatezu? The ability to control the minds of our young, and to expel the minds of the old from their bodies, leaving the husks for your allies to seize and control?"

Milhvar's face changed subtly, and Yabrant pressed him. "That's it, isn't it? You're trying to take over our family by the bodysnatch method!"

"And that," Bheloris said grimly, "is punishable by death." A barbed strangling wire suddenly appeared in his hands; it flashed as he brought it down . . .

. . . around a throat that wasn't there. Milhvar had called on the most precious garment he wore—the real cloak of shadows—and silently faded away.

The three elders looked at each other.

"Right now, *he's* the true Shadowmaster High," Yabrant said angrily.

"He always was," Kostil replied quietly. "He always was."

* * * * *

The cloak spun him through shadows with swift ease, to a place he had chosen beforehand. It had gone badly, as badly as he'd anticipated . . . but not as badly as he'd feared and prepared for.

Milhvar stiffened as a chime sounded behind him, and whirled around. Then he smiled slowly. Hanging in the stasis field he'd set to catch intruders was an unlikely looking visitor: the floating, disembodied head of Old Elminster. The head was watching him.

"Ah, yes," he said pleasantly, "I should have expected you, once your young rabble showed up just walking around our castle. You've been watching all along, haven't you? Laughing at us, to boot. Well, that'll end right now."

He whispered a word, and white fires suddenly streamed around the head, beginning nowhere in the air before it and dying away nowhere in the air behind it. Milhvar leaned forward to grin through the silent, cool, rushing flames at the unseeing eyes.

"Yes," he said softly, knowing a certain distant wizard could hear him. "It's a spell loop. I suspect even the great Elminster won't be able to break free for quite some time. And by then," he said archly, knowing what a cliché it was, " 'twill be too late. *Much* too late."

19
But a Grand Place to Skulk About

The Castle of Shadows, Kythorn 20

The door chimed discreetly once, and then Amdram-nar's gentle voice issued from it. "Are you awake, friends?"

"We are. Please come in," Belkram called merrily. Half-clad, crossed arms shielding herself, Shar stared at him in indignant astonishment. He stuffed her into the top half of her leathers with blinding speed, earning more than one angry growl of promised revenge from her as he merrily laced and snugged, and finished by chucking her briskly under the chin.

"Crude, Belk," Itharr told him, as the door opened. "You're always so crude."

"Ah, but I get the job done," Belkram replied with a smile. "And at the end of the day . . ."

"It's the crudity I remember," Shar said crisply, taking the blue sword into her hand and waving it meaning-fully.

"In hearty spirits, I see," their host said with a smile, as he set down steaming platters of broth flanked by crescent-shaped toasted rolls slathered in butter.

"You've got *more* hearty spirits in your cellar? All that drinking we did last night was for naught?" Belkram asked almost reproachfully.

Amdramnar gave this sally a delighted grin. "This is fun. I must tell you all, I've really enjoyed hearing jests and clever words with every third breath of the day. It's something . . . rare in the Castle of Shadows."

"You get tired of it," Sharantyr told him flatly. "Really you do."

The Shadowmaster spread his hands. "Perhaps after years together, I might, but I've had barely more than an evening to enjoy your company so far."

"We'll be happy to stay with you again this night, if you'll have us," Shar said firmly, "but we'd like to see more of this wondrous castle today. May we wander it freely?"

Their host grimaced and then reluctantly nodded. "With care, yes," he said. "Speak to others with deference, I urge you, and tell them you're . . . my allies, if questioned. Do *not* mention Elminster or the goddess Mystra, and I strongly advise you to refuse all duels, no matter what the provocation. Nor should you surrender that sword." He nodded at the faintly glowing blade in Sharantyr's hands, and then at the plate before her. "But eat first, and drink deep. Water and food will be scarce as you wander. Meals are taken privately among my kin, never consumed in banquets or at set times. Oh, and worry not, young sirs, about controlling your shape-shifting when you leave my chambers. My magic has taken care of that small problem."

The Harpers exchanged uneasy glances at the news they had been bespelled without their knowledge, but shrugged, and smiled again.

"Who heads your family?" Sharantyr asked casually, chewing strong-seasoned buttered rolls, and being surprised at how marvelous they tasted.

"The Shadowmaster High, who sits on the Shadow Throne," Amdramnar replied calmly, perching himself on the edge of a seat as the three rangers ate. What he'd made was very good, and they told him so. He grinned with pride, and Sharantyr found herself warming to their host. He was just like Belkram and Itharr, at heart.

No, lass, Syluné said quietly, in the depths of her mind. *That's what he wants you to think, but that's not what he is. Watch him always.*

"What's he like?" Belkram asked. "I mean, how'll he react if someone complains that three humans are wandering around his halls?"

"He'll do nothing," Amdramnar replied, "because he's dead. The Shadow Throne sits empty."

"Empty?"

"Yes, and don't even approach it when you reach the

Great Hall. It's guarded, and an attempt to sit on it will bring swift death upon you."

"I'll try to remember that," Belkram said dryly. "Help me, will you Itharr?"

"Great Hall . . . don't sit on throne," Itharr murmured. "Yes, I think I've got it."

"Good," Belkram said. "Anything else?"

"Don't mind them," Sharantyr said. "They mean no offense by this flippancy. It's just their foolish way."

"Oh, I realized that early on," the Malaugrym told her, "but I must warn you that some of my kin won't understand it so, or will consider the insult all the greater if they do. Friends, be very careful."

Belkram sighed. "Everyone tells me that . . . aunts, mother, tutors, passing rangers and merchants . . . even you and you and you. Doesn't anyone want me to have any *fun?*"

"During your execution, or after?" Itharr inquired, running a finger around his plate to catch the last of the butter.

Shar sighed. "Just do as Amdramnar says, will you?"

"Heroes never do as they're told," Belkram informed her proudly.

Shar looked at him. "Has it never occurred to you," she asked dryly, "that such stone-headed habits might be why the term 'dead' usually goes in front of the title 'hero'?"

"I thought it was just to make tombstones look grander," the Harper replied.

Itharr sighed heavily. "I'll start work on yours straight away."

* * * * *

Not far away in the castle, a lean and lithe woman embraced a long gray saurian neck. It stretched up from a body as large as twenty of her, but it ended in a tiny head that sported a huge underslung jaw lined with hooked teeth, opening up to well back down the massive neck. The jaw opened now.

"Daughter," the voice came out, as deep and as rough as always, "I must go. Milhvar's schemes run on while we wait and debate and do nothing."

"Be careful, father," Huerbara whispered, so their servitor creatures could not hear. "I don't want to lose you."

"I'm always careful," Ahorga told her gruffly, his stout forelimbs growing long, dexterous claws.

"Be . . . very careful," his daughter replied gravely, and he turned away quickly as he saw tears glimmering in her eyes. Malaugrym should not weep.

He waved a jaunty farewell with his tail as he plunged into deep shadows, and in so doing failed to see the small, dark shape that peeled itself off the wall outside his door and drifted after him, flitting from thick shadow to thick shadow.

But then, he'd been a Shadowmaster elder for long centuries. He'd probably have done no differently had the shadow spy walked along right under his nose. Fear's cold iron taste was something he'd almost forgotten.

* * * * *

"This place still makes me feel . . . uneasy," Shar murmured as they passed the stair post of chained maidens and set foot on a stone floor hidden beneath knee-deep swirling shadows. Close together and warily they began their cautious walk across the chamber known as the Well of Shadows.

"Is this the heart of their power, d'you think?" Itharr asked quietly. "What would happen if you called on your sword and started burning and slicing some shadows, right here?"

"Before I do so," Shar replied icily, "why don't you recite to me just what soothing explanation you'll give to any host of furious Malaugrym who show up to dispute that tactic?"

"Um, ah," Itharr began, "Hello, gentles . . . it occurs to me that you might be wondering what the lady behind me is, ahem, doing. Well—ask her."

His two companions hooted, but their laughter fell away into the deadening maw of muting shadows all around. They exchanged quick glances and fell silent.

Wordlessly Sharantyr raised the blade and held it out in front of her like the prow of a ship. It seemed dull, and dewed with a clinging mist of shadows. Troubled by the sight, the lady Knight quickened her pace into the shadows that hid everything.

All around them, small shadowspawn writhed and spun in the excitements of their birthing, twisting this way and that in the swirling, rainbow surf of shadowborne energy. This was the place of shadows, where all things were spun of shadowmist—and in the end, spun back into shadowy fading dreams. Their skeletons sank forgotten into the glooms where no creatures went but foolish questing mages, dying shadowbeasts, and lurking prowlers-in-shadow. Belkram and Itharr looked at each other, and their blades hissed out in unison. Looking warily behind them at every second or third step, they went on. It seemed to be taking an awfully long time to cross the chamber.

* * * * *

Shadowdale, Kythorn 20

Storm Silverhand sighed and pulled on a boot. Clothing might be optional for a morning selecting stones on the rock pile, but footwear was not.

The kitchen around her seemed . . . empty. Lonely. She missed Syluné more than she'd thought she would.

"Well," she said lightly, "time to start talking to yourself, dearie."

She grimaced at her own imitation of a trembling dodder-wits and reached for the other boot. As she had done after Maxan's death, as she had so many times before, she must put this melancholy aside and go on. Chosen of Mystra always had to go on.

Time to sigh again. She thought about that for a moment, then tossed her head and stood up, stamping both boots firmly on. Pirouetting idly across the kitchen, the Bard of Shadowdale took down the long iron pry bar from its hook on the wall.

And then a voice sounded in her head, a voice that held an unaccustomed note of concern.

Storm, the Simbul asked from half a world away, *do you know what's befallen El? I can't feel him. It's as if he were gone!*

And Storm, standing in her kitchen clad only in boots, armed against the world with an iron bar half as long as herself, felt a swift icy finger run down her spine. She whispered, "No, Sister. I don't know what's befallen him. Do you think—?"

Start looking and asking, her sister told her crisply, every inch the Queen of Aglarond, *but without raising rumors about his death or disappearance. That, as before, we dare not do.* The voice paused, and then resumed with an amused mindtone. *Making folk think everything's fine and you're just casually asking if they've seem Elminster about will no doubt work better if you put some clothes on. I know all you folk are weird up there in Shadowdale, but . . .*

Storm faced west and made a certain gesture with the pry bar that looked almost as impossible as it seemed painful.

Gods above, her distant sister replied, *you've seen him do that? Perhaps I shouldn't be worried after all!*

"Nethreen," Storm said, managing to keep her voice steady, "leave me be for now. Unobtrusively searching all of Toril for Elminster isn't going to be swiftly done."

It may be unnecessary, the Simbul said hopefully. *He may just be off gallivanting in disguise, or hidden in the heart of wild magic somewhere . . .*

"Yes," Storm replied, putting as much hearty reassurance into that word as she could. But as she hung the pry bar back on its hook and sought the stairs to her wardrobe, her heart was dark and heavy, and foreboding ran lightly beside her. She had a feeling it would be at her elbow for a long time to come.

* * * * *

The Castle of Shadows, Kythorn 20

"This must be the Red Chamber," Belkram announced unnecessarily as he strode into the room in front of them.

Sharantyr stayed where she was, gazing around in amazed wonder at a high-ceilinged room as large as the feasting halls of most proud palaces of Faerûn. Every surface—walls, floor, and ceiling—was entirely covered in what looked like red plush velvet. She'd never seen a room decorated in such poor taste, but it looked grand and impressive when done so completely and on such a large scale. "Gods," she murmured, "it looks like the inside of some gigantic beast's stomach."

Belkram spun around. "Do you mind?" he complained, waving his arms. "After I step well into it, d'you have to say something like that?"

The lady Knight sighed. "Belt up," she said calmly, "and put that sword away. You might hit someone with it."

"Well, that *is* the general idea," he agreed, "but—"

"Belkram," she said in silken warning. "*Now.*"

"Well, as you state your view so eloquently and persuasively," the handsome Harper said innocently, returning his blade to its scabbard with a gentle flourish, "perhaps there is something in what you say."

Sharantyr turned dangerous eyes to her other companion. "Well," she asked mildly, "do you have something inane and clever to unburden yourself of at this time? If so, may we hear it and get it out of the way?"

Itharr dropped his eyes from surveying distant corners of the ceiling and said briefly, "A fascinating room, decorated in—Early Bordello, do you think, Belk?"

"I frequent bordellos only when the hour is late," his friend replied smoothly, "but—"

"How do you put up with them, gracious lady?"

They all whirled around. The speaker was a tall man with an elegant moustache and rich robes, who seemed to be melting and flowing out of the wall. Sharantyr eyed that movement of matter with a frown, then raised her eyes to meet his own dark and solemn gaze.

"I manage," she said, lifting her shoulders in a shrug "And you, sir, are—?"

"Charmed to make your acquaintance," the Malaugrym replied, dropping into a smooth bow. As he straightened up, his mouth crooked and he said in a stage whisper to Itharr, "You see? That's how to do it." He waved a dismissive hand at Itharr's leveled sword and added, "And it's Late Bordello, definitely."

"I bow to your superior experience in these matters," Itharr said urbanely, and did so.

The sword in Sharantyr's hands hummed then, and all eyes went to it. She waited until the Shadowmaster's gaze went sideways to her own, and said, "I am Sharantyr of Shadowdale, Knight of Myth Drannor. Whom do I have the pleasure of addressing?"

"Bheloris," the shapeshifter replied, "of this castle. One of the elders of my kin." A half-smile of sadness rose onto his face as the blue blade lifted to menace him. "I am not," he added mildly, "disposed to offer you violence . . . now or at any other time." He eyed the two Harpers, who were watching him tensely with hands on weapons, and added, "That is not a view shared, I'm afraid, by many of the blood of Malaug." He strode forward, gesturing to indicate his intended passage through them. "May I?"

The three rangers parted to let him pass, and Bheloris walked calmly past them, into the soft red heart of the chamber. "I should warn you," he added, "that such fangs as you carry will avail you little against the magic most of us could hurl your way here in the castle. Smooth words and an air of gentle menace will carry you farther."

"Why are y— Are you curious about us, too?" Shar asked him, one eyebrow lifted.

"Of course," the Shadowmaster replied. "So, if you will, I'll accompany you about our halls. Amdramnar must be crazed—or more cruel than I thought—not to have escorted you himself."

"I don't know if I want an escort," Sharantyr said carefully.

"You do," Bheloris told her gravely, "or you will, if you think about it calmly for a moment. Could you handle an attack from an archmage who struck from the other end of this chamber? A being who could melt away into the walls whenever you tried to strike back?"

Shar shrugged.

"So I thought," the Shadowmaster said mildly. "You'd be carrion in short order." He spread his hands. "Go where you please. No place is forbidden except the seat of the Shadow Throne itself."

Shar had a sudden vision of herself hacking at a grand black throne with her blade, a throne that twisted and tried to wriggle away from her blows as she struck showers of sparks from it. Then it was exploding, and she was being hurled helplessly away, whirled to her death against hard, hard walls and pillars . . .

"I'd like to see that throne," she said firmly, lifting her head.

"Soon enough," the Shadowmaster replied. His eyes were on Belkram, who was strolling toward him, looking around. Tall-backed chairs were drawn up around a circular table at the heart of the room, as if for solemn conclaves, all dark wood and gleaming, mirror-smooth polish. "What do you think of this room?" he asked the Harper.

"I don't think I should be impressed," Belkram answered him honestly, "but I am. It's so . . . overblown."

"Your first key to understanding us," Bheloris answered him lightly. Sharantyr's eyes narrowed.

"Do you know why we're here?" she challenged him quietly.

The Malaugrym spread his hands to indicate bewilderment. "You've come a long way, into much danger. Not the act of most idle tourists, nor the achievement of most lost wayfarers. So you must have come for a good purpose, and I'd prefer that whomever you're reporting to have a clear picture of the power you're dealing with, here in Shadowhome. It might steady judgments and save much bloodshed."

"Consider this in turn," Sharantyr replied. "You may be mistaken as to our presumed status as scouts for some invading force."

Bheloris bowed. "I hope I am, Lady of Shadowdale. I merely seek to anticipate the worst and deny it any chance at becoming reality."

Sharantyr stood very still. She'd not told this mild voiced Malaugrym her Shadowdale title. He knew far more about her—about them all—than he should.

Syluné? Sharantyr asked in her mind, but if the Witch of Shadowdale was still resident in her head, she gave no sign.

"Of course," she replied, striding forward to stand be side Belkram. Behind her, she could see that Itharr had noted the little circle she'd made with her sword tip, and was closing ranks too.

The Shadowmaster smiled. "I don't wish to sound men acing," he remarked, "but standing close together is very poor tactics against anyone wielding magic. One spell can so easily harm all."

He shrugged and turned to face the table, calmly turn ing his back on them. "But enough talk of battle and strife. This is where our council met, in the days before ... our last Shadowmaster High, Dhalgrave, dissolved it."

"A council of elders? Were you on the council?" Itharr asked.

The Malaugrym smiled. "You are swift, friend. I was."

"Who rules now that the Shadowmaster High is dead?" Shar asked.

Bheloris smiled. "No one—yet. The more daring among us have begun to act as they please, and things may end in kinstrife. You have come at a most dangerous time, for there is no authority to appeal to if one is wronged. There are many chances for ambitious Malaugrym to enhance their reputations by outdoing each other in acts of ag gression, confidence, and efficient violence . . . and here you are, strolling our passageways, easy meat."

"I appreciate your candor," Belkram told the Shadow master, "but—"

And then the floor beneath his feet gave way. "Whoa!" he cried, grabbing at Sharantyr's arm for support.

Her sword arm. As her elbow was dragged down, a startled Sharantyr thought, *I must keep my feet. My*

*word may be all that is keeping this Malaugrym from
triking us down.

As she set herself, determined not to be pulled over,
*he sword in her hands hummed and drifted firmly up-
*ward, straightening her and taking Belkram's weight.

He got one boot up on the floor again and sprang back.
The punishing weight was suddenly gone from Sharan-
*yr's arm. Together they looked at the octagonal opening
*n the floor. A trapdoor had fallen to one side, opening
*nto emptiness.

Belkram gestured at it. "And is this a friendly wel-
*come? Or one of those little acts of aggression you spoke
*f?"

"Neither," the Shadowmaster replied, striding over to
*he hole. He raised a hand, murmured something they
*ould not catch, and the trapdoor rose smoothly into
*lace. Bheloris promptly stepped forward onto it and
*tood calmly facing them. "My apologies for any distress,"
*ne said to Belkram. "You had the misfortune to step on a
*rap-chute that someone—carelessly or deliberately, I
*now not which—left active."

"Trap-chute?" Itharr prompted mildly, waving his
*lade.

"Swift ways down to dungeon caverns. Long unused by
*he council, but once part of the ceremonial way in which
*Malaugrym who'd displeased us began their punishment.
*Down they'd go upon the instant of their sentencing, an
*mpressive gesture for the benefit of others who might
*lot defiance of the council."

"Are there many such traps about the castle?" Belkram
*sked, looking suspiciously at the red plush around his
*oots.

Bheloris shook his head. "Only here, but there must be
*ighty or more in all, one every few paces."

"Amdramnar didn't warn us about this," Belkram said
*rimly.

Shar shrugged. "He may have forgotten about them, if
*hey've been 'long unused.'"

Bheloris arched an eyebrow. "Oh, I hardly think so."
*Ie met their suddenly riveted gazes and said, "The

moment they master teleporting—for the journey
back up—all children of the blood of Malaug play here
for years before they grow tired of hurtling down stone
chutes. Some never do."

The three rangers exchanged frowning glances.

"I think we've seen enough red plush to last us for
some time," Shar said quietly, "and we'd like to see Glyorgh's Chamber, if you'd be so kind as to conduct us there.
Amdramnar says it's not to be missed."

The Malaugrym bowed. "Certainly, my lady," he said.
"This way, if you please." He indicated the door they'd
come in by, and glided past them. As he went past, Belkram raised a questioning hand. "There wouldn't be any
dangers awaiting us there that Amdramnar might have
. . . ah, neglected to inform us of, would there?"

The Shadowmaster met his eyes steadily. "No, so long
as you stay back of the warning wall of everflame and
don't send any spells over it."

"We weren't intending to," Shar said, "but he gave us
no warnings about this."

Bheloris spread his hands. "In his defense, may I say
that it's something no Malaugrym would think of doing."

"We seem to have made a career, recently, of doing
things no Malaugrym would think of doing," Ithar
mused.

The Shadowmaster turned an expressionless face toward him. "Continue to do so," he suggested. "It may help
to keep you alive."

* * * * *

Shadowdale, Kythorn 20

"Well met, Storm," came the smoky, sultry tones of the
High Lady of Berdusk out of the speaking stone. "How
fare the two Harpers we sent you?"

"Well enough," Storm said to the polished marble
sphere floating in the center of her bedchamber, as she
struggled into the clothes she'd chosen, "when I saw them
last . . . a tenday ago, riding into Daggerdale."

"Good to hear. How can I serve? Pray speak."

"It's . . . becoming increasingly urgent that I speak with Elminster," Storm told her, "and he's off racing around the Realms, as usual. If his path should happen to cross that of any of your Harpers, have them tell him to call on me, will you?"

"Of course. Tell us when to call off our hounds, though. I'd hate to have a few good Harpers turned into frogs because the Old Mage has grown tired of hearing the same message."

"I shall, Cylyria," Storm promised. "Thank you."

"You are always welcome, Storm," the speaking stone replied. "Call on me more often. I grow weary of hearing about the daring exploits of Harpers out east only in minstrels' ballads and tavern gossip!"

Storm winced. "You know I hate using this thing," she said softly. "Yet you're right, Cyl. Expect to hear from me soon."

"Please do. And, Storm—?"

"Yes?"

"If you're lonely, call me and we can sing ballads back and forth to each other."

"Thank you," Storm said huskily, sudden tears threatening to burst up from her throat. "Fair fortune, High Lady."

"Fair fortune, Chosen of Mystra," the stone said, sinking swiftly toward the soft pelts on the floor. Storm caught it deftly and tossed it onto the bed, sighing loudly before she turned away.

* * * * *

Berdusk, Twilight Hall, Kythorn 20

The deep emerald eyes of High Lady Cylyria Dragonbreast were troubled as she turned away from her own stone. Storm *did* hate to use the speaking stone. Something must be very much amiss.

With gods walking Faerûn, magic going wild everywhere, and every petty brigand and marauding orc chieftain on the march from here to the Moonshaes, the Harpers—nay, the good folk of all Faerûn—couldn't afford to lose Elminster.

Her fine features were grim as she struck the little gong built into the head of her bed, took the speaking stone into her hands to keep it from rolling to the floor and shattering, and got up off the bed. Then she smiled at the sound of pounding feet growing swiftly louder down the passage outside. My, but Harper boys were enthusiastic.

* * * * *

The Castle of Shadows, Kythorn 20

"It's . . . impressive," Shar said softly, and meant it. They stared down together from the circular balcony that ringed the dome. In the open space below, amid endlessly roiling, glowing blue shadows, a circle of black magical flames—blazing away consuming nothing and never burning out—encircled a shrouded, floating human form.

"Forgive me," Itharr said to the Malaugrym, "but who was Glyorgh?"

"The closest friend of Malaug, a sorcerer of Faerûn who was the first to embrace the way of shadows," Bheloris replied. "He has rested here, in magical stasis, for longer than men have dwelt in any of the Dragonreach lands."

"Where is Malaug's tomb?" Belkram asked quietly.

"No one knows," the Shadowmaster replied. "There are even legends among us that he never died but lives on still, on other planes or in hidden guise somewhere nearby, watching us."

Belkram and Itharr exchanged glances and shuddered together. More impressive still.

The mood was broken when a hitherto hidden door opened a little way along the balcony, and a youngish-looking man ran toward them, his shapeshifting blood betrayed only by the wormlike flexibility of his arms, wriggling at the elbows in apparent distress.

"Is this Malaug now?" Belkram asked lightly, earning

a hard look from the Shadowmaster.

"Bheloris," the newcomer said sharply, after a swift, searching glance at the three rangers and a second, involuntary one at Shar and her sword, "you must come. Ahorga's looking for Milhvar. He's—"

"Enough, Neleyd," the Shadowmaster said quickly. "You can tell me as we go to him." He turned. "My deep regrets, friends," he said, leaving his mouth behind on a tentacle as he rushed to the door. "If you follow me out this door and take the first stair down on the right, the third door on the left opens into the Lute Gallery."

"Thanks!" Sharantyr said hurriedly as the mouth sped away from them. "Itharr—the door!"

"Aye," the Harper said, diving for it. He got there before it could close and leaned against the door frame, looking swiftly ahead and then back at Shar and Belkram. "Well?" he asked.

Shar was looking at Belkram, and Belkram was leaning forward over the rail, looking down at the floating body of Glyorgh. "No, Belkram," Shar said firmly. "Come on."

Belkram looked at her, eyes bright. "But . . ."

"*No*, Belkram," Shar said, taking him by the arm and towing him toward the door. He sighed once as they went out and down the stairs. "What's the appeal of this Lute Gallery, anyway?"

"Enchantments are supposed to play soothing music there all the time," Sharantyr told him. "Many Malaugrym go there to relax . . . strolling about, thinking. Didn't you listen to Amdramnar?"

"Yes, and I didn't hear anything about traps waiting for me in the Red Chamber," Belkram replied, "so I wouldn't place overmuch credence in what he said, if I were hurrying along through the castle."

"My, Belkram, that's the wisest thing you've said in days!" a voice said unexpectedly from Sharantyr's breast.

"Syluné!" they chorused, coming to a halt. "Where have you been?"

"Here all along. I've only just managed to break a spying spell our kind host Amdramnar sent along with us. I didn't dare speak before. Don't get into the habit of talking to me, though. You're going to need a secret ally against these Malaugrym. This place is full of treachery and fey spells."

"Can you stay hidden," Shar asked in low tones, "in a place where so many mages dwell?"

Syluné sniffed. "Of course. Weaving shadows is so easy that they're all lazy and careless."

"Easy?"

"Like commanding an endless supply of fresh, loyal warriors that surround you eagerly wherever you go, waiting to jump at your bidding. To these shapeshifters, spell weaving's more idle thought and whimsy than work."

"So they don't have to work hard to destroy us," Belkram said. "Heartening news." He looked up and down the passage. "So what should we do now?"

"Start looking for gates out of here," Syluné said, "so you have an escape route when things come to battle— and they soon will!"

"Just open doors and look around for gates?" Belkram asked.

"Just go back to Amdramnar's quarters. The passage that leads to the jakes also leads on to a gate, if you go far enough."

"I'm going to have a few words with our friend Amdramnar," Belkram said grimly. "Let's go!" He strode off down the passage, and then slowed to a halt. "Uh . . . which way?"

Itharr chuckled. "Syluné?"

"Turn left as soon as you find something that looks major. You've a fair distance back *that* way to cover," the Witch of Shadowdale directed, one ghostly hand appearing for a moment to point in the proper direction. They set off without delay.

* * * * *

In a room spun of shadow, six Malaugrym sat around a table, gambling. Gems and lumps of gold floated lazily around each of them as they bent forward over the table, studying the intricate pattern of cards laid out there.

Small plumes of colored flame flickered above the cards, dancing here and there as Olorn studied them, his face an expressionless mask. Between two fingers he held the card he must place this turn, tapping it gently on the tabletop.

"If you're trying to win by waiting until we all die off, Olorn," an eagle-headed Malaugrym said sourly, "just remember that I'm younger than you."

"Hold," another of the players said softly. "See who comes."

Something in his tone made everyone turn and look down through the floor of shadow—transparent to them but opaque to eyes below—in time to see three rangers approaching down the length of the long room below.

Olorn cast aside his cards with a joyous snarl and dropped through the floor in a single bound, plunging down to bar the path of the three humans.

"Going somewhere, cattle?" he sneered. "I think not."

"You would be the one called Olorn?" Sharantyr asked softly.

"I am, breeding maiden. We can discuss such things later, when these two lumps of meat with you are dead!" the Malaugrym snapped. As the two Harpers charged him, swords flashing, he brought his hands together. From where his palms met leapt a beam of white-hot, crackling flame.

As it rushed to meet them, Sharantyr didn't even have time to scream.

20
A Sword Against the Shadows

The Castle of Shadows, Kythorn 20

Without thinking, the Knight of Myth Drannor swung her sword. There was a flash of blue radiance, a moment of roaring brightness around her, and the flames were gone.

Olorn glared at her, eyes flat with fear and hatred. "How *dare* you?" he snarled, raising his hands again.

"What, stay alive?" Sharantyr replied. "I dare it every day. I'm even getting good at it. What is your quarrel with us, anyway?" As she spoke, she felt the stone that held Syluné vibrate once . . . and then again.

"Dung! You defile our castle by your insolent presence!" Olorn hissed, his hands moving in the gestures of a spell.

"He sounds like a priest of Bane in full rant!" Belkram commented, drawing in close behind Sharantyr on one side. "Aye," Itharr agreed, taking the corresponding position on her other flank, shielded behind the swing of the blue blade.

Olorn's next attack was a spell to pluck them from their feet and hurl them against the ceiling high above, but it did no more than thrust them a few feet up into the air, wavering, before the sword's magic broke its effects.

The three rangers advanced together, swords raised. The room suddenly seemed to be full of watching Malaugrym standing around the walls. Their eyes were alive with interest, and none of them lifted a hand to help Olorn.

Flames suddenly flared up in a wall before the three Faerûnians, blistering heat rolling out from its roaring to sear and singe. But Sharantyr snarled and flailed about with her sword, and where it cut and slashed, the fire flickered and faded.

Then the air around them was suddenly full of other blades, whirling and flashing, ringing off the Harper's hasty parries in a constant din. Sharantyr cried out as one blade spun across her arm, shearing through the worn leathers. A moment later, another carried away most of her right ear in a burst of blood, along with the hair around it.

Olorn laughed at the sight, then choked and caught at his throat, tearing out the dagger Itharr had hurled. The Malaugrym flung it down in a fury and swept both his hands together, pointing at the burly Harper, and all the flying blades came whirling out of the air around them to hurtle toward Itharr.

The deadly converging rain of leaping points met the sweep of Sharantyr's blazing blue blade, shimmered, and was gone. Only a few weapons glanced aside enough to escape, missing Itharr entirely.

Sharantyr strode another pace closer to their foe, but a table, flaming cards, and chairs suddenly rained down from above as Olorn spun all the shadows of the gaming room into a cloaking spiral, trying to smother the powers of the blade that seemed able to slay all his spells. Shadow would not fail him. It never had.

The table smashed Belkram to the floor. Itharr was flung aside, face bleeding, under the blows of two chairs, leaving Sharantyr standing alone, struggling to keep hold of her blade as shadows roared and wheeled around her, clawing and tugging.

Olorn smiled triumphantly at the lady ranger, a smile that slowly grew fangs. Shar's eyes fell from the glistening teeth to the Shadowmaster's hands, and saw that they'd become tentacles. As she gasped at the terrible ever-growing power of the shadows mounting against her, he reached forward. He'd tear one man limb from limb, and then the other. By then the maid should be disarmed and he could have some fun.

Then the whirling blades were back, making bloody ruin of the tips of his tentacles. Olorn recoiled, hissing in pain. Could the sword drink spells and then spew them back? He'd b—by the blood of Malaug!

A shimmering barrier of swirling rainbow hue had appeared in front of him, spanning the entire breadth and height of the Hall of Stars, walling him away from the three humans. How could they have such power?

The rainbow wall bulged, and out of the bulge stepped Amdramnar, smiling tightly at him. "Fingers burned, Olorn?" he asked. "That's what happens when you pick fights with innocent folk who've no quarrel with you."

"And just what are they to *you?*" Olorn snarled, growing tentacles at a furious rate.

"They are guests of mine, idiot kin," Amdramnar said meaningfully. "I observe the rules and courtesies of our family, if you do not. They remain under my protection." Many glances were exchanged among the watching Malaugrym.

"And you let them wander the castle freely, to poke and pry where they may?" Olorn raged, drawing his tentacles up before him like a nettled giant spider, ready to strike.

"What can they see, Olorn, but shadows, doors, chambers, and walls? What is there to learn that can hurt any of us?" Amdramnar answered, adding lightly, "What cards you still held in your hand, perhaps?"

There were chuckles from several Malaugrym, and Olorn's eyes turned flat, dark, and dangerous. "You've gone too far," he said softly, "and have become a traitor to our people. I must do what Dhalgrave no longer can. *Die,* traitor!"

A forest of tentacles shot forward, only to vanish in a welter of gore about halfway to Amdramnar, writhing and disintegrating in a mist of blood. Olorn screamed and staggered back, hauling away what was left of his rubbery arms. They left a trail of glistening gore to where he whimpered against a wall.

"You don't learn, do you?" Amdramnar asked incredulously. "Did you not see my blades? Did you actually think me so weak or careless a mage that I'd have to dispel them in order to raise a barrier against you? Nay, I just made them invisible, you dolt. I should finish you."

He gestured as if to move the invisible blades closer to Olorn, but that worthy Malaugrym was dwindling and flattening, air whistling out of him from twenty places in his haste to flow out the door at the back of the hall. Amdramnar took a pace forward as if to pursue him, but other Malaugrym shook their heads and closed ranks to block his route.

"No, Amdramnar," one elder said. "I care nothing for your quarrel, but I'll see no kin slain in the very halls of our castle, fighting over custody of mortals! Keep better watch over your humans in future. If they wander, troubles are bound to befall."

"I bow to your wisdom, Cortar," the young Malaugrym replied, "and I'll see to their whereabouts." He withdrew a few paces, and the rainbow barrier fell away around him.

Several Malaugrym started forward from the walls, but Amdramnar said merrily. " 'Ware the blades—remember?"

They came to abrupt halts and glared at him, and he recognized at least two of Olorn's cronies among their ranks. He gave them soft smiles that held deadly promise as he put an arm around Sharantyr's shoulders—she gave him a glare almost as black as Olorn's had been, evoking more chuckles from the watchers around the walls—and nudged Belkram with his foot.

The Harper rolled over with a groan. "Ye gods an little ground-snails," he gasped, "I think something in my shoulder's broken. It burns like fire!"

"Crawl over to Itharr for me, will you?" Amdramnar asked him. "We'd best get gone speedily. You somehow wandered into the Hall of Stars, where our mages practice spell-hurling!"

"We're going to talk, later," Belkram promised him grimly, wobbling to his feet. Shar laid a hand on his arm, and through it he heard Syluné say, *There's a ring to heal you in her boot, remember. Hang on and do as the shapeshifter bids.*

By your command, Belkram told her mockingly, and began the painful journey to where Itharr knelt, clutching at his forehead, blood still streaming down his fingers. "How are we, old blade?" Belkram asked, collapsing beside him.

"Chairs . . . chairs are beating the soft stuff out of me," Itharr grunted. "The head on the left hurts the most."

"Up, lad. We can stagger off to the graveyard together," Belkram said tenderly, rising and hauling Itharr to his feet by main strength.

"Where's a quiet place we can go?" Sharantyr asked Amdramnar.

"My chambers, of course."

"No, Amdramnar," she said quietly. "Not now."

The Shadowmaster's head swung around, and their eyes met for a long moment. Then he looked away.

"Out this door," he said, "and then through here."

He led them quickly out into a passage and through the first door they saw into a staircase. They went up a flight to another door, across a hall, and through a dusty room full of shrouded human skeletons. They passed through another door into a dank, dark corridor choked with rubble, thence into some sort of storeroom full of huge casks. Amdramnar led them right through the last, false, cask into a small chamber that he lit by making the end of one finger flame until he found a dusty candle lamp. The room was crowded with small, cobwebbed tables, and Belkram promptly rolled Itharr onto one of them.

"Rest here," the Shadowmaster said. "I'll come back for you." He turned to go, then turned back. "Would you like me to work any healing magic before I go? Itharr's head looks pretty bad . . . and your ear."

Take his healing, Syluné said in Shar's mind, *for yourself only, no matter how selfish it makes you look. Act aroused.*

"Heal me," Sharantyr said in low tones, putting out her hand. "Then I can tend my companions with a clear head. Later, when you come back, they'll probably be in need of sleep. And then . . ."

Quite deliberately she reached behind her and set Mystra's sword on a table. Then she put her freed hand to her lips, and licked one finger while she looked steadily at him.

Their eyes met again . . . and slowly, very slowly, Amdramnar smiled. In spite of herself, Shar felt a stirring within her.

He nodded and turned away, murmuring something and making an intricate series of gestures and passes in the air with his fingertips. Then he turned back, extending one finger to touch her ear as gently as possible.

He's added a glamer to make you want him, Syluné told her, a moment before warmth flooded through her and the pain melted away.

"Ohhh, yes," she murmured, and melted against him, turning her cheek to rub against the arm that had healed her. His skin had a strange acrid, spicy scent, but she licked at his fingers avidly, purring deep in her throat.

When she looked hungrily up at him again, she saw laughter and triumph in his eyes. "I'll be back," he said. "Soon."

"If you're quite finished sticking your tongue in his ear, Shar," Belkram roared, "I need you to hold the other end of this. Itharr's still bleeding!"

"I'll have spells that bring slumber," Amdramnar murmured, and was gone out the door.

Sharantyr leaned against it and trembled. *I hope you can do something about that glamer,* she told Syluné, *or I'm going to be a breeding maiden for shapeshifters . . . and love it!*

I already have, little kitten, Syluné's voice told her mockingly. *You did most of the warm and caressing play all by yourself.*

Sharantyr growled as she reached for her boot.

"*Now* what're you playing at?" Belkram snarled. "I'm sure yon Malaugrym'll like you just fine with your boots on!"

Through a wild web of disheveled hair, Sharantyr gave him her best glare—and overbalanced. She fell over helplessly, boot half off, to land hard on her behind. Belkram hooted with laughter as she rolled angrily onto her back to remove the boot.

"He cast a lust-glamer on me, if you must know," she hissed, shaking her boot at him. Then she lifted the sole and snatched the ring she needed, holding it up into his face. "Put this on Itharr. Then when he feels right, wear it yourself."

"This the one that regenerates?"

"Yes," Shar told him, stamping her boot back on, "and hurry! I want to be gone from here before ardent Amdramnar gets back!"

"He'll have put some sort of locking spell on the door, you know," Belkram said warningly.

"Then our secret weapon'll blast a hole through the wall!" Sharantyr hissed.

That won't be necessary. Syluné sounded amused. *There's a secret door at the back of this room that opens into the castle library.*

"The Malaugrym have a library? I'll bet Elminster would give his beard to sit down at leisure and read his way through it," Shar said aloud.

Belkram snorted. "Read it? He probably wrote most of it!" He watched Itharr's bleeding stop, and the gash on the burly Harper's forehead begin to fade. "Syluné's looked around for us?"

"Hush!" Shar told him severely. *Touch and hold him,* Syluné told her. So Sharantyr walked to Belkram, put her arms around him, and kissed him.

He stiffened with a grunt of pain as she embraced his injured shoulder, but as their lips met Syluné said through them, *Well done. Now I can speak to you both at once. Be very careful. Beyond this door is one of the most powerful Shadowmasters, waiting for you to come through. He's too strong to fight but will leave you alone as tools to be used later, if you impress him. Act fearless and mysterious . . . and no clowning, Belkram. If you do this, you just might live. Leave the secret door open behind you—wedge it with that table leg over there—so Amdramnar can come to the rescue if you need rescuing.*

"If he tries what he intends with me," Shar told him darkly, letting go of Belkram, "*he'll* need the rescuing."

"Come back, lass," Belkram said pleadingly, and puckered his lips. "I was getting used to it!"

"Later," Sharantyr told him briskly, taking up her

blade and cutting the air with it a few times. "We've got a castle full of Malaugrym to deal with first!"

"Couldn't I just buy you a nice meal," Belkram offered, "and a little too much wine? No?" He looked mournful. "It *used* to work," he told Itharr wearily. "What went wrong?"

Itharr started to laugh, then clutched at his temples in pain, wincing. A few breaths later, the ring's magic had repaired him enough to sigh, swing himself off the table, and hand the ring to Belkram.

"Heal thyself, dolt," he said, "and hurry, or we'll have a lust-crazed Malaugrym all over her, and that'll sure slow her down when we start running through this place trying to escape."

Belkram put on the ring and looked at Shar. "Ready?"

She lifted her sword in response, and the two Harpers drew their blades again. Shar stepped between them and did as Syluné directed. A part of the wall that looked as solid as the rest grated suddenly aside. Belkram was ready with the table leg.

The room beyond was crowded with ornate bookshelves. The narrow aisle between them ran to the right, and the three rangers followed it cautiously, peering around a corner to look straight into the politely smiling face of a handsome man in a maroon monk's cassock, who sat at a table with several books open in front of him.

"Please be seated and take your ease," the man said, closing a book. It immediately lifted itself off the table and drifted over his shoulder, heading for a gap on one shelf. "No danger awaits you here."

A book floated out of the smooth ranks of tomes in another bookcase, heading for the table. As the volume opened itself for the Malaugrym's scrutiny, the three Faerûnians saw that another book was also on the way. All over the library, volumes were drifting unhurriedly about in a continuous, graceful dance.

"And your name, sir, would be?" Sharantyr asked softly, sitting down. The sword in her hand flashed once.

With smooth effort, the man avoided looking at the blade—beware, this one is very dangerous, Sharantyr told herself—and said, "Milhvar of the Malaugrym. And whom do I have the pleasure of addressing?"

"Sharantyr of Shadowdale, in Faerûn," Shar told him, "and these are my . . . companions, Belkram and Itharr."

"Adventurers come to explore the demiplane of Shadow?" Milhvar asked. "Or do you pursue a private purpose?"

"We came here by accident." Belkram replied, "but have become friends of Amdramnar. Others in this castle have not been so friendly."

"I've just heard talk of a duel or some such unpleasantness in the Hall of Stars," Milhvar said, briefly glancing at the contents of the tome in three places and then sending the book on its way again, "and you do seem to travel with cutting edges in plenty, ready for use. Have you any plans here in Shadowhome that I can help you with?"

"To get home again," Itharr offered. Milhvar raised his eyebrows.

"That's all? Just to leave, before you've seen more than a handful of rooms and a few warring kin? It seems a poor return for the dangers you've faced, surely?"

"I—" Shar began, but broke off, half-rising from her seat, when two other Malaugrym came hastily around a bookshelf.

Milhvar looked at her raised sword, then over his shoulder at the approaching pair, and said to her, "You can safely put that down. We rarely brawl on sight here in the castle, and never in the library. There is too much of lasting value here." He closed another book and let it rise gently over his shoulder.

"Oh," he added, "be known, Sharantyr, Belkram, and Itharr of Shadowdale—a most favorably named place, I must say—to Indyl and Thaune of the blood of Malaug. Have you business with our guests, you two?"

"We do," Thaune said excitedly. "Or at least, we hope so." He sat down on a corner of the table, ignoring Milhvar's pained look. "Olorn's got it in for you. He's raging around the Great Hall vowing revenge and trying to whelm armies of us against you right now. Would you be willing to use that sword on him, if a couple of us cornered him and held his magic in check?"

"It's the only way you'll be safe from him," Indyl put in, lifting burning eyes from a steady scrutiny of the sword to fix Shar with disconcertingly bright golden irises. As if aware of how menacing his blazing gaze seemed, he hastily muted his eye color to a milky brown. "We've been waiting a long time for a chance to deal with him."

"How," Milhvar asked smoothly, before any of the rangers could reply, "will that sword be of any particular use against Olorn? Is it some sort of special blade?"

"It cut through every spell Olorn threw at them," Thaune said.

"Bheloris said it held them both up, when they triggered a trap-chute in the Red Chamber," Indyl added, news that made Milhvar's eyebrows leap upward. He turned his head to watch a third Malaugrym come around the bookshelf.

"Ah, Drelorr," Milhvar greeted him, "we have visitors from Toril."

"Aye," the newcomer said, leaning a leonine body forward to regard the sword Sharantyr was holding. Its tip pulsed with sudden radiance as he drew near. "This is the blade that burns flesh and makes wounds that won't heal."

"Won't heal?" The other two young Malaugrym drew back from the table with almost comical haste.

"Not at all?" Milhvar asked calmly.

Drelorr shrugged. "They can be spell-healed, right enough, but won't knit of themselves just by shifting shape." He looked at Sharantyr. "You wouldn't want to sell this sword to me, would you?"

Sharantyr shook her head.

"Could we borrow it, then? Or rent it for half a day?"

"Sorry," Shar said. "No."

"Or will you work with us," Thaune suggested, "as we suggested before Drelorr arrived? We don't want to part you from your weapon, just bring its powers against Olorn."

"We've no interest in becoming any more entangled in the feuds of the House of Malaug than we have already become," Shar said carefully, "and so I must decline."

She stiffened as the blade flashed, then she relaxed. "Nor will spells dupe or force me into relinquishing it," she added dryly. The next probe was more intense, and she felt the faint vibrations of Syluné working spells of her own.

Sharantyr rose smoothly to her feet, and the Harpers rose with her. "If you're all through trying spells on me as if I were some sort of passing beetle, we'd like to pass on out of the library . . ."

Behind her, Belkram snarled, "Shar!"

She whirled around to see his sword inches from her, his face twisted with strain as he fought against the magic compelling him.

And then she felt the terrible cold of Itharr's blade sliding into her flank.

"Mystra!" she cried, and slashed out behind her blindly. One of the Malaugrym screamed, and she saw fingers flying as she kept turning, striking Itharr's blade out of his hand as she came.

Fire was spreading from the ice in her side, and Shar wondered if this was to be her dying day. *Easy, lass*, Syluné said inside her, and she felt the pain suddenly lessen.

Milhvar was watching her calmly as she staggered, put all the contempt and disgust she felt into the look she gave him, lurched around, and went back through the door into the dusty room full of tables.

Belkram and a weeping Itharr came after her. The Malaugrym were right behind them, flinging out tentacles that Syluné smashed aside with a spell Shar never saw.

The next spell sent a ball of fire crashing through the door into Milhvar's precious library, and they heard his startled shout.

He must have raised some sort of hasty spell-barrier, because the fiery blast came back into the dusty little room, flinging three tortured young Malaugrym with it. Their ashen bodies thudded off the walls amid blazing tables as the three rangers staggered out into the room of casks.

The pain in her side had subsided into a dull ache, now, but Shar didn't resist when Belkram seized her hand and thrust a ring onto one of her fingers. "Your turn," he grunted, and shook Itharr like a frilly lounge cushion. "Stop wailing—she's fine!"

Itharr sobbed, blinked, hiccuped, and fell silent.

And deep within her Sharantyr heard Syluné say, *Trust me,* and felt the sword twitched from her fingers.

There was a momentary flicker of blue light. Then the sword was back, humming and glowing as before but with a subtly different weight to it. Shar cut at the air experimentally as they crossed the room, heading for the door through which Amdramnar had brought them here. No, the sword was somehow different.

And then fire snatched it from her fingers, and shadows howled around her wrist. She grabbed for it in vain and saw it spinning away from her, globed in shadows, to hang near the ceiling.

Light was growing all around them now as Olorn stepped out from behind a cask and waved his hand. Belkram and Itharr froze in midcurse, immobile. Sharantyr grabbed at her belt dagger, but shadows were sliding around her wrists and ankles, thrusting them inexorably apart.

Olorn laughed again and strolled toward her. Behind him, many Malaugrym were entering the room, cruel excitement in their faces.

"I've stood more than enough insolence from mortal wenches in the past," he said to Shar, "and you're just one more. I had breeding plans for you, but you're not good enough to sully myself with." His right hand wriggled then, becoming a tentacle—a long, thin, dark tentacle with eel-like jaws. "So instead," he announced brightly, "I've decided to make a meal of you!" The tentacle rose, like a swaying cobra, then bent and came straight across the room at her, gliding horizontally through the air.

Shar was spread-eagled on thin air by then, floating off the floor in the grip of shadows that had become as hard as iron. Her face was closest to the tentacle, and as it approached her, snakelike, she felt shadows tugging at her lips and the corners of her mouth.

She fought against the steely strength of the shadows, teeth clenched, but the tentacle slid lazily closer and her jaws were being forced apart. No!

A long moment passed, the eager Malaugrym audience silently watching her struggle. She fought in vain. In the end, her mouth was open wide and held that way, jaw quivering with the strain.

The tentacle slid between her teeth, probing ahead with a tip to hold her tongue down. Then it expanded, filling her mouth with its foulness . . . and began to get warmer.

"A little roast tongue to start with," Olorn said jovially, and the Malaugrym laughed in cruel chorus. As the pain began to build, Sharantyr discovered that she could still breathe—but she could no longer scream.

21
Shadows Cloak, but Make a Better Shroud

Tears of helpless rage welled up in Sharantyr's throat, and she struggled frantically against the shadow-bonds that manacled her. They shifted a little . . . and a little more. She could move!

Then she saw that the Malaugrym were laughing at her, enjoying her futile midair squirmings and swayings, and Olorn was sending another tentacle her way with taunting slowness.

"What part of her shall we play with now?" he asked the other Shadowmasters. The tentacle twitched as an eager chorus of suggestions rang out. Sharantyr closed her eyes. She'd never dreamed that dying could be this bad, or this slow. By the sounds of it, midair surgery could go on for days, if they kept her—parts of her—alive with their spells. *Mystra and Tymora hear me*, she prayed fervently, *if you can't deliver me from this, at least make it quick!*

And then the tentacle in her mouth quivered—no, shuddered—and she heard Olorn scream. Her eyes snapped open in sudden wild hope.

A blue blade was glowing in the air, flashing in ghostly hands, flashing through Olorn again and again, transfixing him. Blue flames licked around his body as he struggled to change shape. His tentacle abruptly receded from Shar's mouth but failed to escape the blade that was chopping him apart.

Pieces of the Malaugrym, great writhing lumps, rained down onto the floor in flames. The room was full of wriggling shapes as the Malaugrym shouted and shifted shape and hurled spells at the ghostly swordswoman— Syluné, her hair flying free behind her as she flew about the room, hacking and slashing. The flashing blue blade turned back all the spells sent against her . . . back upon those who'd sent them.

Olorn must have died, because Shar found herself falling abruptly to the floor. As she landed painfully on knees and elbows, she saw the two Harpers stagger out of their immobility. High overhead, the shadow globe fell apart, and the false blue blade it had held began to fade slowly out of existence.

The room was slaughterhouse chaos now, as Syluné dealt death to the Malaugrym. She rose up out of the heart of them for a moment and calmly cast a transmutation spell; the dagger in Shar's hand quivered.

She looked down at it. The good steel now shone with a glossy silver plating, and she could see Belkram's sword and Itharr's dagger were the same. With a shout, Sharantyr raced across the room and buried her tiny fang in the nearest Malaugrym.

He screamed. Sharantyr matched it with a shriek of her own, a shout of anger and disgust as she poured out all she'd held in check since seeing Old Elminster's dripping head snatched away from them in Daggerdale. She waded into shifting arms and tentacles and beaks, snapping fanged jaws and swimming thousands of eyes, hacking at rubbery flesh that smoked and shriveled where her blade touched it.

The room rocked again. She spun around to face the spell-flash.

"This has gone far enough," Milhvar said coldly from where he'd just appeared in the center of the room. At his last word, his prepared spell struck, hurling everyone back against the walls with bruising force.

Everyone except a certain flying ghostly form, who smiled a crooked smile at him and hurled a glowing blue blade through the air.

Point-first it slashed across the room, humming as it went, and Shar saw Milhvar's lips working in frantic haste.

Abruptly he was gone in a cloud of sweat, and another body was in his place. The Malaugrym mage Iyritar screamed as the sword of Mystra tore into him.

Impaled on the blade, Iyritar flailed his hands about vainly, clawing at the air in his agony.

From the wall where Iyritar had been, Milhvar stepped forth, weaving another spell as the three rangers tore free of his fading bindings and launched themselves from the walls with silver blades raised.

Syluné abruptly winked out. Shar stared up at where she'd been in astonished horror, slowing in her run. Itharr's shout of alarm dragged her eyes down to see what Milhvar's magic had wrought.

Iyritar's gore was on fire, blazing with scarlet flames as it sprayed from the dying Malaugrym's body and spread out to form a sphere of blood around the sorcerer's limp form, with the blade of Mystra lodged in it. In seconds the sphere was complete. Milhvar wiped sweat from his brow with one hand and visibly relaxed.

A smile crept slowly onto his face as he stepped forward and held up a hand to slow the charging Harpers with a magical wall. From behind its invisible safety he told them, "Without your precious blade, you're trapped here, to become our playthings or slaves—or carrion, if you prefer. Like all humans, your fates will befall you swiftly."

Behind Milhvar, a faint ghostly form faded into view, lit by the red radiance of the blood-sphere. Syluné was frowning in concentration as she thrust a hand into the red flames.

The three rangers saw her spectral body arch in agony, but it was the sphere that moaned.

"Stop trying to get at the blade, Argast," Milhvar said sharply, without turning to look. "You'll get badly hurt if you persist. The blood-sphere works against Malaugrym just as well as mortals."

The Shadowmaster elder strode toward the rangers, and the invisible wall moved with him, forcing them back. The sphere moaned again as Syluné, her face twisted in pain, thrust herself through it and held herself there. The sword burst free, trailing blood in a long arc of droplets as it soared high into the air.

The ghostly Witch of Shadowdale fell away from the blood-sphere, face pinched with pain, but managed to raise one trembling arm to point at Milhvar.

In silent obedience the blade leapt across the chamber and burst through the heart of Milhvar of the Malaugrym.

"No! No! Not . . . when I have . . . the cloak . . ." he sobbed, doubling over and flickering in and out of visibility. Syluné's eyes narrowed, and she whispered a soft word of power.

Blue flames rolled out of the blade from end to end, licking swiftly up the Shadowmaster's body. He faded from view, but the flames could still be seen. He faded back into visibility, bent over and staggering, trying vainly to reach something only he could see across the chamber, but moving only inches.

He faded from view once more, so that only the blue flames could be seen—flames that rose and rose hungrily, outlining an upright human form at the last as they roared up into a hungry pillar that parted the shadows and ate through the ceiling and kept on burning away shadows, like mist parting before the hot sun.

* * * * *

In a place of chiming shadows, a stream of white fire that gave off no heat faltered, flickered—and ended, leaving a disembodied, white-bearded head floating alone.

The head chuckled and said, "Done, then? Well done, I should say!" and faded slowly away.

* * * * *

"Are you whole?" Syluné asked softly, standing barefoot in the air before them.

Belkram grinned up at her. "I could ask you the same question," he replied. "I can see *through* you!"

She put her hands on her hips and said tartly, "But *I* am the lady of us two, and I asked first . . . so answer, sirrah!"

Shar and Itharr chuckled at that, and fell into each other's arms weak with relief. "Yes . . . we're whole," Shar gasped, "I think . . ."

"Good," Syluné said crisply. "Then have the sense for once to sit still. I've work to do yet."

She raised her hands and cast a spell they'd all seen worked before: a simple telekinesis magic. The blade thrummed happily as it took the spell, and again when the ghostly witch cast an extension spell on top of her first magic.

Then she sank down onto Belkram's shoulder, crossed her legs gracefully, and closed her eyes. Driven by her will, the sword of Mystra spun about and shot to the wall, in the direction of the Hall of Stars.

It struck the wall and hung quivering there, and the shadows around it began to melt and run, flowing away from it.

When the wall was gone, the blade leapt on to the next barrier.

"Gods!" Itharr swore suddenly. "She's burning away the castle!"

They scrambled up, and a look of annoyance crossed Syluné's ghostly face. "Don't let me fall, you great lout," she told Belkram, opening her eyes. "I may weigh nothing, but I don't appreciate being bounced on my head on floors made of shadow. To me, they seem very solid."

"It's all right if we move about, then?" the Harper asked her.

She frowned. "Yes, it's better if you do, I suppose. Follow the sword. If any Malaugrym show up to do battle, it can drink their spells and shield you."

And that is what befell. As the Hall of Stars boiled away into the black emptiness of distant shifting shadows that is Shadowhome, the three rangers saw a tower beyond it topple soundlessly down into the Well of Shadows.

"Don't destroy it all," Shar said to the ghostly form riding on Belkram's shoulder.

"I haven't the time to do so if I wanted to," Syluné told her. "I *am* going to ruin the Great Hall of the Throne, though, and carve up the Shadow Throne. I want the Malaugrym to know they were defeated this day, not just that some lucky humans got loose and managed to do a bit of damage while escaping."

There were a lot of walls between the Well and the Great Hall, and the adventurers soon caught up to the blue blade. It melted away one last wall and then flew down a long corridor into the Chamber of the Veils, the last antechamber before the Great Hall.

As the veils blazed up around the sword, Malaugrym melted out of invisibility all over the chamber. Ahorga, Bheloris, and several others faced them, Malaugrym the rangers knew by sight if not by name. They saw grim determination, and fear, on the shapeshifters' faces.

Syluné spread her hands an instant before forty or more spells crashed down upon them. The room rang with her high, wild laugh of exultation as the spells all flashed back against those who'd hurled them.

The chamber rocked; balconies broke off and crashed to the tiles below. All over the chamber, Malaugrym bodies collapsed, slain by their own spells, or sagged back in pain and flickered out of sight as contingencies and rings took them elsewhere.

Amid the veils, the blue blade began a sudden spiral. Syluné looked up at it and said a very unladylike word.

As they all looked up at her in amazement—and Belkram almost dropped her—the entire chamber shook, pulsed under their feet, and grated into life, joining the spiral. The shadows moved slowly at first, then faster and faster, a whistling drone around them rising slowly toward a scream.

"Syluné! What's happening?" Itharr shouted.

"The blade struck a gate and is taking us all with it in a vortex," the Witch of Shadowdale announced calmly. "Watch this closely . . . you'll probably never be in one again. They're often fatal."

"Thanks," Belkram told her feelingly as they began to whirl around faster and faster. "Are you going to do something about it?"

"I *am* doing something about it, overly muscled one,"

Syluné told him crisply. "I'm calling on the sword's powers to make sure the vortex takes us to Faerûn and not into the fires of Dis, say, or a plane of endless fire or antimatter."

"What part of Faerûn?" Belkram called back over the mounting shriek of the vortex. She turned blazing eyes on him until she saw his teasing grin, then she punched him instead.

And the world fell apart.

* * * * *

Daggerdale, Kythorn 20

The blue blade sizzled deep into the turf of a familiar-looking hillside with a ruined manor house at its top and a decrepit bridge across a stream at the bottom.

As they tumbled to the grass in a last slow spiral, the blade exploded in blue radiant shards that went spinning past them, soft blue shards that dissolved into the shimmering air in moments. The sword of Mystra was gone as if it had never been. As Mystra no longer was.

Three rangers and a spectral sorceress sat up and blinked. Around them, seven other figures rose too, beings who had tails and spike-studded arms and angrily curling tentacles.

"Oh, *blast!*" Belkram cursed, and several Malaugrym flinched, expecting a spell to explode over them at his words.

When nothing befell, they acquired cruel smiles and flexed their tentacles and barbed tails and pincer claws. Then they began the slow climb up the hillside toward the rangers in tattered leathers. The ghostly woman who'd been with them had disappeared.

"To come all this way . . ." Shar said, close to tears, as she saw sure death coming up the hill toward her.

"See the world! Have daring adventures! Join the Harpers!" Belkram and Itharr chorused, in the deepest, most stirring and cultured town crier voices they could manage. And they waved their weapons.

"Hey, breeding maiden!" Belkram called. "Catch!"

His sword—still silver—came flashing through the air to her. Sharantyr caught it, tears in her eyes at his gesture, as she saw him draw a boot dagger, salute her with it, and stand beside Itharr. Each them held two drawn daggers to use against seven ever-changing monsters.

"Mystra and Tymora," Shar said between her teeth, "this is not fair!"

She raised the sword wearily, resolved to die well—and white light broke over the hillside, fire that raged briefly across the Malaugrym.

The shapeshifters danced in agony. When the fire subsided, all stood in human form. There were gasps of horror from the Malaugrym, and frantic cries as they tried to shift shape and could not.

Ahorga, face streaming sweat with the effort, finally managed to produce wings. He sprang back, retreating down the hill, and cried, "I go now, cowards! Know that you've made a foe forever this day! I'll be back!"

"Don't hurry," Belkram called to him as the shapeshifter flapped his wings and climbed heavily into the sky. As Ahorga turned into the wind, to rise, Belkram thought he saw that great shaggy head bare its teeth in a cold answering grin. Then the Malaugrym mounted the winds and soared aloft.

Two more shapeshifters, panting and groaning with the effort, overcame Syluné's magic and managed the same trick. They wasted no breath on proud exit lines because by then their audience was gone.

Men and women were rolling over and over in the grass, tearing at each other in desperate fury, one side trying to snatch weapons and the other, smaller side trying to use them.

While the two Malaugrym flew frantically away from any place where that ghostly sorceress might be able to see them, Syluné used her last forcebolt to blow apart the head of a Shadowmaster who was throttling Belkram.

As the smoking, headless body toppled sideways, Belkram rolled to his feet to find Itharr and a blood-drenched but unhurt Sharantyr doing the same thing.

They stood looking soberly at each other across the corpses.

"Well," Itharr said with a sigh, "we're back."

From out of the ruins of the manor atop the hill, something small and dark came flying. Belkram snatched up a fallen dagger to make a throw, but the object banked smoothly past him and he saw that it was a pipe. A curved, familiar-looking pipe that trailed wisps of smoke and drifted to a halt in their midst.

"Back, are ye?" The voice that issued from it was even more familiar, and as testy as ever. "A fine mess ye leapt into, and stirred up further, to be sure!"

"That wouldn't be who I think it is, would it?" Belkram asked wearily as Sharantyr groaned and covered her eyes.

"Aye," Itharr replied. "It would be."

FORGOTTEN REALMS

FANTASY ADVENTURE

An Excerpt

Daughter of the Drow

Elaine Cunningham

PRELUDE

There is a world where elves dance beneath the stars, where the footsteps of humanfolk trace restless paths in ever-widening circles. There is adventure to be had in this land, and magic enough to lure seekers and dreamers with a thousand secrets. Here there are wonders enough and more to fill a dragon's lifetime, and most who live in this world are content with the challenges life brings.

A few, however, remember the night-told stories that terrified and delighted them as children, and they seek out the whispered tales and grim warnings so that they may disregard them. Intrepid or foolish, these hearty souls venture into forbidden places deep beneath the lands of their birth. Those who survive tell of another, even more wondrous, land, a dark and alien world woven from the fabric of dreams—and of nightmare. This is the Underdark.

In gem-studded caves and winding tunnels, turbulent waterways and vast caverns, the creatures of the Underdark make their homes. Beautiful and treacherous are these hidden realms, and perhaps chief among them is Menzoberranzan, fabled city of the drow.

Life in the dark elves' city has always been dominated by the worship of Lloth—the drow goddess of chaos—and by a constant striving for power and position. Yet in the shadows of the temples and the grand ruling houses, away from the academy that teaches fighting and fanaticism, a complex and diverse people go about the business of life.

Here the drow, both noble and common, live, work, scheme, play, and—occasionally—love. Echoes of their common elven heritage can be seen in the artistry lavished on homes and gardens, the craftsmanship of their armor and ornaments, their affinity for magic and art, and their fierce pride in their fighting skills. Yet no surface-dwelling elf can walk among her dark cousins without feeling horror, and earning a swift and terrible death. For the drow, fey and splendid though they are, have been twisted by centuries of hatred and isolation into a macabre parody of their elven forebears. Stunning achievement and chilling atrocity: this is Menzoberranzan.

In a time some three decades before the gods walked the realms, the chaos and turmoil of the dark elves' city achieved a brief, simmering equilibrium. Wealthy drow took advantage of such intervals of relative calm to indulge their tastes for luxury and pleasure. Many of their leisure moments were spent in Narbondellyn, an elegant district of the city that boasted broad streets, fine homes, and expensive shops, all crafted of stone and magic. Faint light suffused the scene, most of it from the multicolored glow of faerie fire. All drow were able to conjure this magical light, and in Narbondellyn the use of it was particularly lavish. Faerie fire highlighted the carvings on the mansions, illuminated shop signs, baited merchandise with a tempting glow, and glimmered like embroidery on the gowns and cloaks of the wealthy passersby.

In the surface lands far above Menzoberranzan, winter was beginning to ebb, and the midday sun struggled to warm the harsh landscape. The Underdark did not know seasons and had no cycle of light and dark, but the drow still went about their business according to the ancient, forgotten rhythms of their light-dwelling ancestors. The magical warmth deep in the core of Narbondel—the natural stone pillar that served as the city's clock—was climbing toward midpoint even as the unseen sun reached its zenith. The drow could read the magic timepiece even in utter darkness, for their keen eyes perceived the subtlest heat patterns with a precision and detail that a hunting falcon might envy.

At this hour the streets bustled with activity. Drow were by far the most numerous folk in Narbondellyn. Richly dressed dark elves wandered down the broad lane, browsed at the shops, or paused at chic cafes and taverns to sip goblets of spiced, sparkling green wine. City guards made frequent rounds mounted on large, harnessed lizards. Drow merchants whipped their draft animals—most often lizards or giant slugs—as they carted goods to market. And occasionally, the sea of activity parted to permit passage of a drow noble, usually a female riding in state upon a slave-carried litter or a magical, floating driftdisk.

A scattering of beings from other races also made their way through Narbondellyn: slaves who tended the needs of the dark elves. Goblin servants staggered after their drow mistresses, arms piled high with purchases. In one shop, bound with chains and prompted by three well-armed drow, a dwarf smithy grudgingly repaired fine weapons and jewelry for his captors. A pair of minotaurs served as house guards at one particularly impressive mansion, flanking the entrance and facing each other so that their long, curving horns framed a deadly arch. Faerie fire limned the nine-foot creatures as if they were living sculpture. A dozen or so kobolds—small, rat-tailed relatives of goblins—lurked in small stone alcoves, and their bulbous eyes scanned the streets anxiously and continually. Every so often one of the creatures scurried out to pick up a bit of discarded string or clean up after a passing lizard mount. It was the kobolds' task to keep the streets of Narbondellyn absolutely free of debris, and their devotion to duty was ensured by an ogre taskmaster armed with whip and daggers.

One of these kobolds, whose back was lined with the recent marks of the ogre's whip, was busily engaged in polishing a public bench near the edge of the street. So anxious was the slave to avoid future punishment that he failed to notice the silent approach of a driftdisk. On the magical conveyance rode a drow female in splendid robes and jewels, and behind her marched in eerie silence threescore drow soldiers, all clad in glittering chain mail and wearing the insignia of one of the city's ruling houses. The snake-headed whip at the female's belt proclaimed her rank as a high priestess of Lloth, and the haughty tilt of her chin demanded instant recognition and respect. Most of Narbondellyn's folk granted her both at once. They cleared a path for her entourage, and those nearest marked her passing with a polite nod or a bended knee, according to their station.

As the noble priestess glided down the street, reveling in the heady mixture of deference and envy that was her due, her gaze fell upon the preoccupied kobold. In an instant her expression changed from regal hauteur to deadly wrath. The little slave was not exactly blocking her path, but its inattention showed a lack of respect. Such was simply not tolerated.

The priestess closed in. When the driftdisk's heat shadow fell upon the laboring kobold, the little goblinoid grunted in annoyance and looked up. It saw death approaching and froze, like a mouse facing a raptor's claws.

Looming over the doomed kobold, the priestess drew a slender black wand from her belt and began to chant softly. Tiny spiders dripped from the wand and scurried toward their prey, growing rapidly as they went until each was the size of a man's hand. They swarmed over the kobold and quickly had it enmeshed in a thick, web-like net. That done, they settled down to feed. Webbing bound the kobold's mouth and muted its dying screams. The slave's agonies were brief, for the giant spiders sucked the juices from their victim in mere moments. In no more time than the telling might take, the kobold was reduced to a pile of rags, bones, and leathery hide. At a sign from the priestess, the soldiers marched on down the street, their silent elven boots further flattening the desiccated kobold.

One of the soldiers inadvertently trod on a spider that had lingered—hidden among the bits of rag—to siphon the last drop of juice. The engorged insect burst with a sickening pop, spraying its killer with ichor and liquid kobold. Unfortunately for that soldier, the priestess happened to look over her shoulder just as the spider, a creature sacred to Lloth, simultaneously lost its dinner and its life. The drow female's face contorted with outrage.

"Sacrilege!" she declaimed in a voice resonant with power and magic. She swept a finger toward the offending soldier and demanded, "Administer the law of Lloth, *now!*"

Without missing a step, the drow on either side of the condemned soldier drew long, razor-edged daggers. They struck with practiced efficiency. One blade flashed in from the right and gutted the unfortunate drow; the strike from the left slashed open his throat. In the span of a heartbeat the grim duty was completed. The soldiers marched on, leaving their comrade's body in a spreading pool of blood.

Only a brief silence marked the drow soldier's passing. Once it was clear that the show was over, the folk of Narbondellyn turned their attention back to their own affairs. Not one of the spectators offered any challenge to the executions. Most did not show any reaction at all, except for the kobold slaves who scurried forward with mops and barrels to clear away the mess. Menzoberranzan was the stronghold of Lloth worship, and here her priestesses reigned supreme.

Yet the proud female's procession kept a respectful distance from the black mansion near the end of the street. Not a house like those known to surface dwellers, this abode was carved into the heart of a stalactite, a natural rock formation that hung from the cavern's ceiling like an enormous ebony fang. No one dared touch the stone, for on it was carved an intricate pattern of symbols that shifted constantly and randomly. Any part of the design could be a magic rune, ready to unleash its power upon the careless or unwary.

This stalactite manor was the private retreat of Gromph Baenre, the archmage of Menzoberranzan and the eldest son of the city's undisputed (if uncrowned) queen. Gromph of course had a room in House Baenre's fabulous fortress castle, but the wizard possessed treasures—and ambitions—that he wished to keep from the eyes of his female kin. So from time to time he retired to Narbondellyn, to enjoy his collection of magical items, to pour over his vast library of spellbooks, or to indulge himself with his latest mistress.

Perhaps even more than his obvious wealth and famed magical power, Gromph's ability to select his consorts was a testament to his status. In this matriarchal city, males had a decidedly subservient role, and most answered to the whims of females. Even one such as Gromph Baenre had to chose his playmates with discretion. His current mistress was the youngest daughter of a minor house. She possessed rare beauty, but little aptitude for clerical magic. The latter gave her low status in the city and raised her considerably in Gromph's estimation. The archmage of Menzoberranzan had little love for the Spider Queen goddess or her priestesses.

Here in Narbondellyn, however, he could for a time forget such matters. The security of his mansion was ensured by the warding runes outside, and the solitude of his private study protected by a magical shield. This study was a large high-domed chamber carved from black stone and lit by the single candle on his desk. To a drow's sensitive eyes, the soft glow made the gloomy cave seem as bright as noonday on the Surface. Here the wizard sat, perusing an interesting book of spells that he'd acquired from the rapidly cooling body of a would-be rival.

Gromph was old, even by the measures of elvenkind. He had survived seven centuries in treacherous Menzoberranzan, mostly because his talent for magic was matched by a subtle, calculating cunning. He had survived, but his seven hundred years had left him bitter and cold. His capacity for evil and cruelty was legendary even among the drow. None of this showed in the wizard's appearance, for thanks to his powerful magic he appeared young and vital. His ebony skin was smooth and lustrous, his long-fingered hands slender and supple. Flowing white hair gleamed in the candlelight, and his arresting eyes—large, almond-shaped eyes of an unusual amber hue—were fixed intently upon the spellbook.

Deep in his studies, the wizard felt, rather than heard, the faint crackle that warned him that someone had passed through the magic shield. He raised his eyes from the book and leveled a deadly glare in the direction of the disturbance.

To his consternation, he saw no one. The magical

shield was little more than an alarm, but only a powerfu
sorcerer could pass through with an invisibility spell in
tact. Gromph's white, winged brows met in a frown, and
he tensed for battle, his hand inching toward one of the
deadly wands on his belt.

"Look down," advised a lilting, melodic voice, a voic
that rang with mischief and childish delight.

Incredulous, Gromph shifted his gaze downward
There stood a tiny, smiling female about five years of age
easily the most beautiful child he had ever seen. She wa
a tiny duplicate of her mother, whom Gromph had re
cently left sleeping in a nearby suite of rooms. The child'
face was angular, and her elven features delicate and
sharp. A mop of silky white curls tumbled about he
shoulders, contrasting with baby skin that had the sheen
and texture of black satin. But most striking were th
wide amber eyes, so like his own, that regarded him with
intelligence and without fear. Those eyes stole Gromph'
annoyance and stirred his curiosity.

This, then, must be his daughter. For some reason tha
thought struck a faint chord in the heart of the solitary
evil old drow. He had no doubt fathered other children
but that was of little concern to him. In Menzoberranzan
families were traced solely through the mother. Thi
child, however, interested him. She had passed through
the magical barrier.

The archmage pushed aside the spellbook. He leaned
back in his chair and returned the child's unabashe
scrutiny. He was not accustomed to dealing with chil
dren. Even so, his words, when he spoke, surprised him
"So, drowling. I don't suppose you can read?"

It was a ridiculous question, for the child was littl
more than a babe. Yet her brow furrowed as she consid
ered the matter. "I'm not sure," she said thoughtfully
"You see, I've never tried."

She darted toward the open spellbook and peered
down at the page. Too late, Gromph slapped a han
over her golden eyes, cursing under his breath as he di
so. Even simple spells could be deadly, for magic rune
attacked the untrained eye with a stab of searing light

Attempting to read an unlearned spell could cause terrible pain, blindness, even insanity.

Yet the little drow appeared to be unharmed. She wriggled free of the wizard's grasp and skipped over to the far side of his desk. Stooping, she fished a scrap of discarded parchment from the wastebasket. Then she rose and pulled the quill from Gromph's prized bottle of everdark ink. Clutching the pen awkwardly in her tiny fist, she began to draw.

Gromph watched her, intrigued. The child's face was set in fierce concentration as she painstakingly scrawled some wavering, curly lines onto the parchment. After a few moments she turned, with a triumphant smile, to the wizard.

He leaned closer, and his eyes flashed incredulously from the parchment to the spellbook and back. The child had sketched one of the magic symbols! True, it was crudely drawn, but she had not only *seen* it, she had remembered it from a glance. That was a remarkable feat for any elf, at any age.

On a whim, Gromph decided to test the child. He held out his palm and conjured a small ball that glowed with blue faerie fire. The little drow laughed and clapped her hands. He tossed the toy across the desk toward her, and she deftly caught it.

"Throw it back," he said.

The child laughed again, clearly delighted to have found a playmate. Then, with a lighting-fast change of mood, she drew back her arm for the throw and gritted her teeth, preparing to give the effort her all.

Gromph silently bid the magic to dissipate. The blue light winked out.

And the next moment, the ball hurtled back toward him, almost too fast for him to catch. Only now the light was golden.

"The color of my eyes," said the little girl, with a smile that promised heartache to drow males in years to come.

The archmage noted this, and marked its value. He then turned his attention to the golden ball in his hand. So, the child could already conjure faerie fire. This was an innate talent of the fey drow, but seldom did it manifest so early. What else, he wondered, could she do?

Gromph tossed the ball again, this time lobbing it high up toward the domed ceiling. Hands outstretched, the precocious child soared up toward the glowing toy, levitating with an ease that stole the archmage's breath. She snatched the ball out of the air, and her triumphant laughter echoed through the study as she floated lightly back to his side. At that moment, Gromph made one of the few impulsive decisions of his long life.

"What is your name, child?"

"Liriel Vandree," she returned promptly.

Gromph shook his head. "No longer. You must forget House Vandree, for you are none of theirs."

He traced a deft, magical pattern in the air with the fingers of one hand. In response, a ripple passed through the solid rock of the far wall. Stone flowed into the room like a wisp of smoke. The dark cloud writhed and twisted finally tugging free of the wall. In an instant it compressed and sculpted itself into an elf-sized golem. The living statue sank to one knee before its drow master and awaited its orders.

"The child's mother will be leaving this house. See to it and have her family informed that she met with an unfortunate accident on her way to the Bazaar."

The stone servant rose, bowed again, and then disappeared into the wall as easily as a wraith might pass through a fog bank. A moment later, the scream of an elven female came from a nearby chamber—a scream that began in terror and ended in a liquid gurgle.

Gromph leaned forward and blew out the candle, for darkness best revealed the character of the drow. All light fled the room, and the wizard's eyes changed from amber to brilliant red as his vision slipped into the heat reading spectrum. He fastened a stern gaze upon the child.

"You are Liriel Baenre, my daughter and a noble of the First House of Menzoberranzan," he announced.

The archmage studied the child's reaction. The crimson glow of heat and warmth drained from her face, and her tiny, pale-knuckled hands gripped the edge of the desk for support. It was clear that the little drow understood all that had just occurred. Her expression remained stoic, however, and her voice was firm when she repeated her new name.

Gromph nodded approvingly. Liriel had accepted the reality of her situation—she could hardly do otherwise and survive—yet the rage and frustration of an untamed spirit burned bright in her eyes.

This was his daughter, indeed.